Praise for THE QUANTUM SPY

"A fascinating, beautifully textured thriller. . . . For inside dope on the day-to-day work and personal lives among America's espionage personnel, Ignatius is unbeatable." —*Washington Post*

"[A] fascinating thriller. . . . Mr. Ignatius, a prize-winning journalist for the *Washington Post*, supplies plenty of up-to-date technical information in the course of telling his involving and realistic-seeming story." —*Wall Street Journal*

"David Ignatius gives readers a thrilling spy caper and a look into the future of espionage and war." —MPR News, "Best Fiction Picks of Fall"

"Ignatius combines deft storytelling with insider information about spycraft honed over decades as a respected journalist specializing in explaining that complicated world." —*Washington Independent Review of Books*

"*The Quantum Spy* is David Ignatius at the top of his game! A truly thrilling, superbly crafted spy novel that focuses on pivotal contemporary issues—the competition to achieve quantum computing technology, the high-stakes rivalry between the U.S. and China, and the conduct of spycraft in a digital age. It is certain to top the bestseller charts!" —General (Ret.) David Petraeus, former director of the CIA (2011–2012), commander of the surge in Iraq, and commander of coalition forces in Afghanistan

"A thrilling window into the future world of high-tech espionage. David Ignatius may call it a novel, but for those of us who know the work of the intelligence community, this book is nothing less than a real-life insight into the ongoing battle for dominance in the digital world. The names may be fictitious, but what they are fighting about is very real!"   —Leon E. Panetta, former director of the CIA (2009–2011) and secretary of defense (2011–2013)

"A work for now and forever. A contemporary adversary: China. A contemporary problem: quantum computing. And the ageless battle of spy versus spy. Couldn't put it down."
—Michael Hayden, former director of the CIA (2006–2009) and NSA (1999–2005)

"Ignatius's realistic peek into the inner workings of the CIA and its Chinese counterpart shows why he's at the top of the thriller pack."
—*Publishers Weekly*

"The story moves along well, weaving in the author's extensive research without slowing the pace. While the science gets geeky in spots, it's still fun—and the complex intrigue will please thriller fans."
—*Kirkus Reviews*

"Ignatius demonstrates again his superior storytelling skills. This engrossing tale of spy vs. counterspy rockets back and forth from Washington, D.C., to CIA headquarters in Langley, VA, to Beijing. . . . In this sly, fast-moving story, everyone is hiding something. . . . Ignatius's latest is up to his usual high standards and should appeal to all lovers of spy fiction."   —*Library Journal*

THE
QUANTUM SPY

ALSO BY DAVID IGNATIUS

The Director

Bloodmoney

The Increment

Body of Lies

The Sun King

A Firing Offense

The Bank of Fear

Siro

Agents of Innocence

DAVID IGNATIUS

THE QUANTUM SPY

A THRILLER

W. W. NORTON & COMPANY

INDEPENDENT PUBLISHERS SINCE 1923

NEW YORK LONDON

Copyright © 2018 by David Ignatius

All rights reserved
Printed in the United States of America
First published as a Norton paperback 2018

For information about permission to reproduce selections from this book, write to Permissions, W. W. Norton & Company, Inc., 500 Fifth Avenue, New York, NY 10110

For information about special discounts for bulk purchases, please contact W. W. Norton Special Sales at specialsales@wwnorton.com or 800-233-4830

Manufacturing by LSC Harrisonburg
Production manager: Lauren Abbate

Library of Congress Cataloging-in-Publication Data

Names: Ignatius, David, 1950– author.
Title: The quantum spy : a thriller / David Ignatius.
Description: First edition. | New York : W. W. Norton & Company, [2018]
Identifiers: LCCN 2017015373 | ISBN 9780393254150 (hardcover)
Subjects: | GSAFD: Spy stories.
Classification: LCC PS3559.G54 Q36 2018 | DDC 813/.54—dc23
LC record available at https://lccn.loc.gov/2017015373

ISBN 978-0-393-35624-3 pbk.

W. W. Norton & Company, Inc.
500 Fifth Avenue, New York, N.Y. 10110
www.wwnorton.com

W. W. Norton & Company Ltd.
15 Carlisle Street, London W1D 3BS

1 2 3 4 5 6 7 8 9 0

For Candy Lee and Joseph Ward

As part of its mission to address some of the most difficult challenges in the Intelligence Community by investing in high-risk, high-payoff research, IARPA sponsors several applied research programs that explore the potential and possibilities in quantum computing.... IARPA is always seeking novel ideas aligned with our mission, and quantum research is a specific focus.

—INTELLIGENCE ADVANCED RESEARCH PROJECTS AGENCY,
  "QUANTUM PROGRAMS AT IARPA," FEBRUARY 2017

Chinese scientists are developing the world's first quantum computer, which will be much faster than current supercomputers and is expected to come into fruition in a few years, according to a top scientist.

—CHINESE ACADEMY OF SCIENCES, PRESS RELEASE, APRIL 2017

Everything we call real is made of things that cannot be regarded as real.

—ATTRIBUTED TO NIELS BOHR,
  NOBEL PRIZE–WINNING PHYSICIST

THE
QUANTUM SPY

PROLOGUE
SEATTLE, WASHINGTON

A cold mist hovered over Lake Washington, a vaporous green after a morning of rain, when John Vandel arrived in Seattle. The CIA official had traveled from Washington to visit an electronics engineer named Jason Schmidt, who ran a small, privately owned computer company that hadn't yet built its first product. The plant was a low-rise brick building on the southern end of the lake, near the Boeing factory in Renton. A sign announced the initials of the company, "QED," short for Quantum Engineering Dynamics, etched in cobalt blue.

Vandel rang the buzzer. He was a lean, putty-faced man with a bad haircut that spiked short gray hairs in odd directions. His complexion was scarred; his body had an elastic bend at the joints. The only things that sparkled were the slate-gray eyes that retained an intense focus even when the rest of him was slack. He was wearing a rumpled black suit and carrying a briefcase.

The doorbell stuck for a moment; it was answered eventually by a young woman in a black t-shirt with three small diamond studs in one ear and a silver piercing through her eyebrow. The building had a musty odor, as if it had once been something else.

A round-faced man wearing a knit shirt and a jacket bearing the company logo walked toward Vandel. He looked like he hadn't been outdoors in a year.

"I'm Jason Schmidt," he said shyly. "I guess I'm the boss."

"I'm Mr. Green," said Vandel. "Do you have someplace quiet where we can talk?"

Schmidt led him down a nondescript corridor to a conference room that had a view across Rainier Avenue to the southern shore of the lake. On the way, they passed the detritus of a start-up that hadn't yet made its start: rows of grubby cubicles; glowing computer screens flanked by pallid faces that hadn't gotten enough sleep, ever; the strange sounds from a nearby recreation room for over-caffeinated employees—the click-click of Ping-Pong balls and the knock-knock of foosballs scudding toward the goal.

Vandel had a loose, ambling gate as he strolled down the corridor, peering into doors and windows. He had the gift of a good case officer, which was that he looked harmless. In his wallet, he kept a card on which he had printed the advice he had received from his first station chief in Damascus: "Always remember that you are a snake handler, not a snake charmer."

Unkempt as he appeared at first glance, Vandel was meticulous in his work as the CIA's deputy director for operations and acknowledged as the agency's top spy even by the many people who feared or disliked him. He had come to Seattle to do the essential, manipulative business of a case officer, which was to recruit a reluctant agent.

"I'm here because of your letter," said Vandel when he was seated. His eyes wandered the room for a moment and then locked on Schmidt. He removed a two-page letter from his briefcase and read the opening sentence aloud:

"'I am writing to the Central Intelligence Agency because I have information that is important for our national security.' That rang our bell."

Schmidt was nervous. He cleared his throat. "You must think I'm a crank, you know, or a kook, or something." He was fumbling for words. "You probably get crazy letters from people all the time."

"We do. But not like this. And we knew about your company. The NSA checked you out months ago. So when this letter arrived at the CIA, it interested people. Someone sent it to me, and I wanted to come see you myself."

Schmidt mumbled an apology. He was embarrassed at having summoned a senior representative of the U.S. government all this way.

"I wasn't sure who to contact. There are so many intelligence agencies. But I have a cousin who works for the CIA. Maybe I'm not supposed to know that, but I do. So I sent the letter to my cousin and told him to give it to the right person. I guess that's you, Mr. Green. Although that's probably not your real name."

Vandel shook his head. No, "Green" was not his real name.

"I need to talk about two things in your letter, Mr. Schmidt. First, you said you had made a breakthrough in building a quantum computer. I think your exact words were, *'I've solved the puzzle.'* Our engineers looked carefully at the paper you sent. They're not convinced, but they don't think you're crazy, either."

"I promise you, I'm not crazy."

Vandel scratched his head.

"You understand what a big deal this is, Mr. Schmidt? We're spending billions on quantum research. This is a race. The White House pounds on me every week wanting to know where the Chinese are, and we say relax: It'll be ten years before anyone builds a machine, probably twenty, and we're way ahead. And now you say bang, you've done it. I won't pretend to understand what you wrote about 'liquid electrons' and how they interact near absolute zero. That means absolutely nothing to me, but our computer scientists say it's plausible."

Schmidt held up his hand. He was an engineer. He didn't want to overpromise.

"It's still a prototype. It has a lot of bugs. It's not a fully programmable machine. It needs work."

"Details," said Vandel. "Here's the issue. It's not just that you think maybe you have a breakthrough, but that someone wants to steal it. That's the bell-ringer in your letter, about the venture fund that wants to buy you."

"I don't know anything about them except their name. 'Parcourse Technology Partners.' I've never heard of them. Nobody around here has. But their fund manager said they would pay cash for control of QED. When I asked for a number, he said a billion dollars, maybe more.

I mean, we're still beta testing our first machine. It didn't make sense. Who are they? Do you know?"

"They're Chinese. They have an office in Menlo Park, owned by a nameplate company in Panama. The Panama shell is a front for the Chinese Ministry of State Security. I'm assuming the Chinese government is so impressed with what you're doing that they want to buy you out. So I'm here to make you a better offer."

"I don't want to sell the company, to anyone," said Schmidt. "I just want to make my machine work. QED. Quantum Engineering Dynamics. We think we have a shortcut that can give quantum solutions, now. The purists say it's not really quantum computing, but I don't care. If it does what I think it can, then everything else will take care of itself. So just let me build it. I don't want to sell the company to anybody, not even you."

"We don't want to buy it. We just want to be your customer. Everything you make, you sell to us. We'll agree on a price that will make you very rich, I promise, and you keep control. There's just one rule we have for all the people we buy things from, Mr. Schmidt, and you have to follow that. Otherwise, you'll get in a lot of trouble."

"I don't like rules. I'm a scientist. If I wanted rules I could work for Microsoft up in Redmond. But tell me anyway: What's the rule?"

"As soon as we make our agreement, starting today, I hope, everything you do is classified. Your company goes black. It doesn't publish papers. It doesn't have a website. When it gets inquiries from outsiders, it contacts the FBI."

"Ugh! That sounds horrible. Why would I do that? It sounds like going to prison."

Vandel fixed his gaze on the gifted, fragile computer scientist across from him.

"Because it will help your country. Your government needs the ideas that are in your head. It needs to make sure that other people don't get them. Like I said, this is a race. If we lose, we have a nightmare ahead. You must understand that, or you wouldn't have written the letter to your cousin at the CIA."

Schmidt sighed. Of course, he understood. He wasn't a man who had romantic ideas about a technological Arcadia. He thought that Edward

Snowden was a self-deluding traitor. But still, he didn't want to sign away his career for indentured servitude.

"I thought something like this might happen when I sent my letter. I dreaded it, but I did it anyway. And do you know why? Albert Einstein."

"Come again?"

"Einstein wrote a letter to Franklin Roosevelt in 1939. Two typewritten sheets of paper. He wanted the president to understand that scientists in Europe were turning uranium into a new kind of energy. Here, I have a copy in my desk. Wait a minute."

Schmidt rummaged in his desk and retrieved the sheets he had copied. He held them as if they were a piece of scripture.

"It's 1939, remember, sir. Here's what Einstein said: 'Certain aspects of the situation which has arisen seem to call for watchfulness and, if necessary, quick action on the part of the administration.' *Certain aspects of the situation.* My God! And then he says, listen to this, 'This new phenomenon would also lead to the construction of bombs, and it is conceivable . . . that extremely powerful bombs of a new type may be constructed.' *It is conceivable.* What if he hadn't written the letter? That's what I asked myself. What if he had said: 'I'm just a scientist. Science has no flag.' What would have happened then?"

"You know the answer."

Vandel paused, then he repeated: "We want to be your customer. Your only customer."

"I need to think about it. You haven't even seen my laboratory. Come, I'll show you. Then I'll think about the other business."

"We need to make a decision now. Today. I need to tell the White House science adviser we have this locked. People will come see your lab later. We'll learn everything you can tell us. But right now, you need to do the right thing. Which is to sign a nondisclosure agreement that I have brought along, so we can get started with everything else."

Schmidt had clasped his hands. His arms were trembling slightly. His lips were parched dry, suddenly. His voice had gone hoarse.

"I need a bit more time, really. This is such a big step."

Vandel tilted his head. The light through the window illuminated some of the ancient scars on his face, momentarily. He reached across the desk and took the big man's hand in his own, and held it still for a moment. Schmidt's face softened.

"I brought you some presents," said Vandel. He reached into his briefcase and pulled out three objects, each wrapped in blue paper. He handed them across the desk. Schmidt quickly unwrapped the first and removed a translucent box that contained an ochre-red substance that seemed to have come from a kiln.

"What the hell?" asked Schmidt.

"It's fused sand. It was taken from the crater of the first nuclear-bomb test at Alamogordo, New Mexico. James B. Conant kept one of these as long as he lived, to remember what the Manhattan Project had been. There are just a few of these sand samples left in the government. I wanted you to have one of them. Because you're in a Manhattan Project, too."

Schmidt nodded. He didn't speak as he unwrapped the next box. Inside was a jagged piece of concrete marked with spray paint. It was mounted atop a marble base that had been inlaid with the CIA's seal.

"What is this? It looks like junk."

"That's a piece of the Berlin Wall, my friend. Not many of those left either. So many people sacrificed to see that damn thing come down. I don't want to be too corny about this, but we're in that kind of struggle again. When you're in your lab and you think everything is turning to shit, I want you to look at that shard of concrete and remember that the good guys can win if they work hard enough. Okay?"

"Okay," said Schmidt. He was softening.

"Open the last one," said Vandel. "That's the one I thought about the most."

Schmidt began tearing at the paper. Inside was a book. He saw its back jacket first, and he didn't recognize the title. He looked quizzically at his visitor.

"It's a biography of the leading computer tycoon in China. This guy's mother was a factory worker in Chengdu, and his company now competes with Microsoft and Google. Look on page seventeen, where I put the yellow sticker."

Schmidt opened the book to that page. Vandel had underlined a quotation from an American business executive. Schmidt read it aloud.

"If you are one in a million in China, you're one of 1,300 people."

"The numbers say they're going to win this race," said Vandel. "Read what I wrote on the title page."

Schmidt read the words, written in Vandel's sinuous hand:

"*Your country needs you.*"

"So do we have a deal?" asked Vandel.

Schmidt paused, but only for a moment.

"Yes," he answered. "Of course."

On the flight back to Washington, John Vandel began planning his operation against the Chinese intelligence service. He was taking the "red eye," to make a meeting at the White House the next morning about Russia. Washington had become obsessed with Moscow. Not Vandel. Russia was a declining power. It was China that worried him. He took a pill, but he couldn't sleep.

So he curled his long, elastic body around a pad of paper so that nobody could look over his shoulder and began scribbling notes: He wrote "Ministry of State Security," underlined it, and then put a question mark.

It offended Vandel that the Ministry was operating so boldly inside America. The MSS was once thought to be cautious, stealing America's technology secrets by debriefing Chinese scientists or hacking into computer systems. A thousand grains of sand, one at a time; that was how they were said to collect intelligence. But their attempt to capture QED in Seattle had been brazen, and it had nearly succeeded: A greedier owner would have taken the money rather than write to his cousin at the CIA.

Vandel wrote: "Risks," followed by another question mark. Why was the Ministry taking so many chances? Vandel had a stack of analysts' reports back at Headquarters that said the MSS was a target of the Party leader's anti-corruption campaign. Perhaps it was desperate for success and taking more chances to stay in business. But there was another, more frightening possibility: Maybe the MSS knew where to look. Maybe its operatives had found a portal into America's garden of secrets. Vandel wrote the word "mole" in small letters, and then scratched it out.

Vandel wanted to own this case. The China "mission manager" was not managing her mission. Agency operations had been "modernized" so many times that people had forgotten how to run an aggressive counterespionage program. But Vandel remembered. And he had just enough authority as chief of the operations directorate, even in the labyrinth of the new organization chart, to make something happen.

Through the night, as Vandel flickered in and out of consciousness, he saw in his mind the strands of what might be a successful operation against the Ministry—one that would exploit its vulnerabilities and turn it upside down; not just stop it, but break it apart. He was just dozing off, late in the flight, when the scattered thoughts formed themselves into a pattern as clear and bright as a runway landing.

Vandel sat up in his seat, took that pad again, and wrote the rough sketch of an operations plan, boxes and arrows, like a flow chart. The CIA had been lucky in Seattle. He didn't like having to depend on luck.

1.

SENTOSA ISLAND, SINGAPORE

Dr. Ma Yubo had flown six hours from Beijing, and he was tired. His banker had booked him a villa at a luxury hotel near the golf course on Sentosa Island. He would play the next day, after he had met the banker. And then, two days later, he would attend a scientific conference as the representative of the Ministry of State Security.

But now, Dr. Ma wanted to relax. He opened a miniature bottle of Glenlivet single-malt whiskey from the mini-bar and put his feet up on the coffee table. He wanted ice, but he didn't want to call room service. He drank it down and walked toward the window. In the distance, he could see the freighters at anchor in the Singapore Strait, ready to unload their cargoes.

The suite seemed to float in a shallow pool of indirect lighting; the couches and chairs were little islands in a beige, tufted sea. A Rossini opera was playing quietly on the music system, put in play before the guest arrived by the room attendant.

Dr. Ma was a slim man in his early fifties with a refined, sculpted face and fair skin, the color of straw. The first specks of gray showed in his hair. His wife had told him to dye it like any other "big man" and, perhaps for that reason, he resisted. For a Chinese computer scientist, he was elegantly dressed in an Italian sports jacket he had bought when he attended a symposium in Rome.

He opened the sliding door to his garden. The air was the sweet, steamy broth of Southeast Asia. A lizard was crawling to the edge of his private swimming pool. Where was that banker? He was the reason that Dr. Ma had traveled all this way.

Dr. Ma took his *"mijian"* from his briefcase. It was a small, leather-bound diary, in which he made his most private notes. His secret book. Every senior official in the Ministry had one. They were safer than electronic records; that was what everyone said. People wrote the things in their *mijian* that were never, ever to be shared—to protect the Ministry, people said, but really, to protect themselves.

Dr. Ma was going to put his *mijian* in the safe, but then, he thought, that was the first place anyone would look. He put it under his mattress.

Dr. Ma was thinking about his money, and it made him nervous. He shouldn't have accepted so much of it, not so quickly, but he had to worry about his daughter at Stanford, his mother in Shanghai, his annoying wife and her relatives, and the uncles and cousins who contacted him now that he was a powerful man, a "science adviser" on loan from the Chinese Academy of Sciences to a ministry whose name nobody ever mentioned. The overhead light blinked off for an instant and then came back on, as if there had been a momentary power failure.

He looked at his watch. What time was it in Vancouver? That was where his mistress had gone; to wait for him, she said. He was paying for her apartment. She would not dare to be unfaithful. Wasn't that right? No, people always betrayed. That was the law of life. That was why no matter how much money Dr. Ma had obtained, it wasn't enough.

The banker was five minutes late. His name was Gunther Krause, and he was a private-wealth adviser for Luxembourg Asset Management's branch office in Taipei. They had met in Macao, introduced by a friend from graduate school. "Safe," he said.

If Krause was ten minutes late, Ma would fire him. No, that was risky. He would reprimand the banker, severely.

Dr. Ma opened his briefcase. He had brought along the latest issue of *Spectrum*, the journal of the International Association of Electrical and Electronic Engineers. He was a member, or he had been, until he was sent to the Ministry of State Security as a technical adviser five years ago and had to disappear from the visible academic world.

The magazine's cover story was titled "Lessons from a Decade of IT Failures." That worried him, slightly. The Ministry stole so much from the kingdom of American technology, assuming it was all useful. "Explore the many ways in which IT failures have squandered money, wasted time, and generally disrupted people's lives," said the article. That was not true in Dr. Ma's department, surely. It would be a loss of face to steal things of no value.

In two days, Dr. Ma would gather more artifacts of the West at a conference on the esoteric subject of cryogenic computing, the problem of operating a computer at close to absolute zero. The Ministry wanted Dr. Ma's advice on cold machines, but Dr. Ma was thinking about hot money.

Harris Chang waited in the car outside the hotel while an officer from the Singapore station disabled the security system. Chang closed his eyes, rehearsing in his mind one last time the operational plan. He had reviewed the details a half-dozen times with John Vandel. The only hiccup had come when Vandel assured him that his Chinese ancestry had nothing to do with him getting the assignment. "Give me a break, sir," Chang had said, and Vandel, after a moment of stony silence, had laughed.

Chang focused his attention on the alcove off the lobby where the local station officer was positioned. When he raised his hand, Chang nudged the passenger beside him in the back seat, a beefy European man in a suit that strained at the button. They emerged from the car in tandem, Chang walking a step behind the other. Chang wore a blazer and a well-cut pair of slacks, no tie. He had the body of a Chinese gymnast, muscular up top but lean. He had short hair, almost a crew cut, and wore a pair of sunglasses that rimmed his face. They walked together toward the hotel entrance. Chang signed his work name in the hotel register.

The doorbell rang in Dr. Ma's suite. He peered through the spyhole and saw the familiar, fleshy face of Gunther Krause. There was a shadow beyond the door, but Ma barely registered it, he was so eager to get Krause into his room where they could do business.

Dr. Ma opened the portal and Krause entered. Behind him, moving too quickly for Ma to block him, was a second man, younger and fitter, with Chinese features. The second man pushed the door shut behind him and put his finger to his lips. He was no taller than Dr. Ma, but his physical presence was dominating.

"Who is this shit egg?" asked Dr. Ma, pointing to the unexpected Chinese visitor. "Get him out of my room now, or I will call the police."

As soon as Ma made this threat, he realized that it was unwise. He should not call the police with these two in the room. The younger Chinese man knew it, too. He was shaking his head.

"Let me introduce my assistant," said Krause smoothly, trying to pretend this was a normal encounter. "He will be handling your account now."

Krause handed over his briefcase to his companion.

"*Feihua,*" muttered Dr. Ma.

Bullshit.

Dr. Ma turned away for a moment, wanting to maintain his composure. His eyes were burning at the edges.

"This is unacceptable," said Dr. Ma as calmly as he could. "I forbid it. This 'assistant,' whoever he is, will leave now. Mr. Krause will stay. Otherwise, I will close my accounts and your firm will have nothing."

"My assistant is handling your account now," Krause repeated.

Krause walked toward the door. Dr. Ma went after him and then stopped.

Harris Chang stood in his way. The younger Chinese man had removed his sunglasses; his eyes were as clear and focused as those of a sharpshooter. He was shaking his head again, and he had raised a cautionary finger. His manner conveyed authority. He looked like one of the members of the "special projects" staff at Dr. Ma's ministry.

Krause put his hand on the doorknob. He turned back toward Dr. Ma.

"I'm sorry," he said. "Do what my assistant says and you'll be fine. Nobody wants to hurt you. We want to help."

Krause reached out to shake Dr. Ma's hand good-bye, but the Chinese man was immobile. Krause turned the knob and let himself out into the liquid heat. The two Chinese men stood alone in the salon. The younger one went to the wall and pushed a button that closed the curtains in the sitting room and the adjoining bedroom.

"Who are you?" asked Dr. Ma.

The younger man smiled. "Let's sit down," he said, gesturing toward the couch and chair. Dr. Ma didn't move.

"Who are you?" he repeated.

"My name is Peter Tong," lied Chang. "I am a private-wealth specialist with Luxembourg Asset Management." His English was flawless with an American accent.

"What's your real name?" asked Dr. Ma, more sharply. "Who do you work for? I am not a fool."

Chang gestured toward the couch. "I think we need to be comfortable with each other. Have a seat. You like whiskey. So do I."

The visitor walked to the mini-bar. There was only one left of the single malt, so he gave that to his host and poured himself a Johnnie Walker. He moved with the confidence of someone who knew the layout of the room.

Dr. Ma was seated in the chair. He took the glass of whiskey and drank it down in two long gulps.

"Another," he said.

Chang removed the last bottle of Johnnie Walker from the mini-bar and handed it over.

"Tong isn't your name, is it?" said Dr. Ma.

The younger man shrugged.

"You work for the Americans." Dr. Ma spoke the words almost in a whisper, but his visitor put his finger to his lips.

"Of course not. I work for Luxembourg Asset Management. I am taking over supervision of your portfolio, just as Mr. Krause said. You will be very happy with my service. We will have a good client relationship, I promise. A 'win-win' situation, as your president likes to say."

Dr. Ma winced at the mention of the Chinese leader. It was a reminder of the danger in which he had placed himself, dealing with a foreign banker. And now this, whatever it was.

"I can walk out of this room and go to the Chinese embassy on Tanglin Road. You wouldn't dare stop me. It would be too messy."

Dr. Ma stood, as if he was actually preparing to walk out.

"Sit down," said Chang, quietly but firmly. He pulled back his blazer to reveal a small revolver in a shoulder holster.

Dr. Ma stared at the gun. He looked at the door, then back at the weapon. His head trembled slightly.

The visitor spoke slowly in his American English.

"You must understand, sir, that you do not control this situation. You have violated Chinese law, I am afraid. As you know, an anti-corruption drive is underway. As a member of the Academy of Sciences and an adviser to the Ministry of State Security, you would be a prime target for the discipline committee. You understand that, I am sure."

Dr. Ma nodded. He tried for a moment to speak, but no words emerged.

"It is a difficult time," continued Chang. "If there were any suggestion of connections with outsiders, your career would be in danger. Your family and everything they have would be at risk. You need a friend at such a time. You should think carefully."

"*Hun dan*," whispered Dr. Ma.

Asshole.

"I am offering you the chance to survive and to prosper even more than you have already," Chang continued. "But it is not really a choice: You lost your freedom to maneuver the moment that you began to receive payments from those seeking influence with your ministry. I sympathize with your situation."

Dr. Ma made a thin sound, unintelligible.

"I am sure you understand," said the visitor. "There is so much evidence." He patted the briefcase. "We could look at it together. But that should not be necessary. You know the facts better than I do."

Dr. Ma looked down. He dabbed at his eyes with a napkin and then looked up. His face was a death mask.

"I understand," he said.

"Good." Chang took a sip of his whiskey. "We're going to get along fine."

"How could you?" asked Dr. Ma, his voice tremulous, in another register.

"What do you mean, Dr. Ma?"

"You're Chinese. How could you work for these barbarians? How could you harm your motherland in this way?"

Chang laughed loudly.

"I *am* a barbarian, sir. I'm an American-Born Chinese. 'ABC.' I grew up in Flagstaff, Arizona. China is a foreign country for me. Just so we're clear on that."

Dr. Ma shook his head. The worst thing that could happen to someone who works for an intelligence service was happening to him.

"So here's what we're going to do," said the visitor, standing. "I'm going to leave now. In two hours, you're going to meet me at this address downtown. The Holiday Inn. Room 1028."

Chang handed the older man a card. It had the hotel's address near a downtown mall called Orchard City Centre. It was an innocuous, unmemorable location.

"Memorize it," he said.

Dr. Ma studied the card, then nodded.

"You will come alone. Be wise: We will have people watching you the whole way. Please do not stop anywhere. We have coverage of your two phones. If you try to call anyone, the calls will not go through. It would not be wise to alert the Ministry. That would bring ruin, certainly. We have filmed this encounter in your room. For your protection."

Chang gestured toward the big mirror over the desk. He was so polite. Respectful, helpful. His courtesy reinforced the truly catastrophic nature of this event.

"I'm sure you see that caution is sensible," he continued. "For yourself. For your family. For other loved ones."

Chang looked at his watch.

"I will meet you in, let me see, one hour and fifty-eight minutes. Do not be late, please."

The visitor turned and walked out of the room.

Dr. Ma sat in the chair, his head cupped in his hands. He whispered an ancient curse. *"Cào nǐ zǔzōng shíbā dài,"* which literally means, fuck your ancestors to the eighteenth generation.

But he was talking to himself. He thought of his mistress in Vancouver. *Molihua.* Jasmine. She would tell him to survive, prosper, go to the meeting with these Americans and protect his piece of the dream.

Eventually he rose, washed his face, and changed his shirt. He looked at the bed, where his *mijian* was hidden. He couldn't take it with him; he couldn't destroy it. He left it where it was.

Harris Chang called John Vandel on a safe phone when he had left the hotel. It was dawn in Washington.

"*Man man de*," said Chang. Slowly, slowly.

"Get the book," said Vandel. "I need the book."

"Just to make sure, sir: You want me to take the book. Not copy it."

"Yup. The book itself. And I don't care if they know it's missing. Correction: I *want* them to know it's missing."

"Got it."

"Don't tell Winkle you called me. He'll be pissed."

"Sure," said Chang.

Chang lied a few minutes later to Warren Winkle, the Singapore station chief, and said he hadn't talked to the boss. This was the case Chang had been waiting for since he joined the agency. The only way he could get in trouble, he thought, was to upset John Vandel.

2.
ORCHARD CITY CENTRE, SINGAPORE

A faint ochre wash hung over downtown Singapore. The concrete and glass of the metropolis couldn't quite hide the sweet decay of the jungle, carried on the wind. Inside the cars and buses, every face was opaque. At the freight terminal just north of Sentosa Island, great cranes and derricks squatted over the metal containers. The city was an ordered web, frantic with people and cars, but each with a purpose and destination. This was a place where nothing happened by accident.

Dr. Ma Yubo glumly took his seat in the back of the "Comfort" taxi. Three other cabs had been waiting in the queue, but this one had moved to the front when Dr. Ma stepped out of the lobby, and the other drivers deferred. Dr. Ma had changed into a blue blazer and a raincoat and was wearing dark glasses. He gave the driver the address of the Holiday Inn on Cavenagh Street, and the man grunted back in Malay, but he didn't put any coordinates into his GPS. Dr. Ma settled into the passenger seat; his hands were trembling.

The driver took a roundabout route, turning left instead of right after traversing the causeway and meandering through an upland park before turning east toward downtown. He pulled over once, reversed course, and then doubled back. Dr. Ma was in someone else's control, entirely.

The driver deposited Dr. Ma at the back entrance to the hotel on a narrow side street. He kept the passenger door locked for a moment and then emerged with an open umbrella, which he held low over Dr. Ma as he escorted him past the green Holiday Inn sign that marked the rear door to the hotel. Inside waited another man, a dark-skinned Malay dressed as a porter. He bowed and then put his hand on Dr. Ma's elbow and steered him toward the elevator. He stepped inside, inserted a key-card, pushed the button for the tenth floor, and then withdrew.

The elevator creaked and shuddered as it ascended. Dr. Ma had an urge to abort the trip. He tried punching the button for another floor, but it wouldn't illuminate. The door opened on the tenth floor and Dr. Ma stepped out. He walked slowly, as if to delay what he knew he could not escape.

Dr. Ma found Room 1028 at the end of the corridor. He knocked once, softly, and was about to rap again when the door opened. The man who had called himself Peter Tong took his hand and drew him inside in one firm motion. The room was a small suite, overlooking the expressway and, in the distance, the park where the prime minister and cabinet had their offices.

"Sit down, please," said Chang, motioning to a chair. "You're right on time. That's a good start."

The American was dressed casually in a blue knit shirt and gray slacks. His sharply cut muscles stretched the ribbing of his short-sleeve shirt. The shirt just covered the tattoo on his upper forearm that bore three words: Duty, Honor, Country.

Mozart's "Jupiter" symphony played softly from a speaker some-where. That was one of Dr. Ma's favorite pieces of music. How did they know that about him, or any of it?

Dr. Ma was motionless, frozen in place just inside the door.

"Come on," said Chang, smiling, taking the older man's hand again. "Take off your coat. This isn't going to hurt. We're just going to have a little talk. Have a seat. I'll make you a drink."

"*Gou pi*," said Dr. Ma, distastefully. Dog fart.

"Give me your coat and sit down, please. We have so much to discuss."

Dr. Ma waited another long moment and then removed his raincoat and handed it to his host. He sat in the big chair and folded his hands. Chang patted the coat as he took it, just to make sure that Dr. Ma hadn't put the *mijian* in one of the pockets. Then he closed the curtains and went to the bar, returning with two glasses of whiskey. He handed one to Dr. Ma.

"Speak Chinese with me," said Dr. Ma. "Can you do that, at least?"

"Your English is better than my Chinese. You went to MIT. Sorry. I don't want to use a translator."

Dr. Ma shook his head. "*Pantu*," he muttered.

"'Traitor,'" said Chang, with a little laugh and a knowing shake of his head. "I know what that word means. But Brother Ma, we shouldn't insult each other. We're going to be friends. We have no other choice."

Chang winked at his visitor. As he narrowed his eyes, he looked the more Chinese of the two, darker of hue, and coarse-featured.

"*Ganbei*," he said, raising his glass. "Chin-chin."

Dr. Ma stared at the glass for twenty seconds. Then he took a long swig, and then another, and then a third.

"Slow down. We have a lot to talk about. Let's start with your job. You work at the Ministry of State Security."

"You already know that."

"Which bureau?"

"You tell me," said Dr. Ma with a faint smile, the first that had crossed his face in several hours.

"Very well. Tenth Bureau. Scientific and Technical Information. You're technical adviser to the chief of the bureau. Chief technology officer, we'd say."

Dr. Ma clapped his hands, soundlessly, in pantomime.

"Very good," he said. "What else?"

"Your specialty is supercomputing. That's what you studied at MIT, and then at the University of Maryland, when you got your doctorate in computer science. At MIT, you studied with the great Peter Shor. The man who showed that a quantum computer could break any code. You did research with him on quantum computing. When you came home, you were appointed to the Chinese Academy of Sciences. You're a star."

Dr. Ma assayed the Chinese-American man across from him.

"Peter Tong isn't your real name, is it?"

"No." The American shook his head. "I can't tell you my real name, but it doesn't matter. I'm nobody famous." He winked again.

"Where do you work?" asked Dr. Ma.

"The Central Intelligence Agency. I'm a spy. Obviously. Just like you. But now we're going to work together on a common cause."

Dr. Ma shook his head. "I'm not a spy. I'm a scientist, who temporarily works for spies. So you have the wrong man."

"I don't think so, doctor."

Chang smiled. His manner was serene, but his body was taut and insistent.

"We've been watching you for a long time," Chang continued. "Even back in America, when you were in grad school, you were on our list. Not mine. I was still in the Army then. But other people's. They knew you had great promise. We've been waiting for our chance."

Dr. Ma snorted. "A Chinese man in the U.S. Army? Not possible."

Chang sat back in his chair and crossed his arms. "Think again. 101st Airborne. You know what that is? I served in Mosul and Baghdad. And I am not a Chinese man. I'm an American."

Dr. Ma stared, and then nodded grimly.

"I have the greatest respect for you, doctor," said Chang, smiling genially again. "I know this must be difficult. But we have lots of time. Your return flight to Beijing isn't for three days. So let's start with some easy questions. We'll get to the hard ones later. But I must be honest with you, sir: We know the answers to many of these questions already. Let me refill your glass. You like Mozart, right? I can play something else."

"Mozart is fine. If you know the answers, why ask?"

"It's what we do." He filled the older man's glass and topped up his own. "So where were you born?"

Dr. Ma laughed. "In Shanghai. My mother still lives there."

"Of course. And your father was a senior cadre? Where did he work?"

"All over. He was in Beijing when I was born, and then he was sent down to the countryside, to Wuhan, in the bad days. But he came back. He always had friends in Shanghai."

"He was a rising star, your dad, when he died. Isn't that right? And his friends helped arrange for you to stay in Shanghai, at the best schools, while he was moving around, so you could study science."

"My father saw the future." Dr. Ma raised his head slightly, a gesture of respect for his father and self-respect, too. "I studied mathematics and physics. They had no more teachers for me at the high school, so they brought in a professor from Fudan University to give me instruction. I received the physics prize and the mathematics prize."

"And you won a scholarship to MIT."

"I hope I was worthy of my father."

Dr. Ma smiled distantly. He was softening slightly with this talk of his family and school days.

"Yes." The CIA officer spoke quietly now, his words as soft as the flap of a butterfly wing. "That's when you were recruited."

"What?" Dr. Ma was startled.

"Recruited. Reminded of your patriotic duty. The State Security Bureau in Shanghai contacted you. They asked you to report for them when you went to America. Every Chinese student is interviewed, but only a few of them get special treatment. The lucky ones become valued contacts for the Ministry of State Security. Like you."

Dr. Ma lowered his head. These were secrets. He was uncomfortable.

"Here's what we think," ventured Chang. "Probably, you had two meetings in Shanghai, so they could assess you. Then they asked you to come to Beijing, where they gave you a two-week course before you left. Because you were such a clever boy, they knew you would succeed. So they gave you an address in China and told you to send a message every three months. They gave you twenty-five hundred dollars and a plane ticket to catch the flight to America. Am I right?"

Dr. Ma looked toward the door, the curtained window, the young man facing him. The room was even smaller now.

"I wasn't their agent. Not at MIT, not at Maryland. And you made mistakes about my preparation. It was a one-week course, not two. And I was supposed to write every six months, not three. I think you are guessing. How would you know anything about the Ministry's procedures?"

"Because it's our job. I told you, we know a lot. Do you think you're the first Chinese scientist who came our way? We know how it works. The meetings, the trip to Beijing, the twenty-five hundred dollars. Otherwise no MIT. That was the deal for a bright young man. You had no choice. You had to cooperate."

Dr. Ma shook his head. He looked tired.

"What do you want from me, if you know so much already?"

"You need to use the toilet? Are you hungry?"

"No," said Dr. Ma. "I just want this to end."

"Of course, you do. But we must think carefully about how we can work together. Otherwise, it will be hard for me to help you. I know that I'm a bit younger than you, sir, but I am very good at what I do, and I can be a very useful friend."

Dr. Ma exhaled slowly. There wasn't air in the room or time on the clock. Why had he been greedy? Everyone else was doing it, of course, but he had known that he might get caught. Be a man; take the risks. That was what his wife told him, late at night.

His father had warned him: Beware. Bad luck is always hiding inside the doorway, down the next *hutong.*

Dr. Ma had tried to armor himself against misfortune, as his father had advised. But success and power make us relax. We make mistakes. Our luck runs out.

"Excuse me," said the CIA officer. "I need to use the toilet. Help yourself to another drink. I'll be right back."

Chang exited the sitting room of the suite and walked through the bedroom into the bathroom. He closed the door and turned on the faucet. He took a covert communications device from his pocket and called the operations room of the Singapore station. He asked the watch officer to connect with the ops officer on site at the hotel on Sentosa Island.

Chang spoke quietly into the phone.

"Sentosa One, this is Singapore Ops One. Do you copy?"

"Copy, Singapore One." It was a woman's voice. She was the junior officer who had been sent to watch Dr. Ma's suite at the hotel. This was her first big assignment. She tried to sound calm.

"I need you to do something, Sentosa One. I want you to find the target's *mijian*. He didn't bring it with him. It must be in his room. Find it."

"What's a *mijian*, Singapore One? I don't copy that at all. Is that some kind of clothing?"

"It's a diary. A datebook. It should be filled with Chinese writing. Look for it in his room, very thoroughly, but very gently. Collect it and put it in an evidence bag."

"Roger that, Singapore One. What do I do with it when I find it? Should I photograph the pages?"

"Nope. Take it. Send it to Singapore Station and have the watch officer give it to the chief, immediately. He'll pouch it to Headquarters."

"Okay, copy all that. And I learned a new word."

"Listen, Sentosa One. You find this guy's *mijian* and get it out safely and you're a hero at the Culinary Institute of America, for at least the next twenty-four hours."

"Uh, roger that," she said.

The junior officer was inside the suite several minutes later. "Singapore One" went back into the sitting room of the suite to deal with Dr. Ma.

3.

ORCHARD CITY CENTRE, SINGAPORE

Harris Chang walked to the window of the sitting room and pulled back the shades. Night had fallen. The Central Expressway, just below, was a six-lane flicker of headlights and taillights. Beyond was the thick green foliage that guarded the government's central offices. The world was a window away but unreachable. An illuminated sign above the expressway reminded motorists that it was courteous to signal before changing lanes. To the north of this pleasant robot of a city was the Malay Peninsula; to the west, the jungle of Sumatra; to the east, the untracked wilderness of Borneo. And here, this thriving, regimented safe zone. A world in a box.

He turned toward Dr. Ma, who had remained motionless in his easy chair, encased in worry. His eyes were fixed on the window. The case officer pulled the curtain closed.

"It's a long way down," said Chang to his guest.

The older man closed his eyes. He was not courageous. He was a technical man, who enjoyed fine clothes and wine. He liked having money for his mistress in Vancouver. He wanted to be a big man who could have his way.

Chang remained by the curtained window a moment more. He stretched his arms, tilting his head back and forth, flexing the cords of muscle in his neck and shoulders. He watched Dr. Ma. The older man was nearly spent. Chang went to the bar and poured a bottle of Coca-Cola for his guest and switched on the tea kettle. He returned to the couch across from Dr. Ma and handed him the soda.

"Drink this. It will pep you up."

Dr. Ma took a halfhearted sip.

"Nobody's coming for you. You know that. We're good at our work. No rescue team is on the way. It's just you and me."

"I understand."

"Okay, let's start with an obvious problem. Why is a top scientist like you working for the Ministry of State Security? Why did the Academy of Sciences send you? And why does the Ministry need its own expert on supercomputing? I don't get it. The Ministry usually leaves the details of technology to the People's Liberation Army. That's the system."

"If you say so."

"But not in this case. With you, they took a top computer scientist at the Academy, a man with his name on many papers, and made him special adviser to the chief of the Tenth Bureau. Why is that? It must be something very important. We think that the Ministry has been learning things from America, and they needed you to explain what it all meant."

"You flatter me, Mr. Tong. Maybe I am not as valuable as you think."

"Do you think I'm *bai mu*? Blind? Yes, I know that word. Or *bai chi*? An idiot? Do you think I'm an idiot, Dr. Ma?"

"I think you are smart. The CIA is smart."

"Okay, then don't treat me like a fool. Tell me: Why did the Ministry need one of China's top computer scientists as a senior technical adviser?"

Dr. Ma looked down.

"They had a special project, perhaps. I don't know."

"Of course, they had a special project. But what was it?"

"I cannot say. I don't know."

"I want to be respectful, doctor. But I need answers."

"No." Dr. Ma shook his head. He was at the edge of betrayal now, his feet slipping beneath him, but he must resist.

"Please, sir, don't push your luck. This is not a committee meeting or a self-criticism session. I can help you with your . . . problem . . . but only if you are honest."

"If you know so much already, then it doesn't matter what I say." He was trying to find space.

Chang stepped toward the older man and leaned toward his ear. He spoke in a low whisper, each word carrying a weight.

"You have made a mistake, Dr. Ma. You have stolen money. That has consequences. What I say is not a request. I must inform you respectfully that it is a requirement. So listen carefully. As I said, it's a long way down, so to speak. One must be very careful."

The CIA officer was gentle, even in his threats, but the Chinese man understood.

"Please," said Dr. Ma quietly.

"So tell me: What is the special project being run by the Tenth Bureau of the Ministry of State Security? Why is the Ministry involved and not the Second Department of the PLA? What are you advising them about?"

"I'm sorry?" Dr. Ma cupped his hand to his ear as if he hadn't heard.

Chang's hand came down like a hammer, rattling the glasses on the coffee table.

"Listen!" he said.

"Yes, sir."

"What is the special project? You're helping them run something in the United States. What is it?"

Dr. Ma looked down. He took a drink of his Coke. His palms were wet. Tears had gathered in the corners of his eyes. He wished he could show a better face. But he felt trapped in this room, by this man. He didn't know how to escape.

"Maybe you are right. But I cannot say. Look, sir, young man, you are asking me to commit a crime against the state. They will kill me if I cooperate with you."

"You are wrong, Dr. Ma. Here's the truth: They will kill you if you *don't* cooperate with us."

Dr. Ma flinched.

"Are you crazy? That's upside down. What are you talking about?"

"I'll show you."

Chang rose and went into the bedroom. He returned with two files. One of them was the Luxembourg Asset Management folder that Gunther Krause had brought to the villa earlier that day. The other was a sealed FedEx envelope with an address written in Chinese. Chang opened the private-wealth management file and laid it on the coffee table in front of Dr. Ma's chair.

"Here is your dossier, doctor. Your foreign accounts, all neatly assembled by your good banker, Mr. Krause. He works with us, as you have discovered. But he keeps good records. Would you like to take a look?"

"No."

"Sure you would."

He flipped open the binder and pointed to the columns and rows of numbers.

"You have over forty million dollars now. Most of it is in the Cayman Islands, but some is in Vancouver, to help your friend. What's her name? Oh, yes, Li Fan. I think you have a special private name for her. 'Jasmine.' Isn't that right? Sweet name."

A tear trickled down Dr. Ma's cheek. He was frightened, and not just for himself.

"Isn't that right, Dr. Ma? 'Jasmine.' Answer me, please."

"Yes. *Molihua.* Jasmine. Don't hurt her."

"We don't want to hurt anyone. Especially not you. But these are very serious mistakes, taking forty million dollars in unauthorized payments—let's be honest, in bribes—and giving them to a foreign money manager you met in Macao. That's illegal in China. Isn't it?"

Dr. Ma nodded.

"It would be a crime, whoever did it. But if it was done by an official in the Ministry of State Security, well then, that would be a very serious crime. Punishable by death, maybe. The Party is very unhappy with your ministry. How many vice ministers have been fired at the MSS recently?"

"Two," whispered Dr. Ma. He had known them both. One of them had introduced him to Jasmine.

"Two fallen men! Bad luck. That is why I am worried for you, Dr. Ma. You need our help. You need our protection. Because people in Beijing would be very angry if they knew the truth. They are looking for people like you."

"What do you want?" asked the Chinese man feebly.

"I already told you. I want to know about the special project for which you were technical adviser."

Dr. Ma thought a moment, as if pondering the endgame in a chess match. Then he nodded. There was no exit. He rubbed his eyes and then began.

"The special program started six years ago, one year before I came to the Ministry. It is called 'Xie.' The Scorpion. It is operated jointly by the Tenth Bureau, which oversees all scientific and technical intelligence, and the Eleventh Bureau, which specializes in computer technology. It is a special-collection operation, outside the normal procedures because of its sensitivity. The PLA has no choice but to let the Ministry do its work."

"You're running an agent in America. You can say it."

"Yes. We are running a network in America. That is the Scorpion."

"But why is it so sensitive?"

"Because we collect information about the biggest secret, the one that can give us access to all the other secrets."

"Cryptography. Communications intelligence."

"Well, yes, of course. We always look for that. This program was more focused."

"On what? Come, Dr. Ma, you're still avoiding me when I'm trying to help you, and I don't like it. What was the program focused on?"

"Quantum computing."

"I'm sorry?"

"Quantum computing. My specialty. This is part of our China Dream. A machine that can break any code. We must know everything America knows. This was a directive from the State Council. A national priority. I was sent from the Academy. There is a joint group that coordinates all the collection. All the agencies."

"What's it called, this quantum program? Has your joint group given itself a name?"

"We are connected to a big group called Galaxy. In Chinese it's Xingxi. It collects information about supercomputers. But we are the smaller part, more secret. Xie. The Scorpion."

"Okay, got that. But I still don't understand what you were doing at the Ministry of State Security. That's an intelligence agency, not a technical committee. It runs spies. This sort of tech stuff is usually run by the PLA."

"We don't need 2PLA and 3PLA," said Dr. Ma, scornfully. These two intelligence departments of the People's Liberation Army were the Ministry's great bureaucratic rivals. "This is our case."

"But why does Scorpion need the MSS? And why does it need an academician like you? What are you doing there? I don't get it."

"That is a hard question."

Chang pointed his finger at Dr. Ma.

"Answer it. Please."

Dr. Ma nodded, helplessly. He was delaying his capitulation, giving up information one secret at a time.

Chang looked at his watch. He was becoming impatient. "Time's up," he said. "You won't like what happens next."

Dr. Ma sighed. He bit his lip, paused, and then began speaking.

"They need the Ministry because we run the agents. 2PLA and 3PLA don't have the goods. We do. The PLA hates us, but they can't stop us. This is our ticket. Isn't that what you say? Our 'ticket.' Our card. It keeps us in business."

"What's your mission? Come on, professor. No point in delaying. Let's get you back to the villa, tucked in your bed."

Dr. Ma exhaled again. When you have begun talking, it's hard to finish. He adjusted his glasses, trying to maintain a bit of dignity.

"We try to penetrate the American quantum programs that become classified. The ones that 'go black.' Isn't that your word? Those are our targets. I help the Ministry think about where to place our contacts. Where to collect. What to watch. The technical details. This knowledge keeps our ministry in business. They can fire all the MSS vice ministers they want. But as long as we have this knowledge, we survive. You see?"

Dr. Ma sounded almost proud. This was his gift. His special thing. Chang took a deep breath. His man was nearly there.

"That's very good. How would you say it in Chinese? 'Holy fuck!'"

"*Wo cao!*" said Dr. Ma. Yes, holy fuck. A transaction had just been made. Now he wanted compensation. Reassurance.

"Now, I have a question for you, Mr. 101st Airborne. How will you protect me? You promised that I would be safer, but how? I feel that I am more vulnerable."

"Listen, *Lao Ma*. You have begun a secret relationship with the most powerful intelligence agency in the world. Believe me, you're safer now than you were twenty-four hours ago. We will help you protect your money, and we're the best in the world at that. We can monitor every computer and every financial transaction on the planet. As powerful as you think we are, we are much more so."

"Very nice, I suppose." Dr. Ma made a slight, almost imperceptible bow.

"We will also give you money. A lot of money, as a 'thank you.' We will assist your friend in Vancouver, invisibly, so that she never knows. We can help your daughter at Stanford in finding the best graduate school. Like her dad. We can even help you with your work by giving you information to guide you in the Ministry. We want our friends to succeed. You'll be a hero. They'll promote you."

"I am happy with my current position. When can I return to my hotel?"

Chang raised his hand.

"Not yet. We need to know a few more things. You understand? And we need to arrange procedures for communication."

"I've already told you what you wanted to know. The Scorpion. That's the special project, Mr. Tong. There is nothing else."

"Call me 'Peter,' please. I'll call you Yubo. We're brothers now. We can't have any secrets. That ended when I walked into your room today. Okay?"

Chang was trying to talk gently. He knew that the Chinese scientist was exhausted and that, if pushed too far, he would freeze. But nothing Dr. Ma had said so far was really actionable intelligence. They were still at the level of generalities, which would turn to mush when Chang compiled his reporting cable.

Mark Flanagan, S&T's best tech, was down the hall with a bull-necked assistant from Support. They could intimidate the scientist even more, but that would be a mistake. Dr. Ma was a frightened man; under duress, he would say whatever he thought people wanted to hear. The nuance of his scientific understanding would disappear.

"Let's have some tea. Green tea or black?"

Dr. Ma didn't answer, so Chang made two cups of Lipton and brought them over with milk and sugar.

Dr. Ma let his tea sit, steam rising above the cup. He had started to cry. Not sobs or sniffles, but silent tears running down his cheeks.

"I'm sorry, Dr. Ma. This will be over soon. Here's what I need before we break for the evening, so that you can go back to your hotel and get some rest. I need to know the names of your American agents in Scorpion."

Dr. Ma wiped his eye with a tissue and tried to look dignified.

"I don't know their names. We use code."

"Yes, but you know where they work. Otherwise how could you give them instructions and evaluate their work? Help me out, and then we're done."

Dr. Ma shook his head. The tears seemed to have brought a new stubbornness, or self-pity. It was hard to read the man's face.

"I have gone far enough. I have given you the clues you need. The rest, you can discover for yourself."

Chang sat back in his chair. He cupped his chin in his hand while he thought for a moment about how to develop this case. The East Asia Division veterans said it was a mistake to squeeze the Chinese too hard. They would crack. But in this case, gentle wasn't going to work. Ma was too fragile to last much longer.

"I'm sorry, Dr. Ma. That's not how it works. You don't give us clues. You give us information. Otherwise, bad things can happen."

Chang reached down to the FedEx envelope that he had brought from the sitting room thirty minutes before. It was under the Luxembourg Asset Management dossier, but now he took it in his hands. It contained several dozen pages. He laid the envelope before Dr. Ma.

"The express package is addressed to someone in China. Can you read the address?"

Dr. Ma read the script. "No," he said.

"Yes, of course, you can read it. The package is addressed to the head of the Central Commission for Discipline Inspection in Beijing. It is to be sent directly to his private quarters in the leadership compound. You know who he is, I assume?"

The Chinese scientist tried to speak, but he choked on the words at first, so the CIA officer answered his own question.

"This gentleman is the enforcer of your party's anti-corruption campaign. He has prosecuted generals and admirals, even a minister of public security who was a member of the Politburo Standing Committee."

Dr. Ma shuddered. He knew all too well the purge that was swirling around the upper levels of the Chinese bureaucracy.

"And you know, Dr. Ma, that the Discipline Commission is always looking for new targets, new symbols of the abuse of power and rot in the senior levels of the government. The chief of the commission hates your ministry. He hates everyone from Shanghai. He would find what's in that envelope to be a small treasure."

"What have you put in the package?" Dr. Ma spoke the words so quietly they were almost inaudible.

"You know what's there. It's the story of Dr. Ma Yubo, a very prominent Chinese scientist, who grew up in Shanghai with all the privileges of the elite and stole money from the people. It has all the information in your investment dossier, and more."

"No."

"Yes. I think this matter would be of great concern to the Discipline Commission. I think they would be very upset. You would be destroyed, I am afraid to say, and I fear that would also be the case with all of your family and friends. This shame would endure, as long as people remembered your name."

Dr. Ma reached for the folder but the case officer had already pulled it away. He held it aloft in his hand. The Chinese scientist was crying again. He bowed his head. He was submissive now, entirely. He choked back a sob and then, after a long pause, spoke words coated in black.

"What do you want? I am lost. I have no face. I have only shame."

Chang reached out his hand to Dr. Ma's elbow, as if to a bolster a man who had lost his balance.

"Save yourself, doctor, and those you love. Talk to me. You will remember this as a day of happiness and relief from your burdens."

Dr. Ma held his head in his hands and swayed in his chair. He didn't believe a word of what the American said.

Chang let him rock, silently, for twenty seconds. The Chinese man would come across this final bridge. He had no alternative.

"Very well." Dr. Ma sighed in despair and then continued.

"The primary agent in Scorpion is referred to only by a number, which is regularly changed. I do not remember the current number, but it would be useless to you. Soon it will be something different. Handling of the cables about this agent is very restricted, even within the Tenth Bureau. Very few within the Ministry even know of the case. They keep it from the joint group and the PLA. It is their secret. The PLA is very angry, but they have no choice but to accept. We have the asset."

"What do people say about him? How do they describe him?"

"Among those who know, he has an informal code name in Chinese. It is 'Rukou,' which means 'The Doorway.' That is the way the Ministry thinks about him, as a door."

Chang took a shallow breath. He didn't want to break the mood, now that the information was finally flowing.

"Does he work at the CIA, this agent *Rukou*?"

"Yes, I think so. He has access to all the different scientific programs that your government runs, the 'IARPA' and the 'In-Q-Tel' and the different directorates. That is why he is so precious. He sees all the traffic back and forth. He is the door."

"And you help evaluate the projects that *Rukou* tells you about. How does that work?"

"So much is public. This the biggest science project in the world, but no one understands what works. We can see all the unclassified grants that IARPA is making. We know about the work all the private companies do. Microsoft, Google, Apple. They all are doing things in this 'quantum' space. They publish papers, we read them. They fund joint research. They travel to conferences. That's where I help."

"How? What's your job as adviser?"

"To advise. I understand technology. I have worked with many of the universities and private companies. We have hundreds of Chinese students who work on related projects. When we need to find out what is working and what isn't—the things that aren't published in the papers—we can."

"In the middle, a Scorpion. And beyond that, a Doorway."

"We have a thousand men! That's what they call these big collection programs now. A thousand men. Maybe these days it is ten thousand."

Dr. Ma emitted a grunt that was almost a laugh. "You are very generous with your research grants."

"But what about the classified part?"

"I told you. That is why we have The Doorway."

"To go places that would be closed."

"Yes, of course. When things go dark, we know that the Americans have found something important. A grant recipient disappears from the open list, so we assume that the research is now classified, meaning that it is productive. So we ask *Rukou* to help us find where things went in the dark. I help write the questions and then interpret the answers for the Ministry, so we can use our asset wisely."

Chang was going down his list, mentally checking the boxes that John Vandel had given him. There were a few more items.

"Have you ever heard of a company called 'Parcourse Technology Partners'? It's a venture capital fund. We think your ministry runs it."

"Yes, maybe. Parcourse. I think so. There are so many names and fronts, I don't follow them all."

Chang shook his head in mock disgust. "You're stealing our biggest secrets."

"We are sharing. Science is for everyone. And you make it so easy. We have a wise helper in *Rukou*, a person who believes in global peace."

"You must know who this *Rukou* is, Dr. Ma. I don't believe that you are unaware."

"I don't know the identity. I never wanted to ask. You can believe what you like. I have nothing left to hide from you. What does it matter? Already people would say I am *bùyàoliăn de dōngxi*. I have no shame and I am less than human. Why would I lie?"

"Just tell me the truth, even the little pieces that sound like gossip. What have you heard about *Rukou*? Is he a senior official? Is he married? Does he travel?"

Dr. Ma shook his head. It was almost a shiver.

"I am so tired," he said. "So tired of everything."

"I know. A little more. We're almost there. Then you can rest."

Dr. Ma closed his eyes, as if he could not bear to watch.

"*Rukou* is a senior person. If he were not high level, he would not have so much access. *Rukou* does travel. Sometimes we meet him over-seas. I don't know where."

"Who meets him?"

"Eh?" Dr. Ma was resisting again.

"Who meets him, Dr. Ma? This is important."

"A senior officer. Quite senior. I don't know who. This is a very big secret. They do not even tell the PLA about this case."

"It's that important?"

"The Ministry has lost so many battles with the PLA. This *Rukou* is our most precious asset. Maybe our only one left."

"What else have you heard about *Rukou*? Things about his personal life. His past assignments. Anything that can help us . . ." He broke off.

"Find him?" Dr. Ma snorted, weakly. "Good luck."

"Yes, find him. I need anything you can remember. A personal detail that you heard in the corridor, at lunch, or from a friend down the hall."

Dr. Ma closed his eyes again. This was the last shred of betrayal.

"*Rukou* has a relative within the CIA. An uncle, a brother, a cousin, a something. I don't know. My bureau director said it once, several years ago. That was why *Rukou* knew so much. He had family in the intelli-gence business."

"Thank you." The CIA officer's face was still set hard, but it betrayed a trace of satisfaction. He looked at his watch. "It's late."

Dr. Ma shrugged. He had given up more than the information. His soul had gone out of his body. He was a spirit person now.

"I know you're tired. Maybe it's time for you to go back to your hotel. We have a cab at the stand that can take you back. You'll be safe. We have reserved the villas on either side of you."

"And what then, the day after tomorrow?"

"You'll attend your conference and then go back to Beijing and return to your job."

Dr. Ma shook his head. "Impossible."

Chang reached out again toward the computer scientist, who looked as if he had aged twenty years in the last hour.

"We can do this, together. Tomorrow we'll go over the communica-tions procedures. We'll give you a device. It will look like your iPhone.

It can't be opened or broken or cracked. It uses wireless signals that can't be captured either. It's called a SRAC. Short-Range Agent Communications. It has always worked in Beijing."

Dr. Ma was looking away. "Bah!" he said.

Chang wasn't sure whether the older man's response meant that the Chinese had broken the SRAC system, or that he didn't believe it would work, but he would save that conversation for later. Dr. Ma was on the edge.

"We'll discuss communications tomorrow in another location. We'll have a whole condo for you on Beach Road. You see how much we like you?"

Dr. Ma didn't laugh. He looked dispossessed. He shook his head.

"I am *zhao si*. Looking for trouble. Looking for death. I am no good to you."

"Come now, Dr. Ma. You're just tired."

Chang took a communications device out of his pocket and buzzed Flanagan in the next room, who had been recording every word.

"It's time," he said.

He stood and offered the scientist his arm. Dr. Ma remained sitting until the younger man tugged at his elbow and he rose.

"We'll take you back to your hotel, Dr. Ma. Have a good dinner from room service and a drink. Get some rest. Don't do anything stupid, because we'll be watching. Okay? Then we'll think about the future. I'll explain the payments we will make, and how they will be hidden."

"I cannot do it."

"Sure you can. We'll talk about a new treat for Jasmine. How would she like a Mercedes-Benz? Or a BMW convertible? We can arrange for you to bring it to her in Vancouver. Drive it to her door. How does that sound?"

Dr. Ma studied the younger man's face.

"You are *wen shen*. Do you know what that means? It means you are a troublemaker. Someone who plagues god."

"I'm your friend," said the CIA officer, steering his new asset toward the door. "Your best friend. You'll see."

Dr. Ma stopped at the door. Two Support agents had already arrived, dressed as hotel staff, to get the Chinese man down to the car and back to Sentosa. But he had something more to say.

"I feel sorry for you," he said, looking his host directly in the eye for the first time since he had come to the Holiday Inn. "I tried to make you a compliment when I first met you. I spoke to you as a Chinese man. But I see I was wrong. You are a banana. A man who has Chinese skin but is white inside. You are a high nose. You look Chinese, but you are not. How sad."

Dr. Ma turned and walked out the door, framed by the two men from Support. He was unsteady at first, and the officer worried that his recruit's legs might collapse under him. But the Chinese man steadied, and his posture became erect and his steps firm. It was as if he had seen the future and was walking deliberately toward it.

4.

GRANGE ROAD, SINGAPORE

Harris Chang sat down on the couch in Room 1028 after Dr. Ma had departed. He was flushed with the exhilaration of pitching the Chinese scientist, but even more with its implications. When someone says your agency has been penetrated, what do you do? He closed his eyes, but only for a moment. His body was tingling. He needed to move quickly.

His first call was to Mark Flanagan, the S&T technician next door.

"Jesus, Mary, and Joseph," exclaimed Flanagan. "That was pretty damn good, Harris."

"You think?" Chang considered what had just gone down. "I guess you're right. That was pretty good."

"Never heard a cleaner pitch," said Flanagan. "That guy was so scared, he gave it all up."

"We need to hold this tight, Mark. Airtight. Watertight."

"Tight," said Flanagan from next door.

Flanagan was a lanky red-haired man whose long legs always made his pants seem too short. He had survived his two decades in the Science and Technology Division on pure competence and a black Irishman's talent for staying out of the way of career-killing superiors. He regarded the younger Chinese-American case officer as a smarter kid brother.

"I guess I should take custody of the recordings," said Chang.

" 'Originator controls.' Come down to 1026 and get the drives, monitors, everything."

"I'll be right there. I'll let the COS figure out the distribution list when I get to the safe house."

"Better you than me, brother," said Flanagan.

"I'll be there in twenty seconds."

Chang grabbed a fat legal-size briefcase. Before heading to the next room, he made another quick call on the covert communications device to Warren Winkle, the Singapore station chief.

"What's up, hotshot?" asked Winkle when the Ops Center patched through the call.

"I have to see you right now, sir. We need to put a hold on any distribution of what just went down. No transmission, even restricted handling. Can you meet me now?"

"Chill out, Chang. Let Flanagan handle it. I just got the *mijian* from Sentosa One. I'm going over it now. Pretty juicy stuff. I need to write a cable tonight. Some of it could go stale in a hurry."

"Seriously, sir, I need to see you. This guy bled secrets."

"Flanagan said you banged him. Nice job. Surprisingly adept."

Winkle was famously grumpy. This was supposed to be his last assignment after a career in East Asia. He had been waiting for something big to happen, and here it was. He said he'd meet the young case officer in thirty minutes at "Safe House Orange," which was on Grange Road, near the embassy.

Chang made one more call to a number in Washington. John Vandel answered. Chang was suddenly flustered.

"It came up aces," said Chang. "Pretty . . . amazing." He couldn't cover the emotion in his voice.

"*How* amazing?"

"He spilled his guts. Everything on our list."

"Are they inside the Starship Enterprise?"

"Yes, sir. No ID on their penetration, but enough to work on. And we got the book. Winkle's translating some of it now."

"Good boy," said Vandel.

"Thank you, sir," said Chang. The phrase stuck in his ears.

Harris Chang gathered the digital audio monitor and backup recording gear from Flanagan. He put it all in his briefcase, which he locked.
Flanagan called the driver of a car down below, waiting on a side street.

Chang tried to unwind in the Toyota sedan as it snaked through the
downtown evening traffic. He was hungry. All he had was a granola bar,
stuffed in his jacket many hours before. He gobbled it down and took
a bottle of water from the driver. He waited for the anxiety to leach out
of his body.

The driver followed a brief surveillance detection route, east toward
the airport and then north toward the reservoir, but it was halfhearted.
The Singapore police had so many cameras in place that there was no
such thing as anonymity in this microchip of a country. Singapore was a
liaison partner, but its service was laced with "friends" of China.

The Toyota slid through a dozen intersections as it made its way
back toward Grange Road. This was the embassy district, skirted to the
south with large residences for foreign diplomats and civil servants and
to the north with modern high-rises. The car slowed as it approached
an oval-shaped tower. The driver took the rear entrance to the garage,
punched in a code at the gate, and deposited Harris Chang by the basement elevator.

The "safe house" was an efficiency apartment on the fourth floor of
the building. The station got it cheap because the Chinese detested the
number four, which sounded like the Chinese word for "death."

Chang knocked twice. One loud, one soft. Warren Winkle opened
the door. He was a short man with a low belly and bushy white hair
around his bald spot. Chang entered the room, lugging his legal briefcase. Winkle turned on the radio. He pointed to the couch.

A black notebook was open on the table. Next to it was a tape
recorder, into which Winkle was dictating his translation of what the
book contained.

"What's in the *mijian*?" asked Chang. "Anything good?"

"Pure gold. This guy has been taking notes on all the dirty deals made by his friends at the MSS. There's enough in there to burn half the Ministry. Vandel's going to eat it up. Give me the headline on the good Dr. Ma."

"The MSS is running a penetration inside the agency."

"Fuck me," Winkle said again. "You're kidding, right?"

"No, sir. The penetration is helping the MSS collect intelligence about our black supercomputing projects. Quantum computing, specifically. He's just what Vandel was looking for. He's the technical adviser of a program they call *Xie*, the Scorpion. He helps plan its operations."

"I know what *Xie* mean, Harris. You may be Chinese, but I fucking speak it. Cut to the chase. Who's the mole?"

"Ma doesn't know the penetration's name or where he works at the agency. He has a crypt, but it's a number, and our man doesn't remember it. He says people in the Ministry refer to their asset as *Rukou*."

"The Doorway," said Winkle. "Hell of a code name for a mole. What else does he know about him?"

"He says the penetration is high up, because he has access to so many technical programs. He's handled by someone very senior at the ministry, but Ma said he doesn't know who. And Ma says this *Rukou* has a relative who works at the CIA."

"Everybody at the CIA has a relative at the CIA. What else?"

"That's it, pretty much. We're going to talk again tomorrow. The station is babysitting him at his hotel. Officers in place on both sides of his suite."

"I *know* that," said Winkle. "I put them there, for god's sake. Is this guy going to flip on us? Back out. Try to make a run for the airport?"

"I don't think so. He's terrified of what the MSS would do to him if they found out. I told him we could take care of him. Money, mistress, kid at college, the works."

"He's going to panic when he gets back to the room and can't find his *mijian*."

"Maybe. But that's the way Vandel wanted it. He thinks our man will understand that we own him."

"He should be scared. He's a dead man if their *Rukou* finds out."

"We need to talk about that, sir. Who do we inform about this?"

"You got it all recorded, right? Where's the audio?"

Chang tapped his briefcase. "I told Flanagan not to share anything with anyone."

"Okay. So you're not a complete moron, even if you did serve in the Army."

Chang fought the urge to roll his eyes.

"Just joking. Let me get you a drink. It's Scotch, right?"

Winkle walked to the bar of the well-stocked safe house. He came back with whiskey for his case officer and a big vodka on the rocks for himself. He opened a can of Planter's mixed nuts. Chang waited for him to speak, but for a long moment the station chief was silent.

"Here's how it's going to go down," Winkle said eventually. "Vandel has created a special compartment for this case. Until you hear otherwise, it will have five people in it. You, me, Vandel, Kate Sturm from Support, and the Director. If you need any tech support, you can add Mark Flanagan. He already heard everything on the audio feed. But otherwise, that's it. We're not telling anyone else at the Fudge Factory."

"What about Amy Molinari? She's your boss. She's the China 'mission manager.' Can you keep her out?"

"Yup. I just did. I report to Vandel, the deputy director for operations, not a goddamn mission manager. She's excluded until the DDO says otherwise."

"Why?" asked Chang. He was inwardly pleased, but he wondered if Winkle could get away with it.

"Because I'm a mean old bastard, that's why. I've worked with Molinari for twenty years and I still don't know anything about her, except that she's smart and ambitious, and she doesn't like flaps. And there's another thing, my friend."

"What's that?"

"Amy Molinari doesn't like *you*. She thinks you're not a team player. Meaning that she's jealous of your boyfriend, Vandel. She thinks the DDO has been reorganized out of existence, and she resents the fact the director approved this operation. She told me to handle it 'strictly by the book,' which meant minimal support."

"And you ignored her."

"Of course, I did. Molinari doesn't like ops. She came up as an analyst, and not even a good one. The woman she replaced, 'Amber,' now she was an operator. Not Molinari. When she was chief in Beijing, she was the liaison queen, but the station was in lockdown. That's a fact. She doesn't *like* spying on the Chinese. The congressional committees think she hung the moon. But that doesn't mean I have to like her. Or include her in this compartment. You good with that?"

"Sounds like mutual career suicide, but you're the station chief. It's your call."

"Finish your drink. Then sober up. You have to write an intel report, personal to the DDO. Most important of your career. Maybe mine, too."

"What's our ops plan for tomorrow?"

"Tell Dr. Ma that you love him. Give him the coms. Tell him you don't know what happened to his *mijian*, wink-wink. Say you'll handle him personally. You'll meet him outside the country. *Rukou* won't know anything. Tell him that even Beijing station won't know. That's how tight it will be."

"Is that true? That Beijing won't know?"

"Sure. We make whatever rules we want on this one."

"What about money? I need to tell the guy something. He's greedy."

"Start the money flowing, right away. Like, tomorrow. Pay him the max, one hundred thousand dollars a month, into a new bank account. Show him the receipts and then burn them. Dramatic. He'll like that."

"And Molinari? She knows I was meeting the target today. She'll want to know what happened."

"I'll tell her the operation was a bust. The guy wouldn't play and he had a dog whistle to call the Ministry. I'm good at lying. Years of experience."

"People really are going to hate me," said Chang.

"Not if they don't know anything about the case. And we're not going to tell them. Until we have this all trussed up nice and tight. And then, my friend, we are going to seriously mess with people. Vandel is going to take down the Ministry of State Security before he's through. Mark my words. And look at you! A semi-competent former military officer who turned out to be better than expected at busting someone's balls."

"You're pissing me off, Warren."

"Good. Now get to work on the cable. I'm going back to my *mijian*."

Winkle toddled off to a study and returned with a laptop computer for Chang. He took a large swig of his vodka and then went back to the secret notebook and his dictation.

Chang plugged in his earphones and began transcribing key details from the interrogation of Dr. Ma.

5.

SENTOSA ISLAND, SINGAPORE

Emily Jones-Rodriguez, the officer designated as "Sentosa One" who was monitoring the suite next door by video, realized just after 2:00 a.m. that something was wrong. Dr. Ma Yubo had risen from bed and ruffled underneath the mattress, looking for his secret notebook. Through the audio feed, she'd heard a sound like a sharp wail, then silence. Earlier that evening, she had asked for guidance in case he discovered the *mijian* was gone, and she had been told to do nothing. Let him stew. That was direct from the station chief.

And it seemed okay at first. Dr. Ma had returned to bed for five minutes and then gone to the bathroom. But he hadn't come back.

Jones-Rodriguez was blind. The Office of Technical Services hadn't had time to rig a video camera in the bathroom that evening, before Ma's return. What worried Jones-Rodriguez wasn't just that the surveillance target was taking so long in the john, but that she'd heard a loud noise on the audio feed, a sharp crack and a brief sound like a muffled human voice.

"Did you hear that?" she asked her colleague, the tech who had rigged the bugs. He had flown in with Flanagan from the regional S&T base in Japan.

"Roger that," said the tech. "Sounded like someone fell off a chair."

"Shit," said Jones-Rodriguez. She grabbed for her phone and called the special number for the ops watch officer at the station.

"This is Sentosa One. Request permission to enter subject's room," she said. "Urgent."

"What's up?" asked a sleepy voice.

"Code Blue," she said.

"You sure?" responded the ops officer.

"No. That's why I want to check. He went into the bathroom and I can't see him. Our video is shit. I heard something I didn't like. I want to check it out."

"Go," said the station representative. He paused while he looked for written guidance, then came back. "ROE says no firearms."

Jones-Rodriguez took her gun anyway. She slipped out her door and inserted the master key card into the lock for Dr. Ma's suite. The lights were dimmed. Mozart was playing softly on the sound system.

She entered the bathroom, gun raised, and then lowered it.

Dr. Ma's body was hanging from a noose he had crafted from a power cord.

"Shit, shit, shit," she muttered, staring at the body. She cut him down and felt his pulse, but it was gone.

Jones-Rodriguez called the ops hotline again.

"We have a major flap situation here. We have a dead body, I think. He tried to hang himself. Succeeded, it looks like. We need to extract him or something."

The watch officer made a quick call and then came back on the line.

"Get the tech in from next door. It says in the ops profile that he has medic training. Let him work on the body. Otherwise do not touch a goddamn thing. Got it?"

"Copy," said Jones-Rodriguez. Thirty seconds later, the tech was pounding Dr. Ma's chest and breathing into his mouth. He kept at it for nearly five minutes, until the phone buzzed with a call from the ops center at Headquarters.

"Target is gone," said Jones-Rodriguez into the phone. "Like dead. We've been working him since the last call. Nada. What do you want us to do with him?"

"Nothing. Listen to me very carefully. Clean up the room so there's not a trace of anyone but the target. Nobody else has been in the room. Wipe it down good, and then wipe it again. Copy?"

"Yes, sir. What else?"

"Clear out of both the adjoining villas. Everything. No trace. Wipe it all down, and wipe the wipes. If you all were too dumb to wear latex gloves, put them on now. Copy?"

"Roger that. We have the gloves on. Or at least I do. What about the body?"

"Leave it just like you found it. Noose, chair, whatever else he used. The guy killed himself. That's the way it should read. Just like it happened."

"Roger that. There are abrasion marks on his skin and lacerations on his face, and probably his neck is broken."

"Good. Just put him back the way you found him and then get the fuck out. Station is sending officers in Singapore police uniforms to get your team out the back way, by Palawan Beach Road. Copy all that?"

"Yes, sir."

"Is there any note?"

Jones-Rodriguez took a quick tour of the suite.

"Nothing that I can see. There's a bunch of torn-up shit in the trash, but it's not a suicide note."

"Okay, one last thing. You see anything that says 'Luxembourg Asset Management' lying around the room?"

"Wait one, Singapore Ops."

Jones-Rodriguez went back to the trash basket and double checked.

"Sentosa One back. That Luxembourg thing was what was ripped up in the trash. There are six or eight pages, with a bunch of numbers. He tore them up, but not very well. What should I do with the scraps?"

"Nothing. Leave it just like you found it, torn up, in the trash. Don't touch a thing. And for god's sake don't leave any DNA."

"I think I have that part, Singapore Ops. Anything else?"

"No. Out now. No tracks. Bring everyone and everything with you. No more fuck-ups, please."

"Roger that, Sentosa out," said Jones-Rodriguez. In that instant, considering the possibility that her CIA career was effectively over, she wondered if it was too late to go to law school.

"He's dead. The fucker," muttered Warren Winkle when he put down the phone after getting the urgent, disastrous call from the ops chief at Singapore station. He and Chang were still sitting at their computers in Safe House Orange, typing out their cables. Winkle cursed again, loudly, and then pointed his finger at Chang.

"Did you do this?" Winkle demanded.

"Do what? What happened?" Chang was just taking off his earphones. He looked at Winkle quizzically.

"The SOB just killed himself. That's what. The late Dr. Ma. He made a noose out of a power cord. The watchers, evidently, were not watching. What the hell did you tell him at the end of your meeting? I thought this guy was solid. How the fuck could this have happened? I mean, seriously: Tell me, goddammit."

Chang was numbly shaking his head. He was dazed. His new agent was dead six hours after he'd been recruited? He had no idea how that had happened. Was he that stupid, that he had missed the signs?

"I don't know, Warren. When he left the Holiday Inn, he seemed okay. Resigned. Not happy, but not on a suicide watch. Maybe he flipped when he saw that his *mijian* was missing. All his secrets gone. Who knows?"

"Did he say anything? Like: I'm going to kill myself when you bastards take me back to the hotel. Something like that?"

"Fuck off," said Chang angrily. The last thing he needed was the station chief's obnoxious needling.

"Sorry," said Winkle. "I know you're upset. This is your guy. Or was. Talk to me."

Chang searched his memory, trying to find stitches of fact that would explain this catastrophic outcome.

"He was depressed, for sure. He said I was a troublemaker. Something like that. He said he had lost face and now he had nothing. He said some Chinese words, like he was 'looking for death.' Or 'looking for trouble.' I wasn't sure which he meant. I thought he was exaggerating. He was pissed at me for betraying him."

"Betraying him how?" Winkle had his hand cupped to his ear.

"Because I'm Chinese. He thought we were on the same team. I told him that was bullshit. I was an American. Obviously."

"Obviously." Winkle pondered a second too long. "He thought you were on the same side. That's typical Chinese bullshit."

"Exactly." Chang waved his hand dismissively. He had three generations of American-ness in his bank account. But it was never enough.

"Ma was ashamed," said Chang. "He said he had lost face. He had no face. Something like that. He was afraid of what would happen to his family. Everything he said is on the tapes. But I don't think you'll find what you're looking for."

Another call came in for Winkle. It was the ops chief again, passing along a clarification from the officer at the hotel. The target had rummaged around in his bed, looking for something, probably his notebook, before he went into the bathroom to kill himself.

"Un-huh," said Winkle into the phone. "Tossed the bed. No book. Cries out. Then sayonara. Sad case. What a waste."

Winkle closed the phone and turned to Chang. He stuck out his hand to the shaken case officer. It was a soft handshake, there-there, which made Chang feel even worse.

"You'll excuse me, Harris. I have to clean shit up. You finish writing your cable. It will be shorter now, without the future agent-handling stuff. But they need to know about the penetration now. I'll write up the *mijian* so Vandel has it by close of business. And I'll call him personally, in a minute, and tell him we shot the pooch."

"Maybe Vandel knew this would happen," said Chang quietly.

"Maybe. But probably he doesn't care, one way or another. He plays a long game. He's got everything he wants. In any event, it's not your problem, Harris. You should take the rest of the night off."

Winkle walked away leaving Chang alone at the desk, his cursor twinkling on an unfinished operations report about a newly recruited asset who was now dead. What had he done wrong?

Chang would ask himself the question a hundred times in the hours and days to come. But the answer would remain the same: Nothing. It had been a perfect operation except for one thing: Some people cannot live with betrayal and ambiguity. They don't feel the exhilaration of a double life, only the shame. They escape the only way they can.

6.

ARLINGTON, VIRGINIA

"You need to give me a free hand on my China operation," John Vandel told the Director. They were sitting in his private dining room eating breakfast. The Director had ordered Raisin Bran, mixed with All Bran, and skimmed milk. Vandel had requested scrambled eggs and bacon, but he barely touched his food while he made his pitch. He gesticulated when he talked, extending his loose-jointed arms and pointing his long fingers for emphasis: The Director should scrap the agency's new organization chart, with its mission centers and overlapping roles, and let Vandel run the search for the Chinese penetration agent. Vandel would create a special compartment under his sole authority, and he would take all the blame if anything went wrong.

The Director backed away slightly from the table as Vandel talked. The steward brought him a decaffeinated cappuccino. Through the doorway, a forty-year-old oil portrait of Richard Helms gazed down at them, a limpid, skeptical look on his face.

"Can you promise me you'll catch the Chinese mole, if that's what it is, if I do it your way?"

"No, Mr. Director, I cannot. Nothing is ever one hundred percent. What I *can* promise is that if you turn it over to Amy Molinari and her mission center, and to the FBI counter-intelligence division, you'll have a public mess on your hands."

"What do I say to the White House?"

Vandel reflected a moment, scratched his head, while the Director chewed his bran. That was the issue, always, for any director. Political risk. Would the national security adviser go along? Would there be blowback from other agencies? Would Congress complain that it hadn't been notified? The trick with intelligence policy was making it seem to fit with what the president had already decided to do, so that everyone assumed it had been approved and kept their mouths shut.

"Tell the White House that it's about protecting America's edge in quantum computing," Vandel offered, leaning across the table toward the Director's long, lean face. "That's the flavor of the month downtown. Tell them the CIA has its own secret pathway to building a quantum computer. Tell them that if this operation works, we will destroy China's effort to steal our breakthrough quantum technology. They'll like that."

"Is that true, about protecting a secret pathway?" asked the Director.

"Absolutely," said Vandel. "If people knew all the details of this case, they would give you a medal. This is like completing the Manhattan Project and catching the Rosenbergs, all at once."

The Director took a sip of orange juice and dabbed at his mouth with his napkin. There was just a hint of a smile under the white linen.

"The president is obsessed with quantum computing, that is a fact," said the Director. "He doesn't understand it, but he has briefers from Yale and MIT stacked up over the West Wing like airplanes over Dulles. They all tell him the same thing: Quantum computing is a paradigm shift. It's like Galileo and Newton. He listens to these professors, and then he tells everyone around the table in the Sit Room: 'This will change *everything.*' He may not know a lot, the president, but he loves the idea of winning a race. Is that true, by the way? Will it change everything?"

"Beats me. I'm just a spy. But, yeah, that's what everyone says about a real quantum machine. It will own digital space."

Vandel had been hearing the agency's gearheads talk about this super-super-computer for twenty years: Problems that would take the lifetime of the universe to solve with a conventional computer could be computed in a few hours with a quantum machine. Networks that were manipulated every hour of every day by bad people would become safe, thanks to quantum encryption. Impossible miracles of science, like designer drugs to cure any disease, would become routine.

"And your breakthrough, will it do everything that these professors are swooning about?"

Vandel smiled. He wasn't a professor. He stole secrets for a living.

"Probably not. What we're working on is a kind of backdoor version. It cuts some corners, maybe. But we think it will actually work, while all the fancy stuff is just equations on somebody's whiteboard."

"Will it stop all these damned hacks? The Russians and WikiLeaks are making us look ridiculous."

"Maybe. Quantum computing can help us dominate cyber again. And if China gets it first, it will make the Russia problem seem puny by comparison."

"Approved," said the Director. He wrote an eyes-only memo later that morning for the national security adviser to cover himself. The rest, he didn't want to know. The Director was a former member of Congress. Letting the staff do the dirty work was a way of life.

One day after Harris Chang returned home from Singapore, John Vandel convened the restricted-access compartment he had created to handle the case of Dr. Ma Yubo, deceased, and related matters. He gave it the obscure, anodyne name of "DDO Small Group," and it had no electronic existence in the agency's central computers. The information drawn from Dr. Ma's debriefing and his secret notebook was held personally by the DDO in a server in his office that didn't connect with anyone or anything.

Vandel turned over logistics of this special compartment to Kate Sturm, the deputy director for Support. Sturm had the unobtrusive, tight-lipped competence of the agency's best managers. She had come up in the blue-collar Support directorate, starting as armed protective agent with the Global Resource Staff and then being promoted to manage air transport, administration of covert real estate, and then finally, the entire housekeeping system on which the CIA's operations depended. She was a big, broad woman, habitually dressed in a black pants suit, and she was as close to universally respected as anyone in the agency.

Chang spent his one free day back home sleeping and reading Anthony Trollope. Vandel had opined once in a staff meeting that nobody could understand how Washington works unless they read the Palliser novels, chronicling the political machinations of nineteenth-century Britain. Chang was now dutifully on the fourth, *Phineas Redux*. He wanted to identify with Phineas Finn, the mildly nonconformist Irish-born outsider making his way in the capital. But that was silly. Harris Chang was a Chinaman from Flagstaff. He spent his spare time on cross-fit training, not fox hunting.

The members of the "DDO Small Group" gathered in an office building in the Courthouse section of Arlington that the agency used for sensitive business. It had a big picture window that looked out across the suburban skyline toward the Potomac and the low-rise maze of Washington, a few miles downriver. It was fall, and the trees were shedding their acid-bleached leaves, falling in piles of dull tan and yellow, rather than the blazing red and gold of the pre-carbon age. Vandel closed the shades.

The mole hunters took their seats around a small conference table. Warren Winkle joined by an encrypted satellite audio link. He had remained behind in Singapore to take care of any fallout after the discovery of Dr. Ma's body and to avoid arousing the suspicions of Amy Molinari, the China mission manager.

Vandel wrapped his elastic frame into a chair. He had gotten a haircut, down almost to stubble. With his sallow, scarred face, he might just have been released from a Russian prison.

"So, you know the joke about the guy who has good news and bad news, and really bad news," Vandel began. "Well, that's us. The good news is that we recruited a Chinese agent. The bad news is that he told us his service is running a penetration inside the agency. The really bad news is that our agent is dead, and their mole is alive."

"Ha, ha," said Winkle.

"Shoot me now," said Sturm.

Chang was silent, staring down at the table.

"Okay, all joking aside," continued Vandel. "Harris hit a home run in Singapore, as far as I'm concerned. It would be nice to have had a live agent in place in Beijing, but frankly, it would also have been a pain in the ass running him, and we've got what we really needed. Which is confirmation that the agency has been penetrated. Hats off to Harris for eliciting this information on a cold pitch."

Vandel fastened those pewter eyes on Chang and gave him a wink. Maybe he had planned it this way, so the agent would be self-terminating, maybe he hadn't. He certainly didn't seem unhappy with the way things had turned out.

"Now comes the hard part," Vandel continued. "Good intelligence is like a piece of ripe fruit that's been around a week. If you don't eat it quickly, it rots. Meanwhile, the MSS rodent at Langley is still feeding and covering his tracks. Needless to say: We have to find him soon. People's heads are exploding about this quantum computing thing. If they knew someone was stealing our secrets, they would eat us alive."

Heads nodded. They knew they had to move quickly and keep their mouths shut. Amy Molinari had been told that the attempt to recruit Dr. Ma had failed, and that the Chinese scientist had committed suicide because of personal financial difficulties. That version seemed to be holding up in the corridors on the Third Floor, where Molinari's Asia team had its offices. But it wouldn't keep forever.

The Chinese embassy in Singapore had collected the body, after it was "discovered" by the hotel, and shipped it back home. The Chinese Academy of Sciences issued a brief statement expressing condolences to the family of Academician Ma Yubo, Doctor of Science in Electronic Engineering, who had died in an accident while preparing to attend a scientific convention overseas. It was in everyone's interest to pretend that everything was okay for the moment, but this wouldn't last, either.

"Let's start with the golden notebook, my friends," said Vandel. "It's a mystery why these guys write all their secrets in their datebooks, but they do, and this may be the most perishable stuff we have. Warren, walk us through what was in this man's diary."

"Dr. Ma loved his *mijian*!" snorted Winkle. He voice sounded tinny on the satellite line, and there was a slight echo.

"He must have thought it would be his insurance policy," Winkle continued. "He kept dirt on a dozen of his colleagues at the Ministry of State Security, alongside their business contacts. The juiciest morsels

I've found are a hotel group linked to the Ministry and two investment companies that laundered hot money for MSS officers."

"Nice," said Vandel.

"Ma also wrote a careful chronology of an incident involving the fatal crash of a Ferrari coupe in Beijing and the deaths of some hookers who were on their way to a party hosted by one of his MSS colleagues. Next to that, he put the name of a man who was on the Politburo Standing Committee until recently, with a little star. Isn't that cute?"

"The MSS is rotting from the inside out," said Vandel.

"There's other nasty stuff. Who's sleeping with whom; how much someone's real estate is worth; parts of it are like 'Real Housewives of Beijing.'"

"Why did he keep all this?" asked Vandel. "Any chance that it's fake?"

"Probably he wanted protection. Maybe blackmail. Maybe he wanted to make sure that other people were even more corrupt than he was. Who knows? But this was one scared puppy. Am I right, Harris?"

"He was vulnerable," said Chang. "He liked his nice clothes and his fancy travel. He liked having his forty million dollars in Luxembourg. He was sweating the moment I walked in the door. He wasn't a tough guy; he was a scientist. He was caught, and he knew it."

"Why did he kill himself?" asked Sturm. "Was that our fault?"

"Maybe," said Chang. "Probably we could have done a better job of babysitting him. But I don't think he would have made a very good agent in place. He didn't have the nerves for it."

"Nobody screwed up," said Vandel, emphatically. "Understood?"

Chang and Sturm nodded. From the audio speaker, Winkle's gruff voice muttered, "Tell that to the Senate Intelligence Committee." Then he added: "Agreed."

"So, friends, we have two items of business," said Vandel. "The first is what to do with the information in the notebook. The second is how to identify the person the Chinese have code-named *Rukou*. Let's take the second problem first."

Vandel looked around the table, waiting for dissent, and hearing none, he continued.

"Going over Harris's cable, there are three facts that could help us identify this '*Rukou*.' Ma told us, first, that the asset is a relatively senior person with access to the agency's technology programs across directorates. Second, the asset travels outside the United States, at least occasionally, to meet with a handler from the MSS, who is also a senior person. Third, the asset has a relative who works for the agency. That's basically it. Right, Harris?"

"Yes, sir," said Chang. "He may have known more, but that was all he said."

Vandel opened a locked briefcase and removed three folders, each containing four sets of computer printouts. He handed the folders to Sturm and Chang, who began leafing through the pages while he talked.

"So here's what I've done," Vandel continued. "I'm not Mr. Organization, so I turned it over to Kate. She had the Office of Security collect data about our esteemed workforce and then we sliced and diced. The first set of printouts lists everyone with access to IARPA, In-Q-Tel, Digital Innovation, and S&T programs. That turns out to be just over four hundred people, too many, if you ask me, but there it is. The second printout lists people who have a close relative currently working at the agency. That's a disturbingly large eleven hundred people, listed in attachment two."

"Ha!" came a crackling voice from the audio speaker. "The Central Nepotism Agency. We're like one of those back hollows in West Virginia where everyone is related. No wonder we're so dysfunctional."

"Speak for yourself, Warren." Vandel suppressed a smile and continued.

"The next thing I did was to run List 1 against List 2. That is, who has the necessary access and also has a current relative at the agency. That pares the list down to just over eighty people, who are identified on attachment three. The final thing I did was to run that merged list against a roster of agency employees who have traveled overseas in the last year. That cuts it by more than half, to thirty-four people. That's attachment four. Warren, a copy should be in your queue. Open it now. The rest of you, take a look at the last item in the folder."

The thirty-four names were laid out on seven pages, five names on a page: jobs, clearances, career histories, brief summaries of fitness reports, educational backgrounds.

"So, friends, I would submit to you that somewhere on this list is the name of the Chinese penetration. It's not a very big haystack. Ideally, I'd like to narrow this down to a half-dozen people and check them out, in-house, before we take anything to the Bureau. Let's go through the list together and see if we can discard any names or highlight ones that deserve closer attention."

Vandel called out each name in turn, starting with "Anderson" and "Applewhite," "Bellinger," "Borowitz," and so on through the letters. Some names fell off by common consent. Applewhite, for example, was an administrative officer who knew a lot about renting safe houses but wouldn't have a clue about occupying one. Same with Borowitz, an agency psychiatrist, who had high clearances and a brother who was a longtime Latin America analyst, but who was a very unlikely technology wrangler for a foreign power.

More than a dozen names were dropped that way; the group agreed that they were implausible as penetration agents for a foreign intelligence service.

Vandel interrupted his alphabetical scan about halfway through the list. He extended a long finger and wagged it at his colleagues.

"There are two people I want you to look at very closely. Marilyn Lee and Franklin Ye-Win Shu. They're on pages three and five. See them?"

The group scrolled through the attachment. There were "yups" and "un-huhs" from Sturm and the disembodied voice of Winkle.

Chang had mostly kept silent until now. He didn't have the same years of experience or network of contacts as the others, so it was harder for him to form quick judgments about most of the names. He didn't really know Lee or Shu, either, but he thought he knew why they were on Vandel's special-scrub list.

"Why Lee and Shu?" Chang asked. "What makes them suspect, John? Other than the fact that they're Chinese."

Vandel shrugged. "Well, I mean, that's just it. They are Chinese. And if there's one thing we've learned about the MSS over the years, it's that they like to work on overseas Chinese. Isn't that right, Warren?"

"Pretty much," said Winkle through the speaker. "They flirt with anything that looks Chinese to see if they can get a sympathy fuck, so to speak. But I'm not sure that would apply to recruitment of a senior CIA officer. I think the China First stuff goes out the window at that point."

"Larry Wu-Tai Chin," said Vandel, naming China's most famous penetration of the agency, who was indeed Chinese.

"Katrina Leung," said Sturm. "Ran operations against the FBI for nearly twenty years. Classic MSS case."

"Hanson Huang. Dongfan Chung," said Vandel, citing two more Chinese-Americans who had surfaced in FBI espionage investigations.

Chang sat stiff and silent. His color was rising, barely visible on his skin. He should have kept his mouth shut, but again, he didn't.

"Point taken," said Chang. "But I can play this game, too, guys. Wen Ho Lee. Los Alamos scientist. Practically water-boarded because the Bureau was so sure he had given the Chinese the design of a nuclear warhead. But guess what? He didn't. They busted his ass just because he was Chinese."

"They had collateral information," said Sturm. "And they knew the MSS was trolling for overseas Chinese."

"Chinese-Americans is what we call ourselves, Kate. 'Overseas Chinese' is their term."

"Chill out, Harris," said Vandel. "Obviously the fact that they're Chinese doesn't prove anything. It just means that we should eyeball them. That's all. Don't go P.C. on me. You may have saved my life, but that doesn't mean you get to act like a dickhead."

Chang stared at his shoes. He was embarrassed by Vandel's invocation of a long-ago moment in Iraq. He gave himself a quick, hundred-volt charge of American-ness.

"Okay, you're right," he said quickly. "They deserve a close look. They both have engineering degrees, if you hadn't noticed."

"Duly noted," said Vandel, putting asterisks beside the names of Marilyn Lee and Franklin Ye-Win Shu.

"*Da Shouqiang*," said Winkle. He didn't bother to translate the Chinese phrase, but it meant "jerking off." It happened to be a phrase that Harris Chang understood. He wasn't sure whether Winkle was talking about him, Vandel, or both of them.

7.

ARLINGTON, VIRGINIA

John Vandel led the members of his "DDO Small Group" through several more hours of vetting. He was getting tired. He yawned, tugged at his earlobes, and scratched the gray fuzz atop his head. He asked for coffee and then ordered out for pizza, which was cold by the time it had passed through all the security checks. The shades were drawn on the secure room, so it wasn't until the little group adjourned for a bathroom break that people realized there was a pelting October rain outside. Vandel kept pushing them through the names. They cut the list of thirty-four in half, tossing out people who seemed implausible, and once more, and then again.

The final cut left five people with high clearances, technological savvy, recent overseas travel, a relative in the agency, and a profile that might fit. Vandel read aloud the names: Maeve Bingham, a senior analyst who had worked on East Asia and was now attached to the Weapons and Proliferation Center; Roger Kronholz, a Science & Technology officer on temporary assignment as a program manager at IARPA; Marilyn Lee, a former station chief in Brunei who now was deputy chief of congressional liaison; Franklin Ye-Win Shu, who was a branch chief and senior data scientist in the recently created Directorate of Digital Innovation; and finally, Andrew Toomey, the agency's liaison to the National Geo-

Spatial Intelligence Agency, whose wife worked in Russia House, or what was left of it, in the Europe and Eurasia Center.

"That last name, Andrew Toomey, keeps ringing a bell," said Kate Sturm. "Didn't he get in some kind of trouble?"

Vandel shrugged. So did Chang.

"It was, like, ten years ago," continued Sturm, struggling to place the name. "Some kind of flap. Does anyone remember that?"

"I was in Iraq then," said Vandel. "So was Chang. We don't remember shit."

"Hold on, I'm brushing away the cobwebs," said Winkle through the speaker. There was a long silence before his voice came back. "'Looney Tooms.' That was his nickname at Russia House. He got fucked over, that's what I vaguely recall. Sorry, long time ago."

"Come on, think," said Vandel. "How did he get screwed? What happened?"

"I think he got caught up in a Russian mole hunt. His wife had family there. Jewish scientists, refuseniks. People thought Toomey had been compromised. It turned out to be a dry hole. The leak was at the FBI. But they reamed Toomey good. Took away his clearances for a while. It nearly ruined his career."

"That's the flap I'm remembering," said Sturm. "People thought Toomey was rotten. But then it turned out he wasn't."

"Maybe Toomey's still for sale," ventured Chang. "Maybe he decided that Russian mathematicians are so far ahead in quantum computing that he should help the Chinese."

"Forget about the Russians," said Vandel. "They're not ahead in anything that has a 'Q' in its name. We diddled them. Kate knows. She's been briefed."

"Yes, sir. That was a nice piece of work."

"What are you talking about?" implored the distant, amplified voice of Winkle. "Tell the class."

Vandel stretched his long arms behind his head and leaned back in his chair.

"Okay, short version, to be forgotten: The Russians went down a rat hole on quantum computing a few years ago. We found out, thanks to some nice work in S&T, by somebody, I forget who. It wasn't hard to bait the Russians further down the hole, they were so convinced they were geniuses. And that's where they are now: Stuck. It will take them years to climb out."

"Pretty slick," said Winkle from the ether. "That operation sounds too competent for the CIA, but I'll take your word for it."

"Focus on the Chinese," said Vandel. "*Rukou* is real. We have five names."

Sturm raised her hand.

"Our suspects are all technicians. Do we have enough expertise to decode what all of them do?"

"Probably not," said Vandel. "What do you propose as a fix?"

"Maybe we should get a techie who can help us," said Sturm. "Someone who knows the intelligence community and can answer questions without asking too many."

"I'll buy that. Got any suggestions?"

"No, but let me think about it. Maybe I can find an underemployed tech person who can help us if we get stuck."

"Suggestions welcome. In the meantime, I want the Office of Security to do surveillance on these five. Basic stuff that we can do anyway. Read their mail; examine their calls; look at their travel to see if it matches up with any trips by Li Zian or the other leading 'barbarian handlers' at MSS. Any other suggestions?"

"Maybe Flanagan could help with legwork," offered Chang. "He was there with me in Singapore. He knows the case. He's read in."

"Flanagan is already on his way to Washington, my son, on temporary assignment. Amy Molinari thinks he's visiting his mother. I may look stupid, Harris, but I'm not. So that's the order of battle. In the meantime, 'no talkee,' please."

"No talkee," said Chang with a thin smile. He wondered if Vandel even realized it was a racist comment.

"*Hong mao guizi,*" said Winkle.

"What does that mean?" asked Vandel.

"It's basically a slur against white people," said the Singapore station chief through the speaker. "Literally, it means 'red fur devil.'"

"Is that true?" Vandel asked Chang.

"I'm stumped. Warren's Chinese is much better than mine."

Vandel chuckled. "It's you, isn't it, Warren? Obviously. You're the mole. You've been out there so long you're thinking in Chinese."

"Busted! Meanwhile, what about 'item number one'?" said Winkle. "What to do with the notebook. You never got back to that part. I put a lot of work into translating that screwy *mijian*. What's your plan for it?"

"My plan." He smiled and stroked a mottled cheek. "I want to put that information to work. Place it where it would do the most good."

"What's that supposed to mean?" asked Winkle, an electronic crackle in his voice.

Vandel played his answer out slowly, staring at each of them in turn.

"I think . . . we should give it . . . to the Second Department . . . of the People's Liberation Army."

There was a long pause, while they all considered the boss's proposal to give the CIA's new windfall on corruption inside the Ministry of State Security to the military behemoth that was the MSS's biggest enemy inside China.

Winkle eventually broke the silence.

"That's diabolical," he said appreciatively. "PLA Second Department hates the MSS. They'd gut them like a dead fish."

"Precisely," said Vandel. "Our Chinese friends will take action much more quickly and aggressively than we ever could. The MSS is at the edge of a cliff. This could push them over. What do you think, Harris? This is your case."

"Very Chinese," said Chang. "The Tao of Deception."

"Thank you," said Vandel. "What about you, Warren? Does this make sense?"

"Sure. If we put the MSS out of business, a lot of East Asia station chiefs will lose their jobs, but I'm ready to retire, anyway. One warning, John: You need a very discreet back channel with 2PLA. Otherwise this will blow up in your face."

"Please! Of course I have a back channel. For five years I have been feeding a PLA general with targeting data about Uighurs in Al Qaeda and ISIS. The channel is greased and ready to go."

"Well, good luck, Darth Vader," said Winkle sardonically. "Singapore is signing off. It's the middle of the goddamn night here."

"I'll be away for a few days," said Vandel. "I have a notebook that I need to share with someone. Meantime, all of you, please, keep it buttoned. Seriously. The MSS may be weak, but they are inside our quantum computing program. Their 'scorpion' has stung us on the ass."

Three voices said "roger" at the same time.

"Meeting adjourned," said Vandel.

As they were walking out of the clandestine conference room, Kate Sturm turned to Vandel. She knew him better than anyone did. She was tougher than he was, and he knew it.

"What does your gut tell you about the mole?" she asked him. "You went over that list of names carefully. Who's the most likely candidate?"

Vandel slouched against a doorframe as he pondered his answer.

"Who knows? Could be this kid Kronholz. He's got his fingers on all the goodies. Could be the old guy, Toomey. He has an ax to grind. But if I had to make a bet right now, I'd guess Frank Shu. He has access, profile, possible motive. If it's him, we're screwed."

They spoke loudly enough for Harris Chang to overhear. Once more, he spoke up when he might have kept his mouth shut.

"Hey, boss, I'll make you a bet it isn't Shu. Frank is one of the rising stars around this place. He'd be the last one to work for the losers at the Ministry of State Security. The Chinese asset will turn out to be somebody funky. A falling star, with nothing to lose. Wait and see. A hundred dollars says I'm right."

"What a cheap-ass bet. But you're on." They shook hands.

Vandel moved toward Chang as they neared the elevator. He put a conspiratorial hand on his shoulder.

"When I get back, I need to talk to you, Harris, privately," said Vandel. "I have a crazy idea about how to make this whole play much tighter. But it would put you on the firing line again."

"That's where I like to be," said Chang.

Chang took the elevator down.

Sturm stayed behind to share one last thought with the boss. Vandel was itching to go, but Sturm put up her hand.

"You asked me about technical support," Sturm reminded him. "I thought of someone who could help us sort through the drawers and closets in the tech space."

"Fire away. Who is he?"

"She, actually. The person I'm thinking of is Denise Ford. She's working over in S&T now. Her title is assistant deputy director for S&T, but it's kind of a backwater job. She is the person you were trying to think of before, the S&T officer who got the ball rolling on the Russia quantum computing deception. She's very smart about this stuff, and she knows where all the bits and bytes are."

"Hell, I remember Denise. She used to work in operations. Something happened to her. She got splashed. In Germany or Switzerland or something."

"It was Paris. People blamed her for a flap there, but I don't think it was her fault. She's good people. I'd love to give her a chance to help out. She'll like feeling appreciated, even if she doesn't know what for."

"Fine by me, Kate. You're my GPS system."

Sturm shook her head at Vandel. He was particularly unconvincing as a flatterer.

"I'll talk to Ford while you're in Dubai," she said with a wink. "Have a nice flight."

Harris Chang went to the library at George Mason University after the meeting. He still had library privileges after taking a night course there two semesters before.

He requested books about quantum computing. Most of them had too many equations and algorithms for a non-technologist, but a few tried to explain what a quantum computer might be able to do, if one were ever built. These layman's explanations described a machine that could simultaneously explore every possible answer to a problem, creating a tool of immense, almost infinite computational power.

Chang let himself imagine what the possession of such a tool might mean for the hyper-ambitious new colossus of China. Dr. Ma had spoken of a quest involving not just a thousand men, but ten thousand, guided by the American asset they called "The Doorway." At least, thought Chang, the Chinese were pursuing a prize that was worth the risk.

8.

DUBAI

General Wu Huning traveled on an Emirates flight from Hong Kong to Dubai International Airport. He wore an open-neck shirt and a sports jacket, and he wheeled his own roller bag through passport control and customs. He had not carried his own luggage in nearly a decade. He had a square-jawed face, just beginning to sag at the jowls, and the buzz cut favored by military men around the world. He walked with a powerful, deliberate gait. Other Chinese officers were said to be afraid of him because he had no vices other than his love of command.

The general had received an urgent message via the Chinese military attaché in Washington. It had come from an American using an alias, but whose identity the Chinese officer knew. They had met on two previous occasions to plan the targeted killing of Uighur Muslim members of the jihadist underground. This channel had resulted in the deaths of several dozen enemies of China. No reciprocal favor had been requested at the time by the United States or offered by the Chinese. It was just business.

General Wu didn't like or trust Americans, but he respected the man who had sent him the message proposing the urgent meeting in Dubai. He responded through the military attaché, using a special cipher that was to be decrypted personally by him. Before he departed from Beijing, General Wu informed the vice chairman of the Central Military Commission that he was making a clandestine trip to meet with an American liaison officer; he told none of his subordinates in the Second Department of the PLA where he was going or the reason for the trip.

John Vandel arrived in Dubai a few hours after the Chinese general, on an Emirates flight from Dulles. Like General Wu, he was traveling under an alias identity. He had brought along an agency officer who spoke fluent Chinese and could act as translator. Otherwise, he was alone. He did not inform the station chief in Abu Dhabi or the base chief in Dubai. Back at Langley, only Kate Sturm knew where he had gone.

In Vandel's worn briefcase was the secret notebook that had been kept by Dr. Ma Yubo. Vandel had thought at the last moment about holding back the original and giving a partial transcript as a tease. But he decided that would only arouse suspicion about what might have been falsified or left out. Either do it, or don't: So he brought the *mijian* itself.

The two men had agreed to meet at a hotel along Dubai Creek, near the airport, in a part of town that had become unfashionable and was unlikely to draw curious onlookers. Vandel had reserved a large suite on the top floor, overlooking a golf course and the creek beyond. Food had been spread on the conference table, along with ashtrays and a carton of American cigarettes. In the pantry were bottles of vodka, whiskey, and cognac—the classic furnishings of a Cold War safe house.

Vandel heard the knocks on his door at 10:00 p.m. One loud, two soft. Vandel opened the door. General Wu was holding a bouquet of flowers that he had bought in the lobby. That wasn't part of the recognition protocol; Vandel smiled and handed them to the translator, just inside the door.

"Welcome, my friend," said Vandel, escorting his visitor safely inside the suite. "You are kind to pay me a visit. And on such short notice. *Xièxiè*. Thank you."

Vandel's translator began to repeat this greeting in Chinese, but the general waved him off. His English was better than he normally liked to admit. He had studied in America, like so many Chinese officials.

"When an old friend calls, it is best to come soon. We do not ask why. A friend would not make such an invitation if there was no reason."

"I forget that your English is so good, *Lao* Wu. Shall I send my assistant away?" Vandel gestured to the translator.

"Yes, please. Then it will be just you and me. If I get stuck, you can bring him back."

"Good. He can put the flowers in water, so they stay fresh."

The translator retreated toward his room next door, taking the bouquet with him. Vandel was happy to keep the meeting one-on-one. The fewer people in either country who were aware of the transaction that was about to take place, the better.

"Come join me, old friend," he said, taking the general's elbow and steering him toward the salon, with its view of Dubai at night. "I am certain you will find this trip was worth the trouble."

They took seats on a couch that overlooked the city's otherworldly skyline. To the northeast was the billowing white sail of the Burj al Arab and, further west, the impossible stiletto needle of the Burj al Dubai, surrounded by the twinkling lights of a hundred skyscrapers.

"How can the Arabs be so smart, and so stupid?" said General Wu, admiring the view.

"You might ask the same question about America," replied Vandel. "Usually, we take the stupid part of the Arab world for ourselves, and leave the smart part for China."

"Ha!" said the Chinese general. It would be impolite to agree.

"It's cognac, if I remember. And Marlboro Lights."

Vandel retreated to the adjoining room and ambled back with a pack of cigarettes and two glasses of fine brandy. Under his arm was a thick manila envelope. He set down the liquor and lit a cigarette for the general, who was a chain-smoker.

"You are most welcome," said the general, just off in his expression of thanks.

Vandel smiled. He wanted to slow the evening, build a little anticipation. Too eager a presentation might make the Chinese officer suspicious. He scratched his head, studied his glass, waited for the other man to speak.

"Have you brought me a new target set, perhaps?" asked General Wu after a long minute of silence. He had taken several draughts of his cognac and smoked his first cigarette almost down to the filter.

"No, not this time," said Vandel.

"We admire the skill of your special operators. We are a poor country, as you know, so it is not always easy for us to find these enemies, and track them so effectively, in the way that a great power can do."

"Right," said Vandel, elongating the word an extra beat. This Chinese humble pie was part of any Sino-American interaction, but it was tedious.

"Find, fix, finish," said the general, repeating the mantra of the Joint Special Operations Command, which he knew had been the source of the previous two transmissions of intelligence about Uighur terrorist networks.

"Just so," said Vandel. The American sat back on the couch and sipped his brandy. After a few more long moments of silence, he reached for the manila envelope, which he had placed on the coffee table.

"I have a present for you, *Lao* Wu."

Vandel removed the leather-bound notebook from the envelope and held it in his hands, feeling its weight.

"It's a *mijian*," the American said. "Am I pronouncing that right? It's a secret notebook, of the kind that members of your brother service, the Ministry of State Security, often carry."

Wu shrugged.

"Perhaps that's the word. I wouldn't know. Why should I care about such things?"

"Maybe I should explain. I suppose you have heard the sad story of Dr. Ma Yubo. I am told that he passed away in Singapore recently. A suicide. My condolences."

"I do not know the man."

Wu lit another cigarette and finished the last of his brandy. He looked uncomfortable. Vandel retreated to the pantry and returned with the bottle, pouring more for the general and himself.

"It's very stressful, isn't it, our line of work," said Vandel. "Sometimes people do things they shouldn't. They get greedy, or pushy, or careless. They make the wrong friends. It's sad. Sometimes the only thing they can do is write down their secrets. Keep a diary, you know? The way young girls do. So that someone else knows. But sometimes, that's not enough. The secrets get so heavy, they pull us down. Maybe that's what happened to Dr. Ma. Do you think so?"

The general's discomfort had become acute. He stood up, and then he sat down again. He was losing face, listening to these secrets. The American had power over him. Vandel could see his distress. He wanted to ease it.

"Forgive me, general. I don't mean to make you uneasy. I asked you here because I want to return something that doesn't belong to me. The *mijian* of Dr. Ma has many details that might be embarrassing to China, if they became public. So I thought you should have them. For safekeeping."

Vandel handed the volume to Wu. He took it warily, but when he had it in his hands, he opened the book and read a few notations. He inhaled sharply, several times, as he leafed through the pages. The general composed himself. He looked at Vandel severely.

"Why are you doing this? What is the trick? Why do you betray me in this way?"

"I don't betray you in any way, my friend. There is no trick. Have your experts look at the book, check for microphones, chemicals, whatever you like. You'll find nothing unusual. Check the fingerprints. They're Dr. Ma's. But I do want you to understand what these pages contain. Perhaps then you will understand why I am giving this book to you, after it fell into my hands by accident."

"Tell me. And then I will leave. With the notebook. Which is stolen property. Shame on you."

"Here is what you will find when you study the book, old friend. Dr. Ma was like too many officials of the Ministry of State Security. He was doing favors for powerful businessmen and taking money from them. It is a problem that greatly troubles the wise leader of your country, isn't it?"

Vandel waited for an answer.

"Yes," Wu said eventually. "Our Commission for Discipline Inspection works night and day to find such people. We have uncovered them in the Ministry, it is true. Very shameful."

"Too many temptations at the Ministry of State Security, I guess. Too many contacts with foreigners. Too many favors to bestow. You know, you'd think the minister himself, Li Zian, might be infected. But there wasn't any sign of that in the notebook, I must tell you, even though Dr. Ma and the minister were friends."

"Li Zian is a strong tree," said Wu quietly. "But the ground under him is soft, I think."

"You'll read the story in the dossier, my friend. Pretty graphic. Dr. Ma listed the names of people with whom he had such corrupt dealings," continued Vandel.

General Wu's eyes widened. "Oh, really?"

"Yes. I won't bother you with the details. Many prominent names, from Shanghai, especially, which will interest your commission. But there is one matter that I wanted to bring to your attention, in particular. As friends. It involves the chief of staff of the Party's central committee, Hu Liu. Such a sensitive position. I thought you should know, personally."

"This is not your business. Or mine. Do not play more games with me."

"General Wu, my friend, I am sorry to say this, but Comrade Hu was involved with some personalities who were very unpleasant. One of them is a vice minister of state security. I know the Discipline Commission has already cleared away two men from this position, but here is another, it seems. He did dirty deals with a big tycoon from Sichuan. And it seems that Comrade Hu wanted a girl, but not a nice Han Chinese girl. No! He wanted Tibetan girls, two of them, for his bed."

"Enough," said Wu. He put his hands over his ears, still clutching the notebook. But he couldn't stop listening. He savored this tale of the corruption of the Ministry of State Security, his bureaucratic rival.

"Yes, indeed, they were Tibetan girls. That's what Dr. Ma wrote in the *mijian*, anyway. Comrade Hu's son was sent to procure them, quickly. He drove them in his fast Italian car, a Ferrari. Too fast! The car crashed. Young Hu and the girls were killed. What a scandal, if anyone knew. To hide the secret, they had to pay the Tibetan girls' families with money from one of the big energy companies. That's what Dr. Ma wrote, anyway. You'll find out the truth."

"I am a military officer. This is for the Discipline Commission. If there are any irregularities involving officers of the Ministry of State Security, the commission will discover the truth."

"The truth will out! That's what we like to say. So you can understand why I, as a friend of China, did not want to spread these rumors and allegations about the Ministry, which can only damage good relations between our two countries, but wanted to put them into the hands of a friend, whom I know and trust."

Wu looked at the American with perverse admiration. This was a poison-tipped gift that he had brought. But Wu could not deny that it was valuable, especially to his colleagues in military intelligence, who labored day and night to diminish the power of their "brother" service.

"I think I understand you well, Mr. Vandel. And I thank you for your gift. Does it feel better, to give back stolen property?"

"Beats me," said Vandel. "I never stole anything in my life."

"It is time for me to go," said the general, rising from the couch. "Past time, really. Maybe I should not have come. You are a tricky one, sir. I cannot call you a friend tonight. But you have been helpful to China in the past. And perhaps you will be, again. But please, do not interfere in our internal affairs, ever. That is a very dangerous course."

"I agree, entirely," said Vandel. "Recruiting agents inside a foreign power and sowing mistrust is the devil's work."

General Wu walked to the door. Vandel thought at first that he wasn't going to shake hands, but at the door, he turned and limply held the American's palm. In his other hand, tucked tightly at his side, he held the black-leather notebook.

9.

BAGHDAD, IRAQ

Lieutenant Harris Chang first met John Vandel on a hot fall day in late 2005 in a makeshift bomb shelter in Baghdad. Chang was making his way from Camp Phoenix to the Republican Palace when the siren went off that signaled a rocket attack on the Green Zone. The incoming rounds were heavy caliber, and Chang was out in the open. He made a dash for one of the improvised bunkers that had been installed every hundred yards or so around the zone, after the insurgents had decided it was open season on anything American.

Vandel was heading in the same direction when the siren began to wail. He jumped into the shelter just after Chang and cursed, "You mother-fuckers!" in the direction of the incoming fire.

Chang was in uniform, body armor, and rifle; the whole kit. Vandel was wearing civilian clothes under a light armor vest but carrying a side-arm. He studied Chang with sharp gray eyes that conveyed empathy and suspicion at the same time. Vandel was fit, like a soldier, close-cropped and hard-muscled, but his body had a loose, rubbery set.

Chang made an instant guess that his new bunker-mate probably worked at the CIA station, which was near the MNSTC-I headquarters at Phoenix, on the eastern side of the zone. He was too self-assured to be a contractor.

A rocket landed about fifty feet away. Chang, wearing his armor, instinctively fell on top of Vandel to protect him. They felt the percussion of the blast, bending the air with its force. Shrapnel flew into the sides of the bunker and embedded deep in the concrete, but they were both safe. Several other rounds landed further away, and then a minute later, the all-clear sounded.

"I owe you one, lieutenant," said Vandel, standing up. His buzz cut was covered with fine, powdery dust. "I don't forget a favor."

"I had the battle rattle, sir," said Chang, modestly. "You would have done it for me."

"No fucking way," said Vandel, giving the young officer a pat on the back. He stuck out his hand. He looked like a gray ghost come to life.

"I'm John Vandel," he said, brushing the sand from his pockmarked face.

"Lieutenant Harris Chang, sir." They shook hands, and then smiled, each of them, at the formality of the greeting after they had been clawing at the dirt together as the rounds landed.

They emerged from the shelter and walked together toward the monstrosity of the Republican Palace. Vandel fell into the instant brotherhood of having survived an encounter with a rocket shell. He put a hand on the young officer's sleeve patch, marking him as a member of the Multi-National Security Transition Command—Iraq, whose acronym, pronounced "min-sticky," made it sound like a sweet roll.

"MNSTC-I, right?" asked Vandel. "Over at Camp Phoenix."

"Yes, sir," said Chang. "How about you, sir?"

"Other Government Agency. I run the shop there."

"I'm sorry, sir. I shouldn't have asked."

Vandel laughed. A man emerging from a bunker in the Green Zone didn't think so much about secrets. Vandel continued walking with the young Army officer. He had a loose, loping gait. He was a forty-year-old, going on thirty. He didn't like to waste time.

"Is that training program of yours as screwed up as I think it is?" asked Vandel. "It's costing us a fortune, but the results still seem to be crap."

Chang didn't know how to answer, but he wasn't a good liar. In Iraq, it was a relief that someone was actually asking him to tell the truth.

"Yes, sir," he said. "It's a mess."

"How so?" pressed Vandel.

"Well, that's why I came to Baghdad today, sir, actually. Normally I work up at Camp Taji. But we're just getting deeper in the hole up there, and last week I caught one of my Iraqi officers stealing new equipment and trying to sell it. The major I work for thought I better come down and tell the lieutenant colonel about it."

"What did your colonel say?" asked Vandel.

"He said to keep it zipped. The new commanding general just told the president that the Iraqi Security Forces are a success story. So he thought this would be the wrong time to tell the general that it's messed up and people are stealing stuff."

"FUBAR," said Vandel, rolling his eyes.

"Yes, sir."

They were nearing the hulking gates of the palace. They each stopped at a sand-filled barrier to unload their weapons and then proceeded toward the entry. It was midday. The Baghdad sun was as merciless as the people under it.

"You hungry?" asked Vandel.

"Yes, sir. Most definitely."

"Let's grab some food. Follow me. I think they're serving Alaska King Crab legs today. Or maybe it's wild boar." He chortled at the absurdity of the Green Zone's lavish cuisine and everything else about this misbegotten American enterprise in Mesopotamia. At the entrance to the dining facility, they washed the grit off their faces and arms and walked together toward the chow line.

Maybe it was the enforced comradeship of being in a war zone. Maybe it was Vandel's belief that the young lieutenant had saved his life. Maybe it was something else, a yearning in Chang to find someone to whom he could tell the truth, and an eagerness on Vandel's part to hear it, after so many months of upbeat lies from his colleagues.

They talked far longer than the polite thirty minutes of a thank-you lunch, and by the end of their conversation, a relationship had formed. It proved to be a decisive meeting; like so many things that matter in life, it was the result of an accidental encounter.

Chang knew people were often embarrassed about mentioning his ethnic background, so he raised the topic himself. He wanted to feel comfortable in his skin. That had helped him in the Army, dealing with people who said "Gook" and "Chink" behind his back, even though he was a first lieutenant.

"I'll bet I'm the first Chinese-American officer you've met in Iraq, sir," said Chang.

"Not the first. But maybe the second or third. Where are you from?"

"Flagstaff, Arizona." Chang beamed with genuine pride of place. "I was an all-state defensive back for the Flagstaff Eagles. High-school football. How American is that?"

"Delusional. How long have the Changs been in America?"

"Four generations on my father's side. My great-grandfather came over to work on the railroad. He ended up in Flagstaff when it was a depot for the Atlantic and Pacific. His son ran a laundry, his grandson ran a convenience store, and his great-grandson went to West Point. That would be me."

"You were a cadet?"

"Yes, sir. West Point. Then Ranger school. Then in Mosul with the 101st Airborne Division in 2003, and now back here for a second tour. Lucky guy, huh?"

"Your folks must be proud of you."

Chang bowed his head. Not just in humility.

"My dad passed away last year. He and my mom liked me being in the Army. When I got my appointment to West Point, they both cried, they were so happy. They weren't so sure about Iraq."

"Smart people, your parents. I'm sorry about your dad."

"He lived the dream, sir. How about you, sir? Where do the Vandels come from?"

"I'm German on my father's side, from Swabia. Lithuanian on my mother's. Cold and colder. My father came here just after the war. Too many scars from the old country. We grew up with a lot of things unsaid. The agency was a natural fit."

"Chinese are like that, about secrets. My mother's family had nothing but secrets. They were from Chinatown in San Francisco. Something shadowy. I always worried my grandfather was in one of the 'tongs.' My mom would never tell us. Showing emotion was bad. Unless it was fake, then it was okay."

Vandel laughed. He liked the kid. Harris Chang had an easy way of talking with strangers that was unusual in anyone, let alone a Chinese-American first lieutenant.

"What's Flagstaff like?" asked Vandel.

"It's like America, except more so. There's desert on either side, but Flagstaff is up in these big mountains that rise out of nothing. The climb is so steep coming up from Phoenix that people get altitude sickness. Not really, but it feels that way. We have trout streams and forests, and a ton of snow in the winter. We have cowboys and Indians, for real, especially Indians. And we have a little Chinatown, about half a block long. Nice place."

"And now you're in Iraq, you poor bastard."

"I'll be here nine more months. Mom says that when I come home, they're going to give me a parade. People are very patriotic in Flagstaff. They feel guilty when they see soldiers."

"The whole goddamn country feels guilty. I'm not sure why. Maybe it's the flip side of patriotism."

Chang looked away. He wanted patriotism to be unambiguous.

"Deep water, sir," he said.

"Forget it," said Vandel. He paused. They were finished with their meal. "I need to clean up before I see the boss." He had an appointment upstairs with the ambassador. He started toward the door, then stopped, and came back.

"Listen, lieutenant, when your tour here is up, you're going to be thinking about what to do. The Army can be a great life, especially for someone who's gone to Ranger school and punched the right buttons. But my outfit needs smart people like you. We challenge people. We color outside the lines."

"The CIA?" asked Chang. He had never thought about working for the agency until that moment.

"Yes, indeed. We pay better, promote faster, and give more responsibility. Plus, we're habituated to secrets. We're eastern in that way. We almost never tell the truth."

Vandel laughed to signal that he was joking. But Chang just nodded.
"I never considered it, sir, to be honest."

"Well, do think about it. My gut tells me you'd be good at the work.
You've got a talent we call 'rapport,' which is really just the ability to
talk to people. You've got it, and a lot more, I suspect. We've got a
special transition program for military officers who want to join the
agency. We have an associate director for military affairs who oversees
paramilitary stuff. But I'm thinking you're an operator, like me. Plus,
you've saved my life. So I have to be nice to you. You'd have the wind
at your back."

Chang's eyes were wide as silver dollars. He was shaking his
head. Two hours before, listening to the self-enforced ignorance of his
MNSTC-I colleagues, he had been thinking to himself that the U.S.
Army might not be his dream job, after all. And now here was someone
offering a serious alternative.

"That's a lot for me to think about. No parades in your line of work."

"Nope. No parades. No black and white. No bullshit. Or at least, less
of it than you have to deal with in the military. Mostly just life."

Vandel stood. He shook the young lieutenant's hand. His gray eyes
studied Chang one last time.

"Let's stay in touch," he said. "Something tells me you might be
our guy."

Well before Harris Chang's nine months were up, he began filing the
paperwork for military officers to apply to the agency. A lot of it involved
HR crap that Chang ignored, about annual leave, credit for years of service, and transfer of his savings plan.

What interested him was the description of what an operations officer does. It included a series of questions: "Do I thrive on challenge and
significant responsibility? Am I self-reliant, self-confident, adaptable,
and flexible? Do I work effectively on teams and individually? Am I open
to critical feedback? Do I learn from it and adjust?"

Harris Chang knew that he fit the description. It might have been
written for him. It helped that John Vandel, the Baghdad chief of sta-

tion, appended a personal recommendation to his application, and that he forwarded it personally to the drones at Headquarters who handled military transitions. He copied the then-deputy director for operations.

It was fate. Harris Chang was a natural. He had the wind at his back.

10.

OLD TOWN, ALEXANDRIA

Kate Sturm called Denise Ford and asked if she could stop by her home that evening after work. She didn't say why, and Ford was worried at first. Sturm was a player: She had an office on the Seventh Floor and was said to be the closest adviser to the deputy director for operations, a man who navigated the corridors at Headquarters like a barracuda through a coral reef. Why would Sturm want to pay a visit out of the blue? She was a fellow member of the Old Girls club, but they hadn't talked in months.

Ford lived alone in a town house in Old Town, Alexandria. It was a fine two-story brick home built in the early nineteenth century, back when the city was a thriving port. She had painted the façade a creamy off-white, the shade of tapioca pudding, and affixed a plaque next to her doorbell designating the house as part of the Alexandria Historical District. She had filled it with the fine things that a CIA officer with a keen eye can bring back from overseas: Chinese silk draperies, antique rugs from Persia, a fine Federal-style dining table with Hepplewhite chairs and sideboard.

Denise Ford was a handsome woman in her mid-fifties, with a round face and a high forehead. She took good care of herself. Her skin had a smooth glow that hinted at artful maintenance. That evening, home from work, she wore a well-fitting pair of jeans and a tailored tweed jacket she had bought at Max Mara. Her hair was pinned up above her long neck. She wore wide-framed tortoiseshell glasses that were both stylish and bookish.

Ford sat in her study waiting for her visitor. Open on her lap was a new translation of Simone de Beauvoir's autobiography, *Memoirs of a Dutiful Daughter*. She wished she could still read it in the original, but her French had gone soft. "I retain only one confused impression from my earliest days: It is all red, black, and warm," she read. Ford tried to concentrate but the words blurred. She thumbed the pages, looking for the passage where the young woman first met her brilliant but unreliable lover, Jean-Paul Sartre, and then put the book aside.

The doorbell rang eventually, and Ford welcomed her guest. Sturm apologized for late-breaking developments that had kept her at the office. She was a big, reassuring woman, less particular about her appearance than Ford, but someone whose form conveyed robust health and power. She was dressed in her customary black pants suit, set off this evening by a string of pearls. Nobody who handled as many critical secrets as Sturm did could be described as serene, but she had a steady calm and self-confidence.

"The house looks beautiful," said Sturm as she walked into the small, well-appointed living room. "I haven't been here since your Christmas party two years ago."

"I have time to putter," answered Ford.

The place was indeed immaculate, the silver frames on the family photographs were all polished, the annuals were planted just so in the garden. She was a woman who thought about appearances.

"Let me get you a glass of something," Ford offered. "What would you like?"

"I'll have a beer," said Sturm.

Ford retreated to the kitchen and returned with a tray carrying a bottle of Sam Adams, a glass of Napa chardonnay for herself, and a plate with cheese and crackers. She brought a glass for Sturm's beer, but her guest took a first swallow from the bottle.

"I'm sure you're wondering why I called," Sturm said. "It's nothing bad."

"That's a relief. I thought you might have come to tell me I was fired."

"The opposite," said Sturm. "We were talking about you today at work. Me and John Vandel and some other people."

"I'm surprised he even remembers who I am," said Ford. "Our paths don't cross too much."

"We were talking about something you did a few years ago, when we were trying to figure out what the Russians knew about super-computing."

"Oh, that." She laughed. "I gather it worked out. I never got all the details of what you folks did with it, but I'm glad that people haven't forgotten. That's nice."

Ford smiled, warmly, and took a sip of her wine.

"Remind me of how that went down. You were inside the Russian quantum computing program, right?"

" 'Inside' overstates things." Ford laughed again. "We had a program at S&T that we were running with IARPA to monitor all the technical journals in Russian. We used machine-learning algorithms to digest the journal articles and predict what the Russians were doing. I made some good guesses about where the secret labs were and what they were chasing. Then we threw it over the wall to Operations."

Sturm rapped her knuckles on the coffee table, in gentle approval, and took another swig of beer. Ford handed her the cheese plate, but Sturm wanted to keep talking.

"Vandel remembered that this program of yours showed that the Russians were chasing the wrong rabbit in their quantum research. I don't get this stuff, but is that basically right? Explain it for the non-science major."

Ford peered over the top of her glasses, curiously, cleared her throat, and then began talking, slowly and carefully. People didn't usually ask her about her work.

"You know what 'qubits' are, right? Quantum bits that are zero and one at the same time. The problem that has been driving scientists crazy is how to assemble enough of them, and keep them stable long enough, to do real computation. So, the Russians decided that rather than trying to add more qubits, they would increase the dimensions of these bits. So, rather than having just two states in a qubit, they would have three in a 'qutrit,' or four in 'ququart,' all the way up to the hypothetical number 'D,' in a 'qudit.' Does that make any sense?"

"Not entirely, but I gather the Russians made a mistake with this 'qudit' hypothesis."

"A serious mistake. One of our black projects had tried the same approach a few years before, and we knew it was a blind alley. But the engineers at the Moscow Institute of Physics and Technology and the Russian Quantum Center were in love with the idea. The Russians are chess players. They're addicted to complexity. I found the lab in Kazan that was doing most of the work, and the names of the engineers there, and I passed the information on to Vandel's people. They chummed the water."

"You got all this from reading journals?"

"Pretty much. The computers did the reading. I supplied the intuition."

Sturm clinked her beer bottle against Ford's wine glass.

"You should have gotten a medal. Or at least a promotion."

"Right." Ford's voice trailed off, far away. Defeated.

"Pisses me off, sometimes," said Sturm after another drink of beer. She loved the agency, but she hated the way women got shunted off into marginal areas, where they were glorified "reports officers," serving the male "case officers."

"Lots of people wanted credit on this one. They had more friends on the Seventh Floor, I guess. But hey, welcome to my world. People always remember your screw-ups better than your successes. Story of my career."

"Yeah, so can we talk about that? You used to be in Operations, before you went to S&T. But there was a problem in Paris. What happened?"

"Is this a job interview?"

"Sort of. I'll explain in a minute. Tell me about Paris."

Ford sat back in her chair. "Oh, you don't want to hear that. It's ancient history."

"Yes, I do want to know. Vandel asked me about it today, when I proposed you as a resource person for a special compartment we're creating. He said you got 'splashed,' but he didn't say why."

Ford nodded, warily. She sat back in her chair. She didn't really want to tell this story, but now she had no choice.

"Here's the short version: I had integrated cover in Paris at the International Energy Agency. I was developing a French nuclear scientist. I was getting ready to pitch him when he tried to have sex. When I said no, he got suspicious. Eventually he went to the French security service, they ran surveillance, and I was cooked. The interior minister called in our ambassador and told him that I was persona non grata. If we behaved, no publicity. End of story."

"The sex part is infuriating."

"Maybe. But that's life for a woman case officer: If you get close to a man, he assumes you want to screw him. I could have played along. I was recently divorced. Ambitious women COs sleep with their agents all the time. Probably that's what I should have done."

"Outrageous." Sturm shook her head. "But why did you leave Operations and go to S&T?"

"My cover was busted. And after Paris, the DO seemed to think I was 'accident prone.' They offered me jobs, but they were crap. When I complained, they decided I was a troublemaker. It seemed easier to get a new start with S&T. I've always been kind of a gadget-girl, anyway. And now I have my own lily pad."

"You're now assistant deputy director for external programs, right? What does that involve?"

Ford laughed.

"I go to meetings, basically. I talk to scientists who are getting funding. I clear stuff with other agencies. Whatever the S&T director thinks is too boring for him to listen to, he sends me."

"Perfect!" said Sturm. "I mean, I'm sorry you're stuck in this dead-end job, and I'll try to help fix that, but you're the ideal person to help us with the special project I was telling you about. We need a tech road map."

"Great. But I still don't know what you're talking about. Can you explain?" Ford was leaning forward in her chair now.

"Sorry. I can't read you into the details. Not yet, anyway. We need technical support, basically. We need someone who knows computer science. In particular, we need someone with expertise in quantum computing. Could you handle that?"

"Sure." Ford shrugged. "I deal with quantum projects all the time. Overt funding and covert, both. I'm not an engineer, but I know my way around."

Sturm took a last gulp of her beer and rose from her seat. She shook Ford's hand, and then she gave her a sisterly hug.

"This will be good. It will get you back in circulation. Hopefully, it will lead to other things. Please don't tell anyone about our conversation. Sorry to be so vague, but I'll come back to you soon on this. I think we can use your talents on something important."

"I'm glad you came," said Ford, as she walked Sturm to the door and let her out into the cool October evening. And Ford was glad, as she sat back in her chair and finished what was left of her wine. But she was also uneasy. Being put on the shelf, overlooked and ignored, had become comfortable, in its way. The anonymity suited her. Being noticed again came with baggage she wasn't sure she wanted to carry.

She poured herself another glass of wine and walked back to the living room. She turned off the lights and sat in the dark, her face illuminated occasionally by the beam of headlights from a passing car on Prince Street. Her mind flickered among many times and places, but her first thought was of Paris, where things had begun to go bad.

11.

OLD TOWN, ALEXANDRIA

Denise Ford worked in the unfashionable 15th arrondissement, just downriver from the Eiffel Tower. At lunchtime, she liked to get a baguette sandwich from a *boulangerie* on the Avenue du Suffren and find a place on the grass in the Champs de Mars where she could eat her lunch and read a book. It was a short walk from the International Energy Agency. She loved the commotion of tourists along the Quai Branly, the slow chug of the barges moving upstream, and the view of the old Beaux Arts buildings that framed the park. She was in her early thirties; her divorce had been an emancipation; her colleagues envied the Paris assignment and teased her about how soon she would become a station chief.

She met Jean-Christophe Arras the first time at one of those *déjeuners sur l'herbe*. She saw him sitting on the Champs, eating his own baguette, and she said hello and sat down nearby. After an awkward minute, they began talking. They worked together, it turned out, on different floors. Fancy that!

It wasn't as accidental as it looked. Ford had targeted the French scientist from the moment she arrived at the IEA. He was one of the French technical representatives on the IEA secretariat, with a doctorate in nuclear physics. The station ran his traces; he had served in the military with the Force de Frappe. At that time, the CIA didn't run many operations against French government targets. But in the case of Monsieur Arras, Denise Ford requested that this rule be suspended.

The station chief didn't like the operation. He was a heavyset, hard-drinking dinosaur who wasn't convinced that women case officers were useful for anything other than spotting potential recruits. Honey traps, he understood. Recruiting prostitutes, he understood. Women case officers who recruited foreign scientists to spy for the CIA, he didn't understand. But he approved Arras as a "developmental." Soon, after more lunches with her French colleague, Ford began filing intelligence reports. Her developmental got a cryptonym. The EUR division chief sent her a cable commending her and urging her to take the case to the next level.

She had planned that night carefully: She wore a black dress she had bought at Dolce and Gabbana. That was a mistake, probably. She chose a restaurant on the Avenue Rapp and asked him to meet her there. It was a small, intimate place, a neighborhood secret for people who lived in the 7th arrondissement. Another mistake. He was waiting when she arrived; he seemed startled by how elegant she looked. When she sat down, she knew that he thought she was coming onto him. Men are vain; when a pretty woman suggests dinner, they think they understand what's going on.

How do we remember the moments when our lives begin to go off track? A series of little misjudgments, small moments that have big consequences. After dinner, she asked if he wanted to come back to her apartment, which was nearby on Rue de l'Université. She was thinking that she could draw him out on French nuclear consultations with Moscow. In her mind, she was an intelligence officer doing her job.

But that wasn't what Jean-Christophe Arras thought, or even considered, until she shoved him away when he pushed her down on the couch in her apartment. She was strong; she had been trained in hand-to-hand combat at the Farm. When he tried to come at her again, she hurt him. He limped away from her apartment. And then things began to come apart.

"You didn't do anything wrong," said the operations chief at the embassy. When people say that, they usually mean the opposite. He told her to put the recruitment on hold. The French FBI, known as the DST, put surveillance on her, and it wasn't hard, really, for the French to assemble a dossier.

The ambassador was summoned by the interior minister, who complained bitterly about a covert American attempt to recruit a French scientist and demanded the departure of the undeclared CIA officer working at the IEA. The ambassador screamed at the station chief; the station chief told Denise Ford to pack her bags. She was gone twenty-four hours later.

"I knew this wouldn't work," said the station chief as he drove her to the airport. He congratulated himself later for managing to keep the story out of the French newspapers.

When Denise Ford came home from Paris, her father met her at the airport. That was meant kindly, but it deepened her sense of failure. He had served in the government, too. He knew what she did for a living, and he understood what not to ask. He took her for dinner to a restaurant on K Street that had dim lighting and black-leather banquettes with a maître d'hotel who sang Puccini and Verdi arias in a liquid baritone voice. She didn't mean to, but she started to cry.

Before returning to work and the reassembly of her career, she traveled to New Haven to see a faculty mentor. It wasn't to visit the history professor who had pitched her to apply to the agency, but to see his wife, Marie-Laure Trichet, a lecturer in French literature. Ford had always wondered if it was this woman who had really spotted her as a potential intelligence officer, rather than her notoriously well-connected husband.

Ford brought a gift for her French teacher. It was a first edition of *Aden, Arabie*, a memoir published in 1931 by the philosopher Paul Nizan, chronicling his youthful dreams and despair in what is now Yemen. She had found it in an antiquarian bookstore in the 5th arrondissement, beyond the Luxembourg Gardens. She treasured the opening line of the book, which she had quoted in one of her undergraduate essays. *"J'avais vingt ans. Je ne laisserai personne dire que c'est le plus bel âge de la vie."* I was twenty. I will let no one say it's the best time of life. Ford was fourteen years older, but she felt Nizan's premature exhaustion.

"You look very sad," said Madame Trichet, after she had received the visitor in her study and accepted the book. "What has gone wrong?"

Ford explained what she could, starting with the rupture of her marriage before Paris. She had dated George Ford at Yale, where he was regarded by most of her friends and family as an ideal match. He was part of the upward path that she was meant to ascend in her personal life and at work. But the threads had come undone so quickly, they obviously hadn't been stitched very well from the beginning. The silences got longer. Ford always felt that she was making little mistakes, putting the shirts and socks in the wrong drawers. She was relieved when she discovered that he was cheating on her.

"I never thought he suited you really," said Madame Trichet. "He was not supple. His head was flat. But what about your work? We have had such high hopes."

"You know, then?" asked Ford.

"Of course, I do. I was the one who recommended you. Ewing thought women were wasted on the agency, and vice versa. I said you were different."

"I had some bad luck in Paris," said Ford. "It wasn't my fault, but things happened. It will be hard for me to go overseas again, probably. I can't really go into the details."

"Of course, you can't," said Madame Trichet. She looked at the handsome, gifted woman sitting across the table, her shoulders bowed slightly. "May I give you some advice?"

"Please. That's why I came, I think."

"Never settle for the lesser ambition. The job, the title, the conventional loyalties and rewards. Stay focused on the larger ambition, which is making a difference in the world."

"Should I keep working for the government?"

"Probably. But only if you think you are doing good things. That's what you must promise your teacher. That you will have the big ambition, and forget the rest. It's too easy in this world to say yes to mediocre people and ideas. Remember what Voltaire wrote. I taught it to you in this study: 'L'homme est libre au moment qu'il veut l'être.'"

"Man is free at the instant he wants to be," said Denise Ford, translating her professor's words. How far she was from freedom.

———

Denise Ford roused herself from her chair in the living room in Old Town, and from her reverie. She had another opportunity to be useful in an intelligence operation. But really, she had never stopped trying; it had just been hard to get her colleagues to give her the chance.

When she was ready for bed, she turned on the bedside light and opened the memoir of Simone de Beauvoir. It was easier to read, now. Every word was incendiary. "I was choking with fury. Not only had I been condemned to exile, but I was not even allowed the freedom to fight against my barren lot; my actions, my gestures, my words, were all rigidly controlled."

She fell asleep with the book open, but when she awoke the next morning, she felt oddly refreshed.

12.

COLLEGE PARK, MARYLAND

Roger Kronholz worked in an unadorned, white-concrete office in Prince Georges County, Maryland, just inside the Beltway. It had the deliberately uninteresting name "Office Park 2." The sign in the lobby said the occupant was the National Oceanographic Institute. The chief tenant was in fact the Intelligence Advanced Research Projects Activity, better known by its acronym, IARPA. Its presence was suggested by the armed guard just inside the door who barred entry to anyone who didn't have a security clearance.

Because Kronholz was involved directly in quantum computing projects, Kate Sturm had ordered the Office of Security to immediately begin monitoring his phones and computer for "anomalous behavior." Security stationed a plainclothes officer in the parking lot to observe Kronholz's comings and goings. The watcher's suit and tie were incongruous. This was a new-age intelligence facility, with two parking spaces allotted for fuel-efficient vehicles and two more for "mothers-to-be." The security officer removed his jacket and tie.

Upstairs, in an office that had a grand view of the parking lot and little else, Kronholz was unaware of his new status as a subject of a counterespionage investigation. He reviewed a portfolio of research projects with names that were comprehensible only to engineers and computer scientists. His job was to direct government funding toward quantum computing projects that could revolutionize computing. "If it exists," Kronholz always added, with a wink.

To convey its official skepticism about quantum computing, IARPA had added a new logo to its quantum PowerPoint presentations: "The Gap Is Even Larger Than We Thought." This mantra had been repeated so many times that many computer scientists had begun to suspect that the search for the breakthrough computer might, indeed, be folly. But were the skeptics cleared for the real information? If you doubted the technology could work, did that simply demonstrate that you were looking in the wrong place?

Kronholz looked annoyingly like a computer scientist: He was male, bearded, bespectacled, and spoke bewilderingly fast. He read graphic novels, drank craft beers, and played nth-level computer games on his Xbox. Fifteen years ago at MIT, he had been a prankster, one of the undergrads who calculated how to paint a big red nipple on top of the MIT dome. But he wasn't actually an engineer, and he was suspect among his new IARPA colleagues who knew that he was on temporary assignment from the CIA's directorate of Science and Technology and feared that he was snooping on them.

Like many technologists, Kronholz had become something of a loner. In his nearly ten years with the CIA, he had punched tickets in various program management jobs. He was the sort of person who kept his office door closed and sat alone reading a book in the cafeteria. His brother, who worked in the CIA general counsel's office, had advised him not to transfer to IARPA. This was the kind of interagency collaboration that intelligence managers loved, but staff officers usually resisted.

Kronholz made the transfer anyway. He told his brother he needed a change, and he assured his new manager that he would enjoy overseeing the sorting process through which some projects were openly funded and others were taken into the dark. His first IARPA performance review had been generally favorable but included several negative comments. Kronholz's attention wandered. When he was bored with his own work, he asked questions about other people's projects.

Kronholz's world at IARPA was labs and grants. His research projects had unpronounceable names and missions that were difficult to explain. "Quantum Computer Science (QCS)," project number BAA-10-02, was providing funding to Georgia Tech, the University of Southern California, and Raytheon for basic research on the algorithms and error-correction techniques that would allow programming of a quantum computer, if it could ever be built.

"Coherent Superconducting Qubits (CSQ)," project number W911NF-08-R-0011, was funding a half-dozen companies' research into the materials and fabrication techniques to create the physical architecture of a quantum computer, if it could ever be built. "Multi-Qubit Coherent Operations (MQCO)," project number BAA-09-06, was funding research at the University of Maryland, Duke University, and the University of California at Santa Barbara to combine many hundreds of qubits into a quantum computer, if it could ever be built.

The slogan at IARPA was "fail fast." The government didn't mind spending money on blind alleys and dead ends, so long as it discovered a few promising paths through the maze. On his first day as an IARPA program manager, Kronholz had been given a piece of paper with this formula: Expected Utility = Probability × Consequence. That meant that even if the chance of building a real quantum computer was low, the benefit of succeeding was so large that the research made sense.

On a crisp fall Friday, as the Maryland Terrapins prepared to host Ohio State, Kronholz received an urgent message from the Physics Department. Research into a multi-qubit architecture known as an "ion trap" had finally succeeded in "entangling," or combining, many dozens of quantum bits in the magical "superposition" state that was both zero and one. In other words, their pathway might conceivably, just possibly work.

Success was a mixed blessing. Quantum computer research chugged along happily at IARPA so long as it was theoretical. But once something seemed as if it might actually succeed—might help capture the holy grail of information dominance—then changes had to be made quickly. The program had to disappear off the open-source grid and go "black," in the jargon of the intelligence world.

When Kronholz read the message, he thought at first that it was a mistake. He read it twice more and felt a prickling on his skin. He wanted to see the quantum effect happen, live in the lab, before pulling the IARPA alarm.

Kronholz grabbed his jacket and scrambled down to the parking lot and his new toy, a sky-blue Jaguar convertible. He kept it secret from his bike-riding and Prius-driving colleagues at Office Park 2. The car had a 320-horsepower engine and a carbon footprint as large as New Jersey. Kronholz parked far from the building to avoid stares from expectant mothers and Chevy Volt drivers. But the Security officer at the perimeter noticed the fancy new car and made a note to have his colleagues investigate how it had been purchased.

Kronholz drove west to the University of Maryland campus, where the "ion-trap" researchers had reached their seeming breakthrough the previous night. He dumped his car in the parking garage and clambered up a back stairway toward the office of Dr. Gwen Warren, who ran the ion-trap lab. Outside her study was a knot of post-docs who were working on the project: One was Dutch from the University of Rotterdam, another was from Humboldt University in Berlin, and two more, a Chinese husband and wife team, had studied at Tsinghua University in Beijing.

Kronholz glowered as he pushed through this international gaggle of post-docs. Gwen Warren greeted him jubilantly with her arms held aloft above her head. She had short black hair and a runner's body and wore big, black-framed glasses pushed up on her forehead, like sunglasses. Her eyes were alight.

"I think we did it, Roger. We actually did it."

The students outside her office, who could hear through the thin wall, burst into applause.

"Who *are* these people?" Kronholz rolled his eyes. "You've got to get them out of here for a little while so we can talk. We need some privacy."

"Don't rain on their parade, Roger. They're so excited."

"Sorry, but it's not their parade. Uncle Sugar paid for it."

Warren stepped out into the hallway and spoke with the grad students. Most of them had been up all night, and they had the crazy energy that goes with having achieved something most people had told them was impossible. Warren told them to go down to the cafeteria and celebrate with coffee and donuts. She returned to Kronholz and gave him a fist bump.

"Did you really get it to work?" he asked.

"Oh, yeah. This is the real deal. Isn't that what you say? A big 'f-ing' deal! We had enough qubits entangled to factor a pretty big number."

"How big?"

"Three digits."

"That's definitely an improvement over two digits."

It had been a "big deal" not long ago when they had held the qubits together long enough to factor the number 15, identifying the two prime numbers, 3 and 5; and then, another "breakthrough" when someone factored 21. A three-digit number was certainly an advance.

"And the qubits didn't de-cohere?" pressed Kronholz.

"Nope. You want the details? We tried something a little different with the targeting lasers that manipulate the ions to get less noise. And we added more backup, so every time de-coherence degraded the quantum state, we could use extra qubits to fill in. We call it 'Quantum Error Connection.' And it's stable. Really."

"Good for you," said Kronholz. "Less noise means more computing."

"Noise" produced de-coherence, which was the enemy of every quantum computing lab. Normally, researchers could push the fragile qubits into the superpositioned state that was both one and zero and entangle them for a few milliseconds. In that moment, they were both on and off and their power to compute was immense. But then flutter—heat, light, magnetic field fluctuations, even the jitters caused by the lasers themselves—would disrupt the array and the coherence would collapse. If Warren had solved that problem, she might be on the way to something real.

"Look, Roger, this isn't 'it,' but maybe it's what 'it' would look like. The qubits were stable and entangled for long enough to do some real computing. Eventually they de-cohered, sure. But I think this is going to work."

Kronholz nodded, taking mental notes of what she said.

"This is so good, it's bad," he answered after a moment.

"What do you mean, Roger?"

"You still have your SCI clearance, right?"

"I just had it renewed. I sent the notification to the Office of Safe and Secure Operations in your building."

Kronholz lowered his voice.

"We're going to have to take this into another space, if what you say is true. It has to go black."

"What about my lab? What about my post-docs and grad students?"

"We'll keep them on until the contract runs out. But they can't do the serious stuff anymore. We have to cover your tracks. We'll work up some 'glitches' that prove last night's breakthrough was a false start. The foreigners will have to go home; the rest can apply for security clearances and keep working on this, if they pass. How's that?"

Warren shook her head.

"That's terrible," she said. "They'll be crushed."

"Penalty for success. Sorry. You knew the rules when you started."

Warren's eyes were flashing. She had done what she had always dreamed of, and she was being penalized.

"This is why scientists hate the government. It's bullshit!"

"Write your congressman. But you've got to show me it works, before I pull the plug. Maybe you'll get lucky and it will fail!"

Warren scowled at Kronholz. She grabbed her purse and her security badge and bustled toward the door.

"Come down to the lab, Roger. Seeing is believing."

The corridor outside Warren's lab was crowded with the post-docs, doctoral students, and even a few undergraduates. Kronholz shook his head: No, he didn't want everybody crowding around when he made his assessment.

"Sorry, everyone," said Warren glumly. "We're going to have a private session with our visitor. I need a helper, please. Andrew, you come into the lab with me. Everyone else, sorry. We'll be out in a bit."

Andrew Klein stepped forward, thin as a knitting needle, a sprout of black hair topped by a kippah perched on the back of his head. He was the only member of the group who, like his boss, had a security clearance. He had been a cryptographer at the National Security Agency before joining Warren's lab in quest of a doctorate.

Warren punched a code into a lock and the metal door of her lab clicked open. She entered the control room and, with Klein, began turning on the various parts of her ion-trap system. Kronholz studied their den of invention; he made some notes in a pad he had brought along.

The lab had a homemade, science-project look. Spaghetti strands of wires emerged from processors and monitors in the control room. The door to an interior room was guarded by a red sign that warned: "Danger! Visible and/or Invisible Laser Radiation. Avoid eye or skin exposure."

Atop a big table inside this second room was a forest of mirrors and lenses, several score of them, of different sizes and calibrations, mounted atop small stainless-steel platforms. This network focused down the laser beams that were used to target the positions of single ions of ytterbium. The ions were trapped with electrical fields at super-cold temperature that avoided the de-coherence effects of heat. Then other lasers bumped these trapped particles into a quantum state, one particle entangled with another, to build the array.

As Warren tuned her magnets and lasers, Kronholz watched it happen: Inside the forest of mirrors, you could barely see the beams of laser light as they focused down to the infinitesimal bands needed to target the ions. But the tiny tools did their work inside the atomic structure of ytterbium: They were fixed, excited to superposition, and then assembled into entanglement. Two particles appeared on a monitor in the control room, each one representing a fixed ion in a quantum state; then four, sixteen, sixty-four, and so on. More of them, entangled for longer, with greater stability, than people had thought possible.

It wasn't everything, but it was something.

"I'll be damned," said Kronholz quietly. "It looks like you did it. Maybe."

Warren sat next to him, watching the dots that represented the trapped particles, glowing like ghostly planets on the screens. "Spooky action" was how Albert Einstein had imagined such entangled particles that behaved identically at separate locations.

"Beautiful, isn't it? And now you're going to kill it."

"Not kill it. Protect it. Make it flourish. Turn it into a real machine. But in secret."

"I really hate this."

"I know you do. But you love it even more. Now come with me and do the right thing. The sooner you get your smart post-docs out of here, the sooner they can start doing other research back home in Rotterdam or Shanghai. Right?"

Warren nodded. She had indeed known the deal when she started the lab and agreed to accept government money. She had just let herself forget. They stayed in the lab another half hour, removing disks and drives that recorded the previous night's efforts and their own moments before. After a few minutes, the digital record of success was gone. They could write whatever they wanted into the space.

Warren told Klein to enter data from twenty-four hours earlier, when they hadn't been able to get the array to work. He tapped his kippah into place and busied himself typing instructions and shifting files. He had worked at No Such Agency. He knew the deal.

Warren made one last check of the monitors and control machines. She put a hand on the casing of the laser generator as if it were a living thing and gave it a pat. Good-bye. See you somewhere else.

She took her briefcase, headed toward the door, and punched the lock again, opening the door to a buzz of noise. The group of students and post-docs in the corridor had swollen to several dozen now. They began a cheer, but Warren held up her hands. There was deep sadness in her eyes; her jaw was set, accentuating the lines of her cheekbones.

"It didn't work," she said.

"What?" demanded half a dozen voices. "Impossible." "It worked last night." "Something's broken." "Try it again." It was a cacophony of disappointment and denial.

"It didn't work," she said again. "Last night's readings were wrong. Andrew and I reviewed the data. It wasn't robust. We were getting false positives. We'll never get peer review."

"What does that mean?" asked one of the post-docs in the front.

Warren set her jaw. For the sake of kindness, she couldn't be kind. Kronholz was right: The sooner the non-U.S. researchers were released, the better it would be for their careers.

"Because I couldn't reproduce last night's result, we have a big prob-lem. This gentleman"—she pointed to Kronholz—"is from an organi-zation that's one of our funders. I hoped I could show off, but instead I showed him a picture of failure. If that holds up, we lose our money. Is that right, sir?"

"I'm afraid so," said Kronholz. "If something doesn't work, we need to cut the cord."

"Andrew and I will see if we can fix whatever isn't working," said Warren, with mock reassurance. "But we all have to be realistic. I am available starting tomorrow afternoon to speak to the post-docs individually."

"Bullshit," muttered one of the post-docs. Most were too stunned to speak. Working in a lab was like betting at a casino. If you had all your chips on red and it came up black, you were out of the game.

Long before the unclassified grant for the ion-trap experiment expired, a new grant was issued by an interagency group that included representa-tives from the National Security Agency and the CIA. The new funding would support the same work that had been done at the University of Maryland but at a highly classified lab at Fort Meade, behind barbed wire and with background checks and layers of secrecy.

The number of the new contract was a jumble of letters and num-bers: S204GV-71-P-2067. This contract number and confirming docu-mentation were transmitted on an encrypted intelligence community network that had no link with the dirty wire of the Internet. It could not be hacked.

Within days, a full report about contract S204GV-71-P-2067 was on the desk of Li Zian, the director of the Ministry of State Security in Beijing.

13.

BEIJING, CHINA

Li Zian did not like to be observed by his colleagues at the Ministry of State Security when he was digesting bad news. They were so attentive, waiting on each hint of how the boss reacted or what he might do. They encouraged the worst qualities of leadership: the loud braggadocio of command, the appearance of clarity when it did not yet exist. Better the logic of the masters of the Qi dynasty twenty-five centuries ago: Appear weak when you are strong, and strong when you are weak.

Li was a tall, ascetic man. The natural set of his face was a Mandarin disdain. He felt himself surrounded by little men, courtiers and flatterers and crooks. That was the price of Party discipline; it weeded out the ones who might tell the truth and make trouble.

The police had come that morning to arrest the vice minister. Li didn't ask why. He had heard the rumors for weeks about the crash of the Ferrari. And then when he was briefed on the "incident" in Singapore, he had understood why his ministry was too weak to protect its own. It was filled by frightened, little men. The looks in the corridors showed anxiety and greed. MSS officers wondered if they should escape, now. The ones who thought they had leverage asked for meetings with the minister; Li refused.

Li sent meddlesome questioners to see his acting deputy, Xiao-Xi, a man who had a nervous, high-pitched giggle that became more pronounced when he heard or conveyed bad news. Your mother has died, ha-ha-ha. That was the way Xiao-Xi would deliver the message.

The corruption investigations were a mortal threat. Li pretended otherwise, but the ground was shaking under his feet. There were cracks in the walls; the portraits were askew. He had heard the rumors in the corridors outside Central Committee meetings: Why did China need an intelligence service, and a broken one at that, when it had the efficient and disciplined cadres of the People's Liberation Army, Second Department, to conduct intelligence operations?

Li's world had been darkening for many months; now the dreadful "incident" in Singapore, followed by the ouster of his colleague.

Li called a staff meeting. To show face. They would all be talking behind his back about the arrest of the vice minister. But in public, they would pretend they never knew the man.

"You are the wise analyst, Li *Buzhang*," said his flattering, gibbering deputy as the staff meeting began, attaching the honorific word for "minister" to Li's name. And it was true: Li Zian had been the Ministry's top analyst of the United States before he was appointed minister in charge. He assessed the main enemy in the way that an all-source analyst does, putting together the bits of evidence to reach a balanced judgment. But when danger struck—a scientist attached to the Ministry ended up dead in a foreign country—Li wished for the instincts of an operations officer: See it, own it, crush it.

Li looked over at Wang Ji, the head of the American Operations Division. Wang sat silently in a corner of the room, as usual, smoking, listening, and radiating disdain. His nickname was "Carlos," from his many years of working in Cuba and Mexico City, where the American target was more accessible.

Wang was an oddball in a service that liked predictability. Because of his many years working in Latin America, he had taken on the traits of that culture. He was at once a reticent Chinese and a macho Latino, a Party man and a ladies' man; it was a rare and precious combination in the MSS, and for that reason he was resented by more conventional, less talented colleagues. There was another thing about Carlos Wang. He wasn't corrupt. He was still, in his peculiar way, a leftist revolutionary.

Li Zian passed Carlos a note saying they would talk later in the week when the dust settled. Carlos nodded and took another long drag on his cigarette.

The Ministry of State Security occupied a protected compound at Xiyuan, on the northwest edge of the city. It was hidden away in an array of gray brick buildings, beyond two locked fences. It was in an area of Beijing known as "Academic City." Beijing University was nearby; so were the technical schools that did intelligence and military work. The Higher Party School, the campus-like retreat for senior cadres, was nearby, too. All secrets in China were subordinate to the great secret of the Party's rule.

Li excused himself from his giggling deputy and the other briefers and said he wanted to take a walk, alone. The Ministry compound was a sheltered and manicured enclave, and usually it afforded the privacy that Li needed to reflect and consider his next moves.

But on this day, he encountered in the lobby an old friend from Fudan University who was paying a visit, and in the front courtyard a visitor from the Foreign Ministry. He had to be polite to both, but their eyes had solicitous, worried looks. They had heard about the vice minister's arrest, undoubtedly. Li hated their pity; how happy they must all be to see him take a fall.

When Li finally found the solitude of a bench in a garden behind the main building, he was approached by the ambitious young man who had just been promoted to run the Sixth Bureau, which was responsible for counter-intelligence. This was the very last person Li Zian wanted to see on that morning, so he excused himself abruptly and exited the compound altogether.

A guard pursued him, assuming that the boss would want his limousine if he was leaving the Ministry gate. Li loped away in long strides, past the outer perimeter, and hailed a taxi. He told the driver he wanted to go to the Summer Palace, a half mile distant. It was full of tourists, which promised anonymity and a chance to think. They rumbled past the Xiyuan subway stop. Across the intersection stood a KFC, Pizza Hut, and McDonald's, like America, inescapable.

Li entered through the gabled roof of the Eastern Palace gateway, head down, hands in his pockets, his tall form bent forward as if to cut the autumn breeze. This was a morning when you could at least see the clouds above and didn't have to chew the air in your mouth.

"The ruler who rules benevolently will live a long life," read the inscription on the pavilion just inside the gate. How much help was that to a man who ran a spy service, whose trade was thievery and deceit? Benevolence was for another kingdom.

Li escaped the tourists at the gate and took a seat by himself. Finally alone, he turned over in his mind the case of Dr. Ma Yubo, the chief science adviser to the Tenth Bureau and a man whom Li had actually liked, in contrast to so many of his colleagues.

Li had been troubled by Ma's death the moment he heard about it. They were both Shanghai boys; that was part of it. The whole of the Ministry of State Security was a kind of Shanghai Mafia; they recruited from the top ten percent of Fudan University every year; they had the everlasting patronage of the former Chinese president and clique godfather, whose name, like that of the fictional Lord Voldemort, was rarely spoken.

This Shanghai-ness was part of the Ministry's problem, Li understood. But he could no more sever the MSS-Shanghai connection than you could take Harvard and MIT out of Cambridge.

And there was the deeper stain: The Ma case involved foreign hands. It came at a time when the Ministry was under assault from those who said it was too western, too corrupt, too clumsy, too infected with the arrogance of Shanghai. The new Party leadership did not like the Ministry of State Security; the Discipline Commission took down its senior leaders, one by one, like the targets in a shooting gallery. Li survived, to their annoyance. They waited for him to make a fatal error.

The investigators had concluded that Dr. Ma had committed suicide. The toxicologists in Beijing had worked the body every way they could, but the answer came out the same. He had hung himself with a plastic cord in his bathroom. His neck had snapped. His body had fallen to the tile floor. The abrasions didn't lie; they couldn't be faked that well. Dr. Ma had killed himself, all right. But why? How had the Americans gotten to him? What had he said?

Li Zian stopped to admire the cast-iron sculpture of an imaginary beast called the Kylin, which guarded the temple grounds. Its magic was that it transcended nature: It had a dragon's head, a lion's tail, a deer's antler, a cow's hoof. Combining things—sun and moon, light and dark—brings power. Simple things that are all the same, that all go in one direction, are not so strong.

Dr. Ma's death was explained clearly, perhaps conveniently, by the evidence found in his suite. Sheets of his hidden bank accounts were found, torn, in the waste basket. They were foreign accounts, held and managed abroad. The logic train was evident: He was stealing money; he feared he would be caught; the banker had demanded a higher cut, perhaps, and threatened to expose him. Dr. Ma panicked; he feared exposure and ruin, so he killed himself.

That was the story the room told, to the Singapore police, and then to the MSS investigators who were quietly allowed access to the scene when they advised the Singaporean security service that Dr. Ma had been there on "special" business. It all read clearly; too clearly, a suspicious man would say. But Li knew the additional, essential fact that MSS investigators had discovered: The Americans had sent a clandestine team to Singapore. This had been an operation targeting Dr. Ma.

And there was the one, last, horrifying fact: Dr. Ma's secret notebook had not been found. An MSS officer never moved without his dossier. It hadn't been found in his home or office; he must have taken it with him to Singapore. And now it was in someone's hands. Weirdly, perhaps, Li hoped the Americans had the scientist's *mijian*. That would be less dangerous to him than the alternative.

The Doorway was still safe and wide open, at least. Only a day before, another report had come in from America via the special MSS satellite communication channel. The message identified another computing project that was disappearing from the open world into the secret.

Li would have taken this information to Dr. Ma and asked what this new quantum computing idea, "ion trap," was about. Dr. Ma would have explained the technology and used his secret contacts in the Academy of Sciences to fund a new, parallel Chinese effort. Perhaps Li would have allowed Dr. Ma to join him in registering for the reward, the many millions that went to the individual and agency that delivered new technology secrets. But Dr. Ma was gone, so Li could keep the money for himself, if he wanted it. But he didn't. That was part of why his colleagues feared him. Money bored him.

Li strolled down the hill toward Kunming Lake. The crowd was thinning out. Tourists were queuing to enter the Summer Palace with its four delicate floors atop a forbidding stone plinth a hundred yards square. How Chinese, to put a precious structure atop an insurmountable block of stone. Li descended toward the murky blue-black waters of the lake.

Coincidence was possible. The simplest explanation might be correct. But you had to assume the opposite; you had to consider that the picture of what happened in the villa on Sentosa Island had been composed and arranged to send a message that was not the real message.

Li Zian reviewed once more the details of the problem as he walked toward the Marble Boat, the vast structure that anchored the eastern shore of the lake, splendid and immobile.

The Ministry's best officers had investigated the case carefully at Li's direction. The team included members of the Sixth Bureau, responsible for counter-intelligence, the Ninth Bureau, which oversaw anti-defector and counter-surveillance activities, and the Third Bureau, which handled matters in Hong Kong, Macao, and Taiwan. They had done their work carefully, at least. The paperwork was what it appeared to be.

The investigators confirmed that a firm called Luxembourg Asset Management had an office in Taipei and a branch in Macao, which did business under-the-table with many Chinese officials who wanted to get money out of the country. They confirmed that Gunther Krause, whose name was atop the torn documents, was a German national who worked as a portfolio manager with the Luxembourg firm, and that he had traveled to Singapore for a meeting with a Chinese client, presumably Dr. Ma Yubo. By examining Ma's personal email traffic, they confirmed that he had made an appointment to visit with Krause, during a trip whose nominal "official" purpose was to attend a one-day symposium on cryogenic computing.

It had all seemed annoyingly simple, until an officer in the MSS station at the Chinese embassy on Tanglin Road in Singapore began working his best contact at the Security and Intelligence Division, a man who saw all the paperwork, internal and external.

There were some peculiarities to the Ma case, confided the Singapore intelligence officer. Informants at Ma's hotel on Sentosa Island reported that the German, Gunther Krause, had been accompanied to his meeting with Dr. Ma by a Chinese man. The security staff made him sign in before they allowed him to go down to Dr. Ma's villa. His name was "Peter Tong." There were no pictures of him; the hotel's surveillance tapes were blank for the afternoon of his visit.

The Singaporean source man had one other detail, courtesy of the police's network of informants. The two villas on either side of the one occupied by Dr. Ma had been rented, urgently. The renter had paid a bribe to the reservation clerk to obtain those rooms on short notice. They had been booked for three nights, but the guests had only stayed for one, then left abruptly. The rooms were empty. No prints, no other biometric evidence; the Singaporean authorities had checked carefully. The photos taken by the hotel's surveillance cameras were all erased for the twenty-four-hour period of their stay. The SID professed to have no explanation for that.

When Li Zian had heard the briefing that morning, his deputy Xiao-Xi had tittered when they got to the part about the missing surveillance records.

And a final odd detail. The evening Dr. Ma Yubo had died, he had taken a taxi across the causeway into downtown. The taxi had been ordered for him by someone outside the hotel. The Singapore police had tried to trace the cab, but its plates had turned out to be false ones. The surveillance tapes that should have revealed the cab's destination were inconclusive; that's what the police said, at least.

The simplest explanation sometimes suffices. But not in this case.

It was Li Zian's obligation to consider the most dangerous possible rationale for these events. Dr. Ma knew of the existence of the most important American agent that the Ministry of State Security had ever recruited. Ma didn't know much; nobody did. But he knew just a bit, and Li Zian was certain of that because he had been the one who told the scientist about the existence of the American agent he called *Rukou*.

Li stopped and sat on a bench, in the lee of the marble vessel, so sleek with its curved prow and gaily decorated wooden passenger quarters above, yet fixed forever in this spot. He lowered his head and closed his eyes.

Should he contact *Rukou* to warn of the danger? That would be too risky, surely. If the agent had been identified, the warning would come too late. If the agent was not yet a prime suspect, the warning could be a tip-off. *Rukou* knew the agency better than Li Zian did. When it was time to reestablish contact safely, *Rukou* would do so. Let the agent evaluate the risks and make the choices.

Good ideas fall into our minds when we are still. And so it was that morning with Li: The Chinese-American agent, "Peter Tong," was the person that Li Zian should identify. It would take a few days or weeks. The Chinese services weren't as good at electronic collection as people imagined. But eventually, the analysts would obtain an airline reservation, a passport-control record, and then a picture, and they would eventually establish who this Peter Tong really was and take action, creatively.

Li had the man for the operation: Carlos Wang. He knew how to move in the darkness. He understood the Americans. He had taken dozens of overseas Chinese who thought that they had no link with the mainland and had bent them, subtly and sometimes harshly, to China's purpose. Li made a note in his diary to schedule the meeting with Carlos Wang at the end of the week, when the information was clearer and it would not be a loss of face to ask for help.

The Americans had set in motion an attack on the Ministry of State Security. Li would counter-attack in a manner they would not expect. Most Americans did not think like Chinese; they would be unprepared. Or so Li believed.

Li had an eccentric habit. He liked to collect rocks. That day, he had gathered one from near the path down Longevity Hill toward the water. It was a fine-grained piece of granite that he found under a mulberry tree. He took it from his pocket now and, as was his practice, he inscribed the time and place he had found it, in tiny characters, on the rock. He would add it to his collection, hundreds of stones neatly aligned on his shelves at home, so that he could remember this day.

14.

WASHINGTON AND VANCOUVER

John Vandel proposed a location for his meeting with Harris Chang that was out of the building and off the books. He sent the rendezvous coordinates before leaving Dubai and advised Chang not to tell anyone else in the Small Group. It was a coffee shop on Wisconsin Avenue near the Maryland line in northwest Washington. Chang came forty-five minutes early, wanting to stake out the turf. That was supposed to be good tradecraft.

Vandel had arrived even earlier. He was sitting at a corner table outside, one long leg dangling over the edge of his chair, reading his newspaper. A briefcase was propped against the leg of his chair. It was an unseasonably warm fall morning, the sky a hazy Carolina blue and the falling leaves spinning in the breeze. The photo-gray lenses of Vandel's reading glasses had turned dark in the sun, hiding his eyes. He looked up from his newspaper at Chang.

"You're early," said Vandel. He was drinking a black coffee. A half-eaten scone was resting on a napkin. He pulled back a chair for his guest.

"Not early enough," answered Chang.

"I got confused about the time. Couldn't remember if I said 9:00 or 10:00."

"Right," said Chang, smiling at the tradecraft one-upmanship. "You said at our last meeting you had an idea for me. What's up?"

"How would you like to take a little trip out West? Two days, maybe three."

Another customer eased by their table carrying an iced coffee. She was in her forties, dressed in a sleek, sky-blue warm-up suit. She was on her way to the gym or, more likely, returning. She had the look of virtue, rewarded.

Chang waited for her to pass and then answered.

"Absolutely. Does it involve the deceased doctor?"

"Most definitely." Vandel spoke under the sound of the traffic on Wisconsin Avenue. He took off his glasses and leaned toward Chang.

"First, I want you to go see his lady friend in Vancouver. The one you were needling him about. Miss Tiger Lily."

"Jasmine," said Chang. "That's what he called her. Her Chinese name is Li Fan."

"I want you to pay her a call at her apartment in Vancouver. Tell her you're a friend of the doctor's. If she doesn't know he's dead, then break the news. Watch her reaction. Express sympathy. Give her some money. I've authorized ten thousand dollars to break the ice, but if you need more, just message me. Tell her that her boyfriend had a lot of money and that she'll be getting some of it."

"Who's she supposed to think I am?"

"Peter Tong. A friend of her boyfriend. Someone who knows all about her and is looking out for her interests."

"What do we want from her? How hard should I lean?"

"We want to know if anyone else has been in touch about her boyfriend. If she already knows he's dead, someone from the Chinese government must have told her. Even if they haven't, they'll probably be watching her. Scare her a little, if it helps."

"But won't they make me, if I go to see her?"

"Undoubtedly, they have made you *already*, Harris. Jesus! They're not stupid. They've been running the traps just like we have. They'll find tailings of your 'Tong' identity in Singapore if they look hard enough. If you show up on her door, give her a card, give her some money, it confirms to them that bad shit is happening. They'll get nervous. They'll do stuff. They're in a bad way right now. Their ministry is quaking. I want to make it worse."

"You're the boss. What's the second stop?"

"Palo Alto. I want you to go see the doctor's daughter at Stanford. Her name's Ma Daiyu. I'm sure she's heard her dad has passed away. Probably she's gone home for the funeral. Make some inquiries. Talk to her Chinese friends. Let them know that we're watching. If you need help, we can get some people from San Francisco to come down. A bunch of the Stanford professors have worked with National Resources. We can set it up."

"Am I Peter Tong again?"

"Yup." He nodded, the mottled chin moving up and down. "Be visible. Be obvious. It will all get back to the Ministry. I want them to know that the doctor had some weird juju going with somebody. Their top guy, Li Zian, is Mister Cool. I want to spook him. See how he jumps."

"You could just send someone from San Francisco station. Save Uncle Sam the air fare."

"Nope. Don't forget, this case isn't on the books yet. You're one of five people who are cleared for it. Plus, you're the right person."

Chang cocked his head. The morning sun was in his eyes, but it wasn't that. He felt uncomfortable.

"Why? Is it because I'm Chinese, and they're Chinese?"

"Sure. It's partly that. You can talk to these folks more easily. But the main reason I want you to do it is because I trust you. I know you won't fuck up."

Chang nodded. The personal vote of confidence shouldn't have mattered so much to him, but it did.

Vandel opened his briefcase and handed over a thick folder.

"Here's the stuff you'll need. The analysts gathered a file on Jasmine before the Singapore op. The Bureau had a file on the daughter at Stanford."

Vandel drained his coffee and ate the rest of the scone. "Yum," he said.

"How soon?" asked Chang.

"United has two flights that connect to Vancouver this afternoon. Go home, get your Peter Tong kit, and go to Dulles. This is the black budget. Live it up. Martini and steak dinner. Shrimp cocktail, too. Stay out late. Relax."

Chang took the packet. He tried to laugh, but it was forced.

"When do I get to do some operational work that doesn't involve Chinese people?"

"Give me a break. You want to go back to Iraq? Fine. *Ahlan wa sahlan*. I hear they're looking for a new C.O.S. in Baghdad."

"I'm joking," said Chang pushing back his chair and rising to go. "This is my case. I want to nail it."

Harris Chang caught a 4:07 flight from Dulles that connected through Denver, and he was in Vancouver just after 9:00, local time. He checked into a cheap hotel near the airport. He didn't want a steak and he didn't want a martini. He found a late-night ramen shop near the hotel and read *Phineas Redux* while he ate his noodles.

Li Fan, who had been known to Dr. Ma Yubo as *Molihua*, or "Jasmine," lived in a new apartment building in an upscale Vancouver suburb called Burnaby. Harris Chang drove his rented car up Granville Street, past grand mansions barricaded by dense shrubbery. Once they must have belonged to timber or shipping barons who had made their fortunes in the Canadian Northwest. Now many were owned by Chinese tycoons who had begun moving their money out of the Middle Kingdom at the first blush of the great boom.

Chang called Li Fan's home number. When she answered, he hung up. He parked his shiny Kia sedan behind her building on Lougheed Highway and jimmied the freight elevator so that it would take him to her apartment on the twelfth floor. He knocked on her door. When she opened it a crack, the chain still in the bolt, he spoke gently.

"Jasmine, it's Peter Tong. I'm a friend of Dr. Ma's. He asked me to come see you."

She sniffled, and then a tear rolled down her cheek. Obviously she already knew that her lover and protector was dead.

"May I come in?" he asked gently, switching to simple Chinese. "I have something for you. From Dr. Ma."

Li Fan unbolted the door. She was wiping her tears with a tissue; she let her hand drop, turned modestly away, and then looked her visitor straight in the eye.

Chang took a startled step back, and then forward into the room.

"Jasmine" was almost a caricature of Chinese beauty. She had long, lustrous black hair that brushed her neck and shoulders. Her face had been sculpted as if by a makeup artist. The thinnest hints of eyebrows traced across her forehead; long lashes accentuated her almond eyes; her cheeks seemed to glow beneath the skin; her were lips full and red. She was wearing a silk dressing gown, high-waisted, with a long, full skirt. The embroidery around the bodice moved with her as she breathed.

Chang had kept his distance from Asian women. When he was growing up, they so often seemed to be bustling to the lab or the library or wherever success beckoned. Chang had dated Caucasian girls through high school and college. It was part of his "American-ness."

This Chinese woman was like a distant memory. Her face and figure reminded him of a book in his father's house back home in Flagstaff about Chinese nightclubs in the 1930s and 1940s. The book was one of his father's secrets. It was hidden at the bottom of a bookshelf. Chang had thumbed through its pages often enough as an adolescent. This woman resembled one of the showgirls at the "Forbidden City" on Sutter Street.

Li Fan backed gracefully toward the couch. She was wearing slippers with heels. Chang pushed the door of the apartment closed.

"I heard the news," she said, dabbing again at her eyes. "They told me my dear doctor had an accident while he was traveling abroad. Is that true?"

"Yes," lied Chang, switching back to English. "He was in Singapore when he died. He was a fine man. He loved you very much. He spoke about you."

"You knew 'Yu-Yu'?" She used this diminutive word for her deceased lover almost as if she were talking about a pet.

"Just a little. He wanted you to be happy. He wanted you to be taken care of, here in Canada."

"They told me not to talk with anyone."

"Who told you?" asked Chang. He looked around the room. They had probably put a bug in her phone. Maybe a camera in the wall.

"The man from the consulate. He said there would be a problem for me if I talked with anyone about Dr. Ma."

Chang stepped toward her and took her hand. The fingers were thin and fragile. The nails were painted ruby red. As he held her palm, he could feel the fingers tremble slightly. This wasn't just tradecraft. He let the hand go and looked into her eyes. She nodded. What did that mean? Keep going, he told himself. See where this leads.

"I was his friend," said Chang. "He would want you to talk with me. He said that I should give you money if anything happened to him."

She began crying again at the reference to the doctor's passing, tears dripping down her cheeks. She was such a polished performer, it was impossible to know if it was for show. Chang had brought along a pack of tissues, and he handed her one.

"I'm so alone."

"I'm here. I'm your friend."

"You're not Chinese?" she asked, appraising him. "You look too big."

"No. I'm American. Dr. Ma had many friends in America, from the time he was a student here."

Her hand was still trembling. She held it with the other, to keep it steady. Whoever had visited her from the consulate had frightened her.

"Are you a scientist?" she asked.

"Yes, in a way. But I'm really here because I was a friend of Dr. Ma. I have money for you. If you have a bank account, I can wire it to you."

She shook her head.

"I brought along a little gift, then. In memory of Dr. Ma."

He removed a packet from his coat. It was wrapped in brightly colored paper. Inside was the ten thousand dollars.

She took the packet and felt its weight.

"Thank you," she said. She laid it down on a side table. "I cannot say that I do not need help."

"We can send you more money," said Chang.

She cocked her head. She had a courtesan's appreciation of value and nuance. She knew that nothing is free.

"Who is 'we'? And what do I have to do in return?"

"We is just me," said Chang, taking her hand again. "And you don't have to do anything. We want you to be able to stay in Vancouver, if that's what you want. Did he leave money for you?"

"Yes," she said. She pursed those red lips when she had spoken the word.

"Is it enough to last?"

"I don't know. Probably not forever. We'll see."

She was weighing him. She would be talking to the Chinese consulate again soon to see if they could make a better offer.

"Don't play games with me," said Chang. "No back and forth. I have friends in Canada. If I tell them you are untrustworthy, they will make you leave."

"Ah!" She stepped back. "So you do want something."

Her big eyes widened, and the lashes flicked up and down. She took a seat on the sofa. The hem of her silk dressing gown parted slightly, revealing the inner slope of her calf.

Chang felt hot under her gaze. He didn't like using people. The one time he had hated his father as a boy was when he learned the old man had informed on some Chinese migrants in Flagstaff and turned them over to the police.

"You must be tired," she said softly. "Men are always tired. You should relax. I will bring you something to drink."

Chang looked at his watch. It wasn't noon yet. Too early for booze. Maybe it would take away this odd feeling of vertigo, this momentary shiver of lust and shame.

"What do you have?"

"Whiskey. I was keeping it for Yu-Yu. But I will share it with you."

She stood, gave him a teasing look and walked off. Her heels clicked on the wooden floor.

Jasmine returned carrying a glass of whiskey, full to the brim, which she placed submissively on the coffee table. She motioned for Chang to come sit next to her on the couch.

"I hope we are going to be friends," said Jasmine. "I need a friend."

The tradecraft manual didn't have instructions for this situation. Chang waited a moment and then walked firmly toward her. He was tired of following rules. In his cable, he would call it "establishing rapport."

"You are very strong," she said, feeling his bicep as he eased onto the couch next to her.

"I was a soldier."

"James Bond."

"No. Just a friend of Dr. Ma."

She shook her head and wagged one of her long, red-tipped fingers. She knew better.

"You will bring me more presents," she said.

Before Chang could answer, she had wrapped a gentle arm around his shoulder and pulled him toward her. He could hear the rustle of her undergarments as he bent to kiss her.

Chang woke before she did. It was an hour later, in her bedroom. She had dozed off in his arms, light as a bird. She was lost in sleep. Chang shook his head. Why had he ever thought Chinese girls weren't sexy?

"You're good," he whispered.

Her eyes opened wide, then narrowed. She was sharper, now that she'd had him in her bed.

"You aren't supposed to sleep with ladies," she said, smiling, pointing a long, lacquered finger at him.

"How do you know that?"

"I know."

"Can I see you again? Like tonight?"

Li Fan paused, looking him up and down. If he had given her a packet of cash when he walked in the door, then she should make him work harder.

"I'm busy tonight," she said. "You can come back another time, when you have another present."

Chang smiled. This woman didn't give it away. She thought she had him on the installment plan. No wonder Dr. Ma had been so eager to fatten his account in Luxembourg. Chang knew he had to get back to business.

"I want to visit you again, Li Fan. But right now, I'd like to give you my card, so that you can contact me if you need help."

He handed her a "Peter Tong" card with a number that connected to a voicemail in the Ops Center at Langley. She wouldn't take it at first, but he pressed it toward her again, and she slipped it into the bodice of her gown.

Her hand had trembled as she took the card, and she began to sniffle again, as if on cue.

"Don't be frightened. You're safe here in Vancouver. The Canadian government won't let anyone hurt you, so long as we're friends. I promise you that. Don't let anyone try to scare you. You're not in China now. People care about you."

"You go now, Mister America. You are a hard man, but a soft one, too. I like you. I'm glad you are my friend."

She took his hand and led him to the door.

He leaned toward her to kiss her cheek. Her perfume enveloped him. He wanted to hold her close, so that she could feel him against her. He kissed one cheek, then the other.

"Come back soon, James Bond," she said. "I'm not very good at being alone." She put her hand on his back and stood on tiptoes to give him a last kiss of her own. How many times had she done this, with how many different men? He could hear the brush of her silk gown, as she walked with him the last few steps.

She closed the door firmly. Chang took the stairs back down to the lobby. He saw two Chinese faces by the door. Maybe they were from the consulate, but there were Chinese everywhere in Vancouver these days. It seemed the whole of China wanted a second passport. Chang wondered how much of what had happened he should put in his cable to Vandel.

Not very much, he decided. What was there to say, except that he had delivered the package? What Li Fan would put in her own account of the meeting was another matter. But for the moment, Chang wasn't worried about that, either.

15.

PALO ALTO, CALIFORNIA

Harris Chang caught a flight the next morning to San Francisco. He sat by the window and watched the vast watery desert of the Pacific stretching west to another world. He tried reading his Trollope, but he fell dead asleep and didn't awaken until the plane began to bank over the San Francisco Bay. In his dream, he was still in an apartment in Vancouver, but there were other people there; their identities vanished the moment he became conscious. He thought momentarily of sending Li Fan a message when he landed, but by then his normal caution and had discretion returned.

At the airport, he rented another Kia. The traffic was thick all the way down 101 until he finally reached the Embarcadero Road exit and the splendor of the Stanford campus. The lawns were shamrock green, the stone and adobe buildings glowed a light almond-brown. He parked along the grand oval that fronted the main quad. Students thronged the paths and walkways, pedaling their bikes to classes, talking and flirting in the morning sun.

As Chang entered the campus, he dialed Daiyu Ma's cell phone. It was turned off and didn't accept voicemails. Maybe she was in class or with friends. He walked toward the red-tiled cupola of Hoover Tower until he found an academic building with an open door. Several students called out "Good morning, sir," as he passed, perhaps mistaking him for a professor. In a men's room inside the building, he donned a modest disguise, a wig and a pair of oversized glasses.

Chang strode through the quad to the office of the Dean of Students in an administrative building near the lake that bounded the campus. An assistant dean said she couldn't answer questions about students. Chang thanked her and excused himself.

He walked to Ma's dormitory, a two-story Spanish-style building that overlooked Lake Lagunita. It looked like a resort hotel. The resident fellow said Miss Ma was away, but he wouldn't answer any more questions. Chang smiled and left. He had a simple backup plan ready.

Chang took a seat on a courtyard bench facing the water and waited for Asian students to pass by on their way to or from class. He didn't have to wait long. Within minutes, a stick-thin, beardless Chinese boy walked by, toting a backpack and a skateboard.

"Excuse me," said Chang. The boy had his earphones on and he didn't hear at first. "Excuse me," said Chang, approaching him.

The young man was startled and took a step back. He took the buds out of his ears and squinted at Chang through his glasses.

"I'm looking for Miss Daiyu Ma," said Chang. "Do you know her?"

"She's not here," said the boy. "She went away, I think."

"Do you know when she'll be back?"

The boy looked suspicious. He didn't answer questions from a stranger, even if he was a fellow Asian.

"Sorry," he said. "Don't know. Have to go." He put the skateboard to the ground, planted his feet, and rolled off.

Several clumps of students walked past. Chang waited until he saw a solitary Chinese girl in skinny jeans and pigtails. He ventured toward her meekly, apologetically. Like nearly every student on campus, she was listening to music. She pulled out the white earphones. She was friendly, at first. Yes, she knew Ma; she lived in the same dorm. She spoke English with an accent.

"Daiyu is in China now," the girl said. "She left a few days ago."

"I'm sorry about her dad," Chang said. "He was a fine man."

"Very sad," said the girl, looking down.

"Such a loss," said Chang.

"You're not from the consulate," the girl said warily.

"No. Just a friend of the family. Why do you ask?"

"I shouldn't talk to you." She looked anxious.

"I was a friend of her father's. When Daiyu gets back, maybe you could tell her that I stopped by to pay my respects."

He offered a card. She held it by the edge, as if to avoid contamination.

"I must go," she said, turning away and scurrying down the concrete path toward the dorm.

"Don't be scared," Chang called after her. But she was gone.

Chang stopped a third student a few minutes later. He was tall enough to be a basketball player. He wore square-framed dark glasses and had a hard jaw.

"Hey, can I ask you a question?" Chang called out.

"What about?" the boy asked.

"Daiyu Ma. I wanted to express my condolences to her, but I guess she's away."

The boy stuck out his chin. He removed his shades and glowered at Chang.

"You're the creepy guy who's been asking about Daiyu."

"I'm just a friend of the family." Chang extended a card. The boy looked at it and handed it back.

"I heard about you from my brother and sister. We're all part of SACS. We think you should leave."

"SACS? Never heard of that."

"The Stanford Association of Chinese Students. We don't like being harassed. By anybody. You need to leave this dorm area, or I'm going to call the campus police."

Chang pulled out his wallet and displayed the U.S. government ID. It bore an official-looking seal with an eagle and bunting, but it didn't say exactly where he worked.

"I'm a government official. My name is Peter Tong. I'm not harassing anyone."

The invocation of government authority only seemed to upset the young man more. He took out his cell phone.

"I'm calling the cops," he said. He dialed the campus switchboard. When the operator answered, he asked for the university police. When he was connected, he told the desk officer that a man named Peter Tong who claimed to work for the government but had a phony ID was harassing students. He gave the location.

"Calm down," said Chang. "You're only going to make trouble for yourself."

The young man shook his head. "I don't think so." He took up his phone again and punched a text message, which he sent to a group address.

A burly Stanford police officer arrived within five minutes, followed quickly by two more. Chang showed them his ID and then, quietly, hoping he wouldn't be overheard, asked the campus cops to call the San Francisco office of the FBI. The campus police asked him to explain; Chang said he couldn't in an authoritative, trust-me voice. The cops seemed convinced, and one of the officers went over to the tall undergraduate who had called in the complaint, to tell him that everything was fine.

But by then it was too late. A half-dozen Asian-American students had converged on the courtyard, and they were soon joined by a dozen more. The group formed a semicircle around Chang and the campus cops.

"Stop harassment now," called out the tall student who had summoned the crowd. The other students quickly joined in a rhythmic chant. "Stop . . . harassment . . . now . . . Stop . . . harassment . . . now." Many of the students took out their cell phones and began recording videos of the scene.

"Oh shit," muttered Chang, loud enough for the cops to hear him.

The senior campus policeman put a hand on Chang's elbow and whispered in his ear. "We need to get you out of here."

The three cops formed a cordon around Chang and escorted him away from the gathering crowd, out of the courtyard and toward the main quad.

The Asian students' group was emboldened by its success, and the shouting got louder. An older grad student began shouting, "FBI . . . out . . . now." That was picked up by others and morphed into "CIA . . . out . . . now," mingled with the initial chant about stopping harassment.

The cops walked the visitor all the way to the main headquarters of the Stanford Department of Public Safety on Playa Street.

Chang asked to see the commander of the force privately. After five minutes the police captain, a big man with a shaved head, emerged from his office and extended his hand. A patch on his shoulder identified him as an officer of the Santa Clara County Sheriff's Department, which oversaw the Stanford Police.

Chang handed over his Peter Tong identification badge and asked the captain to check it with the FBI special agent in charge in San Francisco. The captain gave him a big-guy wink and said he used to work for the Bureau himself. The special agent in charge was one of his best friends. He disappeared to an inner office to make the call and emerged five minutes later, smiling and shaking his head as if to say, what are the crazy bastards from the CIA going to do next.

"You're clear, but Jesus, what a mess." The police captain handed back the alias ID.

"Thanks. Sorry to cause such a commotion."

The captain nodded grimly. He was going to have to pick up the pieces on campus, and he was pissed.

"The FBI blew your cover, my friend. I told the special agent in charge that he had to level with me, or I wouldn't let you go. You folks aren't supposed to pull this shit without telling us. What kind of name is Harris Chang, anyway?"

"It's my name. Harris. Chang."

"Sure, but it's so tweedy. Sounds like a sports car. Harris. Not like Mick or Bob, or Ye-Win, or Wu-Tai."

Chang's eyes narrowed. "My great-grandfather came from Canton. The Chinese emigrants from there took British names. Hanson. Anson. Jansen. You have a problem with that?"

The captain punched the CIA officer's shoulder.

"Hey, lighten up, Harris. I'm just teasing you. Don't be so thin-skinned. Otherwise, we'll never get along."

That should have been the end of it, but by then some of the aggrieved students (or to be more precise, the Chinese student association's activists) had gathered outside the police headquarters, demanding to lodge a formal protest.

The associate dean of students arrived, and then the associate general counsel, and then the university vice president for administration. They took turns talking to Chang, consulting the FBI office in the city, and conversing with each other. Chang sat quietly through it, listening to the intermittent chanting. It was hot under his wig.

After nearly an hour of commotion, inside and outside the building, the Stanford vice president for administration met with the leader of the Stanford Association of Chinese Students. The administrator promised to meet with the student group to discuss the issues of unannounced visits to campus by government officials and better protection against harassment of students of color, including Asian-Americans.

While this discussion was taking place, Harris Chang slipped out the back entrance of the Department of Public Safety building, wearing a Stanford hoodie that had been provided by one of the campus cops. He made his way across campus to the parking facility near the Oval, where he had left his little Kia, and motored off campus.

It wasn't until he got to downtown Palo Alto that he stopped and called John Vandel's office at Headquarters.

"What the hell happened out there?" asked Vandel. "We damn near had to call the attorney general to get you released. How did you manage to cause a campus riot in one afternoon?"

"Just doing my job. You wanted to pull people's chains, so I did."

"I thought these Chinese students were supposed to be quiet, passive types. Keep their heads down. 4.0 average. Don't cause trouble."

"Racial stereotypes will get you in trouble every time, sir. I expected that too, for what it's worth."

Vandel laughed. He assumed Chang was joking.

"Well, mission accomplished, in terms of pulling the chain in Beijing. The FBI told me the Chinese student group is already posting pictures of Peter Tong on Facebook and Twitter. They sent me a link. Thank god you were wearing a disguise."

"What do you want me to do now?"

"Come home, for Christ's sake. And don't talk to any more Chinese students."

Chang promised he would be back in D.C. the next afternoon. That night, he did manage to spend some of the operational budget. He checked into the Fairmont and took himself to an Italian restaurant in North Beach, where he had a steak and two martinis.

Chang walked back to his hotel along Grant Avenue, through China-town. His mother's family had lived here for three-quarters of a century, and during the summers he had sometimes come to stay in his aunt's cramped apartment. He hated the smells back then; so much garlic, so many strange cuts of meat and fish; so many little men and women quacking at each other in Cantonese. Chang had been happy to get back to Flagstaff and not feel so entrapped by his ethnic roots.

There was that trace of shame, always. To survive in America, you humbled yourself; you made deals. To keep the Flagstaff cops from squeezing the family business, his father had turned in a crowded house full of undocumented Chinese neighbors. How had that felt, to rat out his own people so that he stayed on good terms with the white man? Chang had never dared to ask. It was why he had been happy never to learn Chinese; it distanced him. And yet this insistently American Harris Chang had twice in the last twenty-four hours tried to manipulate people using his Chinese skin. Identity was something you couldn't escape, shouldn't escape.

This evening, the noisy Chinatown street seemed congenial and welcoming. The whole of Grant Avenue was hung with red lanterns every fifty yards. People poured out of the restaurants and shops, ignoring the traffic as they laughed and traded stories. All the shop signs were in Chinese characters; English was a concession for visiting tourists. Chang stopped at the stores selling jade and crystal imports and colorful knickknacks from the mainland. As Chang passed, people called to him in Chinese.

Chang stopped when he reached an old Chinese-style building with a crenelated red-tile roof and a wrought-iron grill across the balcony. He remembered this building from long ago, and it made him oddly nervous. He tried to recall the name, and it fell into his head, suddenly. This was the "Association," that was the shorthand. The Fung Yee Tien Association, where his maternal grandfather once had friends. As a boy, it had seemed darkly forbidding. No one ever talked about what happened inside. Now it was just an old, run-down Chinese building.

Chang had asked his aunt once to tell him more about his grandfather, what he did and who he was in Chinatown, but she just shook her head and put a finger to her lips. His mother was the same way. She never wanted to talk about her father, even when Chang pressed. He had found a picture of him once at the back of a drawer. He was a handsome young man, dark hair slicked in place, passion in his eyes. Chang figured that he must have been some kind of Chinatown fixer, and after a while, he stopped asking his mother and his aunt any more questions.

Harris Chang walked the rest of the way back to his hotel enjoying the lights and noise, feeling for once at home in this enclave of Chinese separateness. Everyone has a secret in his past. Sometimes it's so well hidden, we don't know ourselves what the secret is.

16.

WASHINGTON, D.C., AND SEATTLE

Jason Schmidt, the founder of Quantum Engineering Dynamics, was better at inventing new technology than at following government rules. He resented having to put his cell phone in a locker every time he went into his laboratory. He disliked the security officer who stopped him at the entrance and asked to see his badge every time he entered the headquarters of his own company. But this was the price of patronage from the intelligence community: Schmidt now worked in a "SCIF," a Secure Compartmented Information Facility. He had an electrified steel fence around his building. His communications were monitored. His only customer was the government, which meant that he was a kept man.

Schmidt rebelled against the rules in small ways. He didn't open letters. He didn't answer messages. He left that to the new people he had been forced to hire, forgetting that they didn't have the authority to respond on his behalf. So the communications piled up in his in-box. He figured that if anything were seriously wrong, the government would pull his chain. And Schmidt's inattention might indeed have continued, if one of the messages he ignored hadn't been monitored by the National Security Agency. It was from a supposed venture capital firm called "Parcourse Technology Partners," which was on the NSA's watch list as a front for China's Ministry of State Security.

John Vandel telephoned Schmidt personally. He called himself

"Mr. Green," the alias he had used when he traveled to QED months before. Vandel began calmly, recalling his visit to Seattle and expressing hope that QED's "breakthrough" research was progressing well. But when he asked Schmidt caustically if he had been opening his mail—and whether he understood the legal penalties for mishandling classified information—the conversation became acrimonious. Schmidt began raising his voice and talking about the First Amendment.

"Stop, right there," said Vandel, an icy control in his voice. "We are not having this conversation over an open phone line. Do what I say, or I will send an agent from the FBI to your office immediately. I'm not joking. You signed an agreement. You have to abide by the rules."

"What do you want me to do, Mr. Green?" answered Schmidt meekly.

There was a pause, while Vandel considered his options. There was only one person he fully trusted in situations like this. He spoke slowly and carefully, in a way that allowed no dissent.

"I am sending my best security person out to see you tomorrow, Mr. Schmidt. Whatever she says, do it. While she's there, I want you to brief her on where your research stands. Your work is very important to us. That's why we have to protect it. Do we agree on this? Otherwise, I am calling the Bureau."

Schmidt muttered his agreement and then said, under his breath, "Jesus Christ!"

So Kate Sturm was dispatched on an urgent trip to Seattle to review the operations of Quantum Engineering Dynamics. She protested when Vandel gave her the assignment. She was an administrator, not a technologist.

When Vandel insisted that she do it anyway, Sturm asked if she could bring along some help. Vandel wanted to know who, and she mentioned the first name that fell into her head, Denise Ford, the assistant deputy director for science and technology. She had all but offered Ford a role as informal technical adviser. She could help decode the QED problem, even if she wasn't read into that compartment.

Vandel, who trusted Sturm's judgment in almost everything, said fine, take whoever you want, just get it done. Sturm phoned Ford a few minutes later.

"What are you doing this week?" she asked.

"The usual," answered Ford. "Meetings about reports. Reports about meetings."

"Then come with me to Seattle. That consulting job I talked to you about is happening faster than I expected. Are you game?"

"Of course. Assistant deputy directors never say no to a new opportunity. What's the rush?"

"We have a housekeeping problem with one of our contractors. Are you on the bigot list for a company called Quantum Engineering Dynamics, QED, in Seattle?"

"Not yet." Ford's voice dropped a notch.

"Well, I'll put in a request. Come with me in the meantime. Part of their work is just 'Secret.' Come along. It will be fun, get you back in the mix. What do you say?"

"Are you sure?" There was surprise and slight apprehension in her voice.

"I'll handle the parts that are 'code word,' where you don't have access. We'll make a good team. And Vandel's fine with it. I already asked him."

They made reservations to fly the next day.

The derelict headquarters of QED had undergone a facelift in the last few months. The electric fence enclosed the perimeter, supplemented by cameras and electronic monitors. The QED sign out front had been removed; a visitor had to guess what went on inside. The haphazard greeting system in the front lobby had been replaced by a bulletproof glass barrier and the implacable guard who harassed even the CEO.

A few of the old employees remained, with piercings and outlandishly dyed hair. But the scruffy "Coldplay" era had ended at QED. Now it truly was Quantum Engineering Dynamics. A few new arrivals from back East even wore jackets and ties. The floors were spotless; paper shredders and burn bags were emptied regularly by the security officers, who also tended the metal lockers into which employees were required to place their personal electronics.

Jason Schmidt greeted his visitors from Washington. He had changed less than his surroundings. He was still round-faced, balding, with a graying fringe that needed a trim. He loyally wore a knit shirt with the company's logo, though that was now a collector's item because the "funders" (meaning the intelligence community) didn't like to advertise the company's name in public.

"Welcome," called out Schmidt when the visitors had passed through the metal detector. He shook their hands and walked them down the corridor to an elegant office that an interior decorator had fashioned for the newly capitalized chief executive. Through a picture window behind Schmidt's desk was the dark blue chop of Lake Washington, edged by the moss green of the fir trees that rimmed the far bank. A front was coming in from the Pacific. The clouds were underlined with the beginnings of rain.

"I'm in the doghouse, I gather," said Schmidt. "Mr. Green sounded upset."

"Mr. Green is worried about security," answered Sturm calmly. "And he wants a progress report. That's why we're here. To make sure everything is shipshape."

Schmidt shook his head. "If we get any more security here, people will have to get cleared to go to the bathroom. Did you see the array at the entrance? I barely recognize this place anymore."

"We know it's a nuisance, Mr. Schmidt. But it's important. Please close the door, so we have some privacy, and I'll explain why." Schmidt dutifully closed his office door and returned to his desk. Sturm and Ford were seated opposite him.

"Mr. Green is worried that a foreign company has contacted you, for a second time, to get information about your research. The company is called Parcourse Technology. They claim to be a venture capital firm, but as Mr. Green told you when he first came to see you, we think they work for a foreign intelligence service. Have you had any recent contacts from them? We can track email, but what about regular mail? Have you heard from them?"

Schmidt looked flummoxed. Ford arched her back in the chair, as if she had a cramp.

"How would I know? I throw any inquiries in the circular file. That's what I'm supposed to do, isn't it? Ignore them. So that's what I do."

"You don't actually throw them away, do you?" asked Sturm, as gently as she could.

"Look, I'm a scientist. I don't handle the paperwork. I leave that to my administrative assistant. She's outside. You want me to ask?"

"Yes, please," said Sturm. Ford was attentive but silent.

Schmidt buzzed his secretary on the intercom. "Carla, can you come in here?"

A young woman quickly appeared. She was dressed in jeans and a billowy top. She looked to be about five months pregnant. She smiled genially at the visitors.

"Listen, Carla, these people want to know if we've kept any of those damned letters from VCs. I told you to ignore them, remember? Did you throw them away?"

"Of course not. I keep everything except junk mail, and I even save some of that. I keep them all in a file."

Sturm stood and extended her hand.

"Hi, Carla, I'm from your funding consortium in Washington. This is my colleague."

"Oh, goodness," said the young woman, worried that she had said the wrong thing.

"Could I look at that file for a moment, the one with the venture capital letters?" asked Sturm.

The secretary looked at her boss, who nodded.

"I'll get the file right away." She vanished out the door and returned in thirty seconds with a thin folder, which she handed to Sturm.

"Is this all?" said Sturm, taking the handful of letters.

The secretary nodded. Schmidt reddened.

"For god's sake! We're not looking for money anymore, so we don't get many offers. That's the way it's supposed to work now, right?"

Sturm flipped through the file, passing over brief notes from well-known Sand Hill Road firms that invested in Silicon Valley and Seattle companies, until she came to a particular letterhead. She read that message carefully. Ford, sitting next to her, peered over her shoulder.

Sturm turned the letter toward Schmidt so that he could see its face.

"This one is from Parcourse Technology Partners. That's the same company that Mr. Green discussed with you. They want to come visit you. They say they are ready to increase their earlier offer. That's not going to happen. As Mr. Green told you, we have concerns about this company. Are we clear on that?"

"Yes," said Schmidt sourly.

"So, if you get any more communications from this company I want you to let us know right away. Not just from Parcourse, but from any VC or private-equity company you haven't heard of. Got that? Carla, you seem to handle the mail around here, so I want you to pay special attention. And if you go on maternity leave anytime soon, sorry for noticing, I want you to tell your temp replacement the same thing. Got it?"

"Yes, ma'am," she answered. Sturm was simple, direct, and intimidating.

"Could I have a copy of this?" asked Sturm, handing the letter back. "My colleague will come with you while you xerox it."

Ford followed the secretary out and returned with her a minute later.

"I made two copies, just in case," said Ford, handing one to Sturm and keeping the other in her hand.

"One is fine, but thanks." She reached out her hand for the second copy, which Ford was starting to fold. Sturm took the two pages and put them in her briefcase and then turned back to the CEO.

"That takes care of that," she said. "Now let's hear your progress report. Carla, you can close the door on your way out."

Schmidt turned warily toward Sturm when his secretary was gone. "Am I in serious trouble?"

"No. Try to look at your mail. You're the only person here who has clearances to know why we're so worried about Parcourse. So keep your eyes open."

"Do I have to sign any more forms, god forbid?"

"No, not now." Sturm reached out across the desk and gave his hand a friendly pat. "Just tell us how you're doing. Are you making any progress? Can you get that machine powerful enough to crack any codes? That's what Mr. Green wants to know."

Schmidt brightened. The inquisition seemed to be over.

"I'll take you into the lab," he said. "That's the easiest way to explain. The baseline is that we're not there yet, but we're getting closer. Come on. I'll show you the coldest place in the universe, just about."

"The *what*?"

But Schmidt had already risen from his chair and was heading out the office door toward the lab where QED did its real work, with Sturm and Ford bustling behind.

"Just what I said, the coldest place in the universe," Schmidt repeated, talking over his shoulder.

"It's cryogenics," said Ford.

"Yes, very good. Someone has done her homework. Come on, I'll show you."

Schmidt led the two women down a corridor and through a locked door into a high-ceilinged room. It was a simple warehouse space with a spotless linoleum floor and bright fluorescent lights overhead. Employees were dressed in white lab coats, tinkering with machines that were arrayed in sixteen chambers. Schmidt took them to a small conference room, flanked on three sides by whiteboards covered with algorithms and equations. He gestured for them to sit.

"So, our concept at QED is adiabatic quantum computing, which people often call quantum annealing. Does that word mean anything to you?"

"Metallurgy," said Ford.

"That's where it originated, yes. Over thousands of years, artisans learned that they could make metal stronger by heating it up and then letting it cool slowly. The purest values emerge as the temperature falls. That's what we do with our quantum chips, but we do it near absolute zero. We let the quantum bits settle into the least-disordered, lowest-energy state. We've shown that if we do it right, we can solve optimization problems that way."

"Time out." Sturm help up her hand, apologetically. "My colleague hasn't been read into the compartmented parts of your research. So please keep this at 'Secret' or below. Sorry, Denise."

"Fiddlesticks," he said. "This was all published in academic journals before we were taken 'black.' I won't say anything that your friend can't find in the open literature."

"Fine," said Sturm. "Then go ahead."

"Okay, Quantum 101. Cold is good. Heat is noise. It's friction. It destroys coherence. You've both heard of Moore's Law. Well, heat is sabotaging it. If you keep doubling a normal supercomputer's speed and memory, it gets too damned hot."

"So you've gone the other way, to super-cold," said Ford.

"Precisely. We use tiny loops of a metal called niobium. At very, very low temperatures, electrons behave differently. They become superconductors, and the current flows clockwise and counter-clockwise at the same time. They take on quantum properties, in other words. Do you understand that, a little bit?"

"No," said Sturm. "I need to see a diagram or something, or I'm not going to get this."

"Better than a diagram. I'll show you the machine. Come on!"

"Hold up," said Sturm. "Is the lab an SCI compartmented area? Because if it is, my colleague can't come."

"Nope. Just 'Secret.' These are the same damned machines we used when our research wasn't classified at all. The only juicy stuff is on some of the readouts, but they're shielded."

"Okay," said Sturm. "Lead on."

Schmidt walked them out of the equation-filled conference room back into the main workroom. He stopped at one of the bays. A conical device that looked like a huge metal ice cream cone was suspended from the ceiling. Nearby stood several technicians, checking screens that registered the temperature inside.

"This is a dilution refrigerator," said Schmidt. "The quantum chip is right there at the bottom." He pointed to a small casing at the lowest point of the cone. "That's what we're trying to cool. It's now thirty millikelvin, or three-hundredths of one degree kelvin. The temperature in deep space, by comparison, is nearly a hundred times warmer. But even that is way too hot for our chip. We have to cut the heat almost in half."

Ford studied the computer array, but there were coverings obscuring the digital monitors.

"Maybe you're wondering how we make it so cold," said Schmidt, hopefully.

"Yes, please," said Ford.

Schmidt took a step toward Ford. At least someone from Washington cared about the details of his research.

"Actually, we pump in a mix of helium-3 and helium-4. These are very cold gases. Helium-4 is the stuff in those balloons that make your voice squeaky. But helium-3 is very rare and costs about three thousand dollars a liter. When these two interact, it gets very cold, less than 450 degrees below zero, Fahrenheit."

"That's cold," said Sturm.

"Quite cold. What happens is that our helium mixture pulls the heat away from the objects we are cooling. It gets colder and colder, and down we go."

"Are your qubits stable at that temperature?" pressed Ford.

"Briefly. And they're not just protected from heat; we shield them from any magnetism, too. They survive for nanoseconds, but then poof: They 'de-cohere.' But it's long enough for them to do our work."

"You folks want to watch it happen?" asked one of the technicians. "We're just testing the cooling cycle on the next machine down."

They walked to the next bay, where a dilution refrigerator was encased in a sealed black vacuum box to prevent any "noise"—heat, light, magnetism—from entering. Schmidt removed a cover from one of the digital readouts. It registered eleven millikelvin. As they watched, the temperature inside the array fell to ten, then nine, and settled at eight point five. Eight point five hundredths of a degree above absolute zero.

"There it is!" said the CEO. "The coldest point in the universe. Actually, that's not quite true, I think a lab in Italy has gone down to six, but close enough."

"Is that where you normally operate?" asked Ford, peering toward the device.

"No. We usually do our quantum annealing at about…" He stopped and looked at Ford. "Oops. I think the exact number is in the SCI compartment."

Sturm gently placed a hand on Ford's shoulder. She hated to exclude her female colleague. But rules were rules.

"Sorry, Denise, but I'm going to finish this up with Mr. Schmidt by myself. We'll go back to the conference room. Wait for us by the door. We'll be out in a few minutes."

"I'll stay here with the refrigerators," said Ford amiably.

Sturm and Schmidt filed off toward the conference room. Sturm closed the door firmly and turned to the CEO.

"This conference room is secure, right?"

"Of course," said an exasperated Schmidt. "Your people check the whole facility every month."

"So now, give me the code-word part of the briefing. Mr. Green wants to know whether you're anywhere near getting these machines to solve encryption problems."

"Slowly, slowly. We just started using a new chip with 512 qubits. The old chip had 128 qubits. So that's progress. Our latest machine has about 2,000 qubits. Next stop, 4,000."

"But will it crack codes? It's dark out there. We need some light."

"I am working as hard as I can," said Schmidt emphatically. "I've found a way to program my machine so that the annealing function can also factor numbers, but it keeps crashing. Tell Mr. Green that I think I know *how* to do it, even though I can't actually do it yet, if that's comprehensible."

"Is there anything you need from us? Do you have enough money? Are you able to hire the people you want?"

"Money is fine. People, well, let's be honest, there aren't enough smart Americans. Life would be easier if I could hire more foreigners. But we know that, right?"

"Yes, we know that. And on the subject of the Chinese, for goodness sakes, don't forget to let us know if Parcourse tries again. And recheck your suppliers, please. Trusted foundries, only."

"Christ, I hate security. It is the enemy of science. But yes, I've got it." Sturm shook his hand. That was what she needed to hear.

Out in the corridor, Ford waited. The moment brought a sense of isolation. In this business, access was everything. And she needed to know, if she was going to do her job. Ford stood by the doorway. The technicians and scientists had gone back to work on machines down the corridor. She stepped a few feet into the first bay and entered the darkened recess. What a beautiful machine it was, a universe in miniature. She wanted to understand it.

The door to Schmidt's conference room was still closed. He and Sturm would be talking a few more minutes, at least. Ford tiptoed near the edge of the machine and the control module that recorded the mysteries inside. So many questions: What were the parameters within which this machine produced its quantum effects? How cold was the chip, precisely? How fast was the processor that ran the machine? What was the architecture of the processor?

Ford edged soundlessly closer to the machine. The digital display panel that monitored the machine's performance was covered by a plastic sheath overlaid with TS/SCI classification warnings. She gently tugged at the plastic cover. As it fell away, she quickly began studying the categories and numbers on the digital displays: precise temperature; active qubits in the attached chip; power required to achieve quantum effects; target time for problem solution.

The machine began a loud, regular electronic beep. Ford bit her lip. She quickly reattached the cap. The beeping stopped, but a red warning light was flashing behind the machine. She stepped away. The technicians were busy at their work, and Ford hoped that nobody had noticed. She eased toward the entrance to the bay, hoping now that Sturm's meeting would end soon.

A technician was striding toward the bay where she was standing. He was wearing a badge that said "Security." He marched past Ford to the machine and its flashing light. He quickly typed a command on the keyboard and waited until the machine reported the nature of the violation of its electronic space.

"Ma'am!" the security officer said sharply as he approached Ford. She paused and then took a step toward him. Nothing looks as guilty as a frightened woman trying to deny what's obvious. She straightened her skirt. She pulled a wisp of hair away from her forehead.

"Did you touch the machine, ma'am?"

Ford opened her palms, in a gesture of mute apology. She was shaking her head.

"I'm so sorry," she said. "I think I may have bumped it accidentally. I didn't mean to do anything wrong."

"Someone tried to remove the protective seal. Was that you?"

"I don't think so," she said. "I certainly didn't intend to. Maybe the casing was loose. I feel terrible. I know how important security is."

Ford removed her green CIA badge from her purse and showed it to the security officer. He studied it, a puzzled look on his face.

"Ma'am, did you see anyone else approach this machine?"

"No, but I wasn't paying close attention."

The security officer's face was impassive. It was impossible to read whether he believed her or not. He hesitated a moment more and then strode to Schmidt's conference room, twenty yards away, and rapped on the door. When Schmidt emerged, the security man whispered in his ear.

"What?" roared Schmidt. "The display access panel? Are you kidding me? Who did it?"

"I don't know, sir." He gestured toward Ford. "The visitor was standing in the bay where the intrusion happened. She said she may have bumped the machine, by accident."

"I am so sorry," Ford repeated, walking toward Schmidt. "I was looking at that amazing machine, and I stumbled, and I must have set something off. Forgive me. This is so embarrassing."

Ford turned to Sturm, who had been watching from the conference room door. "This is my fault," she said earnestly. "I had no business being near that machine. Please apologize to everyone."

Sturm pulled her colleague aside, out of earshot of the others.

"Did you try to access the machine? Come on. This is serious."

"No, Kate. As I said, I was taking a look, I was curious. I must have bumped the wrong thing, or something was loose. I don't know. I didn't take anything. Check my pockets."

Before Sturm could answer, Ford turned the pockets of her jacket inside out, showing each empty one to her CIA colleague.

"Thank you. That wasn't necessary." Sturm turned back to the group.

"My colleague has extensive TS/SCI clearances, even though she has not been read into the details of this program. Please check the computer and file the proper security-intrusion notice. The seal may be defective. It may be sending false signals. Figure that out. Send the Bureau a report. They'll brief me on whatever you find."

"If this is QED's fault, I'm sorry," said Schmidt, shaking his head. "Please understand, we take security seriously. Forget my griping earlier. I know it matters. We'll find out what happened here and let you know, as soon as we can."

Sturm and Ford shook the CEO's hand and walked slowly back down the hall to the door. Schmidt apologized again. Sturm reassured him and gave him a card with her direct number at work; Ford was silent.

Before Sturm boarded the flight back to Washington, she got a text message advising her to call Headquarters. Her deputy at Support said that a man named Jason Schmidt had called to report that he had notified the FBI of the security breach.

Sturm excused herself, showed an airline official her badge, and went to a quiet room. She called the head of the FBI's Seattle office and explained the sequence of events that day. The special agent in charge said that forensics would check for fingerprints on the protective casing as soon as it could, but the lab was swamped and it might take a day or so.

Sturm said she could wait. As soon as the lab could find time. She didn't want a flap. Ford had already suffered enough from rushed judgments.

Ford tried to chat on the flight back. She mentioned a novel she had been reading and a favorite new restaurant. Sturm said she was tired. She closed her eyes and was silent for most of the long overnight trip back across the country.

Kate Sturm debated with herself through those sleepless hours whether to call Vandel when she got back. She was fastidious about security, but she was torn: Denise Ford had been the victim of hasty and unfair treatment in the past. Sturm didn't want to add to that history. Women fought against the odds in the agency; if the "house" could extend them a little credit for once, then that was only fair. Sturm decided to wait until she'd heard more from the FBI forensics team.

When they landed at Dulles early the next morning, Sturm gave a bleary-eyed Ford a sisterly hug and said good-bye.

Sturm was just dozing off at her town house in Reston at 7:30 a.m. that morning when she was roused by an insistent phone call. She had hoped to ignore it and get a little more sleep before going into the office, but the same number called back immediately. This person badly wanted to talk.

Sturm answered her phone with a sleepy hello. It was John Vandel. His usually modulated voice was a breathy shout.

"We got him," he said.

"What are you talking about? Got who?"

"We got him!" Vandel repeated. "It's Kronholz, that son of a bitch from IARPA. We need to lock this down. Meet me at Courthouse at 9:00."

"I just got home," murmured Sturm. "Can we make it 10:00? Or 11:00?"

"Chang and I will be there at 9:00. Mark Flanagan has come back, too, to help with surveillance. Big day! You can sleep later."

"I'll be there," she said wearily. "Of course, I will."

Sturm quickly showered and dressed and by 8:00 she was on the road, fighting the morning traffic to Arlington. She was very glad that John Vandel had found his mole. That meant, among other things, that she could put aside her worry about Denise Ford.

17.

ARLINGTON, VIRGINIA

"Artificial intelligence is no match for natural stupidity," said an exultant John Vandel to Kate Sturm and Harris Chang when they met at 9:00 a.m. upstairs in the secure area at the Courthouse facility on North Glebe Road. His face was glowing. "That's what people forget," he said, wagging a bony index finger. "If they send a message, no matter how careful they think they are being, the chances are that we're going to see it land. And then, pop."

Vandel punched the buttons of the cyber-lock and opened the door. The room inside looked like a motel lobby with a cheap blue carpet, two shiny, red, fake-leather couches, and a mahogany coffee table with a tray of pastries and a coffee pitcher.

He was giddy. He turned to Kate, who was shaking her head. "Behind every great man is a woman rolling her eyes."

"You're in a good mood," she said, laughing despite her fatigue.

"I am in a very good mood, yes ma'am, thanks to our brothers and sisters at the NSA. They managed to intercept a version of an IARPA contract after it had been decrypted in Beijing. And guess who had just signed off on the contract for IARPA? Yes, that's right. Roger Kronholz."

"Congratulations, boss," said Chang, pumping Vandel's hand. It wasn't one of the two Chinese-American suspects, after all.

"We got lucky," said Vandel. "And we don't actually have the hard proof yet. We need to catch him in the act. Speaking of which, where is Mark Flanagan? He's supposed to be here. Harris, go check."

Chang trundled down the hall to the waiting room on the other side of the security barrier. Sitting stone-faced in a corner, reading a tattered copy of *People* magazine, was Flanagan. His face was pallid and puffy from fatigue. He looked up as Chang approached and glowered at him.

"Jesus! Where have you been? I've been waiting here since 7:00 a.m. I fly in from Tokyo, sixteen hours of misery to get here, and the Office of Security says they've never heard of any 'DDO Small Group' and I'm not cleared to be in this location and please go sit in the unsecured lobby. And I don't even know what I'm doing here in the first place."

"Sorry, Mark. Sit tight. I'll get you cleared."

Chang trotted back to the secure office and returned with Kate Sturm, who spoke to the guard and then to the guard's boss. She brought a special badge to Flanagan and apologized for the inconvenience.

"Don't worry," said Flanagan. "I've worked here twenty years. I'm used to being treated like shit." Flanagan had joined S&T directly out of Cornell. He liked to think of his directorate as part of the agency's blue-collar workforce, perpetually abused by the big shots on the Seventh Floor but loyal, nonetheless.

Vandel was slouched on the couch, eating a glazed donut, when the three entered the cyber-locked office. He unbent himself and shook Flanagan's hand.

"Sorry to keep you waiting out there," said Vandel, bits of glazed sugar falling from his lips as he spoke.

"The little people are accustomed to delay," said Flanagan acidly. "What am I doing here, anyway?"

"I have a special assignment for you."

"I don't like 'special.' I like 'regular.' And my wife likes it in Tokyo. Does this involve what happened in Singapore? Because that wasn't our fault."

"I can't talk about it until we have a deal. Don't be an asshole, Mark. Just give me an answer."

"Yes."

"Meaning what?" Vandel's eyes narrowed.

"Yes. Of course, I'll do it. I'm a lifer."

"Good. You had me worried for a moment. It's dumb to be a rebel when you're over sixty. You remember the CIA penetration mentioned by the Chinese scientist in Singapore when he was being debriefed?"

"Absolutely. I was on the other end of Harris's wire. The Chinese guy said they had someone inside."

"So you're now one of the mole hunters. We have a suspect, but we need to nail the case before we take it to the Bureau. This compartment has me, Chang, Kate Sturm, and now you, plus Warren Winkle by VTC, plus the Director, but he's leaving it to us."

"What's the crypt of your, uh, compartment?"

"There isn't one. There are no cables, no files, no cover-your-ass memos, nothing. The China mission manager has not, repeat not, been informed. S&T has been told to let you go for a few weeks. Any questions, refer them to me. Got it so far?"

"Not really. You haven't told me anything. Who's the mole?"

"His name is Roger Kronholz. We think. But we don't have proof. That's why we need you."

"Kronholz at S&T? Shit! I know him."

"He transferred to IARPA. He manages quantum computing programs for them. One of his black contracts just landed in Beijing. It involves 'ion-trap' technology, whatever that is. The point is, Roger Kronholz is IARPA's contract officer on this ion-trap thing. They just had a breakthrough. Kronholz ordered it classified. Two days later, the MSS has the specs and is tasking its people to find out more. He's got to be the leak."

Sturm squinted, and not just from fatigue. "A dozen people must have reviewed the paperwork when this went black. It could have been any of them."

"True," said Vandel. "But Kronholz meets all the other tests for this agent, *Rukou*. He has traveled abroad in the past year, he has a brother in the agency, and he has clearances for our most secret supercomputer programs. We just need to nail his ass."

"Are you sure it's him, sir?" asked Flanagan. "We've worked together on some S&T assignments. Kronholz may be an asshole, but he doesn't strike me as a Chinese spy."

"I'm not absolutely sure," said Vandel. "If I was, he'd already be in handcuffs. We need to catch him in the act. That's your specialty, right, Mark?"

"I guess," said Flanagan.

"Then let's get started. I want bugs in Kronholz's office, car, and home before the end of the day. Then we feed him some intel that the Chinese would want and see if he bites."

"I don't mean to be fussy," said Flanagan, "but isn't that illegal inside the U.S., unless you have a warrant?"

"It's legal enough," said Vandel. "I talked to Miguel Votaw, the FBI deputy director. Walked him through a 'hypothetical.' He says it's probably covered under standard protocol for insider threats. And even if it isn't, the Justice Department would never prosecute this. Never. And if they did somehow, a jury would never convict. And if by some infinitesimal chance there was a conviction, you'd get a pardon."

Flanagan looked to Chang. He opened his palms.

"Hey, Harris, am I nuts? I'm exposed here."

"You're not nuts, Mark," said Chang.

Vandel leaned toward the S&T veteran.

"Okay, straight up, Mark: You're the only person who's read into this and has the tech skills to do it. You're a stand-up guy. And the fact is, you've already said yes."

Flanagan studied the DDO for a moment and then nodded.

"Got it. How do I start?"

Vandel gave the technician a sly look. He scratched his stubbly head.

"Well, if it were me, I'd give my old friend Roger Kronholz a call this morning. Tell him you're home from Tokyo on TDY, you're thinking about your next assignment, and you've asked HR for permission to contact people and get some advice. You're interested in IARPA, and you want to know what he thinks. How does that sound?"

Flanagan, Chang, and Sturm all voiced their assent.

"Let's not screw this up," said Vandel. He looked at his watch and stood abruptly. He had an appointment back at Headquarters. "I'll think about what intel to feed Kronholz. You get the bugs in place. Let's meet back here at 6:00."

Kate Sturm called her deputy back at Headquarters and asked him to collect some surveillance equipment and bring it to the Courthouse building. The gear arrived in less than an hour. Technology made snooping so much easier. Batteries could be woven into fabric. Microphones could be tiny oscillators that operated remotely from their power source. The filament in a light bulb could pick up sounds, if you tuned it just right.

"Don't you love this stuff?" said Flanagan as he packed the gear into a bag an hour later. He talked over with Sturm and Chang where he would put the bugs and how they would be monitored.

Just after noon, Flanagan drove a rented car to the IARPA outpost at Office Park 2 in the Maryland suburbs. He was relaxed, even fighting the traffic on the Beltway: He had installed surveillance devices in a hundred places around the world, many of them hostile environments where getting captured could mean time in prison, or worse. The only hard part about this assignment was that he was bugging a colleague.

Kronholz greeted him like a long-lost comrade from the secret fraternity of S&T. Flanagan scanned the small office. There was a lamp atop the desk with a big, conical shade. It was too translucent to hide a bug. The teak desk had an overhang of six inches on all sides, plenty of room underneath for a microphone embedded in a clear adhesive strip.

"What are you doing here, man? I thought you had turned Japanese."

"Time to come home," answered Flanagan. "I saw that you had defected to IARPA, and I thought that might be a fun place for me. Headquarters is in another state!"

"Don't do it, buddy," said Kronholz. "I thought the same thing: Get some IC experience. Work with real scientists. Pad my resume for when I leave the agency. It sounded like a great idea. But it isn't."

"What's wrong with it? It sounds like the perfect escape."

"It's boring. Most of the shit IARPA puts money into turns out to be a dead end, and the few things that work out we have to bury, which pisses everyone off. As program managers, we're not scientists or even techs. We're paper-pushers. I'd go back to Headquarters tomorrow, if they'd let me. I may just quit and work for a contractor."

"Sad to think of a place more messed-up than Headquarters," said Flanagan.

"Yup." Neither man spoke for a moment. Kronholz broke the silence.

"Check this out, Mark." He took his friend to the window and pointed to his fancy, powder-blue Jaguar convertible in the parking lot, his new toy.

"Nice. Must have cost a lot."

"It cost a ton, but who's counting?" It was a flip remark, something anyone might say, but it hung in the air.

As Flanagan listened to his former colleague, frustrated with his job and seemingly flush with money, it seemed plausible that he might be the person they were looking for. Bored people sometimes do strange things to restore their self-esteem; they seek out others who will value them in the way they feel they deserve; they seek, too, the special, illicit arrangements that can buy a fancy sports car.

As Flanagan rose to leave, he fixed the microphone gently to the underside of Kronholz's desk. He shook the younger man's hand firmly and wished him good luck in getting back to S&T before the tedium of his current job led him to do something rash.

When he had left the building, Flanagan crept along the perimeter of the parking lot until he found Kronholz's new Jaguar, to which he attached a GPS tracking device. After that, he stopped off at Kronholz's house in Arlington, jimmied the back door, and put surveillance devices in four rooms of his house.

Vandel ate lunch in his office. He was puzzling about what intelligence he should use as chicken feed with Kronholz. It should be something about quantum computing that the Chinese would want to know immediately. It had to be real, but it couldn't be truly valuable. He needed technical advice on what might work. He remembered that Kate Sturm had already recruited someone as an informal adviser: Denise Ford, the former ops officer.

Vandel called Sturm's office to get Ford's number and make sure it

was a good idea. But Sturm's assistant said that her boss had left the office
to go home and get some rest before returning for her 6:00 p.m. meeting.
The assistant offered to try her cell phone, but Vandel said not to bother
her, it was something he could handle himself. He didn't want to wake
up Kate twice in one day.

Melanie, his assistant, got Denise Ford's extension and put through
the call.

"Hello, Denise, this is John Vandel," he said when she came on
the line. "Kate Sturm said you could help us out with some technical
problems."

"Yes, sir," Ford said quickly. She was sleepy herself, after the long
flight, and startled to be contacted personally by the deputy director for
operations. "Kate said there was some sort of special compartment where
you needed expertise about quantum computing."

"Exactly. Things have moved more quickly than we expected. Do
you have any time now?"

Ford paused before she answered. She shook the sleep out of her
head. When she spoke, her voice was crisp and assured. She agreed to
meet Vandel thirty minutes later, in the cafeteria between the new and
old Headquarters buildings.

When Ford approached, Vandel nodded appreciatively. She was dressed
in a tweed suit, better cut and more stylish than what most CIA employees wore to work. He hadn't seen her in years, but it was obvious that she
had taken good care of herself.

Vandel straightened his back and adjusted his tie.

"Hey, Denise. It's been too long. Thanks for helping us out."

"Flattered to be asked." She smiled broadly. It was good to be in the
club again.

Vandel moved a little closer. His voice lost its edge. His gray eyes
softened.

"I need something," he said. "I want a piece of intel that's hot, but not
too hot, that I can feed to an adversary. Like what you did a few years ago
with the Russians. Remember that?"

"Oh, yes. Very proud of that one. I thought people had forgotten about that. Where's this new package going?"

"Can't tell you, my dear, but you can probably guess. It's not Moscow. Do we have any new quantum reporting that's just gone into the black box, which it wouldn't kill us to lose?"

Ford thought a moment and then described two recently classified projects. An NSA team working with a university in Connecticut had just developed a new technology for making "Josephson Junctions," which were one tool in the intelligence community's experiments with superconducting. Another team, working with a big defense contractor, had just written a new programming language for pattern recognition and factoring on a quantum computer. Neither would have practical application for more than a decade.

Vandel listened carefully, nodding when he understood and asking for more explanation when he didn't. When she finished, he made his choice.

"The programming language sounds perfect," he said. "Important, but obscure. The right thing to use as bait."

"Yes, sir," said Ford. "I'll get you the details of the programming contract this afternoon. It's a joint project, with money from In-Q-Tel and IARPA. I can bring it by your office, if you want."

"You're a superstar," said Vandel, taking her hand in both of his.

"Send it to Kate. I'll figure out with my team how we'll use it. Maybe we can get you cleared into the compartment, too. That will make it easier, next time."

"Not a problem," she said. "I'm happy to help in any way I can."

18.

BEIJING, CHINA

The sky was heavy as cast lead over the capital. The pollution had rolled in on a gentle east wind and then congealed over the capital, suspending Beijing in a cloud of particulate matter that was the residue of iron and steel and concrete and chemical wastes, and a hundred other things that had made the New China and were now killing it. It was a day when people stayed indoors and coughed out as much of the soot in their lungs as they could before braving the trip back home. Some of the secretaries down the corridor from Li Zian's office were wearing gauze face masks to ward off the bad air that was circulating through the ducts of the heating system.

Li Zian's office looked out on a garden, but today the green was diluted by the acrid brown mist. The walls of the office were spare, like the man. He had no pictures of himself shaking hands with Party leaders, no award trinkets from the banquets thrown in his honor. On his desk was a picture of his wife; behind his desk, atop a credenza, was a picture of the badminton club at the University of Illinois at Urbana-Champaign, where he had taken his undergraduate degree. He kept it there to remind himself of what America was like between its coasts—friendly, trusting, wanting to be helpful.

Li had been dreading this day. But now that it had arrived, he was eager, almost enthusiastic, for events to happen. He gathered a carefully prepared file from his desk, put it in his briefcase, and rose to leave the inner office. With his round glasses and studious manner, he might almost have been one of the young Bolsheviks who went to study before the revolution in places like Paris or Berlin. It was said of him that he didn't eat food, only books.

Today, Li Zian would meet with the leading group that oversaw the special project known as *Xie*, or Scorpion, which monitored quantum computing. Li had hoped to gather the other members at his office at the Xiyuan compound near the Summer Palace. But the Second Department of the PLA had insisted on somewhere else, closer to the center of town. After the fall of another vice minister and the death of the scientist, the generals sensed weakness.

Li proposed that they gather at the Ministry's formal headquarters downtown, near Tiananmen Square. That was accepted.

Li had decided to bring along Wang Ji, the MSS's chief of North American operations. He trusted "Carlos," in his romantic, revolutionary disdain for the PLA and its power plays. The PLA had many things, but it did not have a human sting ray who could speak English with a Cuban accent.

Carlos Wang was waiting downstairs. He was wearing a black leather jacket, a beret, and zip-up leather boots. He had a wispy moustache and a thin goatee. Except for the Chinese features, he might have been Che Guevara himself. Like the American James Angleton or the East German Markus Wolf, he was a man whose eccentric presence and operational success had created something of a legend.

Carlos moved to sit up front with the driver, but Li summoned him to the back seat and pressed a button for the partition screen, so the driver couldn't hear what they said. They needed to talk before confronting the PLA and its evisceration mission. Li placed his briefcase on the seat between them and gave it a pat.

The big Mercedes limousine rolled off, curtains drawn against any curious proletarians. The Xiyuan campus was out beyond the Fourth Ring Road; with the normal, miserable traffic, the trip to Tiananmen would take nearly an hour. Carlos Wang removed his beret; his hair was long and dyed jet black. The fringes fell to the collar of his leather jacket. He lit up a cigarette without being invited. He was a man who pushed the

limits; Li Zian appreciated such bravado, especially this day. He needed
to talk, to order his thoughts.

"Have you read into the case?" asked Li. He had opened the window
on his side of the car to clear the smoke.

"Of course," said Wang. "The Singapore files, and the Vancouver
files, and now the Palo Alto files. I think we have enough information
to understand what happened before the death of Ma Yubo, and after."

"A disappointment," said Li. "I should never have brought him into
sensitive operations."

"He was a weak man, minister. But a strong tree can survive even
when some of the branches are weak."

The limousine crawled along the Fourth Ring Road and eventually
turned south at the University of Aeronautics and Astronautics. Li could
see the tower of a big luxury hotel, just ahead, north of the Ring Road.
He shuddered. That was where the deposed vice minister had invited
Central Committee members for drinks and sex. The vice minister had
tried to invite Li there, too, to bring him into the "club." Li would never
admit it, but he was glad that these MSS thieves were being purged, so
long as the Ministry itself survived.

The traffic slowed heading into town on Xitugeng Road. As a minister, Li could have put on the lights and siren and gone around the other
cars. But he wanted time to plan. And he didn't mind keeping the PLA
waiting, ever.

"What judgments have you reached, now that you have read into the
files? I want your thoughts on the principal case officer, this Peter Tong."

"A puzzling case, minister. Peter Tong is an American of Chinese
descent who had not been known to us before. Regrettably, he did a very
good job with Dr. Ma. The operational plan appears to have set him up
very cleverly with the invitation to discuss investments. But I wonder:
Why did they go to such lengths?"

"To weaken me," answered Li. "I think they mean to bring our house
down. Did Ma betray the service? That is the question that others will
ask us today."

"We cannot know what Dr. Ma told this Tong, but given the suicide,
we must assume the worst. Whatever he knew is gone."

"Were we aware of this Luxembourg Asset Management?"

"I regret that we were not, minister. But honestly, if we chased every MSS officer with an offshore bank account, we might as well shut down the service."

"And there is the missing *mijian*, with all of Dr. Ma's personal secrets."

"Perhaps it is in Chinese hands, minister. A friend at the prosecutor's office, who works with the Discipline Commission, says they used the *mijian* to arrest the vice minister."

"I don't believe it. The Americans have the *mijian*. Our enemies in the Party don't need help, anyway. They have a hundred knives. We have been a target long enough. I want to fight back. I want a counter-strike at the Americans."

"I can help, minister. This Tong has been dropping his handkerchief everywhere he goes. It's a provocation, or stupidity, or probably both at the same time. That is the American style."

"Who do you think he is?" Li pressed his operations chief.

"We know who he is. We finished our review this morning. His real name is Harris Chang. He's never had a diplomatic posting, so he was clean. Before joining the agency, he was a lieutenant in the Army. A Ranger. That makes him in America, you will forgive me, a 'big dick.'"

Wang Ji snorted as he said these last words. It was part of his style to talk dirty, in the way of the West.

"Where's he from in America?" pressed Li. "What kind of Chinese family?"

"Harris Chang has an unusual background, minister. He is from the 'Wild West.' Flagstaff, Arizona. It's near the biggest Indian reservation in America and the Grand Canyon, too. He grew up riding horses and playing football."

"What was a Chinese man doing in Flagstaff, Arizona?"

"His great-grandfather came to build the railroads. We have been doing some research."

Li Zian sat back in his seat, tall and erect, a Mandarin of the twenty-first century.

"I think I despise this man, Harris Chang. Wild West. Football. The Middle West is the real America. The rest is extreme."

Carlos Wang nodded. "Truly, he is a barbarian, minister." In fact,

Wang was indifferent. He regarded Chinese chauvinism as a useful operational tool, but not something that a serious person would believe.

"You said you were puzzled, Carlos," continued the minister. "Why
is that?"

"Here is my confusion: Why is Harris Chang so careless? Why does
he keep leaving cards with his Peter Tong alias everywhere he goes? His
flight records to Singapore were not encrypted. He went to Vancouver
to meet Ma's little whore. And then he announced himself to the Chinese friends of Ma's daughter, Daiyu, at Stanford. Our consulate says he
nearly caused a campus riot. Why is Harris Chang doing these things,
Mr. Minister?"

Li Zian answered the question that Carlos had posed so precisely.

"His service wants us to see him. It can only be that. He means to
draw us out. To invite us to a meeting. To discover what he knows."

"I am sure you are right, minister."

The Minister of State Security stroked his chin. Out the window, past
the opaque screen, they were passing the Beijing Film Academy, and then
they were inside the Third Ring. They had only a little time left to plan
before they reached the old city.

"An encounter with Harris Chang sounds dangerous, Carlos. Why
would I ever approve such an operation?"

"Because it may be the best way to protect your asset."

"You mean *Rukou*. How would this protect *Rukou*?"

"Think of how a magician distracts his audience, minister. The right
hand moves back and forth, tosses a ball, flashes a bit of powder, makes
a flourish, and you don't notice that the left hand has slipped into the
pocket and deposited the marked card."

"If I were to approve such an operation, would you visit with Mr.
Chang? Draw him out, even as he draws us out?"

"Yes, sir. I could do that in Mexico City, where our Cuban friends
can help us control the environment."

"And what would the left hand be doing while this distraction was
going on?"

"Ah, dear minister, at the appropriate time you would meet with the
agent who is everything to us. The agent that 2PLA, for all its conniving,

cannot replace. The agent who makes us the stinger of *Xie*. I speak of our asset, your asset, the irreplaceable *Rukou*."

Li nodded. He gave his briefcase a protective, reassuring pat.

The limousine had passed inside the Second Ring Road now. The car turned east, toward Beihai Park, and then south to the grand boulevard called "Chang'an," the street of Perpetual Peace. As they neared Tiananmen, backed by the brutal splendor of the Great Hall of the People, the limousine slowed and turned into the drive of an old gray concrete building, a relic of Soviet days, dark, forbidding, unmodern. The car stopped at the entrance and the two walked up the steps, Wang Ji a step behind his boss.

A great wooden door opened, and the two entered a large entrance hall, dank and drafty. They were ten minutes late, an eternity for a punctual Chinese. "Greetings, minister," called out the guards and receptionists; late or not, this was an MSS building. Li was the boss, until the PLA contrived to shove him aside.

The lions were waiting inside the main conference room, arrayed around a U-shaped table. At the bottom of the "U" sat the two senior officials who presided over the "leading group" that ran the operation: Dr. Xu Wanquan, a member of the State Council, and General Fang Qilang, representing the liaison bureau of the general political department of the Central Military Commission.

The figures gathered around the table nodded awkwardly and looked at their watches as the MSS men, Li and Wang, made their way to the two empty chairs to the right of State Councilor Xu.

General Wu Huning, the chief of the Second Department of the PLA, sat nestled among the array of uniforms. He was smoking a cigarette. Most of the others rose when Minister Li arrived; he remained seated, puffing on his Marlboro Light.

General Wu dominated the military side of the table; but in the Chinese way, he allowed others to appear to share the lead. Next to him sat the head of 3PLA, which handled communications and cyber-intelligence, and at the end, the commander of what was known as 2PLA First Bureau, which handled the military's assignment of officers abroad under non-official cover.

The civilian side of the table had less firepower. Fanning out from the MSS leaders were representatives of the Ministry of Public Security, which handled domestic security matters, a representative of the Science and Technology Ministry of the State Council, and the chief of the Institute of Scientific and Technical Information, which sought to coordinate acquisition of foreign technology.

In the outer seat on the civilian side, head bowed sheepishly, sat a delegate of the Academy of Science. His body language reflected remorse for the unfortunate actions of the deceased academician, Dr. Ma Yubo.

"You are late, I believe," said Dr. Xu from the head of the table.

Heads nodded in tart disapproval. They waited for Li Zian to apologize, but he said nothing. His demeanor announced that he had not lost face in being late; they had lost face in waiting for him.

There was a long silence, broken by General Fang, the senior military representative.

"The members of the leading group have gathered following the unfortunate death of one its advisers, the academician Dr. Ma Yubo, who was assigned to the Ministry of State Security," the general began. "The members of the leading group fear that the integrity of the program has been compromised. At the suggestion of our PLA comrades, we request a prompt and full report from the Ministry of State Security."

Li Zian, long and sharp as a straight razor, let the silence build again, and then began to speak.

"Dr. Ma committed suicide. He had been compromised by a member of the Central Intelligence Agency, who accused him of keeping money offshore illegally in a fund administered in Luxembourg and run in Taiwan and Macao."

There were gasps around the table, as people pretended shock at the very thought of high-level bribery. It was a fine piece of theater. Every one of them had illegal accounts overseas in the name of a family member. "It is a glorious thing to be rich," Deng Xiaoping had proclaimed nearly forty years before, and certainly nobody in this room dissented.

Li Zian resumed, before anyone else could capture the momentum.

"Although Dr. Ma's actions were shocking, we believe that he chose to end his life to protect one of the most precious secrets of the state. I am not permitted in this setting to disclose all the details, but I believe it is known to senior members of the leading group that the Ministry of State Security is running an operation that gives us unique visibility into decisions of the leading adversary as regards development of Project *Xie* and the technology known as 'quantum computing.' It is this operation that Dr. Ma sacrificed his life to protect, we believe."

Li paused a moment to take a breath, which was long enough for General Wu from 2PLA to interrupt. He was a tough, box-headed general. In uniform, his upper body looked as big and firm as a refrigerator. He spoke with the sharp, guttural tone that was at once that of a military commander and a Party boss.

"This is a fairy tale," said General Wu, looking to each member of the civilian team other than the two MSS men. "Dr. Ma was set up and recruited by the CIA. They sent a case officer from Washington and a technician from Tokyo. Whatever secrets Ma possessed are gone. The rationale that for many months has been given by the Ministry of State Security for its senior role in Scorpion—that it has special 'access'—has been shown, by this incident, to be false."

General Wu bowed, stiffly, toward the State Councilor.

"In light of these developments, I have a request," continued General Wu.

"State the request," answered Dr. Xu, the councilor. The 2PLA leader almost shouted back his response.

"I request that the senior role in this leading group be transferred from the Ministry of State Security to the People's Liberation Army, Second Department, because of the evidence of gross incompetence and corruption."

The demand produced a momentary uproar. Li and Wang, the two MSS representatives, rose from their seats in protest. Several other civilians shuffled papers or moved their chairs.

A bureaucratic coup was in motion. If the MSS could be purged from this sensitive spot, its hold on power was fragile indeed. There were whispers that the Party's general secretary wanted to abolish the Ministry altogether.

"Order, please," said Dr. Xu. "I ask my co-chair, General Fang, for his view of this matter."

The senior general was a little man, dwarfed by his uniform; he was truly skilled in one thing, which was the political infighting that had characterized the PLA since the revolution. The CMC liaison department that he ran was one of the hidden power centers of the new China. He understood that when an animal was wounded, it was time to go for the kill.

"We are among friends, so let us be honest," said Fang. "If this were the first instance in which we had cause to doubt the leading role of the Ministry of State Security, I would say that this incident in Singapore was a matter of bad luck. Just that. Ill fortune."

He paused to look around the room.

"But comrades, it is not bad luck," the diminutive general continued. "There have been too many other instances. This month, for the third time, a vice minister has been removed at Xiyuan. The Discipline Commission is investigating numerous other cases of corruption involving the cadres of the Ministry of State Security. I say 'cadres,' but is that an accurate description? Do these comrades even remember their Party loyalty?"

Several of those around the table muttered comments about disloyalty. The lynch mob atmosphere was growing, but Minister Li Zian, angular and austere, barely moved a muscle.

"We are one country, and yet . . . ," General Fang paused for effect. "And yet, even today, we hear from the capitals of many of our regions a deep resentment at the dominance of the Shanghai clique that persists in the Ministry of State Security. So I am afraid that I cannot see this as bad luck or one mistake. There is a pattern here. It must end."

"What is your proposal?" asked Councilor Xu, in his role as chairman of the meeting.

"I regret that a change of status is necessary. To rescue the essential program that we call Scorpion, on which the future security of the state depends, we must assign the supervisory role in this leading group to the People's Liberation Army, Second Department. I say that not as a member of the Central Military Commission, but as a Chinese patriot."

There were groans and murmurs, and another shuffling of papers, so people at first didn't see the figure of Li Zian rise from his seat. He had the hard, narrow face of one of the early communists.

As Li stood, he opened his briefcase and took out a folder that contained a dozen copies of a document in English, stapled to a companion that was a Chinese translation. He handed a half-dozen to his left, and then to his right, and they were passed around the table.

"Comrades, I regret this breach of normal security procedures," Li began. "But I fear there is no other way to save the program that has been entrusted to me and the Ministry of State Security from imminent destruction. Please look at the documents before you."

The figures around the U-shaped table looked at the pages. The older ones with poor vision held the document close to their eyes. General Wu, the head of 2PLA, gave it a quick scan, immediately recognized what it was—and what it meant—and laid it down, exhaling quietly.

Li Zian continued, holding the document aloft as if it were a torch that might illuminate the room.

"As you can see, this is a document created by a program manager at the U.S. Intelligence Advanced Research Projects Activity. In the document, this manager assigns a new top-secret, Specially Compartmented Intelligence contract number, S204GV-71-P-2067, to a quantum computing project that previously had been unclassified. Check the number on your copies, please."

The members grouped around the U-shaped table duly noted that they were reviewing document number S204GV-71-P-2067. Nods, clucks of approval, and Li continued.

"Let me explain, comrades: After careful study, our analysts have determined that this project involves the so-called 'ion-trap' pathway to creating a quantum computer. The academicians can explain another day how this works. This document tells us that the CIA and NSA believe this pathway is so valuable that it must be protected from the People's Republic of China. Thanks to the heroic work of the Ministry of State Security, we are able to see the very development that was meant to be hidden from us."

General Fang, who could see the mood in the conference room changing, moved to intervene.

"How do we know this is real?" Fang demanded, quivering with indignation. "This could be the work of MSS forgers. Where does it come from, other than your briefcase?"

Li nodded. They had taken the bait.

"Where does this document come from? That, as General Fang says, is the only question that matters. I cannot give you a detailed answer, for reasons that you will all understand in a moment. But the simple answer, which must never leave this room, is that it comes from our penetration of the CIA. We have for several years been running an asset, yes, a 'mole,' inside the highest circles of the CIA. This agent allows us to monitor their progress in the most sensitive areas of supercomputing."

"*Wo cao*," muttered one man. "*Diao Niao*," said another. These were coarse, graphic expressions.

"The code name of our penetration agent is '*Rukou*,' because this operation is the doorway through which we have walked into the most private sanctuary of the leading adversary. We believe we will receive much more information from our special source. Very much more. I regret that for security reasons, we thought it wise to inform only one other person in this room. That is General Wu, the head of our brother service."

"Yes," said Wu quietly.

"I must apologize to others, and most especially to General Fang, the representative of the Central Military Commission, that they were not briefed on the *Rukou* operation. But please be assured, General Fang, that the chairman and the vice chairman of the commission were fully briefed. I am sorry they could not share the details with you."

That was the coup de grâce. Fang rose from his seat and exited the room. He had been humiliated in an especially shameful way and been shown to be unaware of the secrets known to his superiors.

Some of the civilians looked up toward the looming figure of Li Zian and began to clap. Others followed, including most of those in uniform. Dr. Xu, the chairman of the leading group, stood and shook Minister Li's hand and whispered something in his ear. All the while, Carlos Wang, watching this exquisite performance, remained impassive, the thinnest trace of a smile on his lips.

Li turned to the group and raised his hands for quiet.

"For obvious reasons of security, I must ask all members of the leading group to return their copies of the document to me for safekeeping. We will soon have a detailed report on its implications for our programs, budgets, and collection efforts."

The papers shuffled back toward the MSS chief. It was over. Minister Li shook hands all around and escorted the members of the leading group to their limousines outside. The last to leave was General Wu, the head of 2PLA, Li's only match as an intelligence officer.

They shook hands. General Wu was about to say something and then thought better of it. Li walked him down the stairs to his car. As the door opened, Li leaned over and whispered in the general's ear: "I tolerate much from my brother. We are a family. Please don't ever do that again."

19.

OLD TOWN, ALEXANDRIA

Denise Ford mixed herself a cocktail when she returned home the night after her surprise meeting with John Vandel. It was a drink she had learned to love during her too brief stay in Paris, called a "kir," mixing a swirl of crème de cassis with white wine. She took off her heels and put up her feet on the ottoman. As tired as she was after the long flight the night before from Seattle, and the traumatic moments that had preceded it, she felt a deep satisfaction. She put a Vivaldi oboe concerto on the music system and sipped her drink. When she finished the first one, she made another, redder with the blush of the blackcurrant liqueur.

Her mentor at Yale had told her to have the big ambition, always, and she had tried to stay faithful to that advice. And now perhaps she was coming closer, though not in the way that anyone around her would dare imagine. She put on her headphones, so that she could hear the music louder, and closed her eyes.

Her senior colleagues, Vandel and Sturm, valued the fact that a few years before, she had been able to identify a damaging mistake that Russian scientists had made in their quantum computing research. Did they really think that her work was a mere accident of intuition, as she sometimes liked to claim? Or did they suppose that it was just a product of a machine-learning algorithm applied to Russian physics and computer science journals? Even smart people could often be very stupid. That was the fact of life on which successful intelligence operations, in the end, depended.

It had begun as an improvised experiment. She hadn't planned it, really, it just happened. But as the French say, *il n'y a que le provisoire qui dure.* Only the temporary lasts.

She had been traveling to a technical meeting of global computer science professionals in The Hague, sponsored by the Institute of Electrical and Electronics Engineers. The CIA had approved her trip, mainly because nobody else wanted to go. These people were dull. They were too intellectual to be interesting. The meeting offered a rare chance, Ford thought, to exercise the skills of rapport that her tradecraft instructors had admired. And she did, although not just as she had imagined.

At a dinner the first night of the conference, Denise sat next to a tall, well-mannered Chinese man. He spoke perfect English and seemed to have some kind of government position, which he never precisely revealed. Denise imagined that she had spotted him, but life is always more complicated than we think.

They had stayed up late that night drinking in the hotel bar. That was the reason people came to such events, to socialize with people whose work secrets they want to know and with whom they might develop relationships for the future. Denise had an advantage. She was an attractive, divorced woman. Everyone wanted to talk with her, but the Chinese man drifted back several times, always well-behaved, funnier and more relaxed as he drank.

The man spoke about China's future, its need to connect with the world of knowledge and technology. He detested the closed, communist past, he said. When he looked at a country like Russia, rotten with corruption, talented only at belligerence, he was ashamed. The more passionately he talked, the quieter his voice became. Denise felt an excitement that she had almost forgotten. This gifted Chinese man spoke almost as if he wanted to be recruited.

Denise pretended that she didn't notice when well past midnight, among the dwindling crowd still at the bar, the elegant Chinese man slipped a note into her handbag.

When she read the message a few minutes later in her room, she had trouble breathing for a moment. He had proposed in his note that they take a trip the next afternoon, when the conferees had "free time," to another destination in the Netherlands. The gentleman had suggested an unlikely rendezvous, a grand spot in a famous Dutch city, where they could talk without being seen. He said that he was placing his life in her hands. He begged her not to tell anyone from her "company."

Denise lay awake half the night wondering if she should message Headquarters. Normal procedures required that she seek authorization for such a meeting; it was forbidden for a case officer to do otherwise. But she wasn't a case officer anymore. If she contacted Headquarters, they would assign someone else to make the approach to the Chinese man. She was on the shelf. She would be excluded, again. They might even be angry at her, simply for having talked to him. No, it was better to take a risk and ignore the procedural rule; better to have the larger ambition than the smaller.

They met in a nineteenth-century neo-Gothic palace, near the banks of a canal. The Chinese man spoke as if he was making a confession. He could not bear the closed horizon of life in Beijing. He needed to believe in something larger. He knew that Denise Ford worked for the CIA, even though her conference identification described her as a senior researcher for a consulting firm. That was why he had sought her out at the conference, the Chinese man said, because he knew that she could help him.

"I believe in one world," he said. "I believe that scientific knowledge must be shared. I believe that technology belongs to everyone."

"I believe that, too," she answered. "That's the world I want to live in."

The Chinese man took her hand. He was a handsome man, thin-boned, with delicate features and the manners of a natural aristocrat. What she felt for him wasn't sexual attraction but an intellectual bond. That, and the thrill of the chase, returning after so many years.

"I can help you," he said. "I can give you secrets. About Russia, about China, about many things that you will want to know. But you must protect me. Otherwise, I will be a dead man."

She asked how she could keep him safe, and he answered that there was only one way. She must not tell the CIA about their contact.

"I know that you have said nothing to your company so far," he explained. "That is why I trusted you. That is why I came to our meeting today. If you had contacted them, I would not have come."

She looked up into his eyes. He was tall, for a Chinese man, but he leaned toward her, closer than people do usually, in a way that made every word and gesture seem intimate.

"It's true," she said. "I didn't tell them. But how did you know that?"

"Because I checked. I am very careful. If you had sent a message, I would have known."

Perhaps that should have frightened Denise, but it didn't. It deepened the connection. Their sharing of information would be kept in a secret box, opened only by them. She believed him, too, when he said that if she broke her word, he would know. He was a man who seemed to possess such power, more convincing because he didn't explain its source.

They returned separately to The Hague. Before she left the country, he gave her instructions for how he would contact her in the future. He would send her information that would help her, he said. He wanted only what she wanted, which was one world. That was his promise.

The Chinese man contacted Denise a month after her return to America. She almost thought that he had forgotten about his pledge, and she wondered if perhaps that was better. She had mentioned meeting him in the debriefing, when she returned from the conference. Of course, she had; people had seen them together in the bar, and she would face a polygraph eventually, so it was better not to conceal a foreign contact now. But the operations officer who debriefed her didn't seem to care, especially when Denise said she thought the Chinese man didn't have any potential as a "developmental." She was so unimportant, even her contact with a Chinese official didn't matter.

The first package of material arrived by Federal Express, just as the Chinese man had said it would. It was a long list of Russian computer scientists at the Moscow Institute of Physics and Technology, with the names of several dozen highlighted in yellow. Denise Ford had seen this same list before. It had been generated by the machine-learning algorithm that she was using to examine Russian technical journals, as part of a joint project between her directorate and IARPA.

How had the Chinese man obtained this list? Ford could not imagine. But as she turned to the end of the package, she saw a note of explanation. The highlighted names were the ones involved in important, secret work.

Over the next days, Ford subtly put this information to work. It was intuition, she told her colleagues, a feeling that she had from studying the product of the machine-learning search about who might be worth a deeper look.

Two weeks later, another package arrived. The documents in this second installment were more detailed. They listed the engineers at a computer science laboratory in Kazan that was engaged in advanced research on quantum computing. Ford put this to work, too. People were beginning to pay attention to her good guesses. And then there was a third package, focusing on a research pathway the Russians had chosen that hypothesized that there might be quantum bits with more than two dimensions. This, too, was gobbled up in the interagency hunt for information about rival approaches to quantum computing. The operations directorate got involved, too, when the analysts said the Russians were on a path to nowhere. The operators devised ingenious ways to make it appear that the Russian misadventure was actually a success, so that they dug deeper in the wrong direction.

This information helped Denise Ford's career, just as the Chinese man had promised. And in the CIA's hands, it harmed a Russia that he had seemed, genuinely, to despise.

It was a few months later that the first package arrived from the Chinese man in which he asked for Denise Ford's reciprocal help, too, in creating the one world of scientific knowledge in which they both believed.

What to make for dinner, after the delicious wine and cassis that had made her lightheaded? Though she'd had a very long day, Denise Ford decided that she would prepare something special. She'd shopped for the ingredients, after clipping the recipe from the *New York Times*. She made herself a salad of French lentils, topped with shredded Manchego cheese, and after that a breast of roasted ginger chicken. She set an extra plate in the candlelight, for symmetry, but she ate the sumptuous meal all by herself.

Despite the anxiety of twenty-four hours earlier in the computer laboratory in Seattle, Ford fell asleep quickly. She arose the next morning feeling refreshed and newly confident.

20.

ARLINGTON, VIRGINIA

Kate Sturm was in her office the next day catching up on paperwork when, just after noon, she received a call from the Seattle field office of the FBI. The special agent in charge apologized that it had taken him two days to complete the forensics on the compromised machine in the laboratory of the Seattle computer company, QED. The fingerprints had been difficult to lift from the plastic surface of the protective cover on the quantum computing device. And it had taken a few extra hours to process them, because the analysts had initially gotten a false match with another set of prints.

"We have a positive ID," the FBI man said. "Probably nothing, though. It was the lady who accompanied you that day. I see that she has TS/SCI clearances. Denise H. Ford."

"Oh, Jesus," said Sturm. She felt a prickly heat on her skin and a sudden loss of breath.

Sturm willed herself to be calm. She thanked the SAC and asked him to keep this information out of FBI channels for the moment, while the agency's Office of Security assessed the information. He agreed. This was an accident, he assumed, worthy of an administrative reprimand but not a criminal referral.

Sturm let her heartbeat settle. She dabbed away the sweat on her forehead with a tissue. Then she called John Vandel's direct line.

"I need to see you right away, John," she said.

"Not the best time," answered Vandel. "The Director is having one of those days. How about tonight or tomorrow?"

"Can't wait."

"Come now, then," said Vandel. "I'll pour you a Scotch. Sounds like you need it."

"Not in your office. Meet me outside the front door. I don't want anyone else hearing this. I'm leaving for the elevator now."

Sturm didn't give Vandel time to say no. She walked quickly down the seventh-floor corridor and descended to the lobby. She was outside the front door, standing by the statue of Nathan Hale, when Vandel emerged from the building. He walked toward her along the stone path.

"You okay?" asked Vandel. "What's up? Where's the fire?"

He took her hand, to steady her against whatever had put the flush on her cheeks, but she shook him off.

"Listen to me, John. I think we're chasing the wrong person as the Chinese mole. It's not Roger Kronholz."

Vandel took her arm again and gently tugged her away from the entrance, where other employees were now emerging. They walked north, past the bubble-shaped auditorium.

"Why do you think that?" asked Vandel quietly. "We've just started the surveillance of Kronholz. I haven't fed him the chicken feed yet. Let's wait and see if he bites."

"It's not him. I think it's someone else. Someone who wasn't on our list."

"Okay. I give up. Who?"

"You're not going to believe this, but I'm worried that it may be Denise Ford."

"Your pal? I just saw her yesterday. She helped me bait the hook for Kronholz. I mentioned it at the 6:00 meeting, and you didn't say boo. Are you sure? Denise Ford doesn't fit. She's like part of the wallpaper around here."

"Precisely. And I trusted her, obviously. I thought we could use her as a resource person. But I began to get squirrely after we went to the tech company in Seattle. And I just heard something that really spooked me."

"I can see that. But back up. This is the first time I'm hearing that anything bad happened in Seattle. What was the problem?"

"Denise acted weird. She kept asking questions that pushed the line. She wanted her own copy of a letter from the Chinese company, Parcourse Technology. She was nosy, but I didn't take it seriously. And then something really strange happened. While I was off in another room getting a code-word briefing, the protective cover came off the classified monitor of a piece of hardware. It triggered an intrusion-detection alarm. Denise was near the machine. She said it was a mistake, she bumped it accidentally, but I don't believe her."

"Why not?"

"Because her fingerprints were on the protective cover. The FBI office in Seattle just called me with the forensic results. She did it, and she lied about."

"Shit! Why didn't you warn me last night that you had doubts?"

"I didn't want to hurt her career if I didn't have evidence."

"Oh, right. I forgot. She's part of the 'sisterhood.'"

Sturm stepped away, as if she had been slapped.

"Stop it, John. I don't need any crap from you right now. We have a traitor in the building. It's Denise Ford."

Vandel's head froze. His face registered disbelief, then belief.

"Plausible," he said eventually. "She has a motive, which is that she has been fucked over ever since she washed out of her first big assignment."

"I'm sorry, John. This is my fault."

Vandel was rubbing his forehead, thinking about how they had gotten it so wrong. He muttered a curse.

"I am so stupid," he said. "She's divorced. She ditched Ford years ago. Her maiden name was Hoffman. Isn't that right?"

"I think so. What does it matter?"

"This place used to be full of Hoffmans. She may not have a current relative at the agency, but she did once. What a dope I am."

Sturm was silent for a long moment while they walked.

"What do you want me to do?" she asked as they neared the bubble.

"Nothing, for right now, except watch her. Use Flanagan as a bird dog. He works in her division. Does she know he's part of our team?"

"No. We never talked about Flanagan."

Vandel was shaking his head, still stunned by his mistake.

"Do you think she'll bolt?" he asked "That would be catastrophic."

Sturm considered his question.

"No," she said. "She's a cool customer. I'd guess she has a lot of emotional investment in whatever she's doing with the Chinese. This is her operation. She won't give it up easily."

Vandel shook his head one last time.

"We need to confirm this as quickly as we can. I'll ask the DNI for special authority for the NSA and NRO to crunch data on her travel abroad. We'll gather the Small Group again tonight. Even if we don't have proof by then, we can start watching Denise Hoffman Ford very closely."

Vandel put his hand on Sturm's shoulder. He never touched her; it was out of bounds. But this was different.

"I wish the Chinese were stupid," he said. "But they're not. They are very smart. They're doing exactly what I would have done. And they're not finished. But I'm not either."

"What are you going to do, John? We're running out of time. We're going to have to tell the Director, and he'll tell the White House, and they'll tell Congress, and then, kaboom. What's your alternative?"

"I'm going to take Li Zian apart. That's what. He may think he's in control here, but he's wrong. Watch and see. And don't tell anybody anything."

The drab office building on North Glebe Road was hardly a prominent location. It was a few hundred yards from the commotion of the subway stop, and the neighborhood was so full of buildings doing classified work that you could throw a rock in any direction and very likely hit someone with a security clearance. But even so, John Vandel's assistant advised Harris Chang and Mark Flanagan to enter by a back alley into the basement garage.

Chang wore a baseball cap and shades. His gray suit, white shirt, and striped tie were all from Brooks Brothers. Even on the streets of Washington, where nearly everyone is unmemorable, he was especially indistinct. An observer would not have registered his age, profession, or nationality.

Chang was the first to arrive that afternoon. He was escorted down the long hall, past the picket of cyber-locks, to the meeting room designated for the DDO Small Group. Mark Flanagan came twenty minutes later, still early. When the two were gathered in the unadorned, utilitarian meeting room, a tech arrived to dial up Warren Winkle from Singapore on a secure video-teleconference line.

John Vandel appeared at 5:00 p.m. sharp with Kate Sturm. Vandel was wearing suit pants that were low on his waist and his tie was loose, after a long day's march through the bureaucracy. Sturm was wearing the inevitable black pants suit. They both looked tired and unhappy.

Nobody spoke, not even Winkle, the wise guy from Singapore. They all waited for Vandel to tell them what was next in their hunt for the unseen, unnamed enemy. Flanagan, the lanky Irishman, normally so disdainful of authority, sat rigid. Vandel was stroking his chin, not wanting to begin.

"We have a new target," Vandel said eventually. "It appears that I was wrong. It's not Roger Kronholz. It's someone else."

He paused. No one spoke. Was he going to make them guess?

"So who is it?" asked Chang, breaking the silence.

"It's a woman in S&T named Denise Ford, formerly Hoffman."

"No way," said Winkle. The disembodied voice conveyed what everyone was thinking.

"Way," said Vandel. "It's her."

"The niece of Cyril Hoffman—the guy who died a couple years ago, who worked at ODNI?"

"Same one."

"Denise Ford," muttered Winkle, the sound of his voice hardened by the metallic relay of the voice connection. "So senior. So harmless. So yesterday. She used to be a friend of mine. We went on a date once after she divorced, when I separated from the first Mrs. Winkle."

"Too much information, Warren. Thank you," said Sturm.

"I remember her, too, actually," said Flanagan. "When Denise came into S&T about ten years ago, she was like a wounded bird. The word was she got screwed by the DO. People felt bad for her."

"Ancient history, doesn't matter," said Vandel. "The point is that we need coverage, starting now. I want to catch her in the act. Or at least on the way to Dulles."

"Can we take this to the Bureau, please?" asked Flanagan. "I don't want to make a profession of breaking the law."

"Not yet. I don't want to bring in the Bureau until the takedown. Right now, I need to get someone into S&T who can keep an eye on her. Make sure she isn't about to run, but otherwise, keep a loose string. And it has to be someone who already is a member of the Small Group."

"Which means what?" asked Flanagan warily, his voice bumping up a notch. He knew what was coming.

"You were Ford's friend, right? Now you're going to work for her. She needs a deputy. Her boss just told her that, this afternoon. At my suggestion."

"You can't ask me to babysit a Chinese mole. Come on, John."

"I just did. You've worked so long in S&T, you're the one person who would be credible as her assistant."

Flanagan turned to the group, arms upraised.

"Come on, people. I'm not cut out for this. I'll screw it up."

"No, you won't," said Chang. "You're the iceman."

Vandel nodded; he began to pull away from the table, thinking he had accomplished his mission, but Chang put up his hand.

"Something here I still don't get: The MSS is usually so careful. Li Zian took a big risk recruiting her. What's he got on her? How did he convince her to cross over?"

"I have absolutely no idea," answered Vandel. "Blackmail, idealism, probably some combination. But he knows Americans. He understands our vulnerabilities. He lived in Normal, Illinois, for Christ's sake, when he was a college student. He has an American foster family. He still writes them letters, or at least he used to, until the FBI told these folks to stop answering. Li is an artist. For him, even a smart patriotic woman might commit treason. But you know what? Li Zian is not quite as smart as he thinks he is."

Chang looked at his boss and saw the intensity in his eyes and the firm set of his normally loose frame. He remembered that look from Baghdad.

"You want him bad, don't you, sir?"

"Yes, I do. That is a fact, boys and girls. I want Li Zian really bad. He has recruited one of my agency's senior officers. I take it as a personal insult. This is the first time a foreign intelligence service has recruited a woman mole in the CIA. I don't like it, and I am going to burn his ass."

The meeting broke up. Mark Flanagan stayed behind to send his message to Denise Ford, volunteering his services. Chang stayed behind, too, thinking that Flanagan might want company. But when the big Irishman was finished with his work, he was preoccupied and silent. Chang descended to the basement with him, and they departed the building on Glebe Road by separate exits, their caps pulled low on their heads.

21.

LANGLEY, VIRGINIA

Denise Ford's office in the new Headquarters building overlooked the arched roof of the cafeteria and the back side of old Headquarters, where the senior directors worked. It was close to power, but agonizingly separated from it. Ford had filled her office with keepsakes of happier days: pictures of Paris, her college degree from Yale, and her master's in computer science from George Washington. There was a picture of her with Marie-Laure Trichet at a reunion ten years ago. Under it, her former French professor had written in flowing script: "Always the big ambition!"

On the credenza behind her desk, where most people might place pictures of a spouse or children, Ford had a framed quotation from the physicist Richard Feynman: "I cannot define the real problem, therefore I suspect no real problem, but I'm not sure there's no real problem." Nobody had ever thought to ask her what that quotation meant to her, so she had never needed to explain.

On her bookshelf, she had arranged a little display of S&T's handiwork. The division was the CIA's version of "Q" in the James Bond movies. She liked to show visitors the robot mouse that could crawl inside walls in denied areas; the tiny drone, little bigger than an insect, which could buzz in the chimney and fly, unseen, through the ventilation system. Sometimes, when she wanted to amuse a visitor, she would spread them on her desk like a little family of toy animals.

Ford's boss, Bill Grayson, didn't like paperwork, so it had fallen to Ford over the last few years to review technology projects across the expanse of the intelligence community. It was tedious work, mostly, checking boxes and confirming someone else's decisions. The job gave her access to many of the black projects at CIA, NSA, IARPA, and In-Q-Tel. It was a lot of bureaucratic detail, but Ford never complained.

Grayson had suggested twice in the past year that Ford needed help, so she wasn't really surprised when he called her the day before and told her he was giving her a deputy. Grayson said he had already posted a notice on the S&T bulletin board. The timing was mildly suspicious: Kate Sturm had been upset in Seattle, but Vandel had been friendly after that and had even asked for help. So Ford went along with Grayson's proposal, but with her eyes open.

A half-dozen résumés arrived in the first few hours. Grayson's secretary brought them in a stack. Ford was pleased to see that the application on top was from Mark Flanagan, an S&T veteran, who was home on leave.

When Flanagan arrived the next morning for his job interview, Denise Ford shook his hand firmly and then patted him on the back, not quite a hug. He was, like her, a veteran who had never quite risen to the top with the flyboys.

She was dressed in a light blue chiffon blouse and a well-cut leather jacket. Her hair was pulled back from her wide face in a ponytail. She motioned him toward the couch under the window that looked out at the back side of the Seventh Floor.

"Well, you haven't changed, Mark," she said with a smile. "Edith must be taking good care of you. Although she needs to take you clothes shopping."

Flanagan did look like a perpetual undergraduate. He was dressed, as ever, in a tweed jacket, chino pants, and his Bass loafers. He was wearing an especially short pair of socks, so there was a gap of mottled skin between the bottom of his pants and the tops of the socks.

"I've been keeping busy in Tokyo," Flanagan answered. "Headquarters has been so busy reorganizing things, they forgot about my little tech-support hub. But I've been living on airplanes. It's wearing me down. I decided I need a change."

She appraised him; still fit, still irreverent toward management, still enjoying the arcana of espionage. But wanting the calmer, leeward side.

"I got your application. Do you really want to work for an old has-been like me?"

He held back a moment, not wanting to seem too eager.

"Sure. Until we get tired of each other. It's time for me to come home. I need somewhere to land. I don't want to leave S&T, and I don't want to work for an asshole. So you're it."

"Do you really want to be somebody's deputy?"

"Happily, if it's you. I don't want to be thrown in the motor pool by HR and have to work for people I don't respect."

She eyed, him, not suspiciously, exactly, but with a wary curiosity.

"You don't know me that well: I studied French literature. I'm obsessed with computers. And I'm a Democrat. You probably wouldn't like that."

"I could care less."

"Well, well, well." She looked at him, rose from her chair, and walked over to the bookshelf that displayed her toys. She picked up something that looked like a fish and handed it to Flanagan.

"Remember Charlie the robot fish?" she asked.

"Of course. We thought we were so cool when we got it to swim up the Neva River in Leningrad."

"Have you seen the new ones? They release little crawlers that can go anywhere. Jump up trees and telephone poles. Slither into your router. Amazing battery life."

"What's the new fish called?"

"'Willy.' The tech shop can't make enough of them."

She put Charlie back on the shelf and picked up what looked like a mechanical dragonfly. She held it in her hand and then let it drop to the floor. She picked it up and cradled it, head high.

"This one is my pet. She has every sensor you could want, all minia-turized, low voltage. She's beautiful. Aren't you, sweet thing?"

Ford gently stroked the mechanical dragonfly as if it were alive in her hand.

"My little friend has just one problem. Do you know what she misses?"

"Tell me."

"She can't see what people are thinking. She can't tell us about intentions. Or loyalty. The things that matter most. How frustrating, to get so close but never know."

Ford was watching him as she spoke, looking at his face for any sign of recognition beyond the straightforward words and sentences. But Flanagan's putty face was immobile. If he caught any special meaning when she talked of "intentions" and "loyalty," he didn't betray it.

"We'll get along fine, Denise. I'm low maintenance. Long battery life." He spoke like a man who wanted a job.

Ford returned to her chair, sat down, crossed her legs, and leaned toward her visitor to make one more foray.

"What do you know about bats?" she asked.

"Not much. Actually, that overstates it. Nothing, is what I know about bats."

"Grayson told me to read up on bats, for a meeting at the National Geospatial-Intelligence Agency. I thought it would be a waste of time, but it surprised me. The little fruit bat can fly in the dark for thirty miles, straight line, and perfect navigation, to get to its favorite habitat. It seems to have a nearly flawless radar and GPS system."

"The Air Force must be studying that," said Flanagan. "Sounds like their sort of thing."

"The Air Force." A shadow passed across her face, as quickly as the exhaust of a Hellfire missile. "Yes. The Air Force. Probably already in the pipeline."

She was silent, studying the very practical man across from her. Was this a trap? She couldn't know, and it didn't matter.

Flanagan waited for her to continue, and when she didn't, he asked the question.

"So can I have the job?"

"Are you sure you want it? I am one of those quirky people who still thinks she can make a difference in the world. I hate surprises. And I dislike people who undercut their colleagues. If I discover you have another agenda, I will make your life very unpleasant."

"Got it. I know how this place works. One boss at a time."

"How soon can you start?"

"I'm already on TDY in Washington. I can start now, if you want me."

She paused a moment, and then nodded and extended her hand.

"As you'll see, my end of S&T isn't very interesting, compared to what you could do out in the field with Charlie and Willy and the fruit bats. But I'd like to have you. And you won't mind if I'm away, sometimes."

"Sounds good," he said. "Should I tell Grayson?"

"I'll tell him. He won't believe it from anyone else."

She led him to the door. "Honestly," she said, "I need help."

Denise Ford's new deputy began work the following Monday. He went to the DDO Small Group office on North Glebe Road after he had finished work the first day, and each workday after that, to report what he had heard and to check the take from the sensors he had discreetly placed around his boss's office.

The reporting was meticulous and recorded in rich detail the bureaucratic journeys of Denise Ford, the diligent assistant deputy director of Science and Technology. But they could not find a hint, in anything she said, wrote, or looked at that she was anything other than loyal to the CIA. In that sense, she had achieved the highest art of her profession, which is the ability to appear ordinary.

Several days passed before John Vandel received a response from the director of national intelligence to his query for a "restricted handling" review of data collected by the National Security Agency and the National Reconnaissance Organization. Vandel had asked them to mine their massive sound and image archives to find any record in foreign locations for Denise Ford's voice and face. The databases had included camera footage at airports, embassies, and consulates.

At Vandel's request, the surveillance agencies made a similar check for any images outside China of Li Zian, the head of the Ministry of State Security. Vandel had reasoned that Li would never give such an assignment to one of his subordinates. He was the America expert; he understood the leading adversary.

The search was slow but more than successful: It produced too much data. Li had been in Russia several dozen times; he was in Southeast Asia even more often. So Vandel advised the analysts to focus on Li's travels in Europe. It was so easy to operate there with open borders: Fly into Paris, take a train to Milan, or Madrid, or Brussels.

The facial recognition matches taxed the capabilities of the government's supercomputers. There were tens of thousands of camera locations and billions of faces. Some matches appeared for Li in Berlin, and then in Paris, and in Oslo. But those locations didn't fit Denise Ford's travel, so Vandel told the analysts to push again.

Vandel complained about the delay to the DNI's chief of staff. Why did it take so damn long to do the searches? The aide explained the limits of conventional computing power. Even using arrays of servers in the cloud or superfast high-performance computers, many, many hours of computing time were required.

"Jesus!" exploded Vandel. "This is why we need a quantum computer right now, not twenty years from now."

"Excuse me, sir?" asked the DNI man, puzzled by Vandel's outburst.

Vandel apologized. It was a pet interest, he said. He didn't mean to lose his temper.

The DNI's rep called Vandel when the facial recognition matches came back and hand delivered the product in a blue-bordered folder: A police surveillance camera showed Li and Ford entering the same hotel on Avenue Louise in Brussels, an hour apart, in May. That couldn't be a coincidence. Ford was wearing a wig, but the facial confirmation was one hundred percent. The hotel was loaded with surveillance cameras but there was no audio. The subject of their discussion was unknown, but what mattered was the fact it had taken place.

Once the analysts had confirmed the Brussels meeting, they went back and re-queried the Europe databases. It didn't take quite as long on the second run. But it was another full day before they had a shot of Ford wearing the same wig when she met Li six months earlier, in November, in Helsinki, Finland.

Vandel noted the dates on a pad. The two had met in November last year. They had met again in May, six months later. It would be time for another meeting soon. But where?

22.

MEXICO CITY

"Hello, James Bond," began the voicemail message to the Peter Tong alias telephone number in the Operations Center. The woman spoke slowly and carefully in Chinese-accented English. She said she had a "big difficulty from the consulate." She implored Peter Tong, who had been so kind and had volunteered to help, to please call her back. "You are so strong. Can you take care of me now?" Her last words were silk. She left a number in Vancouver.

Harris Chang listened to the message on a secure circuit. The voice was unmistakably that of Li Fan, Jasmine, the mistress of the late Dr. Ma Yubo. The message arrived just before noon, Washington time. Chang's heart raced for a moment when he heard the voice. He bit his lip.

Chang's first move, after digesting her seeming plea for help, was to contact John Vandel. The deputy director for operations was eating lunch at his desk; he had food in his mouth when he said hello.

"My Tong voice-drop just got a message from Dr. Ma's girlfriend," said Chang.

"I know. She's hot for your bod, Harris. Did you fuck her?"

Chang felt a flush of embarrassment. Of course, Vandel had listened to the tape first. He was the boss.

"We established some rapport. Good tradecraft."

"Well, you little sidewinder, you. You left that out of the cable. And now she wants to talk. For openers. Frankly, I'm delighted."

"What do you want me to do?"

"Call her back," said Vandel. "*Tout de suite.*"

"What if it's a trap?" asked Chang.

"It's almost certainly a trap. We want to know who's running it, and why."

"What if she asks me to go somewhere to meet her?"

"Then say yes. Mr. Bond is at your service."

"Okay," said Chang dubiously. "What if she wants to meet somewhere that isn't Canada or the U.S.?"

"Well, I wouldn't go to Beijing. But otherwise, yeah, sure. Why not? You could suggest Iraq."

"Ha, ha," said Chang. "You're not taking this very seriously."

"To the contrary. I am more invested in your rescue mission than you might realize. This is what we want. Keep pulling on the thread."

"What am I pulling? What intel am I after?"

"We want to see their cards. They're running a mole and they're scared we know who it is. They just lost a senior adviser to their service. They must be suspecting that we recruited him. And even more, they must be worrying that he blew their secrets before he died. Like I said, pull on the thread. Eventually, no more sweater."

"And what do *they* want?"

"Who cares? Watch and learn. That's all you have to do. They're not going to shoot you. The Chinese don't do that. Just listen. Whatever happens, it's all good."

Chang swallowed hard and brought the telephone close to his mouth.

"Level with me, boss: This is what you wanted all along, right? That's why you sent me to see this woman in Vancouver in the first place, and then had me go to Stanford, handing out my card. You were chumming the water."

"Guilty as charged," answered Vandel. He rang off, leaving Chang to return the call to the young Chinese woman in Vancouver.

Li Fan sounded more than grateful when she received Harris Chang's phone call. She needed him. She choked back a sniffle when Chang finally said he had to go.

The damsel in distress had been well briefed. She told her rescuer that it was too dangerous to meet in Vancouver and that America wasn't possible because she had no visa. She proposed instead that they meet in Mexico City in two days. She had even picked out a rendezvous: Gran Hotel Cuidad de México.

"Good hotel. Best in town. I made a reservation. Is that alright, my dear? I am so frightened. I will be waiting."

Harris Chang said he would meet her at the hotel in two days at 4:00 in the afternoon. He would call up to her room, and if Jasmine answered with the address of her apartment building in the Burnaby suburb of Vancouver, he would come up and meet her. Any other greeting and he would abort the meeting.

Li Fan repeated the address coolly. This was a setup, stone cold, on both sides. Chang stopped by Kate Sturm's office that afternoon to request Support to make arrangements. She wasn't encouraging.

"We're not well staffed in Mexico, I'm afraid," said Sturm. "It seems like everyone has better operational resources there than we do. Not our turf."

"Well, find some, please," said Chang. "I'm going to need some watchers in two days, no matter whose turf it is."

Carlos Wang slipped into the Chinese Embassy in Mexico City. The front entrance on Avenue San Jeronimo was simply a gatehouse, a façade with five Aztec carvings, the middle one crested with the Chinese seal, and the red flag flying behind. It was covered by constant U.S. surveillance. But the street behind the compound had a back entrance through a big office building.

Carlos checked in with the MSS resident at the embassy when he arrived. He was the head of the American Operations Division—visiting royalty, in effect. Carlos informed the Mexican intelligence liaison officer, too. The MSS wanted to maintain the comradely environment of Mexico City, a city where Chinese money was augmenting the "fraternal ties" of leftist solidarity.

The Chinese had built their embassy not in the fancier, northern districts of the city but in Coyoacán, the place of the coyotes, the historic home of the Mexican left. The Autonomous University was nearby, and just north was the "Blue House," the home of the painters Diego Rivera and Frida Kahlo, red priest and priestess.

For Carlos Wang, there was another spot of veneration nearby, one that he didn't dare mention to his colleagues at the embassy. Carlos left his leather jacket and beret in the closet. He wore a proper blue blazer with brass buttons, pulled his long hair back into a pony tail, and slipped out the back way onto Rio de la Magdalena.

Wang walked northeast. He knew the way by heart because he had made the pilgrimage before. He took side streets and paused occasionally to look for surveillance in the storefront windows. But who would be following him, except for other Chinese? Those he could spot in a heartbeat. He ambled down the alleyways, listening to an old Cuban recording from the Buena Vista Social Club through the ear buds of his iPhone.

He approached the shrine on a frontage road parallel to Avenida Río Churubusco. The house was a museum now, painted bright red with a red picket fence: "Museo Casa de León Trotsky."

Wang entered the courtyard of the old house, unchanged since the day in 1940 that Trotsky was murdered. It was a pleasant villa but topped with a crude masonry watchtower for Trotsky's bodyguards. Trotsky had known they were coming for him; they had tried to kill him once before. But still, he had stayed on, feeding his chickens and rabbits and writing his biography of Stalin that would expose all the secrets of the red monster.

Carlos Wang lingered in every corner of the house. The dining room, with its black-and-yellow tables and chairs, painted like bumblebees—the simple whitewashed quarters for his comrades and bodyguards, the "family" that had braved machine guns in the attack three months before his assassination and had stayed.

And then the study. Carlos Wang was not a religious man, but he did venerate the ancestors. Nothing on Trotsky's desk had been moved since the day the assassin plunged an icepick into his head. His reading glasses were on the table; his typewriter was behind him, awaiting the final revisions of the Stalin exposé; a crude Dictaphone stood next to the desk to record his words.

And the books of his little library, arrayed just so: Marx and Engels, of course, and also several volumes of a Russian encyclopedia. Carlos Wang studied the Cyrillic writing on the spines of the books. Lev Bronstein was a revolutionary theorist, certainly, but also a man of meticulous fact. That was what Carlos Wang remembered, every time he visited this shrine and thought of his own intelligence agency, encrusted in bourgeois wealth and aspiration, and their rivals in the PLA even worse. Like Trotsky, he hated watching a revolution decay.

It was getting near the time Wang should leave for his meeting. He made one last stop in the garden out back. Trotsky's ashes were buried under a granite stone, bearing his name and the hammer and sickle, below a red flag flapping stiffly in the fall breeze. Carlos Wang looked at the marker and remembered a line of Trotsky's he had read years before, when even to say the man's name in China was the rankest heresy. It had been written by the young Trotsky in 1924, before the unraveling, when revolution was still a white sheet of consciousness and the dreamer was trying to imagine the future:

"Man will become immeasurably stronger, wiser and subtler; his body will become more harmonized, his movements more rhythmic, his voice more musical. The forms of life will become dynamically dramatic. The average human type will rise to the heights of an Aristotle, a Goethe, or a Marx. And above this ridge new peaks will rise."

Carlos Wang bowed, imperceptibly, before the tomb. He reminded himself what the stakes were in the project he had embraced. They were seeking a quantum computing machine that would replicate the very essence of human thought, a machine as subtle and ambiguous as the human brain, whose fruits would rise even above the peaks that his secret mentor had imagined. The idea that a venal, corrupted America would possess this thinking machine first was an abomination.

Harris Chang approached the Gran Hotel from the wide expanse of the Zocalo plaza. Behind him, a hundred yards distant, was the splendid façade of the National Palace. In the southwest corner was the turreted tower of the hotel.

Chang was dressed in a pale blue windbreaker over a turtleneck. His eyes were covered by wraparound shades with mirrored lenses. He was wearing a backpack with the gear he had brought with him on the flight from D.C. He had traveled light, unsure how long he would stay. His instructions from Vandel were as skimpy as his kit.

Chang had stopped earlier that day at a safe house near the U.S. embassy on the Paseo de la Reforma. The local operations chief said he had stationed six watchers at the Gran Hotel. He was grumpy: A big station like Mexico City was like a hot-sheet motel; guests in and out, no questions asked.

Chang thanked the ops chief for arranging surveillance, but the team wasn't large enough to do much good if someone wanted to grab him.

Chang fell in behind a group of Chinese tourists gathered in the Zocalo. The Chinese were just off a bus, forming an orderly queue behind their guides. Chang accompanied them toward the southwest corner of the Zocalo and then slipped away. He waited for a knot of visitors arriving at the entrance to the hotel and followed in their wake. Inside, it was as if he had entered another century. Vaulting above the lobby was a delicate ceiling of stained glass.

Chang headed for the concierge desk. He asked the uniformed attendant in halting Spanish to be connected to Miss Li. The concierge answered in English: He asked for identification and Chang handed over his Peter Tong passport. The man at the desk called up to the room, announced the visitor's name, nodded, and then handed the phone to Chang.

"Hello," Chang said. "I want to make sure I have the right room. What is your address?"

"I have missed you, James Bond," the Chinese woman said. "I live on 4200 Lougheed Highway in Vancouver. I am happy that you want to see me again. Will you come upstairs please?"

The concierge, with a knowing wink, pointed Chang toward the elevator.

Chang knocked on the door. Young, helpless Miss Li was standing just inside. She was wearing a form-fitting silk dress. It exposed the curves of her breasts, but she had gathered a shawl around her shoulders. She looked guilty and embarrassed.

Chang entered warily. It was a setup; it had to be. When she closed the door, Chang could see that she had in her hand an envelope.

"A Chinese man was here before you," she said. "He wants to meet you. He said to give you this. I am sorry."

Chang stared at her until she dropped her gaze.

"Maybe I am a bad woman to make you come all this way. But I am Chinese, you understand."

She handed Chang the envelope. It was addressed to "Harris Chang." He opened it and read the computer-printed note inside:

"Dear Mr. Chang: I have a message concerning Dr. Ma Yubo. Please meet me this afternoon in Pachuca district, fifty miles north of the city. It is not safe here for our conversation. For that same reason, I cannot give you the address in Pachuca. A car is waiting for you downstairs, at the corner of Palma and 16 de Septiembre. It has a blue pennant on the passenger-side window. The car will bring you to me. Come alone. If you are followed, the meeting will not take place."

The note was signed in Chinese characters. Below that, the sender had typed "Wang Ji, Ministry of State Security."

"You need to go now," said Li Fan. "They will be waiting."

The car was on the corner, just as the note said, a block from the hotel entrance, next to a Nike Outlet Store. A muscular Mexican man was sitting in the driver's seat, his head nearly touching the car's upholstered roof. Chang read the license plate and then stepped away into the shadows on Calle de la Palma, several dozen yards away, and called Vandel on his secure cell phone.

"I'm at the meeting place, down in the street, outside. Nobody was in the hotel room other than the fairy princess. She handed me a note addressed to me in my real name, not the Tong identity. It was signed by Wang Ji. It says he wants to meet outside the city. If I'm followed, no meeting."

"Sweet! Carlos himself!"

"Should I go? There's a car here waiting to take me someplace up north in Pachuca, toward the Sierra Madre. Or so the note said. What should I do?"

"Go! *Vaya con dios*," said Vandel. "I wish I could come along."

"Can anyone cover me up there? I don't know where we're going."

"Not to worry, Harris. The Chinese won't hurt you. They aren't ISIS. They don't operate like that. Let's just see what the play is. We'll have you overhead. I have a drone up on loan from the DEA. We'll follow you out of Mexico City. We can jump in if you get in trouble. But you won't."

"Thanks, bro," said Chang, sarcastically. "I think the Chinese care more about my ass than you do."

"Don't say that, Harris. Not even in jest. Let them lead. This is their show. If they ask any questions, say you have to check with Headquarters and request another meeting."

Chang sighed. He looked at the car and driver from his perch. "All in." That was what his commander in the 101st Airborne liked to say at the commander's morning huddle every day in Mosul.

"You want the license plate number?"

"Sure. What's the tag?"

"The number is ZHB-43-36. The car is a black Lexus."

"Got it," said Vandel. "Have fun."

Chang went back into the hotel. He put his secure cell phone into his backpack and checked that he was carrying only Peter Tong identification and pocket litter. He asked the concierge to check his backpack, gave him a twenty dollar bill, and took the ticket. He went back on the street and found the black Lexus, still idling on the corner. The blue pennant was fixed to the right window, as promised.

Chang leaned toward the driver to say who he was, but the Mexican just nodded and pointed toward the back seat. He had already gotten confirmation from someone that the Chinese-American in the blue windbreaker was the designated passenger. Chang opened the back door and took a seat. A lock clicked, and Chang found he couldn't open his door. The driver went to the trunk, took a new set of license plates and, after removing the previous tags, fastened the new ones in place.

"All in," Chang told himself.

The Lexus pulled away from the corner and headed north toward Avenida de los Insurgentes and the slow crawl of afternoon traffic. Chang scanned the forest of billboards that skirted the slum neighborhoods on either side. "Will you choose good or great?" asked a whiskey ad. Chang would settle for "alive."

When the car reached Route 85, the main route north, the driver pulled off the road and loosely bound Harris Chang's hands, blindfolded him, and made him lie down flat on the back seat before continuing toward Pachuca.

23.

MINERAL DEL MONTE, PACHUCA, MEXICO

Harris Chang felt the change in altitude as the car rumbled up the Sierra Madre. It was like being back home: high, dry air; the hum of tires on pavement. He could smell the pine forests until it got chilly and the driver closed the window. The driver was playing Mexican pop songs on the radio. For a big man, he seemed to have a taste for ditzy pop music. Over and over the radio pulsed with upbeat, mindless songs and a breathless DJ trilling the names: "Thalia!" "Belinda!" "Anahi!" as if they were goddesses.

The blindfold was tight, so Chang had no sense of where they were, other than the feel of the terrain in his lungs and nostrils. The car began ascending more steeply, up a series of switchbacks, until it finally came to a halt. The driver uncuffed Chang's hands and gently eased him out of the back seat to his feet but kept the blindfold on. He led him up stone steps and into a room where he seated him in a comfy chair. Chang could feel the warmth of a crackling fire to his right and the cool breeze from a window, straight ahead.

The driver removed the blindfold. In the low light, it took a moment for Chang's eyes to adjust. Out the open window was a vista of high hills at sunset, pine forests climbing the hillsides. A half-mile below was a town, the buildings painted in fading, early evening tones of pink and ochre, illuminated by streetlights. A pale stucco church stood in the center of the little town, its twin bell towers fronting on the town square.

Chang didn't see, at first, the man sitting in shadow to his left. But the flicker of the fire caught his face for a moment. He was Chinese with high, hard cheekbones. He had long hair that stretched to his shoulders and a wisp of a goatee. He was wearing a beret, tilted on his head. He was smoking a cigarette, each puff illuminating his features. It was a face that Chang had seen in pictures; up close, he looked more like his reputed role model, Che Guevara, than Chang had expected.

"Hello, Harris Chang," said the voice in the shadow. He spoke English with a Spanish accent rather than a Chinese one. "I am sorry for the long and bumpy ride. This was the only way to meet in confidence. I hope you were not too uncomfortable."

"Wang Ji," answered Chang. He spoke the name slowly. "You are a mystery that lures people from a great distance."

"You will call me Carlos, I hope. I like that name, especially here in my dear Mexico. Do you like this place? I thought it would remind you of Flagstaff, Arizona."

Chang smiled. This was a carefully constructed piece of theater. In the flames of the fire, his skin and Carlos's were the same lustrous tan, sparking when the flames rose like golden wheat on fire.

"Flagstaff is special," said Chang. "No place quite like it. What's this town? Does it have a name?"

"We are in Mineral del Monte. It is high in the mountains, beyond Pachuca. We are in a little safe house I found many years ago. I didn't like to tell anyone, it was so beautiful. I never knew how I would use it, until now."

"Now that you've brought me all this way, what do you want from me? I'm here to listen."

"I want to talk with you about China. About your life as a son of China."

"Come on!" Chang snorted. "Are you shitting me? I am the least Chinese man you ever met. I bleed red, white, and blue. If that's why you invited me, it's a waste of time."

"Really?" asked Carlos Wang.

He took another long puff on his cigarette. The glow illuminated his eyes, bright with intelligence. He said nothing more for a long while, just smoking on the cigarette. He offered one silently to Chang, who refused, so Carlos puffed away until the ash fell to the floor. Carlos rose and went to the pantry of the little mountain chalet. He returned with a bottle of Mexican red wine and two glasses. He poured one for himself and one for Chang.

"Try it," said Carlos. "It's from Baja. '*Único*.' It's very good, I think. Americans don't like it, but as with many things, they are mistaken."

Chang tasted the wine. Carlos was right. It was delicious.

"I know many things about you," said Carlos. "I know that you are from Flagstaff, yes. I know that you were in the Army. In Iraq, too, sorry for that. I know you work for the CIA. I know you were in Singapore. So I know pretty much, you might say."

"You do your homework. That's good. But you didn't bring me here to show off, did you?"

"No, I told you. I want to talk to you about China."

"I have no authority to make any deal. I have to check back with Langley."

Carlos snorted and waved his hand.

"Listen to me, please, young Chang. Here's what I want to tell you. Your great-grandfather came to America to work on the railroad. Do you know where he was from in China?"

"Canton."

"Yes. Guangdong, we say now. He was recruited there with so many other poor men. I know the town he was from and even the village, too. Would you like to hear?"

Chang knew that he should feign disinterest and change the subject. But in fact, he did want to know where his great-grandfather had come from. He had asked, as a boy, and his father had said he didn't know. But he had always been curious. Now this proffer of information. It wasn't free, but the price was elusive.

"All Americans are interested in their ancestry," said Chang. "That's part of what makes us American. We can be proud of our roots and not be embarrassed or worried about where we came from. So, sure, I'd like to know where my great-grandfather came from. If you really know."

"Ah, but we know everything."

Carlos Wang lit himself another cigarette and poured them both another glass of wine.

"Your great-grandfather's name was listed as Chung Hoy Co on the manifest. He was from Taishan County in the Pearl River Delta. It is just west of Hong Kong. The name of his village was Baisha. Many Chinese people went from there to California and Canada. Would you like to see a picture of some of your cousins from Baisha? The Xiang family there?"

"Sure. But don't think this is buying you anything, because it's not."

Carlos Wang shook his head. He would never presume on the loyalty of his guest. He pulled from his satchel a photograph of a beautiful young woman, an orchid of a girl, and then a picture of a young Chinese man, dressed in a PLA uniform—smooth tan features, muscular body—who looked astonishingly like Harris Chang.

"You see? He is a soldier, too, your cousin. His name is Xiang Kun-Ming. He asked me to give you this picture."

"Did he really?" responded Chang skeptically.

"Yes. Take it. He would be insulted otherwise. The woman, too."

Carlos handed over the pictures gently, like fragments of another world. Despite himself, Chang took them, passing his finger over the faces.

"Very nice," said Chang. He tried to hand the photos back.

"Keep them, please. The village of Baisha is very proud of its American cousins. It is part of the story that families tell, how during the famine years at the time of the opium wars, so many brave men went to America. They feel a hole, an empty place."

"Stop it," said Chang. He was fighting the pull of the narrative, but something powerful in him wanted to hear it.

"Would you like to know more about your great-grandfather?"

Chang didn't answer. Carlos waited patiently, and then proceeded, with Chang's silent assent.

"Your great-grandfather worked for the Central Pacific Railroad. He was part of a Chinese labor force recruited in Guangdong by a businessman named Charles Crocker. We found the pay record for Chung Hoy Co in 1866. He worked in Camp 6. His foreman was Mister G. W. Taylor. He worked for 317¾ days. Here. I'll show you."

Carlos passed a copy of a faded ledger book page. Chang found the name of his ancestor, Chung.

"The record does not say how much he was paid, but it was probably thirty-one dollars a month. That was the going rate for a Chinese man on the railroad then. In a year, he would have made $372, if there were no accidents. Not so much. But it was better than starving back home."

"How did you find that? My family looked for those railroad records for years."

"Please, Harris, if I may call you by your Christian name. Please: We are very expert at this work. And we have so many Chinese people to help us. Everyone shares this story, you see. You should not fight it so hard."

"I'm not fighting. I'm listening. But if this is the best you've got, it's not working."

Carlos smiled.

"Your great-grandfather was part of the great Chinese railroad workers' strike in 1867. Did you know that?"

"No. My father told me about the strike but never about his grandfather's involvement. I guess he didn't know."

"Oh, yes, he was one of them. They were proud men, you see. Working in those high mountain passes, blasting tunnels one hundred feet below the surface, for a quarter mile. And in the winter, too, with the snow and the wind, these poor Chinese boys from Guangdong."

"They wanted more pay."

"They wanted dignity. Crocker had raised their pay from thirty-one dollars each month to thirty-five dollars, so they knew that the boss needed them, high up in the Sierra, to dig those tunnels and blast the rocks. They demanded forty dollars a month! Yes, and ten hours a day instead of eleven, and only eight hours in those terrible tunnels. But Crocker said no."

Chang nodded. "So Crocker called out the cops. I read about the strike."

"More cruel. He cut off food and water to the Chinese camp, high in the mountains, bitter cold. For eight days, they starved. Crocker finally said he would take them back, same pay as before, thirty-five dollars, if they stopped causing trouble. Your great-grandfather was one of them. He lived to be ninety, I believe."

"Quite a story."

"Yes. Brave men. Do you know there was a famous strike, right here in these mountains, too, in 1776? The Spaniards mined their silver here. They treated people like dogs, too. But the workers fought back. They weren't Chinese, these ones, they were slaves and Indians. But they were human beings. They went on strike! It's universal."

"Give me a break with the communist crap. And seriously, you're making this up."

"You think so? Why would I do that?"

"I don't know. I'm still not sure why you brought me here. This is all bullshit. You haven't asked me anything yet."

Carlos Wang raised his eyebrows. He gave a thin smile and shook his head.

"I have no questions. You are free to leave anytime you want."

"Thanks." Chang moved forward in his seat, about to stand. "How about now?"

"First, maybe you would like to hear about your mother's family. That is a very complicated story. It will interest you, I'm sure."

"Good luck. My mother didn't talk much. She was from San Francisco. 'It's Chinatown, Jake.'"

Carlos Wang was quizzical. "Who is 'Jake'?"

"It means, 'forget it.' It's a line from a movie called *Chinatown*. A cop tells Jack Nicholson to forget about something, because the truth never comes out in Chinatown."

"Ah, but it does, when people aren't afraid. The problem for your mother was that she knew too much."

Chang was exasperated. Despite himself, he was being pulled deeper into Wang's narrative. He couldn't help himself.

"My mother didn't talk about her father because he was a gangster. I always figured that. Big deal."

"That is not quite right. Your mother's maiden name was Rose Kwan. Am I correct?"

"Yup. Her father was Henry Suh Kwan. My mother showed me the fancy Chinese building where he used to go sometimes as a young man, on Stockton Street in Chinatown."

"The Fung Yee Tien Association," said Wang.

"Yeah. That's right. Fancy balustrade. Red-tiled roof. There's a sign in the masonry that says it was built in 1925. I used to see it as a kid. Just went back, the other week."

"Ah, yes, a building. Very nice. But do you know what this 'association' was? It was a *tong*, a radical organization for self-defense, created to honor four heroes from ancient times, from the time of the Three Kingdoms. Those four heroes were named Kwan, Liu, Chang, and Chu. So it was your mother's family that was part of this association, this band that was pledged to fight the warlords."

"Like I said, we assumed they were a gang. The Chinese Mafia. That was why my mother wouldn't talk about her father. You're telling me what I already know."

"I don't think so. The line between criminal activity and radical politics is a fuzzy one, don't you think? When people are scared by a movement, they say it's an illegal gang. Or a terrorist group! That was what happened with the Fung Yee Tien Association. But your grandfather and your mother were smart. They found another way."

"The more you talk, the less I believe," said Chang. But his eyes remained fixed on the man in the beret, whose face was half-illuminated in the light of the flickering fire. Chang poured them both another drink.

"Your grandfather Kwan knew that trouble was coming. It was the 1950s. There was a 'Red China Scare.' But the police were cracking down on the associations, too, the tongs. Everyone was waving Kuomintang banners and saying to fight for Chaing Kai Shek. But your grandfather Kwan knew that Chinese people were being used by everyone. Police, politicians. He'd had enough."

"My mother said once that her father got in trouble, but she wouldn't explain. What did he do?"

"He tried to be an American. Ha-ha, think of that. He went to the Six Companies, the elders of Chinatown, who formed the Chinese Consolidated Benevolent Association, and said that Chinese people should not be mistreated in this way; they had their rights. But the elders were too scared in that time. He was not scared. You want to see his picture?"

Carlos Wang removed from his satchel a copy of a picture. It showed a handsome young Chinese man, clear-eyed, with a great shock of black hair, wearing a gray cardigan sweater. He was smiling.

"I've never seen this picture," said Chang. "What did my grandfather do?"

"He fought for the truth. He helped start a reform group called The Correct Path. That meant the honest, clean way without the tongs or political bosses. People said it was a radical organization, but your grandfather didn't care. Then, in the 1960s, he and some friends started a bookstore for Chinese people. Just books! It was called 'All-American Bookstore.' They sold books from the Mainland. Even the 'Little Red Book.' Ha-ha."

"Where was it? I've never seen it. Never heard of it."

"It was on Walter U. Lim Place. All the good things in Chinatown were there. All the organizations that fought for Chinese people, so they could be real Americans. Like you."

Chang shook his head. He was uncomfortable. It was as if someone else had taken possession of his life story. He tried to fend off the Chinese officer.

"Nice try," said Chang. "You're making this up. Why wouldn't my mother talk about her dad starting a bookstore? Give me a break."

"Because it was too painful. Too dangerous for you."

"Why? What's dangerous about a civil rights organization and a bookstore?"

Carlos Wang spoke very quietly.

"Your grandfather Kwan served time in prison. They said he was a communist. He spent five years in a federal penitentiary. Here, I will show you the record of his sentencing. And here's the discharge picture of him when he left prison."

Carlos handed two sheets of paper to Chang. As he took them, Chang's hands trembled slightly. He lowered his head. The photograph showed a man who looked like he hadn't slept in his five years of captivity. The eyes that once sparked with confidence were now hollow and rimmed in black.

"Uh-huh." That was all he said at first, as he tried to recover his balance. Then a low mutter: "This is crap."

"It was a matter of great shame in those days, never to be talked about. Your family arranged a marriage. They had distant relatives in the Chang family in Arizona. That is how Rose Kwan went to Flagstaff. To meet and marry your father. He was poorer, less educated. But it was an escape. Her own father had just been sentenced. Children were calling her names in school. She had to leave."

"My mother would have told me later. He was her father. My ancestor. Part of my story."

"How could she, Harris? You were on the football team. You were going to West Point. You were a war hero. Now you're in the CIA. It wouldn't have helped you to know that your grandfather had been a communist. It wouldn't help you now. It's a secret because it has power. It's dangerous."

Harris Chang sat back in his chair and put his glass of wine aside. His face fell into deep shadow. He held the photographs and other documents in his hands and then let them drop to his lap. He closed his eyes. He wasn't an introspective man; his whole life had been about control of emotion. But in this moment of personal revelation, he felt deep sadness, even remorse, for the pain that his mother and grandfather had experienced.

Chang brushed a teardrop with his sleeve. He hated giving Wang Ji, his interlocutor, what he wanted. But sitting there, immensely lonely, suddenly, he knew that this would be a very hard story to explain to his colleagues back home.

"This is bullshit," Chang said again. But his voice betrayed a different emotion.

"You must be hungry," said Carlos. He rose and went to the pantry. His slim form, seen in shadow, might well have been that of the revolutionary he admired.

"I have prepared meat and bread and cheese," Wang said. "And a little more wine, perhaps. And then you can sleep. Tomorrow, you can go home. There's a taxi stand down in the *villa*. They can take you wherever you want."

Chang struggled to recover his identity as a CIA officer.

"What do you want to know about Singapore?" asked Chang. "I'll bet you're wondering what Dr. Ma told me. That's why you brought me here. Not all this Chinese crap. Come on, play your cards. Ask your questions."

Carlos Wang shook his head. He patted the American on the hand.

"We know enough about Dr. Ma. It was you that we wanted to understand. And now, we do."

"You bastard," said Chang. "Maybe you think you have power over me, but you don't. This is a rookie play. I have nothing to hide. From anyone. My whole life story is about loyalty."

"Of course," said Carlos. "It's just a more complicated story than you realized. Now that you know, you must explain it to others. To your agency. To the FBI, maybe. What consequence that will have, I cannot say."

"Nice try. A non-pitch, using precious facts of my life, if they are facts. But honestly, it won't work. As good as you are, I'm better."

Carlos Wang set a plate of bread and cheese and cold sausages before Chang.

"We'll see," he said. He lit another cigarette. The gentle look disappeared from his face. Even in the flickering shadows, the anger in his eyes was clearly etched.

"I don't know what will happen to you when you return home, Mr. Chang. But really, sir, after what you did to Dr. Ma Yubo, you deserve whatever comes. This man was weak, but he was a scientist, a graduate of your own universities. His mistake was that he wanted to be rich and have a pretty girlfriend, like an American."

"He knew what he was doing."

"Not really, sir. You took him apart, like a doll made out of paper and thread. He did the honorable thing, which was to kill himself. I wonder about you."

Chang stared at the plate. He didn't want to engage in the conversation with Carlos Wang anymore. In truth, he had no answer for him.

"Eat," said Wang. "You'll need your strength. Tomorrow will be a long day. And long days after that, too."

Wang left the room. A door slammed shut, and then a car engine fired. Chang looked around the small chalet. There was a bedroom and a bathroom, in addition to the living room and pantry. He was alone, it seemed.

Chang put another log on the fire and ate the little meal that his host had provided. He had no phone to call anyone, and he wasn't sure yet what he would say. He finished the bottle of wine and fell asleep undisturbed in the single bed.

Harris Chang awoke at dawn. His head hurt. In the living room, he saw the pictures that Carlos had given him of his grandfather Kwan and the villagers back in Baisha and his great-grandfather's railroad records, still on the floor by the chair. He thought about burning them, but that seemed wrong. He put them in his jacket pocket, gently so they wouldn't crease.

He walked down to the village of Mineral del Monte and found a taxi outside the Hotel Paradiso. The driver gave him a wink, as if he knew the story. "It is a *senorita* in the hills, isn't it? Now, very early, you must leave her."

"Yes," said Chang. "How did you guess?" The way back seemed a lot longer than the ride up had been.

Chang booked a flight for that afternoon back to Dulles but then canceled it and reserved another flight, twenty-four hours later. He needed time to think. He composed a brief operational message for John Vandel about his trip to the mountains and left the rest for later. He wasn't sure how he was going to explain the hours he had spent with Wang Ji, the head of the American Operations Division of the Ministry of State Security, and he wished that it were possible to say nothing at all.

24.

LANGLEY AND ARLINGTON, VIRGINIA

Mark Flanagan slept badly the night before his first day as deputy to Assistant Deputy Director Denise Ford. There were circles under his eyes and a dull cast to his usual ruddy complexion. He didn't like spying on colleagues, even when they were suspected of disloyalty to the agency. He looked out of place. He wore a gray suit instead of his usual rumpled tweed jacket and khaki pants. He didn't know where to park. He went to the old Headquarters building instead of the new one. On the elevator, he couldn't remember the names of two S&T colleagues he'd known for twenty years.

Flanagan had been assigned a small office just down the hall from Ford's. When he unlocked the door, he found a little stack of books on his chair and a note from his new boss. "To get you started," she had written. The books were about computing. The two on top looked almost accessible: *Quantum Computing Since Democritus* and *Schrödinger's Killer App: Race to Build the World's First Quantum Computer*. The rest were textbooks, filled with algorithms and equations that Flanagan couldn't have read even when he was an engineering student at Cornell.

Denise Ford rapped on his door thirty minutes after he arrived, while he was setting up his computer profile. She might have been a middle-aged professor at a smaller Ivy League school, better dressed than her colleagues; the spark of intelligence in her eyes but a wariness, too. She was carrying two cups of coffee. She handed one to Flanagan.

"Settling in?" she asked.

"Totally," he said, casting off his weariness. "I'll have to brush up on my math and physics, though." He nodded at the pile of books.

She picked up the top book in the stack and leafed through its diagrams of quantum rabbits and coins that were in two positions at once.

"I warned you I'm a quantum computing freak," she said. "The world is about to be turned upside down. That's why I left the books. So you can prepare."

Flanagan took a sip of his coffee. How was he supposed to respond to that? He had been briefed about his mission by Miguel Votaw, the deputy director of the FBI, who had offered some general guidelines: Flanagan should shadow his new boss, monitor who she was visiting and calling, and report any sign that she might be planning to flee. He should pay particular attention to any activities that involved quantum computing, on which, it was believed, she was focusing her espionage on behalf of China.

Flanagan was perplexed. He had assumed that his target would be elusive. But here she was, on his first day in the office, confiding—no, advertising—her interest in the very topic that the investigators thought was most sensitive. Flanagan dangled a question.

"How did you get so interested in quantum computing? That's more an NSA and IARPA thing, right? S&T is still the gadget shop, not the computer science lab."

She took a seat on the arm of Flanagan's guest chair. She wasn't resisting his inquiry. She wanted to talk.

"I couldn't avoid it! Part of my job is reviewing IC paperwork that doesn't interest Grayson. And these quantum projects are everywhere. I just visited one last week in Seattle with Kate Sturm. I wanted to know everything about it because of all the other work we're approving."

"Was it interesting?"

"Fascinating! Maybe I overdid it, asking questions. But I want to, you know, spread the gospel. This stuff is important. My only worry is that with so many projects going black, we'll kill the science."

She was laying an alibi. That was Flanagan's first thought, listening to her explain her interest in quantum computing. All these conversations could be cited later by a lawyer, if it ever came to that.

Flanagan kept the ball in play.

"There's no way to stop stuff going black, is there? I mean, that's what we do."

"But it's stupid. When we put things in compartments, it's like trying to suck up the ocean with a soda straw. Quantum mechanics isn't an intelligence compartment. It's *life*. It's the way the universe operates. We can't *own* it. That would be like trying to own the air."

She stopped, pushed a strand of her auburn hair off her forehead, and took a breath.

"Oh, well," she said. "Don't mind me. I do my job. If they say it's black, fine, into the box it goes. But sometimes . . . ."

"Sometimes what?"

She laughed and flipped into a different gear.

"*Sometimes a Great Notion*, by Ken Kesey. Did you ever read that? I did, in college. Wonderful book."

"You were talking about quantum computing?"

"Was I? Maybe so. Well, I have to go to work. There's a world out there, waiting for the competent woman. That's what my father always said. How wrong was *that*? What are you doing later this week?"

"Nothing. I mean, anything. What did you have in mind?"

"How about a field trip? I have to go to California to talk to some of our grantees. They're in the quantum space, too. They took government money, and now they're unhappy about disclosure rules. I have a little rebellion on my hands. It's one I sympathize with, but don't tell anyone that. The thing is: I need a wingman. Grayson won't come. Why not you? Come on! It's a great boondoggle."

Flanagan played coy. "I don't know. I just got here. Where is it?"

"I'm meeting the scientists in Newport Beach. It's ridiculously beautiful. I need some company, even if he's an old has-been from S&T. Come on: You can listen to the rebels."

"What's the rebellion?" pressed Flanagan. "What are the scientists upset about?"

"Us! The government. They think we're trying to fence off the world.

Sometimes I think they may be right, but I'm a softie. That's why I need an agency veteran to come along. To keep me inside the chalk lines."

"Chalk on your cleats," said Flanagan with a laugh. It was a line that had been used by a former CIA director. She was brilliant. All this talk about openness and sharing. She had made him as an informer the moment he walked in the door. She was weaving her tapestry of defense. Either that or she was innocent.

"Are you sure it's wise for me to go?" asked Flanagan. He worried that he was falling into a trap, racing off with her to a meeting on the subject about which she was supposedly stealing government secrets.

"What a silly question. Of course, it is. We're just doing our jobs."

John Vandel nodded appreciatively several times when Flanagan recounted the conversation with Ford and her travel invitation. They met that night at the hideaway office on North Glebe Road.

"She's good," he said.

"What do you want me to do? I can bail on the trip."

"Hell no. Fly out to the coast with her. Keep her talking. She'll make a mistake, eventually." He paused and shook his head.

"Smart lady," said Vandel. "Her family were screwballs, from what I hear. But they weren't traitors."

Flanagan got up to leave, but Vandel, usually so quick to adjourn a meeting, was staring into space. He looked preoccupied. He hadn't moved even when Flanagan was punching out on the cyber-lock.

"Anything wrong, boss?" asked Flanagan, turning back. "Something I can help with?"

Vandel came out of his bleak reverie. He waved his hand, dismissively.

"No big deal. Harris is late coming home from Mexico. He sent me a cable. I don't know what to make of it."

Flanagan had talked briefly with Chang before his trip. Chang had wanted advice on resisting interrogation, if it came to that.

"Is Harris alright? He said he was meeting a Chinese woman in Mexico City. What happened? I hope they didn't mess with him."

"No. That's just it. Harris says nothing happened. He says everything's fine. An MSS man just talked to him for a few hours up in the mountains. He sent me an ops cable, but there's nothing in it, really. That's not like him. He's usually meticulous."

"How can I help?" asked Flanagan.

"Harris will be home tomorrow. After I debrief him, you should go see him. He likes talking to you. Find out what the hell happened to him in Mexico. I get nervous when people tell me that everything's fine."

Vandel remained seated, head in hands, after Flanagan let himself out the door. He was trying to put himself into the mind of someone else. Not Harris Chang, or even Denise Ford, but Li Zian, the Minister of State Security.

25.

GREAT FALLS, VIRGINIA

Harris Chang brooded on the way back to Dulles. He put on his earphones, not to listen to music but to muffle the noise around him. Self-reflection was not his natural state. From his earliest days, he had been a doer, the Chinese kid who could hit the baseball farther than anyone, do more push-ups, stay later in the weight room, help the other, slower members of his team with their homework. When he thought of himself, he saw a face in the sun in the high plains of Arizona. He didn't see yellow, but a deep, rich tan, like all the boys.

When Chang graduated from West Point, the superintendent had told him he was one of those soldiers who gave meaning to the phrase "the American dream." That had made Harris Chang happy. His personal beliefs were summed up in the West Point motto: Duty, Honor, Country. He didn't know much about his Chinese past; his family went to a Methodist church but not very often. He spoke a little Chinese, but he couldn't read it. The superintendent had been right.

Chang wondered what he should tell John Vandel about the meeting in Mineral del Monte. He knew that until he told the whole story, including the awkward facts about his family history, he would be subtly in Wang Ji's power. But explaining what had happened wasn't as easy as going to a private confessional. If he spoke up, he would set in motion a process that would trigger an investigation that might—no, that would—harm his career.

CIA officers didn't just discover, in the presence of a foreign intelligence officer, that one of their family members had served time in prison for subversive activity. They didn't suddenly disclose, after nearly two decades, information that had never surfaced in scores of background checks and polygraph exams. Facts had consequences, especially when they were previously unknown.

Harris Chang knew that he was a bad liar. Deception was a life skill he hadn't managed to learn at Flagstaff High School. When his pals told little fibs about shoplifting or smoking weed, Harris froze. He knew that if he echoed a lie, he would get caught.

Chang called Vandel when he landed in Washington just after 3:00 that afternoon. The DDO was busy, but he called back a few minutes later.

"I've been waiting," Vandel said coolly. "That wasn't much of a cable."

"I need to see you right away, sir," said Chang. "I wasn't candid about what happened in Mexico."

"Oh, Christ," said Vandel. He exhaled and took a slow breath. "I'm sending a car out to the airport to get you."

"I'll take a cab," said Chang. "I can drop my stuff off at my apartment and then come to the office in Arlington."

"I'm sending a car. Be at the United exit in twenty minutes. They'll come get you. Don't talk to anyone, anyone, until I see you."

Vandel closed the connection. Chang knew that he was, from that moment, under investigation.

The car brought Chang, not to the familiar clandestine location near the Ballston Metro stop, but to a safe house in the Virginia countryside, off Route 193 near Great Falls. The driver put a hand on Chang's elbow as they walked up the front steps. Inside were John Vandel and Miguel Votaw, the deputy director of the FBI, flanked by an armed man and woman from the Office of Security. They ran Chang's briefcase through a metal detector and then handed it back.

"A welcome home party?" asked Chang, smiling, trying to keep himself from feeling guilty.

"You could say that," said Vandel. He extended his hand to Chang, greeted him, and introduced Votaw. His tie was loose and there was a day-old stubble on his face. He looked like he had been brooding. "Miguel and I just want to hear what happened down in old Mexico. You said you hadn't been 'candid.' That worried me a bit."

Chang looked at Votaw warily. Vandel had gone outside the family; he had invited a member of the Justice Department to hear his personal account. Votaw was a big man with a gut overhanging his trouser tops. He was wearing a white shirt and an embroidered silk tie. He looked like he was on his way to church.

"Should I ask to speak to a lawyer?" said Chang.

"Hell, no. Not unless you've done something wrong. But we can play this however you want."

"Shit," said Chang, shaking his head. He pondered the situation, but not very long.

"I'm fine with whoever you want in the room, John. I have nothing to hide. That's why I asked to see you right away. I want you to know everything about what happened. Even the stuff that's going to sound strange. 'All in,' as my unit commander liked to say."

"Good boy," said Vandel.

He motioned for Chang and Votaw to take seats in the living room. A steward appeared. Vandel and Votaw both requested glasses of whiskey. Chang asked for a Coke and then reconsidered and asked for a beer. Only a guilty man would drink soda pop.

"So what happened to you up in those mountains?" asked Vandel. "Did Carlos put a hex on you? Feed you some peyote or something? Tell you his life story? Open a bank account for you in Vanuatu? Inquiring minds want to know."

"He told me about my family," said Chang. "I don't know how the MSS got all the information, but they obviously have been working my file ever since Singapore. You wanted them to be all over me, John. Well, they were. They found some stuff that surprised me."

"Oh, yeah? Like what? You're a war hero. You're Mister America. What's there to know?"

"Let's start with the fact that my mother's father was a communist. He supported Red China. He served time in federal prison. He was a subversive."

"You're shitting me, right?"

"Nope. Wish I were."

"That's not in your personnel file," said Vandel. "Why didn't you disclose that? It's not a disqualifier. There are lots of red-diaper babies in the agency. Or there used to be. You're just supposed to tell us. Why not?"

"I never knew. It was a family secret, apparently. Everyone was ashamed. Nobody talked about my grandfather. I thought he might have been a gangster."

"And Carlos Wang thought he could squeeze you, by telling you this family secret and holding it over you?"

"I guess so. It didn't work. Right? Here I am. Red Chinese commie's grandson faces the music."

Vandel sipped his whiskey and studied Chang's face. He'd "spotted" Harris Chang that day in Baghdad, recruited him into the agency, steered good assignments his way. It was on him, too, if there was something irregular in Chang's story.

"What about the intel? What did he ask about Dr. Ma? What did he want to know?"

"Zip. That was the weird part. He said they already knew everything. I pushed. Believe me."

Miguel Votaw, the FBI man, had been twirling a pen absentmindedly in his fingers, like a slow-turning baton. He turned to Chang. His voice was deeper than Vandel's with a south Texas drawl.

"And that's all this Chinese fellow did, was tell you about your communist granddaddy? Seems like an awful long way to have you come, just to hear that story. He could have sent you a postcard."

Chang sighed. This part was the hardest, because there wasn't any scandalous fact, just the reality of his Chinese-ness.

"He knew everything. About me and my family. It was spooky."

"What do you mean, son?" asked Votaw.

"Wang had my family history on both sides. He knew about my great-grandfather, how he worked on the railroad, and where he came from in China. He knew the village. He even showed me pictures of my distant relatives."

"Well, isn't that nice. Can I see the pictures?" asked Votaw.

Chang stared at him. He reached into his briefcase and removed the photos of the two villagers from Baisha and the railroad records. He handed them to Votaw.

"What about your commie grandfather?"

Something in the FBI man's tone bothered Chang. It was disrespectful. It touched a nerve that had been sensitive since he began work on the Ma case and was now raw. Feeling wounded, Chang did something dumb.

"Sorry, I don't have a picture of him," he lied.

It was a stupid falsehood, so easily disproven. The moment Chang uttered the words, he wished he could take them back. It was mistake ever to deceive a colleague. Especially if you were a bad liar.

"Un-huh," said Votaw, nodding dubiously. He paused. "So I gather all this talk about your family was an effort to appeal to your sympathies. As a Chinese-American."

"American of Chinese descent. And yeah, I guess so. I told him it was a waste of time. I bleed red, white, and blue. Those were my words. It's true."

"Look, Mister Chang," said Votaw. "This is what they do. I've run dozens of cases involving the Chinese service. Katrina Leung. Hanson Huang. I was involved in all of them. And this is the card they play. Loyalty to the motherland. Help out your compatriots. Don't forget your village. Respect your ancestors. This is their M.O. And you know what? It works."

Chang looked at the FBI man and then at John Vandel, who had been his friend and defender until he walked into the door of this house in Great Falls. Chang closed his eyes. He could feel the ground slipping away under him, his career ending, a shame that had been hiding all these years, now devouring him. He opened his eyes.

"I need to tell you something," said Chang, looking directly at Vandel. "I lied about pictures of my grandfather. I kept two of them. They're in my bag."

Chang handed over the two pictures of Henry Suh Kwan: the hopeful young man and the one who had been broken by America. Votaw took them, snorted, and put them in a file next to his chair.

"Now, why did you do that?" asked Votaw, his low voice a bassoon of reproach.

"I'll handle this, Miguel," said Vandel. "Talk to me, Harris. What's up?"

Chang shook his head. He felt exhausted. He wanted to get out of this room, quit the agency, and leave the business of deception.

"I haven't done anything wrong. They tried to work me, just the way Mr. Votaw said. But I didn't bite. I thought my grandfather's pictures were mine, a private part of my life. When you asked for them, I froze. I screwed up. But it was just a mistake. I'm no traitor. Hook me up to a polygraph. Whatever you like. But I promise you, John. I didn't get bent."

They were shaking their heads. Chang wanted to scream, but instead he took off his jacket, rolled up his sleeve, and showed them his West Point tattoo.

"Read it, sir," said Chang.

"I know what it says. Don't push it."

"Duty, Honor, Country."

"Which country?" said Votaw.

"Fuck you, sir."

Once again, the moment Chang had spoken the words, he wished he had kept his mouth shut.

Harris Chang was polygraphed three times over the next two days. He consented to have all his telephone calls and Internet messages monitored, at home as well as at work. He was initially suspended from working on the case, but Vandel decided that was a mistake. If Harris Chang was innocent, so much the better. If he was in play, that might be useful, too.

"I believe in you, Harris, honestly I do," Vandel said when he welcomed the case officer back to the command post on North Glebe Road. Chang had hoped he might really have been forgiven, until he heard the word "honestly."

26.

IN FLIGHT, IAD TO LAX

Most people wear simple clothes on airplane flights: warm-up suits, or comfy jeans, or even baggy shorts. Denise Ford appeared at the airport in a tailored green dress, a blue cashmere cardigan sweater, and low heels. She looked stylish, comfortable, in every way a well-composed picture. Mark Flanagan was dressed casually in chinos and an open-neck shirt. He had booked himself in economy and was standing in line with the other steerage passengers when Ford approached him.

"I upgraded you," she said. "I have an expense budget. You're in business class, with me."

Flanagan stepped away from the gym-suit-clad economy travelers and walked with Denise to the counter, where he received a new boarding pass. They joined the line that said "Premier Access." Flanagan had been planning to sleep on the flight out, and he had packed his good tape recorder and microphone. He excused himself and went to the men's room while she held their place in the boarding line and tested the fidelity of his iPhone recorder. He decided it wasn't good enough in addition to being too obvious. He returned to the line just as "Group 1" was moving toward the door.

"I need to talk to someone," Ford confided, when the flight attendant brought her a glass of wine, thirty minutes into the flight. "I need advice."

Flanagan mumbled assent as the flight attendant handed him a gin and tonic. He didn't want her to confess anything, not when he didn't have the tape recorder rolling and nobody to witness the exchange. He felt in his pocket for his cell phone.

But he had misread her; she wasn't in a confessional mood, but rather one of embellishing details of the portrait she had been painting of herself. Her eyes narrowed; her brows tightened. She leaned toward him.

"I've been thinking the agency needs to invest more in neuroscience," she said in a confidential whisper.

"Say what?" answered Flanagan.

"Neuroscience. We're at the frontier, from what I read. There are laboratories now where scientists can watch people thinking. If you see a movie, they can reconstruct how you registered the characters and stories. Isn't that our business? These neuroscientists say they can detect thoughts we may not be able to verbalize, although I wonder about that. You remember what Wittgenstein said."

"Who's Wittgenstein?"

"Ludwig Wittgenstein. A philosopher of language. I wrote a paper about him in college. One of his precepts was that if you can't say something, then you can't whistle it, either."

"Nice," said Flanagan. "What does it mean?"

"It means that a thought doesn't exist apart from the language that expresses it. If you follow me."

"Sort of," said Flanagan. He lapsed into silence.

Flanagan studied her. He wanted to understand, not just the words but also what motivated them: What would a person say if she knew she was under surveillance? How would she craft her "legend," for best effect? She would talk about her work, of course, her dreams and aspirations. She would design a world that was parallel to her betrayal, but where all her suspect actions had noble motives.

Ford was sipping her wine, still waiting for Flanagan to respond to her neuroscience-funding idea.

"I love these mixed nuts," said Flanagan. "They're the best thing about flying in business class. Lots of cashews and almonds. Brazil nuts, even."

"You can have mine," she said.

Flanagan poured her nuts into his own nearly empty white cup and continued popping them in his mouth.

"What do you think about robots?" she ventured. "Not little ones, like Charlie the fish, but big autonomous systems? The Pentagon thinks they're the future."

"They'll never take my job. I can't see a robot bugging another robot."

"How trusting you are. You think that we'll have only ethical robots that won't steal each other's algorithms?"

"Who said anything about ethics? I just want robot cars that don't hit other cars."

She shook her head and gently pointed a finger at him. Her nails were painted a light aqua blue.

"I don't think you've thought much about this, Mark."

"You're right. I haven't."

"You should: The ethical decisions have to be made beforehand and programmed into the robots. Take driverless cars. What happens when two pedestrians jump into the road from different directions? How is the robot car supposed to decide which pedestrian to hit?"

"Beats me." Flanagan had raised his hand to get the flight attendant's attention.

"Another gin and tonic," he said. "And more nuts."

"I'm fine with my wine," said Ford to the attendant. The glass was still nearly full. She turned back to Flanagan.

"Do you like animals?"

"Of course. Everybody likes animals."

"So how much should a robot care about animals, compared to people? If your driverless car hits a deer, head on, the deer will be dead but the human passengers inside will probably be safe. If the car is programmed to swerve, on the other hand, then the deer will live but the passengers may get hurt."

"Not so easy to be an ethical robot," Flanagan conceded. "I should be taking notes."

"Yes, you should." She smiled. "Have you ever heard of 'The Trolley Problem'?"

"Can't say that I have. Why does the trolley have a problem?"

"My goodness. You really are an engineer!"

"Yes, ma'am. Bugs and plugs."

"The Trolley Problem assumes that a runaway trolley is about to hit five people who are tied to the tracks. If you throw a lever, the trolley will switch to a siding where only one man is tied down. Are you visualizing this? Okay. What's the ethical robot supposed to do?"

"Stop the trolley."

"That's not an option, unfortunately. The question is whether you make the choice and kill one, or let things happen, and kill five."

"One. Duh."

She nodded and tapped her glass with one of those lacquered nails.

"That sounds right. And ninety percent of people give that answer. But to see the problem with that decision, you need to think about 'Fat Man on a Bridge.' You probably don't know that one either. You interested?"

Flanagan was trying to keep his distance, but her intensity and clarity made it hard to stand apart.

"Yes, Denise, I'm interested."

"Okay. Our train is heading down the tracks toward those same five people, but this time you're on a bridge above and you can stop the train only if you throw something heavy in its path. There's a fat man standing next to you. Should you push him off the bridge so he stops the train and saves the five people, even though he'll end up dead?"

"Does it matter that he's fat? Suppose he's a thin man?"

"He has to be fat. Otherwise he won't be heavy enough to stop the train. It could be a fat woman, I suppose, but that introduces other issues. So yes, a fat man."

"Push him," said Flanagan.

"You're the exception," she said with a wink. "It turns out that most people who were willing to kill the person who was tied to the tracks to save the other five don't want to push the fat man off the bridge. Isn't that interesting?"

"What would you do?" asked Flanagan.

"Push him," she said. "Maybe it's something about our line of work."

Flanagan held up his white ceramic cup for the flight attendant to signal that he wanted a third helping of mixed nuts, but the attendant said it was time for lunch.

"Let's go back to robots," said Flanagan. Despite himself, he had gotten interested in the conversation. "Could someone hack an ethical robot and make it a bad robot?"

"Of course," she said quietly. "I believe some of our colleagues are working on that very problem now. The adversary's robots are presumed to be unethical. That's one of the unquestioned assumptions around here, if you hadn't noticed."

Flanagan leaned a bit closer. He lowered his voice almost to a whisper.

"Could you recruit an ethical robot to spy for you?"

"Well, well." She looked away for a moment, out the window to the tabled farmland below. "That's an interesting question. Recruit the robot! I'm not sure. If the robot was ethical, could it allow itself to be reprogrammed? I need to ponder that one."

Flanagan waited for more, but she was rustling in her seat, adjusting the pillow.

"I think I'll have the pasta," she told the attendant. But she barely touched it.

She dozed off after lunch. Flanagan went to the bathroom and recorded on "Voice Notes" as much as he could remember of what she had said. But he wondered, as he whispered the words into the phone, whether he was just helping her cement a studiously crafted cover story.

They rented a car at LAX and traveled down the 405 to Newport Beach and Orange County's version of the Riviera. Flanagan drove and Ford fell asleep in the passenger seat. It was a crystalline fall afternoon; Flanagan savored the ride and hoped his companion wouldn't wake up.

They checked into a fancy hotel in Newport Beach near the headquarters of a big bond-trading firm. Ford said she wanted a comfortable venue for the world-class computer scientists they would meet the next day. She was quiet, talked out; she said she was going to order a salad from room service and get a good night's sleep.

"I hope you read some of those books I gave you on quantum computing," she said before parting. "You're going to need them tomorrow."

Flanagan promised it would be his bedtime reading. He set a monitor across the hall from her door to alert him if she left. She didn't stir until morning.

Flanagan took a run along the beach late that afternoon, as the sun was disappearing into the Pacific. He drove to a stylish restaurant in town and sat at the bar with people who looked like movie stars, and maybe they were. He had a martini—a "see-through," as his Boston Irish father always called them—and a pork chop. He had struggled during the flight to LAX to find the telltale admission in Ford's smart, sinuous talk and failed. Now, his mind was pleasantly empty.

27.

NEWPORT BEACH, CALIFORNIA

Denise Ford convened her meeting with contractors the next morning in a conference room overlooking the sea. The sign outside the door said simply "Computer Science Group." A hotel manager wheeled in a cart with coffee, hot water, soft drinks, and pastries and then promised to leave them undisturbed.

Ford was gracious and demure. She wore a black suit with a white blouse and low heels. Her eyeglasses were perched on the bridge of her nose.

"Welcome, all," she said, rapping a coffee cup with her spoon. The morning sun was bleaching the little room. She held the center of the table easily, effortlessly, looking at each guest and gaining assent as she framed the agenda.

"Thanks for joining us this morning. Before we start, some housekeeping: This conversation will be unclassified but under the non-disclosure agreements that you have made previously. If each of you could please sign the forms at your place, acknowledging that you are aware of the rules."

Ford paused while the grant recipients signed their forms. When they were done, Flanagan gathered them up and she put them in her briefcase.

"So on to business. It may seem strange to sign agreements that you can't disclose your requests for greater openness, but welcome to the world of government contracting. I know from our correspondence that you all share concerns about classification and publication rules for your quantum computing projects, going forward. Right?"

Voices assented around the table.

"I am here to listen to your concerns and answer them, if I can. I have brought along my new deputy, Mark Flanagan, who, like me, is a longtime agency employee. He will help me report back your comments to our colleagues."

Flanagan introduced himself to the group. He apologized that he was a mechanical engineer, rather than an electrical one, but he promised to take careful notes.

Ford introduced the three scientists sitting at the table. Howard Sagan, a professor at the University of California at San Diego, was developing a new approach to building stable, long-lived "qubits." He looked like an advertisement for the California good life, tan and fit, wearing a black t-shirt under his blazer. Next to him was Carson Malloy, the chief scientist of a big computer company that was financing Sagan's research. The third attendee was Andrea Bildt, a blonde woman in her thirties who ran a start-up that was developing new programming languages.

Malloy was the spokesman for this insurgency. He had been designing and building supercomputers for thirty years. He was the only person in the room, other than Flanagan, wearing a suit and tie. He was precise and emphatic.

"We're doing world-changing work on quantum computing thanks to Howard and Andrea," he began. "Breakthrough work! We're making so much progress, in fact, our biggest worry is that you'll insist that it be classified. That would be a terrible mistake. Research is an organic process. It will thrive in the sunlight and wither in the dark. That's why we asked for this meeting. We respectfully must protest!"

Malloy leaned back in his chair and looked over the top of his glasses. Sagan and Bildt nodded vigorously.

"Hold on, folks," said Ford, raising her hand gently. "Before we go to the barricades, you need to explain what this 'breakthrough' is about. Then we can talk about rules. And I remind you: I don't make these decisions. I may not even agree with them. But I'm here to listen, on behalf of the government. So tell us: What do we need to know?"

Howard Sagan, the professor, answered for the group. He had a PowerPoint presentation queued up on his computer, and he now projected it on a screen at the foot of the table. The first slide showed a familiar picture of Albert Einstein, with his electrified shock of white hair, and next to him, a round-faced man in aviator glasses and a bushy moustache.

"Let's begin by recalling what's at stake when we talk about quantum computing. Every schoolchild knows Professor Einstein, the founder of modern physics. But for us in this room, the more immediate ancestor is the other gentleman on the screen, Peter Shor, professor of physics at MIT. He taught us in 1994 that if we could build a quantum computer, it could factor numbers much faster than a classical computer. How much faster? Let's remind ourselves."

Sagan's next slide showed a computer chip above two mathematical formulas for factoring large numbers. The first portrayed a classical computer, whose required calculations would be proportional to ten raised to the power of the number of digits factored, divided by two. The second showed the formula for a quantum machine, whose steps would be proportional to the number of digits *squared*—a vastly smaller number.

"What would this mean in practice?" continued Sagan. "We currently estimate that it would take a classical computer more than ten million years to factor a fifty-digit number, whereas it would take *less than a second* on a quantum computer. No existing cryptographic system could withstand such computer power. All codes could be decrypted and read."

"We know that," said Ford. "That's why we're here."

A new slide filled the screen. "QC May Change Many Aspects of Human Life," read the caption. Sagan summarized the applications that would be transformed by this wondrously fast computer: materials science, chemistry, pharmaceuticals, process optimization, pattern recognition, machine learning. To hear him, the future of global health and happiness would be altered by this magical box.

The slide dissolved into one with a quote from Arthur C. Clarke: "Any sufficiently advanced technology is indistinguishable from magic."

"Understood," said Ford. "It's a digital cornucopia. But to repeat: What's your breakthrough? That's the question."

Sagan flipped ahead several slides. He stopped at one marked "De-coherence."

"Coherence is the problem for quantum computing, as we have all discovered. We have learned that the wondrous, potentially life-transforming qubits in our quantum computers are very fussy. They're vulnerable to heat, magnetism, any kind of energy. They often survive only a few milliseconds. Even the supposed breakthrough with the 'ion-trap' approach will not provide an answer to the problem of de-coherence, we believe."

"We're not going to talk about the ion-trap research." Ford wagged her finger. "Not in this session."

"We don't think it will work," broke in Malloy. "And believe me, we know a lot more about this than your ion-trap friends at IARPA."

"No comment," said Ford. "Let's stick to your research for now, not other people's."

Sagan projected a new slide, marked "The Secret of Topological Qubits—Braiding." It showed something that looked like a Mobius strip. Sagan stood now, looming over the image on screen, as he tried to explain his breakthrough.

"We are convinced that the best way to create a truly stable, error-resistant qubit is by braiding quantum quasi-particles around each other so that they are entangled in a quantum state. These quasi particles hide quantum information just as a cipher hides classical information, and this encryption protects the quantum information more precisely than other architectures. Do you perhaps, possibly understand what this means?"

"No," said Ford. "But you seem to, which is enough for now. But you realize what this means: If it's as good as you say, then my colleagues in the United States government are going to want to take it off the grid so that you can work on it. Quietly. Safely. Secretly."

"But that's a dreadful idea!" exploded Malloy. "You can't keep this secret. It's already public. We're a global company. Everyone knows what we've been doing."

"But they don't know that it works!"

"This is crazy," muttered Sagan. "It's a flat world. You can't fence things off anymore. We are working with labs all over the world. Some of our closest collaborators are in the Netherlands and Denmark. I have members of my lab from Qinghua University in Beijing and Moscow State University. They've moved their families to San Diego. I can't just tell them all to go home."

"Yes, you can. If we tell you to. Those are the rules."

"We don't want to play anymore, then," said Malloy. He was glowering at the two CIA officers. "It's knowledge. It's free. That's America's comparative advantage, for god's sake. The fact that we're open. That's why we get the best grad students from Russia and China."

Andrea Bildt had been silent until now, watching her male colleagues spar with Ford. But now she spoke up. There was a hint of a Swedish accent in her voice. That was where she had started in her travel across the flat world to Silicon Valley. Her blonde hair was knotted in a braid. She looked as if she might have just come in from surfing at Redondo Beach, a few dozen miles up the coast.

"Let me explain my work," said Bildt. "Maybe then you'll understand why you can't keep this technology in a box."

"At last, a woman's voice," said Ford. "I am tired of arguing with alpha males."

"Here is what I do, Miss Ford: I am writing a quantum programming language. Strange stuff. But to someone like me, it is poetry."

"Brava," said Ford.

"I began with a language called F Sharp. It's a very high-level language, good for pattern recognition and meta-programming. But then we began to think, suppose Carson and Howard could build their quantum computer. How would we tell it what to do? We would have to write the instructions in braids to match the qubits. So that is what I have written—a braided language that can provide instructions to our entangled qubits. Does that make any sense?"

"Yes and no," said Ford. "I can't follow the science, but what makes sense is that you're telling me you did it."

"Yes, I did do it. I'm sharing it now with programmers around the world. They want to help. For people like me, this is a very big challenge because nothing in quantum software can be copied, and all operations have to be reversible. Do you see what a challenge that is? It's *hot*. Everyone wants to work on it. If we try to stop them now, they will be upset. And if the world hates us, they won't want to work with us. That would be very bad."

Ford looked at Flanagan, who had been silently tapping at the keys on his laptop, taking notes. Her look said: See? I told you so.

"You make a powerful case. Especially you, Andrea. I'll report what you said. But it's not my call. These rules have been around since the Manhattan Project. They're not likely to change now. I'm not saying I agree with them. I'm just telling you what it is."

"Let me show you one more slide," said Sagan. "Maybe it will help you understand the mystery here. And why you shouldn't try to choke it with secrecy."

On the screen appeared a photograph of a handsome young man in a double-breasted jacket and tie. His dark hair was neatly combed. He had a thin, delicate mouth and piercing dark eyes.

"This is Ettore Majorana," said Sagan. "He was an Italian theoretical physicist, a Sicilian, who studied with Enrico Fermi, then with Nils Bohr, and also with Werner Heisenberg. For a physicist like me, Majorana is a god: Fermi compared him to Galileo and Newton."

The screen dissolved, and the picture of the young Italian was replaced with a page of dense equations.

"Why is this man important to us?" continued Sagan. "First, he gave his name to the subatomic particles that we are trying to braid in our topological qubit. They are called 'Majorana Fermions,' because he predicted them in 1937. These particles are their own anti-particles. They behave the way that entangled qubits do, except that they are more stable. I know that sounds very abstract, but technologists have actually manufactured these strange fermions, at the end points of tiny nanowires that are cooled almost to absolute zero. They are impossible, but real! That is the first reason we revere Majorana."

"What's the second reason?"

The screen dissolved once more, and it now showed a picture of a slightly older Majorana, his eyes haunted, in a picture accompanying an Italian newspaper story with the headline "*Chi l'ha visto.*" Who saw him?

Sagan's voice lost its quick, academic cadence. He spoke slowly, somberly.

"Majorana disappeared at sea in 1938. He was traveling by boat from Palermo to Naples. He vanished without a trace. His body was never found. The day he left, he sent a note to the director of the Naples Physics Institute. I can quote it from memory. 'Dear Carrelli, I have made a decision that has become unavoidable. I realize what trouble my sudden disappearance will cause you and the students. I beg your forgiveness.' And then he was gone. What happened to him?"

"Maybe he fell off the boat."

Sagan shook his head. Malloy put his finger to his lips.

"Many people think it was suicide," said Sagan quietly. "Or that he fled, perhaps to Argentina. Or that he escaped to a monastery. But why did he take these radical measures? What frightened him? Many of his friends thought they knew the answer. When he went to work with Heisenberg, the Nazis had come to power. People were already thinking of war . . . and weapons. Majorana did not want his brilliant work in physics to be used by Hitler and Mussolini. He did not want science to be militarized. So he vanished."

Nobody spoke for a moment. The photo of Majorana stared out at them, from beyond the grave.

"Okay," said Ford. "Point taken. You don't want quantum computing to be militarized. You want it to be for everyone. I've got that. Truly. And thank you very much. Unfortunately, you are grant recipients of national security agencies of the United States government. Which means that when you sign research contracts, you have to abide by the rules."

"We'll quit the program," said Malloy.

"They'll sue you," answered Ford. "And bar you from doing further business with the government. They're not playing around."

"We don't care," said Sagan. "We are scientists. We would rather vanish, like Majorana, than do something we think is wrong."

"The intelligence community is making a mistake," said Malloy gravely.

"Well, it wouldn't be the first time," responded Ford. She looked over at Flanagan, who was motionless for a moment and then nodded. Who could deny it?

Ford paused. She studied a pad she had brought along and then cleared her throat. Her manner was determined and solicitous.

"There's one last item, this morning," she said. "Not to flatter this group. But I have a technical question for all of you. Something that I want to understand better."

"Just ask," responded Malloy. "We're scientists. It's our business to answer questions."

"What can you tell me about the quantum approach that's being pursued by a company in Seattle called QED? Quantum Engineering Dynamics. Do any of you know them?"

Flanagan leaned back on the swivel of his chair as she spoke. He glanced down toward the bag by his side.

"Sure, we know them," said Sagan. "We've been watching their work for a decade. They claim they've already built a quantum computer."

"Are they right?" asked Ford gently. "That's what we want to know. Does their technology work, in your opinion? It's something we're trying to evaluate."

"No," said Malloy flatly. "What QED is doing is quantum annealing, not quantum computing. It's not the same thing."

"But does it work?" pressed Ford. "It may not be a duck, exactly, but can it quack?"

"Sometimes. It can solve some problems. We've read all of Jason Schmidt's papers, back when he was still publishing them. But we don't think his machine is any better than a good supercomputer, and in many ways it's worse."

Ford paused again. She looked at Flanagan, who avoided her gaze.

"Can it factor numbers, this annealing technology?"

"Maybe," said Malloy. "But not very well, as far as we know. But don't ask me. Ask Jason Schmidt. He's your boy, from what we hear. He has entered the black cavern that we're trying to avoid."

The room was still for a moment. The mid-morning sun illuminated the shrubs beyond the window so that they shimmered a hot green. The waves of the Pacific rolled onto the beach beyond. The only sound was the cool whir of the air conditioner flowing through the vents.

Denise Ford rapped her knuckles on the conference table, signaling that the session was over.

"We can't discuss what we may or not be funding, of course," she said. "With QED or anybody else. But I wanted to get your views, unclassified only, and that was helpful. Now let's adjourn for some lunch, and then we'll meet back here for a final session about grant procedures. Thank you all *so* much for coming this morning."

Denise Ford rose and moved toward the door, following her guests out into the hall.

Flanagan stayed behind, checking his tape recorder to make sure it had captured Ford's last words accurately. It took him no more than thirty seconds.

When Flanagan emerged from the conference room, Ford was waiting just outside the door, by the poster that said "Computer Science Group." Her composed, presentational face had hardened.

"What were you doing in there after I left?" she said icily.

"Just gathering up my stuff. You know." Flanagan wasn't a smooth liar. His face reddened.

She fixed him with a look that carried the weight and menace of a woman who had spent decades in study, apprenticeship, and then, when blocked, in a creative reinvention. She was not going to be blocked again.

"Be very careful, Mark," she said. "This is dangerous work we do."

She didn't wait for an answer. She turned and walked down the corridor to the private dining room they had reserved for lunch.

That afternoon, after the second discussion session, Denise Ford complained to Flanagan that she was feeling sick. She took the elevator up to her room before Flanagan could follow. She entered the room, turned on the bathroom fan, and then left, taking the service elevator down to the basement. She walked to a nearby shopping mall and entered a department store. She bought a floppy hat that obscured her face and a raincoat that covered her black dress. She left the store through another door that opened on a parking lot on the other side of the building.

At the far end of the lot was a municipal bus stop. She waited for a bus that took her to the Newport Beach public library, which adjoined the city hall.

Ford pulled the brim of her hat down low on her head. On her face was a smile of pleasure, exhilaration, even. This was the work for which she had trained, for which she had joined the agency. Now, again, she was able to use her gifts for a purpose she had convinced herself was noble.

The library had the empty feeling of a place with too many books and not enough readers. Ford went to a kiosk that had two public Internet connections. She opened a password account at an address she had never used before, on a server in the United States that she had been told was clean and safe.

Denise Ford composed a message to her case officer. Though she wrote in veiled language, to avoid any words that might be on a watch list, she conveyed three essential messages: She was under surveillance by the man who was her new deputy; there were rumors that a colleague was similarly under investigation after a visit to "MC"; and she had learned that a technology of interest, under development by a company in Seattle, might be adapted to complex problems that could not otherwise be solved.

The message, carefully written, was saved in draft form. Denise Ford signed off the account and erased the history of this email session on the library computer. She stopped at a drugstore on her way back to the hotel and bought a medication that induced some of the digestive distress about which she had complained. There were two voicemail messages from an anxious Mark Flanagan, who realized that he had lost track of her. Ford deleted them and took a nap.

28.

BEIJING, CHINA

Li Zian had more than one hundred rocks in his collection, each of them signed and dated to mark its significance. The oldest was a flat, reddish stone from the village in Hubei where his father was sent down by the Red Guards as a "capitalist roader," inscribed by his father when Li was just twelve years old. Next to it was a black fragment of shale that Li had signed in Shanghai on the day his father died in 1979, too young. And another for his late mother, a willowy woman who had never lost her beauty through all the years of travail.

Li's life as an intelligence officer had a foundation stone, too. It was a small chunk of granite that he had taken from the garden behind the Ministry of State Security in 1983, the year the Ministry was created. Before that, China's intelligence service had been the Investigations Department of the Central Committee of the Chinese Communist Party. Li had been twenty-three years old, just out of university and on his way to graduate school in America. He had already been recruited in secret. Li had been present at the creation. Now, under his stewardship, the Ministry of State Security was wobbling. The comrades around him had gotten greedy for their share of the new wealth. That vexed him.

Li summoned Wang Ji on the day that the chief of the American Operations Division returned from Mexico City. He had read Wang's operational cable, but it was elusive, like everything about the man. Li wanted a personal report. He needed to understand where the pieces stood on the game board.

Li had the recent message from *Rukou*, relayed and decrypted, in the inside pocket of his suit jacket. He took it and reread it. It was characteristic of a well-motivated agent to deliver intelligence and warn of danger. *Rukou* should not have taken the risk, but once it had been done, it was essential to put the information to good use.

Carlos Wang arrived five minutes late for the meeting. His collar button was undone, and his tie was loose. His hair looked shaggier than usual.

"I think you need a haircut," said Li. "You look like a musician."

"Yes, minister," said Wang. He took out a cigarette and put it to his lips but didn't light it.

"I want to hear about more about your meeting with the American. He sounds promising. The beginnings of a conscience."

"I planted a seed," answered Wang. "I told him about his Chinese life. I explained the story of his 'Red' grandfather, our comrade. I helped him to understand who he is. He had thought of himself only as an American, but he sees now that it is more complicated: People can be two things at once. This is not a man who can be squeezed. If we try that, we will fail. In sum, minister, he has been destabilized. He doubts his world, perhaps for the first time. We will see if this seed grows."

"I want to water it and fertilize it. We are running out of time."

"I await instructions, minister. But you cannot hurry something that is organic. I believe it was Leo Tolstoy who said that the strongest warriors are time and patience."

"Tolstoy wasn't a communist."

Li looked at his watch. He picked up his phone and told his secretary to have his car and driver out front, immediately.

"Let's get out of the office for a bit. Somewhere private. We need to talk. Or should I say: I need to talk, and you need to listen, and then you need to implement."

"Of course, minister. I will get my coat." He headed off down the hall, the slouch gone from his posture, and met the minister downstairs several minutes later.

"Take us to Yuquan Mountain," Minister Li told the driver when they were in the car.

"To the *Xianghongqi*?" asked the driver, puzzled. Yuquan Mountain was in the "sensitive area," a few miles west. It was one of the most carefully guarded places in China. It held a resort for the Politburo and, nearby, the bunkers where the Chinese leadership would seek safety in the event of a nuclear war.

"Yes, precisely," said Li. "I have all the necessary papers."

Li turned to the head of the American Operations Division, who was also curious about the destination Li had chosen.

"I want the PLA to know we're there," he explained. "But not what we say."

The car headed west toward the Summer Palace and the mountain just beyond. From Kunming Lake on the palace grounds, you could see a graceful six-story pagoda atop a green hill. They drove to a concealed entrance, double-fenced. Burly PLA soldiers blocked the way. They wore special insignia that designated them as members of the Central Guard Bureau, a special unit responsible for protecting the president and members of the Politburo.

Even after Li showed his special MSS documents, the captain in charge of the unit said he would have to contact headquarters for permission to open the gate. Li held up his arm and walked slowly toward the office until he could speak without being overheard by other members of the detail.

"Comrade Captain," said Li, "I see that you are a member of the unit that is code named '8341.' That is a great honor."

"Thank you, minister. But how did you know our code name? It is a secret."

"Well, now, Comrade Captain, I will tell you the story of your code name. But it is a secret, too, so you mustn't repeat it."

"Yes, sir." The captain leaned toward the tall, austere figure in civilian dress, so that he could listen.

"They say that our great helmsman, Chairman Mao, stayed in these woods, on this mountain, when he first came to Beijing in 1949. There were Buddhist temples then, like the one you see atop Yuquan."

Li pointed to the finely wrought towers of the temple, five hundred yards distant. He continued, now in an even quieter voice.

"It is said that Chairman Mao encountered a monk, who came down from the temple; perhaps it was in this very place. Mao said he was going into Beijing and asked the monk if he needed to know anything to safeguard his trip. The monk answered: '8-3-4-1.' Mao asked him what significance that number had, and the monk said he didn't know. It was a message from heaven.

"So Mao proceeded, and you know the rest. He triumphed in our glorious revolution, and he passed away in 1976, the eternal hero of the people. But here is the thing, Comrade Captain. Listen carefully: When Mao died, he was eighty-three years old. He had been serving as leader of the Party for forty-one years. So yes, I think it was a message from heaven. 8-3-4-1."

There were tears in the eyes of the young man who commandeered the Central Guard Bureau. He motioned to a sergeant to raise the gate, so that Li and Wang could pass.

"You honor us with your visit, minister," he said. "I will never forget this story."

The limousine rolled forward, accompanied by a military escort vehicle. After a hundred yards' ascent, Li told the driver to stop and motioned for Wang to join him outside. The trees were densely clustered, but there was a path that meandered uphill toward the pagoda.

"We want to take a walk," Li told the captain. "We'll be a few minutes."

"Would you like accompaniment?" asked the officer.

"No," said Li, striding off toward the path.

The captain stood at attention and saluted. There was nothing in his regulation book that required an escort for visitors admitted to these grounds.

Li walked fifty yards uphill before he slowed his pace and turned to Wang Ji.

"Have you ever been here before?" asked the minister.

"No, sir. This is forbidden ground. I did not hear what you told the guard, but it must have been very persuasive."

"It was a revolutionary fairy tale, that's all. People need myths. Even PLA officers. This is sacred ground for our military and party. Do you know what is underneath our feet? There is a secret railway. It is called the 'Underground Great Wall System.' There are hundreds of miles of track, buried underground, so that our brave leaders can flee in secret if there is trouble. There is a terminal underneath the Great Hall of the People that connects with the bunker here in Xianghongqi. Never forget: Beneath even the greatest secrets, there are other secrets."

"Thank you, minister," said Carlos Wang. "But I hope to die above ground."

They walked another fifty yards before Li Zian spoke again.

"We must discuss matters in confidence," he said. "The walls at our ministry have ears, I am sorry to say. The PLA Third Department has paid us a visit. That would not have been possible without permission from somewhere high up. The wolves are gathering."

"Good intelligence officers are mistrusted most by their own countrymen, minister," said Wang. "This has been our lot since the days of Pan Hannian."

Li smiled. He patted Wang on the shoulder.

"You are a clever one, to mention his name."

Pan was Li's role model. He had overseen Chinese counterintelligence and deception operations against the Koumintang immediately after the revolution and used defectors, double agents, and captured radios to confound the enemy. But his rivals inside the Party framed him, and he was falsely convicted on espionage charges. Pan was rehabilitated in 1982, just as young Li was making his decision to become an intelligence officer.

"Here is what Comrade Pan would advise us," said Li. "You must expand the operation you have begun with the American who calls himself Peter Tong. What is his real name? Harris Chang. He is our beachhead. We must broaden it. I believe that he is already under suspicion, thanks to your skill in Mexico. We must further confuse and frighten our adversary. This is the only way to protect our deep agent, *Rukou*."

"You are the only person who has met *Rukou*. You alone would know."

"Yes, *Rukou* is my burden. But Mr. Harris Chang is yours. I would like to scratch this wound that you have opened in his heart."

"How would you suggest that we do this, Li *Buzhang*?"

"Here is my idea, which might surprise even Comrade Pan: We should behave as if we have already succeeded."

"I do not understand, minister."

"We pretend that 'Comrade Chang' is our asset. We send him a tasking message that will make the CIA suspect him, if they do not already. If we pretend to control him, the Americans will wonder if it isn't true. They will doubt him and themselves. They will be distracted. You understand: Misdirection. False signals. Spreading confusion. This is the Tao of deception."

"All warfare is based on deception," answered Wang Ji, quoting a famous passage from Sun Tzu that was imprinted in the consciousness of every Chinese intelligence officer.

Li Zian, who also knew the passage by heart, simply nodded.

"How do you want to proceed with Mr. Harris Chang, then?"

"I have prepared a message. Have your subagent in Vancouver send it to the Tong phone."

Li pulled a paper from his pocket and read it.

"*'Mr. Tong. We need to meet again, at the place that was agreed at our last meeting in Mexico. Please follow the protocol.'*"

"There is no protocol, minister."

"Of course not. Send this message. Also, I want you to find Mr. Harris Chang's home address. I don't care how you get it. Have a station agent in Washington deliver a satellite communication device to his home. Leave it where he puts his garbage or on the doorstep, I don't care."

"How should the device be programmed?"

"To contact the center. As for a normal agent."

"But it will be discovered. The FBI follows all embassy intelligence officers, ours and the PLA's, both. They will obtain the transmitter."

"Precisely."

Wang Ji bowed slightly, in deference to Li's cunning.

"How should these operational messages be transmitted, minister?"

"Normal cipher protocol. Including to the embassy in Washington."

"The PLA will read them." Wang smiled, seeing another layer.

"Indeed. They will be impressed, confused, and uncertain. They would like to destroy us. The talk is everywhere. The matter was referred to the Standing Committee of the Politburo after the death of Dr. Ma.

They took no action, but the issue will come back. Our survival is at stake. Can I trust your loyalty, Wang Ji?"

"Yes, minister. Eternally."

"You have a brother in the PLA, don't you? He is a senior general now in the Third Department. They tell me you have dinner with him often."

"Yes, of course, sir. My brother's position is well known."

"Does he tell you what role you will play if the PLA is successful in abolishing the Ministry of State Security? A senior one, I am sure."

"We do not talk about our work, minister. We are both very respectful of the division between his service and mine."

"I wonder if your brother knows anything about the listening devices that have been installed at the Ministry. You should ask him sometime."

Wang, embarrassed, said nothing. He reached for a cigarette, then put it back in the pack.

Li Zian, tall and composed, studied his scruffy deputy.

"I wonder, Comrade Wang: Does your PLA brother know that you are a left-wing deviationist? Does he realize that you are a follower of Leon Trotsky and maybe the Gang of Four, too? He cannot know this. He would be shocked, certainly. But I do know. I have indulged you. I have protected your secret, because you are valuable to me."

Wang Ji took a step back. He shook his head.

"This is unworthy of you, minister."

"Just advice from a friend. These are very difficult times. We must stay in our own boats and carry out our duties. Otherwise, accidents will happen, and we may find ourselves in great difficulty."

When Li Zian returned to his office, he found waiting an encrypted personal message from General Fang, the head of the liaison department of the General Political Department of the Central Military Commission. It was a summary of a meeting that had been held the day before with members of the PLA Second and Third Departments.

The Central Military Commission was concerned that American "special activities" had led to the death of Academician Ma Yubo. Such behavior required a response from China. There must be retaliation; power only understood power. The identities of the members of the

American team responsible for the death of Academician Ma Yubo were known to the Central Military Commission. Therefore, working with the PLA Second and Third Departments, the liaison department would consider how best to take a proportionate response to the death of Academician Ma.

The message requested concurrence by the Ministry of State Security.

Li considered the equities of the case: *Rukou* was still operating, but vulnerable and under surveillance. He resented any interference from the PLA, but perhaps there was an opportunity in what General Fang proposed. Li sent a written response on the most secure internal channel. He affirmed the Central Military Commission's judgment that the death of a Chinese scientist was a serious matter and must be avenged. Li offered a few suggestions about proper targeting.

Li sat for a long time in his office with the door locked and the lights out. He thought of *Rukou*, so brave and isolated. An intelligence chief lives for such an opportunity and prays to be worthy of such an agent. Would it be possible to protect the peerless *Rukou* by entangling his true agent with a false one? That would require great skill and courage on the part of the agent, heroic daring, but perhaps this was the challenge that *Rukou* craved. The very best intelligence officers understood that the truth was so important that it must be enclosed in a carapace of deceit.

29.

KYOTO, JAPAN

Mark Flanagan hadn't wanted to leave Tokyo, but now that he was "officially" installed in the executive suite of the Science and Technology division, it was impossible for him to maintain two residences. He had advised his wife Edith a week ago to begin packing; now it was time to go to Japan and bring her home. Edith Flanagan had been upset about leaving their apartment in a fancy high-rise building in Roppongi Hills. As the price of cooperation, she insisted that her husband take her on a last festive trip to Kyoto, her favorite city in Asia. She was a veteran of so many overseas moves that she knew to exploit her moment of leverage.

Before taking the long flight to Japan, Flanagan had stopped to see Harris Chang. He had developed a protective feeling for the younger officer. He admired his skill as a CIA operator, the physical bravery he had shown in the military, and even more, the cheerful, outward-facing optimism he had displayed as an intelligence officer. The agency could be a dark place, but Chang had seemed to carry his own sunshine and self-confidence until recently.

Flanagan hadn't been told any details, only that there had been an "inquiry," which was now "resolved." But it was clear from Chang's demeanor that something was wrong. Flanagan asked if there had been trouble after his return from Mexico City, but Chang cut him off in midsentence. He assured Flanagan that everything was fine.

Flanagan confided that he was going away for a few days to Tokyo and Kyoto with "the Mrs." He said he'd be back soon and wanted to take Chang to a Washington Capitals hockey game. A friend had seats behind the glass. Even that didn't get much of a rise from Chang. Flanagan was worried that something was bothering his friend. He gave Chang his personal cell phone number, which he disclosed only to his wife and the local station chief because the device tracked his movements.

"This is your hotline, Harris," Flanagan said, writing the number. "Call me if anything comes up."

Flanagan called Kate Sturm from the departure lounge, asking her to check on Chang. Something had happened in Mexico. Sturm advised him to leave it alone. This was Vandel's show. Flanagan headed off to Asia with a sense of apprehension, knowing that something was wrong, but not sure what it was.

Flanagan had taken many dangerous assignments in his decades with S&T. Installing and servicing surveillance devices was some of the riskiest work the agency did. As he became more senior, his reputation grew, so that officials of allied intelligence services befriended him and asked for his advice on difficult technical problems. But Flanagan's status in the secret world had its costs. He was "known." His presence was now declared to foreign governments. He no longer traveled under the radar as he had when he was a junior officer.

Flanagan had always refused offers of protection by local services or escorts from the agency's Global Response Staff. He had never carried a firearm. He knew, vaguely, that he could be a target for hostile intelligence services, but as with most things that worried other people, Flanagan found a way to compartmentalize. "That's all bullshit," he would say in his squeaky, Boston Irish voice. And he meant it.

When he arrived in Japan, Flanagan paid a last, melancholy visit to his apartment, which overlooked midtown Tokyo and, a few miles further on, the emerald expanse of the Imperial Palace. He would have been happy to have stretched out his tour running the S&T regional base a bit longer, living in splendor and enduring the occasional operational trips to Singapore and the rest. Asia was a tonic for a senior officer. And he knew how much Edith liked her circle of friends in the American community in Roppongi. She went to cooking classes and jazz-dancing lessons and had even learned how to make little animals with origami paper-folding. But it was time.

The apartment was empty. The movers had come the day before Flanagan returned. They had swept the place like a swarm of locusts. The movers had even wrapped and packed the rags Edith used for cleaning. The couple stayed the night at a nearby, too-American hotel.

Edith Flanagan's consolation prize was Kyoto. They took the bullet train the next morning from Tokyo Station. Edith had reserved seats in the fancy "Green Car," because it was their last trip. The train departed, as always, at the very second it was scheduled.

Flanagan was in a reflective mood. He was happy to see his wife and relieved to be dealing with something other than work. Maybe it was time, after this case was over, to put in his papers. The fun part, living overseas and ignoring Headquarters, was finished. He could probably double his salary in retirement. He had technical skills and a high security clearance. Half the "Beltway bandits" who did contract work for S&T had already sent feelers.

Flanagan had other things he wanted to do, too, besides making money: volunteering in a homeless shelter; counseling school kids; giving back to a world that had been generous to him. During the long flight to Tokyo, he recalled how in college he had considered becoming a priest. He had even sent off an application to a seminary, about the same time he was making inquiries at the CIA. What a long time ago.

"What are you thinking about?" asked Edith, as her husband stared out the train window toward Mount Fuji. She was a compact woman with green eyes and a rosy, carefully tended complexion.

"I was thinking about Father Paul," he said. "He was our campus priest at Cornell. Not much of a parish; everybody was too stoned to think about going to Mass. But Father Paul listened to all my BS. I was a very confused kid."

"You aren't the confused type, honey. You're an engineer. Your first job was at the CIA, for goodness sake. That doesn't sound very confused to me."

"You didn't know me in college. I wanted to save the world, one way or another. Father Paul counseled me. I told him I was thinking about going to a Jesuit seminary. He listened. He even wrote me a recommendation. But he said it would be a mistake."

"You weren't cut out for celibacy," said Edith, giving her husband a nudge.

"It wasn't just that. Father Paul said I wasn't ready. He said it might be a passion, but that didn't mean it was a vocation. I was crushed. It was like getting rejected by Harvard, except it was God."

"Whatever happened to Father Paul?"

"He died a few years ago. I couldn't get back for his funeral. I was on assignment. Story of my life. I stayed in touch with him over the years. Funny thing: He never once asked me what I did in the government."

"He probably knew," said Edith.

"Must have. Who knows? Maybe Father Paul was the agency spotter at Cornell."

Mount Fuji loomed out the right window of the train: perfect, conical, implausibly large. Edith insisted on taking photos of it, even though she had dozens already.

They stayed in a hotel that was directly above Kyoto Station. Flanagan wrangled the luggage through the knots of Japanese who clogged the station passageways and took the bags up the escalator to the hotel. The room was tiny. Flanagan had to turn sideways to enter the bathroom, and his too-long legs dangled over the foot of the bed. Edith was delighted with the little room, as with nearly every aspect of Japan's tidy, fussy lifestyle.

Flanagan checked in with the CIA duty officer at the embassy when they arrived. He always did that, anywhere. The duty officer, a young woman on her first foreign posting, reminded him to keep his phone on and said she would inform the boss. A few minutes later the station chief texted him an animated GIF that showed the Russian president giving the Chinese president a blow job.

They went sightseeing as soon as they had unpacked. The two had traveled to Kyoto twice before, so they had seen all the famous temples and shrines already, but Edith wanted one last look. She bundled them into a taxi, crisply fitted with linen seat covers, and they sped off for an ancient temple in the hills that was famous for its "love shrine." The pilgrim was supposed to walk with his or her eyes closed for fifty feet to assure finding true love.

Flanagan made the walk every time they came to please his wife; he always peeked.

The temple was so crowded that the American couple could only move slowly from place to place. Flanagan had an odd sixth sense that someone was watching him. He caught one man loitering at the entrance to the temple; another moving past them in line and then lingering; a third looking like a man who had been on their train, but wearing a cap and dressed in a different outfit. So many foreigners were visiting the hilltop shrine that nearly every nationality seemed represented in the crowd, but Flanagan had a fleeting thought that there were more non-Japanese faces than he remembered seeing before in Kyoto.

Snap out of it, he told himself. Your mind could always play tricks, if you let it.

Edith wanted to catch one more sight that afternoon, one more Eastern treasure, before it got late. Flanagan was feeling claustrophobic and proposed that they walk in the wide open gardens of the old imperial palace, but Edith said no: She wanted to see the Zen rock garden at Ryoan-Ji, with its thirteen rocks arranged just so on a bed of sand that was swept each morning by the monks.

The monastery was packed. Part of the game for visitors was to traverse the wooden floor of the viewing gallery to check the legend that no matter where you stood in the shrine, you couldn't see all thirteen stones in the garden. There were so many people in the gallery they could move only slowly. Flanagan felt the same sense of being observed. Too many people didn't look like tourists; they were too young, or too fit, or too deliberate.

"I don't get this place," said Flanagan. "Rocks and sand. What's to contemplate?"

"You're not a Buddhist. Shush!"

They made the tour, navigating the human traffic from one end of the rock garden to the other and then back again. Flanagan wanted to return to the hotel. He had made a reservation at his favorite restaurant in Kyoto. He was on vacation. Why did he feel as if he was working? Why did he look at each passing face and wonder if he'd seen the person somewhere else in a different costume?

They queued up to retrieve their shoes at the entrance to the temple. As they were nearing the front of the line, Flanagan felt a sudden, sharp pain in his right calf. An older man had stumbled, colliding with him and hitting his leg on the way down. It seemed to happen almost in slow motion, like a choreographed scene in a modern dance.

The clumsy man mumbled apologies and limped away toward the men's room. He looked to be Korean, maybe Chinese. Flanagan thought the fall was odd, and his leg was throbbing where the man had made contact. He waited a minute for the man to exit the men's room so he could get a better look. But after a minute the man still hadn't appeared, and Edith was tugging at his arm, so they left and took a taxi to the hotel.

Flanagan's leg was still aching in the taxi. He rolled up his right trouser cuff and saw a red swelling and what looked like a small puncture wound. His pant leg, too, seemed to have been perforated. Flanagan was alarmed for a moment, and then put the thought of a deliberate attack out of his mind. No way, he thought to himself. The man who stumbled into him must have been carrying a pen or some other sharp object. This wasn't a movie; real life didn't have assassins walking around Zen temples.

"Everything okay?" asked Edith, watching her husband massage his calf.

"Yeah, fine. That guy gave me a poke. I'll be fine. I'm hungry."

When they returned to the hotel, Flanagan tried to take a nap. He thought maybe he was tired, or suffering from jet lag, or had a bug. He tossed and turned and slept fitfully. His wife kissed him and said he needed a drink and a good dinner.

Flanagan had made a reservation at a teppanyaki restaurant on the top floor of a nearby hotel that overlooked Higashiyama Hills. But he wasn't very hungry by the time they got there. He was sweating, and he had the chills. He looked at his watch; it was now four hours after the incident at the temple.

He ordered a gin gimlet and tried to forget about the pain, but he began to feel nauseous after a few sips, and when he went to the men's room, he vomited. He needed to use the toilet, too, urgently, and he saw that there was blood in his stool. That was when he got worried.

Flanagan walked unsteadily back to the table. As he sat down, he nearly collapsed onto the hot range where the chef was cooking morsels of beef.

"You're not well," said Edith. "We need to call a doctor."

Flanagan shook his head. He steadied himself, found his cell phone, and called the number of the duty officer at the embassy in Tokyo.

"I think I've been poisoned," he told the young woman on the other end of the phone. "I need help right away. I'm in Kyoto. Send whoever there is." Flanagan gave the address of the hotel and stumbled back to the men's room, where he vomited again.

A private ambulance arrived fifteen minutes later, dispatched by the *Koanchosa-cho,* the Public Security Intelligence Agency. A paramedic took Flanagan's vital signs and said his blood pressure was low and falling. They took him to Takeda Hospital, about a mile away.

Flanagan called the duty officer in Tokyo again. He explained where they were taking him and described his symptoms.

"It's probably ricin," said Flanagan feebly. "What's the antidote?"

The officer checked on another line with the ops center at Langley, which had been alerted. There was a delay of about thirty seconds while an agency physician was contacted. The duty officer came back on the line.

"There isn't an antidote," she said. "Get them to hook you up to an IV right away. Lots of fluids. That's all you can do. We're sending someone to Kyoto on the next train."

Mark Flanagan's nausea and diarrhea worsened through that night, and he became severely dehydrated despite the transfusions. After thirty-six hours his liver, spleen, and kidneys began to fail. A urine test indicated the presence of an alkaloid found in the castor bean plant from which ricin is extracted, but it wasn't conclusive. Edith kept shouting at the doctors to *do* something. In thirty years of marriage, she had come to think that her husband led a charmed life. He was one of those men who never got sick or tired or complained of a headache. She thought it must be a mistake; bad things didn't happen to her husband.

Flanagan died at Takeda Hospital three days later. A CIA Gulfstream jet flew his body back to Washington, accompanied by his shattered, grieving widow. They dressed him in the same clothes he always wore: khaki trousers, a worn tweed jacket, a button-down shirt, and penny loafers.

John Vandel met the plane. When he embraced Edith Flanagan, she began to sob.

"Who killed Mark?" Edith Flanagan asked through her tears. "Do you know?"

Vandel shook his head no. It was reflexive for him to lie, and there wasn't enough evidence to be sure even that it had been a murder. There were too many unknowns: Who knew that Mark Flanagan was going to be in Kyoto? Who might have had a motive for killing him? What score was being settled? Vandel could speculate, but he didn't know the answers to any of those questions.

"We loved Mark," said Vandel. "He was one of our best officers. If someone murdered him, we'll find out, and we'll make them pay."

Nearly five hundred people turned out for Flanagan's memorial service and most of them made the trip to Arlington Cemetery for his burial, too. Harris Chang walked behind John Vandel at the funeral. His eyes were red from weeping.

30.

VIENNA, VIRGINIA

Harris Chang studied his face in the mirror as he looped his necktie. He didn't like what he saw: His skin was puffier than it used to be. There were circles under his eyes from lack of sleep and new wrinkles on his forehead and at the corners of his eyes. His mouth at rest drooped down slightly, so that his default expression was no longer a smile. His daily workouts kept his biceps firm and his legs taut, but the healthy body was a sheath. He was forty-three, but he felt ten years older.

Chang was angry and also disoriented after the death of Mark Flanagan. It wasn't a guilty feeling, exactly, but whatever had killed him had begun with their partnership that night in Singapore. Chang had used the older man's skills but had been unable to protect him from the consequences of their actions. Chang felt an unsettling isolation: Army officers are by definition social animals; they move together; they eat, sleep, and die together. Spies are solitary. Their work is a fabric of lies; Chang worried that he had chosen the wrong second profession.

Chang could feel the thinnest strip of fat in his stomach. He had been drinking more since he broke off with his girlfriend a few weeks before. She was an Anglo, a blonde from Phoenix; he had met her on a military dating site: "Feel safe in the arms of a military man" was the logo. The silences between them were too long, and there was too much he couldn't talk about. When they broke up, it left an empty space. He tried a Chinese-American dating site called "2RedBeans" and another called "EastMeetsEast," but the women looked too young, too shy, too Chinese, maybe.

Chang finished dressing. He was dreading everything about this day. He wondered, as he locked the front door, whether there was a way to start a new life without crash-landing the old one.

Chang had been summoned by John Vandel to another clandestine location in the Virginia suburbs. Chang had visited many of these islands of secrecy, but this one was new: The entry was the rear door of a bland office building on Maple Avenue in Vienna.

From the moment he left his home in the District, he sensed that a car was following him. The chase car didn't try to disguise its pursuit. It was as if the watcher wanted Chang to know he was under surveillance and was waiting for him to bolt.

At the entrance to "Evergreen Finance" behind Maple Avenue, Chang went through a metal detector and was then frisked, not a light pat-down but a thorough examination. The guard checked each article in his briefcase and carefully unpacked his wallet. He had to surrender his phone and his watch, too. Past the guard station was a waiting room. It had the dingy look of the holding area in a courthouse where prisoners are kept in transit.

A guard from the Office of Security summoned Chang after a few minutes. He was escorted to a windowless room with a bare table and two wooden chairs. A large mirror stretched across the far wall, barely masking the observation booth behind. A camera was fixed from a metal pole across from Chang's seat. There was a sour odor, a faint smell of decay. Whatever the agency called this room officially, it was obviously a covert interrogation site.

Vandel arrived after Chang had been waiting ten minutes. He shook Chang's hand, but his usual affable manner had disappeared.

"We need to talk, my friend," said Vandel, taking his seat across the table.

"Evidently. What's up? I thought we resolved the issues you had after my Mexico trip."

"We did. I decided to give you a break that time. This is something else. People are telling me to arrest you today. Seriously. But I still want to give you a chance."

Chang rocked back in his chair as if he had been punched.

"What the fuck, John? What have I done now?"

"Maybe you should tell me. This is your chance, before the FBI and the U.S. Attorney get here."

"Are you crazy? I haven't done anything. I kept some pictures that a Chinese intelligence officer gave me. I told you that. I made a mistake. I thought it was over."

"Forget the pictures. This is serious shit, my friend."

Vandel removed a piece of paper from his jacket and handed it to Chang.

"Can you explain this? It was left on the voicemail drop of your alias cell phone, from a number in Vancouver. We took the liberty of intercepting it. Some people think it proves you are a goddamn traitor."

Chang took the paper and read the words, read them twice: *"Mr. Tong. We need to meet again, at the place that was agreed at our last meeting. Please follow the protocol."*

He handed the paper back to Vandel. He felt sick. There was a lump in his throat.

"This is bullshit," he said. "They're trying to set me up."

"It's hard to keep making that argument, buddy. I trusted you after your Mexico escapade. I told the Bureau to cut you some slack, but maybe I was stupid. Fool me once, shame on you; fool me twice, shame on me. Right?"

"They are completely wrong about this, John. A hostile service could do this to any officer in the agency. It's the oldest trick in the book. I don't understand why anyone would fall for it."

"I'm not falling for anything. I am looking at evidence. What about this?"

Vandel dropped a rectangular device on the table. It looked like a cell phone, but it had no proprietary markings.

Chang looked at it. He didn't touch it or leave prints.

"I've never seen this before. I have no idea what it is."

"It's a covert communications device. It was taped to the fence behind your apartment, behind the trash can. Waiting for you to pick up. We waited two days then decided to pull you in. The Bureau thinks you had been warned off."

Chang shook his head. He began to speak, caught himself, and then started again.

"You've been watching me?"

"Yup. The Bureau has had sealed search warrants on you since you got back from Mexico."

"You really think I'm a Chinese spy. Are you fucking kidding? I thought this was a joke at first, but you're serious. For the record, I deny any allegation that I have ever worked for any government, ever, besides the United States of America. Now, I want to see a lawyer."

"The FBI said you would lawyer up. That's why they just wanted to arrest you and be done with it, when they found all this shit. But I said no, give me a shot with Harris. I know Harris. He won't pull the 'call-my-lawyer' routine. Wrong again. But answer me one question, okay, before we go to the mattresses."

"What's the question?"

"Why did you set up Mark Flanagan? He was your partner, for god's sake. He was the one who kept telling me not to worry about you. He kept saying you were a good officer, a good kid. Poor bastard. You gave them his number. How could you do it?"

Chang had struggled to keep his composure, but now he lost it. He pounded the table so hard that he might have broken a bone. As he did so, he let out a scream of rage. A security guard opened the door, but Vandel waved him away.

Chang was near tears. They both waited. Chang finally spoke, saying each word carefully.

"They are playing us, John. Don't you see that? This is what they do. I'm Chinese-American, so they work the Chinese ancestry angle."

"I've considered that. But when I see so much smoke, I have to consider the possibility that it's an actual goddamn fire. And Li Zian isn't playing me. Believe me. His service is falling apart."

"That's why he's doing this, John! He's weak, so he tries to look strong. He's confusing you. Distracting you. Laying a false track. You're hunting for a Chinese mole, so he makes you think he's recruited another one, too. That's their game. Read Sun Tzu."

"Fuck Sun Tzu. How did they know Mark Flanagan would be in Kyoto, unless you told them?"

"Come on! They could have found that out a hundred ways. They probably had eyes on Flanagan the moment he left Singapore. They don't need me to tell them where he is. And honestly, John, if you think I helped them poison Mark, I feel sorry for you. That's sick. I loved Mark. He was like my big brother. If you really think I would have helped set him up, then, yeah, shame on you."

"Why should I believe you? A lot of bad stuff is happening, and you're connected to all of it."

Chang looked at his mentor and friend. Vandel was a selfish man; he was a manipulator; he was a paid liar. But he was the closest thing Chang had left to an ally.

"You should believe me because you're not stupid. At least, I never thought you were. You have no evidence, except what someone is trying to manufacture. I'll take a polygraph every day for a month and the needle isn't going to budge, and the people at the Bureau will look like idiots. That's your problem, but what bothers me is that they're going to get away with it."

Vandel stood up, walked out the door, and returned a few moments later.

"I told the Office of Security guy behind the mirror to turn off the camera," he said. "To protect me, not you. I don't want to look like a dupe later, when they fry your lying ass."

Chang laughed, despite himself. Vandel was so nakedly self-interested.

"So what's the deal that you don't want to say with the tape running?"

"You take another polygraph this afternoon. And yeah, for good measure, we'll repeat it tomorrow. If you pass, then I will consider using you as bait. Running you against them as a double agent."

"How can I be a double agent when I'm not their agent in the first place?"

"Single, double, triple. It's a technicality. Frankly, I don't know what you are. The point is, are you game? Because that's the only way you're going to clear your name."

"What if I say no?"

"In that case, you're fucked. I will make it my personal business to see that you are indicted in the Eastern District of Virginia. And convicted."

"Even if I didn't do anything wrong?"

"That's why we have juries. To decide questions like that."

Chang folded his hands. He closed his eyes and lowered his head so he could think a moment. He didn't really have a choice.

"Okay. I'll do it. Bring the polygraph officer as soon as you can. Let's get started. But before we do, I'll tell you a secret. '*Shu dao husun san.*'"

"What the hell does that mean?"

"It's a Chinese proverb my mother told me. I was thinking about it today."

"Oh yeah? How sweet. Translation, please."

"When the tree falls, the monkeys scatter.'"

"You're talking about me, I presume. Okay, insult registered."

"Actually, John, I am talking about the Ministry of State Security. Their tree is falling, and they're doing strange things. This play with me, for example. The hit on Flanagan. The Chinese are rattled. We need to finish what we started."

Vandel applauded, noiselessly, patting his hands together.

"Good speech. For once, I agree with you, assuming you're not a lying piece of shit. The polygrapher will be here in an hour. I'll tell the Office of Security."

Harris Chang registered no deception when he took the first lie-detector test that afternoon, and the results were confirmed by a second, longer examination the next morning with a new operator and another machine that recorded different measures of stress. They had kept him overnight at the office in Vienna, gave him a toothbrush and clean underwear, but after the second exam, Vandel called Chang and said he was free to go home.

"Am I still under investigation?" Chang asked.

"Yes, technically," said Vandel. "And actually, too. But nobody is charging you with anything. And for now, pending other information, I have decided to believe you, which is all that matters. Go home. Chill out. Don't do anything stupid. I'll call you when we're ready."

31.

WASHINGTON, D.C.

Harris Chang lived on Twelfth Street, just off Logan Circle, in the second floor of a remodeled town house. He sat in his apartment for a day, leaving only to go to the gym. He wanted to unwind, but his anger had only grown at being accused, especially at the suggestion that he had been involved in targeting his Singapore partner, Mark Flanagan. He was relieved that Vandel had decided to trust him, provisionally, but furious that his loyalty had been questioned in the first place. By the second day at home, he was bored with brooding and self-pity and decided to take a long walk.

It was a cool November day with a sharp west wind. Despite the chill, Chang was happy to escape. He walked down Twelfth Street toward the Mall, making no detours, avoiding busy locations where it might seem as if he were trying to lose a tail. When he reached the grassy promenade of the Mall, he was going to turn east toward the Capitol but decided instead on a whim to continue straight across the lawn to a museum he had never visited that specialized in Asian art. He wondered if it might look suspicious, under the circumstances, to visit a gallery filled with Chinese art, and then decided that he didn't care.

The gallery was a revelation for a man who had spent so much of his life ignoring his country of ancestry. In room after room were objects of subtle beauty. He paused five minutes before a delicate scroll painting from the fifteenth century that showed fog-shrouded mountains, spindly trees,

and the thatched hut of a gardener. Down other halls were woven tapestry panels depicting ancient travelers on their quests; a silver mirror from
the seventh century, cast with the forms of magical plants and animals;
portraits of gentle faces painted six hundred and seven hundred years ago;
and then, in the oddest room of all, hundreds of rocks taken from the Yi
River and treasured by some lost collector for their beauty and simplicity.
Chang wondered what sort of person would collect simple stones.

Chang left the gallery after an hour and walked slowly back up
Twelfth Street, feeling refreshed and also unsettled by this visit. When he
reached his town house, he walked up the iron stairway and opened his
door. An unstamped letter was lying on the floor inside, slipped through
the mail slot. Chang opened it and read the handwritten message.

*"Shop for olive oil at the Whole Foods Market on 14th and
P Streets at 4:00."*

The letter was unsigned. It was a summons and possibly a trap. Chang
knew that he should report it, instantly. He looked at his watch. It was nearly
3:30. He tried Vandel's personal cell phone. There was no answer, but the
phone wasn't switched off. He must be away from Headquarters. Chang left
a message, asking Vandel to call him back as soon as possible.

Someone was pulling his chain. Chang wanted to know who. He
went upstairs and unlocked his Beretta M9 handgun, which he had not
used since his Army days. He put on a shoulder holster, checked his wallet to make sure he had his carry permit, and headed out the door.

The market was a quarter mile away. Chang walked a block west,
rounded Logan Circle, and continued down P Street. Now, he was looking actively for surveillance, but none was visible. He stopped under the
blue umbrella of an outdoor café outside the market and entered just
before 4:00. He walked to the aisle that carried oils, canned goods, and
packaged grains. He stood there for more than sixty seconds, studying
the different varieties of olive oil: garlic, basil, extra-virgin, cold-pressed.
He didn't pay attention at first to the person in the Burberry raincoat
who was browsing the products on the opposite side of the aisle. But then
she turned toward him, and he saw her face.

It was Denise Ford. Chang recognized her from pictures. She was wearing a blonde wig and a new pair of oversized glasses. Her demeanor was restrained, her manner unhurried.

"We should talk, Mr. Chang," she said quietly, strolling toward him. "From what I've heard, you need help."

"I don't know who you are," he lied.

"We have no time for that. Meet me across the street at Logan Grill in ten minutes. I'll be in a booth in the back. You need to listen to what I have to say."

She turned and walked down the aisle, stopping to pick up a package of linguine and adding it to her basket before heading to the checkout line. Chang retreated in a daze. It was as if he had fallen into a nightmare version of his CIA life.

He walked deeper into the store toward the butcher counter. He had no idea if he was being followed. He took out his cell phone to see if Vandel had sent him a text message or left a voicemail. When he saw nothing, he pondered a moment. He was at a moment of maximum danger. The mere fact that he had encountered Ford would be damning, if it were known. He needed to report the incident to someone, if only to create a record.

Chang called John Vandel's cell phone again. This time he answered.

"This is Harris. You're not going to believe this, but Denise Ford just made a covert rendezvous in a grocery store. She wants to meet me in ten minutes. What should I do?"

"That depends on whether you're a patriotic American."

"Of course, I am. That's why I called you. I didn't want you to find out about this some other way."

"Then go meet with her. Record it if you can. But remember it, so you can testify about it when she's indicted. Can you do that, Harris? You sound frazzled. You okay?"

"Yes, sir. More than frazzled, actually. Should I ask her about the Chinese?"

"Hell, no. And don't tell her anything she doesn't know already."

"Do I have immunity for all this? I don't want to get burned for doing what you just told me to do."

"I'm not a lawyer. I don't grant immunity. But as the deputy director for operations, I'm telling you to go. We'll sort the rest out later."

"Thanks for nothing." Chang closed the connection.

Chang walked one block up Fourteenth Street and sat down in the out-door patio of a French restaurant, wondering what to do. He would have called Mark Flanagan, if he were still alive. Chang liked to imagine that he had friends. But in this moment, he felt entirely alone.

Chang rose from the barren café and walked back toward P Street. He found the tavern across the street from the grocery and entered warily, looking for a setup. There was an old-timey bar on the right, backed by a mirror and fifty bottles of booze. On the left beyond a big common table was an array of booths. Most of them were empty, but in the last one, behind the wooden divider, facing away from the door, he could see a blonde head.

Chang pushed the record button on his phone and put it in his breast pocket. He walked back and took a seat opposite the woman. She had a martini glass in front of her. It had the light pink tint of a Cosmopolitan. It was untouched.

"You're late," said Ford, "but I won't hold that against you."

"I came. I told you in the market that I didn't know who you were, but that wasn't true. You're Denise Ford. You work in the front office at S&T. You said you needed to tell me something. Why all the mumbo jumbo with the message at my house and the brush pass?"

"Do you have a phone with you?" she asked. "Take out the battery, please."

"It's an iPhone. It doesn't have a removable battery."

"Then turn it off and put it in this bag." She removed from her purse a small phone case that blocked the phone from sending or receiving signals.

Chang handed the phone to Ford, who put it in her quarantine case. She appraised him as he moved.

"Do you always carry a weapon?" she asked, looking at the bulge under his shoulder.

"Not usually. You're special."

"Call me Denise," she said, extending her hand. "You were a friend of Mark Flanagan's weren't you?"

"Yup. We worked together sometimes. I liked him a lot. I miss him."

"Such a nice man. My deputy, too briefly. What happened to him, do you suppose?"

"I don't know. Maybe someone tried to kill him. What do you think?"

"I think he was unlucky. He made a mistake coming to work for me, probably. It was a strain. He was letting people use him. That's always a mistake, isn't it? Being used."

"I loved Mark. He didn't deserve to die."

"Of course not. Nobody does. We went to California together. Did you know that?"

"He told me. He said it was pretty interesting. Computer stuff."

"Quantum computing. I'm not sure that Mark understood it very well. Mechanical engineers are like that. If they can't take something apart and look at the wiring, they don't trust it. Poor man."

Chang stared at her. The blonde wig made her look like a Russian. She had the icy precision that the instructors described in the Career Trainee program, when they were explaining how a case officer should behave. Chang wanted to draw her out; he would have to explain each moment of this conversation to Vandel later.

"Why did you want to see me so badly? You said I was in trouble. What kind of trouble?"

"The worst kind." She laughed, once. "Your trouble is that you don't know what kind of trouble you're in."

"Can you help, Ms. Ford?"

"I don't know. But you're here. That's a good start. You need to get your head straight."

She took a tiny sip of her Cosmo. Chang asked for a beer. She steadied her gaze. She was beautiful in the low light of the bar: round, sculpted face, high forehead, intense and nimble eyes. She leaned toward him and whispered.

"They think you're a Chinese spy. It's just racism, probably. Chinese boy. Chinese spy. But that's what they think."

Chang was startled. "Where did you hear that?"

She gave him a wink.

"Corridor talk. Everyone knows that you and Vandel have been out looking for a Chinese penetration. And now they think it's you. Crazy, maybe. But the fact is, you're in trouble, and I can help. That's what I wanted to say. I can be of assistance, if you'll let me."

"How can you help me, Denise?"

"All sorts of ways. But for starters, I know for a fact that you're not the Chinese spy they're looking for. They're mistaken."

"How would you know that, Denise?"

She sat back in the booth and turned away from him for a moment, arching her graceful neck so that the skin was taut, and then turned back toward him.

"Because you're a good boy. You do what you're told. But you should reconsider. It's obvious that your loyalty isn't reciprocated. You need someone to catch your fall."

"Like you?"

"Yes, just like me. I want you to think about things, that's all. Open your mind. It's one world! That's what I told Mark Flanagan, poor man. Open up! It's a big world out there. Stop holding onto the past. Think for yourself."

"The Chinese killed Mark. That's what I think."

She was startled. Her regal face seemed to sag, as if it had lost its inner pressure. She shook her head.

"That's a terrible thing to say," she said. "How cruel."

She was done, suddenly. She took her wallet from her purse and dropped forty dollars on the table. She removed Chang's cell phone from the case and handed it back to him. Chang was mystified.

"Cruel to whom? To Mark? It doesn't matter to him. He's dead."

"No. Cruel to me. Think about what I said. If you want to talk again, do it carefully."

Denise Ford rose from the booth and walked quickly out of the bar. Chang sat motionless for a moment, trying to sort what had happened, and then rose to follow her. By the time he reached the street, she had vanished. He wondered what to do, but not for very long. He was in serious trouble now, and there was only one exit.

32.

McLEAN AND ARLINGTON, VIRGINIA

Harris Chang walked back to his apartment on Twelfth Street. A homeless drunk was sitting on his front stairs, screaming about Jesus. He asked Chang if he was saved. Chang walked around him and opened the door. The man was still moaning, talking now about the "chinks" and "kikes" who were out to get him. Chang had seen him in the neighborhood before. He wasn't dangerous, just crazy. Chang pulled out his wallet. He held a twenty-dollar bill in front of the man, just out of reach, and said he would give him the money if he got off the stoop and spent it on food rather than booze. The man's eyes were as wild as before, but he stumbled toward Chang and took the bill in his hand. He touched it to his lips.

"Thank you, Jesus," he said, walking down the stairs.

When Chang got upstairs, he put his head in his hands. What was happening to him? Why were the timbers of his life collapsing? None of it made sense. The Chinese intelligence service had tried to recruit him and then pretended it had succeeded. His partner had been poisoned. The Chinese mole he had been chasing had just tried to pitch him. Harris Chang, the person who never made a mistake, had stumbled into a snare that was tightening around him. And the worst of it was that his colleagues, the people on whom he depended, no longer seemed to trust him.

When Chang was a young boy in Flagstaff, he had run away from a fight with a big Navajo boy in middle school who had insulted his family. When he got home, his father beat him with a belt and said it was better to lose a fight than be a coward. Chang had never run away from anything again. But in this moment, the temptation to do so was acute. He thought for a moment about where he would go if he tried to escape, and then put the thought out of his mind.

Chang dialed John Vandel's mobile phone. The call went over to voicemail immediately.

"This is Harris," Chang said into the phone. "I need to talk to you right away."

Chang feared that Vandel wouldn't return the call. He was in the office now, if his cell phone was off. When he picked up the message, he might tell someone from the Office of Security or the FBI that he had been contacted by the subject of an investigation, and eventually someone would return the call on Vandel's behalf, with a tape running.

Chang couldn't wait; a weight had been attached to his body that would drag him to the bottom unless he could get himself free.

He called Vandel's office number and told his executive assistant, Melanie, that he needed to speak to the boss, urgently. She had always been friendly with him when he was on his way up and regarded as Vandel's protégé.

"Hey, I hope everything is okay," she said, hearing the anxiety in his voice. "Let me see what I can do."

Melanie came back on the line thirty seconds later and apologized that it wasn't convenient for Mr. Vandel right now. She didn't say so, but Vandel had evidently refused the request.

"Tell him I'm coming anyway," said Chang. "I'll be at Headquarters in thirty minutes. He can throw me out, or have me arrested, or do whatever he wants. But I have to try to see him."

Vandel's voice broke in. He had been listening on the extension.

"Jesus, Harris, what the hell is wrong with you? I've got it, Melanie." His assistant clicked off the line.

"Nothing is wrong with me, sir. But I need to see you, right now. No bullshit."

"Talk to Kate Sturm. I'm in the middle of a shit storm here."

"No. I need to see you personally. You have to deal with this. It's about the meeting I just had. I can't talk about it on the phone. But I promise, you will regret it if you say no."

"Whoa! A threat. And from a former U.S. Army major. I'm scared."

"Not a threat at all, sir. A warning. You really need to say yes. Otherwise I'm coming to Headquarters. It's the only way I can protect myself."

"You are a pain in the ass, Harris. You know that?" He put the phone on hold while he made another call on his cell and then came back on the line.

"I'll meet you in an hour at that Persian restaurant off Route 123. 'Karim's.'"

"Are you sure that place is private enough?"

"What? You want a Chinese restaurant? This will have to do. I'm not booking a meeting room for you here. Sorry. Too many boxes to check. Too long a paper trail. Maybe you've forgotten, but you're under investigation."

"I haven't forgotten," said Chang. "I'll see you in an hour."

The restaurant occupied a corner of a low-rise shopping mall in McLean Town Center. It had the ambience of a kabob restaurant in Tehran: tile floor, cherry wood tables and chairs with vinyl backs, lace curtains tied at the bottom, the smell of saffron and cardamom permeating the small dining room. Chang parked his car in a supermarket lot a hundred yards away. He knocked on the back door, hoping to conceal his arrival from anyone watching the main entrance, but nobody answered so he went around to the front.

Vandel was sitting at a table in the rear, talking to the owner. The restaurant was nearly empty in late afternoon. Vandel and the owner conversed like old friends; of course, they were. The restaurateur must have been on the payroll once; maybe he still was. Vandel never went anywhere he didn't have a measure of control. He looked up as he saw Chang approach.

The owner retreated. "Nobody will bother you, Mr. John," he said. He locked the door and flipped the "open" sign so that it showed "closed."

"This better be good," said Vandel. "I blew off the national security adviser for you. What did your squirrely girlfriend have to say?"

"Denise Ford tried to recruit me. She said we should work together. She told me I needed a friend, because the agency suspected I was a Chinese spy. How did she know that? Did the MSS tell her? Someone did, because she's targeting me. I need help."

"Calm down, Harris. Did you get this on tape?"

"I tried. But she took my iPhone and put it in a pouch that blocked signals. I want to dictate an affidavit right now, while it's all fresh in my mind. Can I do that? Otherwise, nobody's going to believe me."

Vandel thought a moment. "Yes, but keep it in-house, with Kate Sturm. The FBI already thinks you're a Chinese spy, so if you tell them you had a recruitment meeting, they'll have a fit."

"If you can't turn off the FBI, then I'm calling a lawyer."

"Don't be an idiot, Harris. You'll screw everything up. We need to keep this case rolling."

"How? The lady is dangerous. She's working for Beijing. You have to shut her down."

Vandel absentmindedly rolled the salt shaker back and forth on the tablecloth while he pondered the situation. He kneaded his scarred cheeks.

"I've got an idea," he said eventually.

"Oh yeah? What's that? Because so far, John, your ideas just keep getting me in deeper trouble."

"You should frighten Ford. Miss Ice Water. Tell her that we're about to arrest her and that she needs to run."

"What's the point of that? She has to assume she's under investigation already. She must know we put Mark on her tail."

"But she's still in place, and our evidence is crap. Make her so scared that she'll go to the big boss in Beijing. Bait the trap and then, snap! We've got her, and the Chinese, too. If we do it right, we'll hit the MSS so hard it will splinter, what's left of it, anyway, and we'll have one less collection of assholes to worry about."

"But John, I'm the bait. You're telling me to tip off a Chinese agent that the CIA is onto her. But to the FBI, I'm a Chinese asset, too—and

I'll be sharing highly classified information with another Chinese asset. That means I'm screwed if this goes wrong. I want something in writing from the Bureau."

"We can't tell them. There would be a three-alarm fire. I already told you that."

"Then I want it in writing from you. And the Director. Otherwise, no deal."

"The Director is out of the question. I haven't briefed him on anything for two weeks. He wants it that way, so he won't get blamed later. And for god's sake, Harris, stop pretending that you have leverage in this situation. You don't. I am offering you a way out of the mess that you got yourself into. Nobody made you do anything. Take it or leave it."

"I want it in writing from you, as DDO. A written record, copied to Kate Sturm."

"You can have a memo from me."

"And Kate. Otherwise, I'm not playing. Seriously."

"Christ! What a pussy. Okay, I will copy Sturm. Not that it will make any difference. She'll tear it up if I tell her to. But I won't. Do we have a deal?"

Vandel extended his hand. Chang waited. In that moment, he truly disliked John Vandel, the man who had once been his hero. Did he have another choice? Not a good one. Vandel would do his best to ruin Chang's career, and probably far worse, if he didn't play along.

Chang thought one last moment and then shook his boss's hand.

Vandel gave him a tight grip and a thin smile. Had that glint been in his eye, back in Iraq?

"I'll call Sturm now," said Vandel. "An Office of Security representative will come take your affidavit, except it will actually be a memo, but so what? You dictate everything that you remember about your meetings with Ford. The Security guy will take it back up the road to Disney World and get it transcribed, pronto, and bring it back here for you to sign and date."

"I can't go to Headquarters myself?"

"No! I told you. You're under investigation. Eat something. You need it. You look like shit."

"Thanks, John. I wonder why that is."

"Save the self-pity for someone who appreciates it, Harris. We are on a short clock. I need to go now. I'll get an ops plan ready overnight."

"Where do we go next? After my affidavit, I mean."

"Meet me tomorrow morning at 10:00 at the office in Ballston."

"Am I allowed back in the clubhouse?"

"Not exactly. I'm going to say in the log that I'm interrogating you. But Kate will be there."

"Good. She can be my character witness."

"Dream on. Nobody's going to say anything nice about Harris Chang until you deliver your Chinese brothers and sisters. That's a fact. Sorry if it sounds politically incorrect, but it's true. Be smart. Eat some Persian food. Got to go."

Vandel rose and left. Chang ordered the mixed kabobs. Forty-five minutes later, an officer with a tape recorder arrived from the Office of Security. He suggested that they record the "memorandum" in his car outside, so Chang had to leave the rest of his food on the plate.

33.

ARLINGTON, VIRGINIA

Harris Chang sat on a bench the next morning in a little park near the Ballston metro station, waiting for the meeting to begin. The park was surrounded by office buildings with flat, Virginia-sounding names: Jefferson, Stafford, Avalon. Who knew what happened inside a place with a name like that? Many of the nearby tenants were government contractors; their chief job qualification was that they had security clearances and could send classified information to other people with security clearances.

Chang surveyed his little oasis. The grassy spots were green but the leaves had vanished from most of the trees; there was a wet November chill in the air. Chang drank his coffee. What a sad little place. He missed Flagstaff. The desert sun would be low in the morning at this time of year, the air so crisp that it cleaned your lungs and nostrils with each breath. The Hopi and Navajo traders would be dismantling their roadside stands for the winter; the town would pull a little blanket over itself and sleep, like a hibernating bear, until it got warmer.

Chang rose from his bench and walked the two blocks to the dull façade on North Glebe Road where the agency had its "covert" facility. It took him longer than usual to clear the guard station, but he was eventually sent upstairs and escorted to a conference room, this time with two armed guards from the Office of Security outside the door.

Kate Sturm arrived on time, but Vandel was late, and she didn't want to start without him. Since the entire floor was designated a Secure Compartmented Information Facility, they had both surrendered their cell phones and had no easy distraction to pass the time. Chang had brought along a paperback of *The Duke's Children*, the last of the Palliser novels, so he read about the travails of Lady Glencora and Plantagenet, while Sturm wrote memos to herself in a small wire-bound notebook.

John Vandel arrived eventually with the commotion that is customary when people are late. He complained that he had been up nearly all night framing his operational plans, and the doughy color of his face and the raccoon eyes confirmed that he hadn't had much sleep. His hair was a messy quill of needles. But he was oddly jubilant, for all the physical exhaustion.

"We've got them," he said, pointing his finger at Chang. "So long as you do your job, we are going to clean their clocks, from here to Beijing."

"That's very nice," said Chang calmly. "But I'm not doing anything until you sign an authorization for my mission, at your direction, and give a copy to Ms. Sturm."

"What a little robot you are," Vandel said curtly. "The military mindset." But he had come prepared. He removed two sheets from his briefcase. "Your orders. Read them over carefully. Then I'll sign."

Chang read the short document twice. It said that the deputy director for operations requested Harris Chang, a case officer suspended from the Clandestine Service and under investigation by the counter-intelligence division of the FBI, to conduct a mission targeting officers of the Chinese Ministry of State Security. Upon successful completion of the mission, the deputy director for operations would recommend to the FBI that the investigation of Chang be terminated, without prejudice to Chang's record, and that he resume active duty with the Directorate of Operations.

Chang let the document fall to the table below.

"This is crap. Sir. It doesn't really commit you to do anything. I mean, you direct this and you recommend that. But there's no commitment by anybody."

"Hey, Harris. It is what it is. You want to call it crap, fine, but it's all you've got. You want me to sign it or not?"

Chang looked his boss in the eye. He felt a rising confidence, for the first time in a long while. While the silence built, he took off his jacket and rolled up his shirtsleeve until the tattoo showed.

"No jury will ever convict me of espionage," said Chang. "I'm going to win, no matter what."

"Maybe so." Vandel shrugged.

"Sign it," said Chang. "Have Ms. Sturm sign both copies, to confirm that she's a witness."

Vandel was about to protest that they hadn't agreed to any co-signing, but Sturm waved him off. She had her pen ready; she signed one copy, then the other, a neat careful hand. As she signed, Chang rolled his sleeve back down.

Chang asked for his copy but was told no, the document was classified and he wasn't authorized to have it. He snorted at the absurdity of that and then asked for permission to copy it out in longhand.

Vandel didn't answer, but Sturm nodded assent. Chang wrote the brief text on the inside flyleaf of *The Duke's Children*.

"Okay, book group's over. Now that we've finished trying to cover our asses, can we get down to a little intelligence work, please? And don't get me wrong, Harris. I wouldn't do this if I didn't believe in you. Truly. Are we clear on that?"

Chang stared straight ahead. He felt a wave of disgust hearing Vandel's affirmation of sincerity.

"Good," said Vandel. He removed two more sheets of paper from his briefcase and handed one each to Sturm and Chang.

"This is your ops timeline. When you contact Denise Ford, I want you to follow exactly the same tradecraft that she used with you yesterday. 'Beijing Rules,' so to speak."

Vandel handed the timetable to Chang. It had a map at the bottom of the page.

"Here's the drill. Go to her town house in Old Town. It's on Prince Street, between Fairfax and Lee, just south of the river. The address is on the sheet. Do a surveillance detection run and shake anything the Chinese may have set up. Drop the message just after 7:00 p.m., when she should be home. Put it through her mail slot, the same way she did with you."

Vandel read the text aloud:

"Urgent. It's your friend from the bar. Meet me 8:00 tonight in the Safeway on Royal Street. I'll be in the canned soup aisle. I have information that you need to know."

Chang took the message and nodded.

"I'll run the whole play back at her, in reverse. Note, brush pass, meeting."

"Exactly."

"Okay," said Chang. "What next?"

"For the hour after dropping the note, get lost. Go bowling. I don't care. The Safeway is three blocks from her town house. Get there a little before 8:00 and then start looking at soup labels. When she shows, brush her this little piece of paper."

Vandel handed Chang another sheet, this one no larger than a supermarket checkout receipt. Chang read the words:

"Hotel Luna restaurant. King Street. 15 minutes."

"We'll have the Luna staked out. Nobody's getting in except you and her and the extras we'll have on scene. Take a booth in the corner, facing the window. It will be wired. If she wants another table, don't fight it. We can get sound and pictures from anywhere in the restaurant."

"Suppose she smells a rat and wants to go somewhere else?"

"No problem. She can go all the way to West Virginia but we're going to monitor this meeting. And don't forget, little buddy, you'll be wired, too."

Vandel handed him a tiny button microphone, embedded in adhesive.

"Put that under your shirt. Next to your heart. Or near your bad-ass Army tattoo."

"What do I tell her when we're at the Luna?"

"Scare her. *Confide* in her. You're her friend. Tell her we have her nailed. Tell her Vandel is ready to have her arrested. If she wants out, now is her last chance."

"Why am I warning her? Is she supposed to think I'm accepting her pitch?"

"Yes. You're ready to come over. You're sick of the CIA. You put your trust in John Vandel and it was betrayed. You're worried that this is the last chance for both of you. You're a pro, Harris. You know how to recruit people. This time, do it in reverse."

"What if she wants more information? Bona fides."

"Tell her the story. Describe the meeting with Carlos Wang in Mexico. Describe the family pictures. Make it bleed. Tell her what a bastard I am. Tell her you're sick of racist crap about China. Somehow, I think you can do this. Just make it real."

Chang shook his head.

"If you had trusted me when I came back from Mexico, I wouldn't be in this situation."

"Self-pity is your worst enemy, Harris. It makes you weak. And you're wrong, by the way. You're in exactly the position I hoped you would be, before I sent you to Vancouver and Mexico. This isn't an accident. It's an operation. Wait for the punch line."

"You really are a bastard."

"No. I am an intelligence officer. It's a fine line, but there's a difference."

Chang looked at his boss with a strange mix of anger and admiration. Maybe this was the thing that people like Vandel and Ford and Li Zian understood. You couldn't be in their world and not get caught in the undertow.

Chang nodded his head slowly.

"How do I close the deal? Suppose she balks. How do I convince her?"

"This is where it gets sweet: The deal closer is you!"

"I don't know what that means."

"You tell her that you're ready to come over. But you need personal assurance from the big boss, Li Zian. Otherwise no deal. You need to meet him soon, somewhere overseas. If not, there's no deal. You're taking all the risk. It's too dangerous. You might go to the FBI."

Chang closed his eyes and spoke the words of the script.

"I want to defect. I hate John Vandel, and I hate the agency. But I want to meet my new case officer, Li Zian. Otherwise, I can't do it."

"Just right," said Vandel.

Chang opened his eyes again. There was a faint glimmer of a smile.

"Okay. I'm there. How do Ford and I communicate, if Li Zian agrees to meet us? We're two suspected Chinese spies. We can't just meet in the cafeteria."

"Work out the tradecraft with Kate. She's better at it than I am."

Vandel looked at his watch. It was his habit that when he wanted to end a meeting, he pretended he had run out of time.

"Let's get out of here before any of us has second thoughts. You'll get a medal for this, Harris, assuming it works. Otherwise you'll get ten years, with time off for good behavior. Just joking. Good luck."

Vandel strode off, face set, feet splayed, hands thrust in his pockets. He looked like a baseball manager, walking off the mound after deciding to leave his starting pitcher in the game despite a few bad innings.

Kate Sturm walked Chang through the operations plan one more time. When they had covered all the details and were walking toward the door, she turned to him and, after an awkward silence, she apologized to him. Chang asked her what she meant but she wouldn't answer. She just said that she was sorry.

34.

OLD TOWN, ALEXANDRIA

Harris Chang began his surveillance detection run with a stop at a bar in his neighborhood. There was an empty seat next to a cute redhead in her mid-twenties who was drinking a margarita. She had a girlfriend on the other side, but the friend was talking to the guy next to her, so Harris introduced himself and asked the woman what she did. It sounded like a pickup line, even to him, but she didn't seem to mind. She said she was a graduate student at Georgetown who wanted to go into the "foreign service."

"Don't do it," said Chang, without thinking. When she asked why not, he mumbled something about low pay.

She asked him what he did and he said he had recently gotten out of the Army and was looking for work. She scrolled through more questions that he didn't want to answer. She spoke a little Chinese, she said. Chang changed the subject. He talked about the local hockey team and its playoff chances, but she didn't follow any sports except golf.

Nobody who looked like a watcher had come in or out of the bar; Chang found the redhead annoying, so he paid the tab and left. The woman looked mystified. What had she done wrong? Chang wanted to apologize for making her a decoy; he wanted to apologize for everything. But another guy quickly took his chair at the bar.

Chang took the subway west toward Vienna, then east toward Old

Town. He got off two stops after his destination and took a cab back to Ford's town house on Prince Street. It was a well-kept neighborhood of brick town houses and cobbled streets, a less crowded version of Georgetown, with fewer people on the streets and less dog shit, too. Ford's two-story brick house was nestled among larger dwellings. The curtains were drawn. From inside, there was the sound of classical music.

Chang read the note a last time and wondered at Ford's reaction. Did she imagine that she was the hunter or the prey? Chang folded the note and slipped it into the slot. He heard it clank shut as he walked away, quickly, south toward Fairfax Street. He heard the door open behind him but didn't turn back.

Chang kept walking. She wasn't coming after him, and there was nobody on the street. He slowed his pace as he neared the thoroughfare of Washington Street. There was a curious statue in the middle of the intersection. Chang waited for the light to turn and walked toward the bronze figure. It portrayed a Confederate soldier, hat in hand, head down, shoulders slouched as he looked south. It was called "Appomattox." An inscription under the figure said: "They died in the consciousness of duty faithfully performed." It was a monument to defeat. Chang had never admired the Confederacy, but in that moment, he empathized. Defeated cultures behave strangely.

Chang paced the streets for the next hour, slowly tacking toward the rendezvous at the Safeway. He arrived ten minutes before the meeting. The market occupied a one-story brick building at the less fashionable end of town.

Chang navigated toward the aisle that displayed the canned soups. He began looking at the Campbell's section and then, after a minute, wandered down a few feet to the array of Progresso cans. He had counted nineteen different kinds of chicken soup when he caught sight of Ford across the aisle, looking at vegetable oils. Without making eye contact, he moved toward her and brushed her purse, depositing his note gently in the open sack.

Ten minutes later Ford was sliding into his booth at the far end of the Luna hotel dining room. She was wearing a tailored black leather jacket over designer jeans. She didn't look worried; if anything, she looked exultant.

"I knew you were a good man," she said quietly as she took the seat next to Chang. "You're sick of the lies and arrogance. You want a new world."

Her face radiated the fusion of belief and action. Chang pulled back toward the banquette.

"I don't know what I want, yet. But I need to tell you something. Urgently. The CIA knows you work for the Chinese. They have you cold. They're ready to arrest you."

She closed her eyes. She pressed her lips together tightly. When she opened her eyes again, they were ablaze.

"Why are you telling me this? Did they ask you to do this?"

"No," he lied. "I want to help you. I think you're right about, I don't know, everything. I want you to escape."

"You mean you want to work with me? That's the only thing we need to discuss."

Chang paused. Every word he said was being overheard and transcribed. His main feeling was that he needed to finish his mission.

"Maybe. But I need to meet with the Ministry's top person. The one who handles you. I didn't like the case officer they sent after me in Mexico. All he wanted to talk about was my Chinese-ness, my duty as a Chinese person. I didn't like that."

"I hate racism. In any form. I sympathize. That was wrong."

Her chin was arched upward. The soft leather sleeve of her jacket grazed against Chang's arm. Vandel had told him once that the best lies are the ones that you believe. Chang let her arm rest against his, as he formed the words.

"The only thing I ever wanted was to work for America."

"Me, too," she said. "I still do. It's just for the American future, not the past."

"They think I'm a traitor. I told them they were wrong, I let them polygraph me, over and over, but they still didn't believe. I listened to all their bullshit racist comments. Something broke. I can't take it anymore. I have to get out."

"I understand," she said. "They betrayed you."

"I don't hate my country."

"Of course not. Our Chinese friends would never assume that. At least not the ones who run the show. They understand how complicated loyalty is."

"I need to meet the top guy. I can't make a commitment to someone lower down who can't keep it."

"Maybe. Maybe. They travel very quietly. They don't like to rustle the leaves."

Their arms still touched. Two hunters; two prey. Chang's head trembled slightly. Her gaze remained firm.

A waitress arrived. She had the hard body of someone who had graduated from a paramilitary training program. She asked if they'd had a chance to look at the menus.

"Give us a few more minutes," said Chang.

Ford took Chang's hand in his. Her soft skin covered his taut fingers.

"How much time do we have?" she asked.

"We need to move quickly. They could arrest you anytime. Tomorrow, the next day. They say they have everything they need. You need to set up the meeting with your friend. I'll only come if you're there. I don't trust anyone else."

"This isn't easy," she said. "They're very careful."

"You're trying to do what's right. So am I. But they need to show that they're serious. Otherwise how can I take the risk?"

"I get it," she said.

"We need to go soon. You're being watched. So am I. This is dangerous."

She took one last careful look at Chang, weighing him. She could control herself, but not him. This was a wager she didn't like to make.

"How will they know this isn't a trick? That's what they will ask. And they should. How can they be sure this Chinese-American man isn't showing a double face?"

Chang thought a moment. What would Li Zian want most? He moved his lips close to her ear. He was improvising, but he could tell from her reaction that he had made a good guess.

"The Ministry of State Security is under attack. Unless it fights back, it will be destroyed. I know how your friend can save himself. I know the secret weaknesses of his adversaries. Tell your friend that. Tell him that we need to meet in the next week, somewhere outside China. Otherwise it will be too late. You and I will be gone, and soon, he will be, too. Tell him I will bring him the information he needs."

Her eyes were hard as agate marbles. She nodded.

"Yes. That would make a difference to my friend. But you must deliver. If this is a false promise, it will be a fatal one."

"I'll deliver."

She squeezed his hand. A sure, confident smile formed on her lips.

"I was right about you, Harris. You are a citizen of the world. The true patriots, people like you and me, are vilified, but we're right. You are very brave. I am so proud of you."

"We have to move fast. Do you have a clean alias passport and credit cards?"

"No. But my friends can get me out of the country if they need to. They've already told me that."

"Okay. Use the most secure communications you have. Make sure there's nothing anyone could find that would give you away. When you hear back from your friend that he can see us, leave me a message."

"How should I do that? We're both under surveillance."

"I thought about that already. Go to the CIA employees-only website and post online on the swap-mart that you're selling your car."

"In the classified chat room? Under their noses?"

"It's the one place they would never look. What kind of car do you drive?"

"A 2014 Lexus Hybrid SUV. Light green."

"Offer it for sale. I'll check the swap-mart every few hours and look for your post. As soon as I see it, I'll know we're on. In your post, say where you bought the car. That's the city where the meeting is set."

"Okay. Purchased in Berlin means meet in Berlin."

"Then say how many miles the car has on the odometer. The first digit is the number of days until the meeting. So, if you say five thousand miles, that's five days. If you say three thousand miles, that's three days."

"Pretty good tradecraft," she said. "Mine would be better, but we don't have time."

"I will meet you in that city, on that day. I will check into the Hilton

Hotel, in whatever city it is. Leave a message for me under my Peter Tong alias. That's it: Hilton Hotel. Peter Tong."

"Why the Hilton?" She was wary about ceding control.

"Because they're everywhere. And it's easy to remember. When I get to the hotel, who should I ask for?"

"Audrey Fingerhut. That's my alias name."

"Okay, Audrey. We need to arrive a day before the meeting, so we have a chance to plan."

"What if my friend says he won't meet us?"

"Then don't contact me. The deal's off. You get out of the country however you can. But I'm not coming."

"Hard bargain. You're good at this, aren't you?"

"Yes, I am. But I'm nervous. If either of us makes a mistake, we're both dead."

She took his hand again.

"This is what we do." She waited a long moment. "I always hoped there would be someone like you, who understood." She gave his hand a last squeeze.

"We're out of time," said Chang. "I'll see you downrange."

"Don't play any games," she said quietly. "I may look nice, but I'm not."

Denise Ford walked easily toward the door. She thought she had won.

Harris Chang strode past the reception desk to the men's room at the end of the corridor. He was just zipping up when John Vandel strolled in and parked himself on the marble bank of sinks. He was shaking his head and clucking his lips.

"You deserve an Oscar," said Vandel. "Seriously, that was pretty damn good. She bought it. And I'll wager that she can sell it to her friend at the Ministry."

"Thanks," said Chang. He was exhausted from his moment on stage. He didn't feel ebullient. "I'm going to need some collateral."

"What collateral? You're the trophy. Li wins. He doesn't need anything else."

"I told Ford I would give Li secrets about his enemies in the PLA. What if he asks for them? I don't have anything to give him."

"Don't worry. We'll have him in our hands by then. All he's going to ask for is asylum."

"I need something. Just in case. Otherwise you need to find another Chinese-American defector."

"Christ! You are a pain in the butt." Vandel thought a moment, then gave Chang a wink.

"I do have a little something. Some pictures we took in Dubai of me and General Wu Huning, the archenemy of the Ministry of State Security."

Chang gave a thumbs-up. "That will work. I'll tell Li you recruited him. Photographic proof."

"I didn't realize you were such a conscientious liar, Harris. It gives me a whole new insight on you."

"Inscrutable Chinese, right?"

"You're just being cranky. Go home and get some sleep. And pack your bags. You may be leaving in a hurry."

Vandel gave him a jocular punch on the arm.

"I feel sorry for that woman," Chang said.

"Fuck her. She deserves whatever she gets. Don't get moody on me. We're in the red zone here. Get the ball across the goal line. No mistakes. Is that understood?"

Chang wanted to say more, but as usual with Vandel, he simply assented.

"Yes, sir. No mistakes."

For once, Chang was the first to leave. Vandel sat for a while on the sink top, congratulating himself, and then returned to the dining room to dismiss the brigade of CIA security officers he had assembled. He had a proprietary air when he sent them off, as if he had set in motion a lucrative business scheme. Chang had vanished, out the door and into the November night.

35.

BEIJING

The enemies of Li Zian within the bosom of the Party had become increasingly bold. They had bugged his office at the Ministry of State Security, as well as his residence and his limousine. When he walked outdoors, vans moved slowly behind him on the streets; when he ventured off the sidewalks into parks or wooded trails, pedestrians followed him at a measured pace. His rivals did not bother to hide their tracks anymore. Li was in retreat; his enemies sensed his weakness and took advantage of it.

Li turned for help to an old friend who was the chief of the Beijing Municipal Bureau of State Security, the MSS's branch in the capital. Li called him "Ali," as a kind of personal code, because he had served for nearly a decade in Tehran. Ali understood surveillance technology, and how to counter it, because his bureau oversaw technical operations against the U.S. embassy in Beijing. Li asked him to arrange safe places for conversation using the resources of his bureau. It worked for several weeks. But in the middle of an early December night, Ali was arrested on orders of the Commission for Discipline Inspection. Like everyone around Li, his friend had been greedy and incautious.

When the officers of the Central Guard Bureau searched Ali's apartment in northwest Beijing, they found something that astonished even those who feared and hated the Ministry of State Security. Hidden behind a false wall of Ali's penthouse were several thousand pages of transcripts of private telephone conversations of the president of China. Ali had been bugging the leader. Li swore to his comrades that he knew nothing about it. Whether they believed him or not didn't matter. He was running out of string. His deputies had been purged, one by one. Power was draining from Li's network. He needed to recharge himself somehow, soon, or his power would flicker out.

Li summoned Wang Ji the morning he heard the news about Ali's arrest. He had been up much of the night, puzzling about a message that had arrived the day before with his unique cipher, which he had decrypted himself. As he lay awake at 3:00 a.m., turning the puzzle over in his mind, he received the news of the arrest of his friend and confidant, Ali. Li could think of only one person left whose advice he could take. He was uncertain of Carlos Wang's loyalty, but he had nowhere else to turn.

Carlos had cut his hair. He had restrained his machismo swagger. It was no longer the season for ostentation. Luxury was dangerous. The authorities were closing the golf courses that had become so popular with Party officials only a few years ago. Sales of fine French wines and Iranian caviar, products for which China had become a principal market, had almost stopped. Party officials no longer entertained each other with lavish banquets. Before, stealing money had been part of the "China Dream," but now, it seemed, no one wanted to look rich.

It was a December morning, bitter cold, but Li asked Carlos Wang to walk with him outside in the garden behind the gray brick of the Ministry. They wore bulky overcoats; Li covered his head with a red fur hat. Their breath condensed in the chill. Li brought along an old analog tape player, whose tinny sound covered their conversation.

"You have heard the morning's news about the arrest of the director of the Beijing Bureau of State Security, I suppose," Li ventured.

"Yes, minister. Bad news travels fast. I am sorry for him. My brother told me this morning that people are very angry about the tape transcripts."

"I didn't know about the tapes," said Li. "He did that for someone else. Or for himself."

"Of course, minister," said Carlos Wang. "Placing bugs in people's office is not your manner. That's what I told my brother."

"What we discuss is not for your brother's ears. Or anyone's. Is that understood? Do not think you can escape, *Xiao* Wang, if this house collapses."

"Yes, minister."

As he often did when he had something especially sensitive to discuss, Li shifted the conversation to the solid, reassuring foundation of Chinese history. It soldered the present to the eternal past.

"In intelligence matters, there are always rivals," said Li. "It is our Chinese way. Today it is the Second Department of the PLA that combats our ministry. In other times, it was the same story with different names."

"Tell me, minister. My understanding of history is not as good as yours."

"The imperialist puppet Chang Kai Shek had two sources of intelligence. The *Zhong Tong*, the central investigation bureau, was like our ministry. But he also maintained the *Jun Tong*, which we might compare to 2PLA."

"And in our era?"

"After the revolution, inevitably, there were also two factions. There were the cadres that had fought in the countryside, the military men. And there were the cadres in the city, the secret fighters, led by the revolutionary comrades in Shanghai. My father was a Shanghai man. I am his son. We cannot change who we are. Who are you, Carlos?"

"I am your deputy, minister." He bowed. "If you fall, I fall with you."

Li nodded. He was silent. He removed his glasses and polished them against his jacket and then continued.

"What we never imagined, Comrade Carlos, was that China would become so rich. That is the source of our good fortune and also our difficulty. Do you know what Deng Xiaoping said before he died in 1979?"

"No, minister. Those secrets of our party's history are hidden except to the most senior cadres."

"Deng summoned Jiang Zemin, who was general secretary of the Party and paramount leader. He warned Jiang that as China had grown rich, corruption had become widespread and asked what he was going to do about it. Jiang requested advice, and here is what Deng told him: 'If you don't fight corruption, China will collapse. If you fight corruption, the Communist Party will collapse.'

"Our leader has decided to fight corruption," Li continued, "starting with our ministry. He believes he can have both, China and the Party. But he has too many enemies now. The internal fighting cannot stop. It will not stop. It makes me sad that I must watch."

They continued strolling through the garden, leaving a circular trail on the frost-hardened grass.

"Let me tell you something, Carlos, a secret that I have never told anyone. When our leader came to power, he had a problem with his relatives. We all have problems with our relatives, don't we? They see that we are powerful, and they want to profit from it. So when our leader knew that he would become general secretary, he told his sister, who is head of the family, to sell anything that could cause trouble. She sold nine real estate ventures in Hong Kong, which were worth $260 million. Very quietly, very carefully."

"But you learned of it."

"Yes, I did. One of the Ministry's assets was the family butler, who knew all the secrets. I obtained the details from him. I have the files in a safe place. I have never used them. I hope that I never have the need."

Carlos Wang nodded. His boss had just taken out an insurance policy, but it was late in the day to do so. A more ruthless man, or one less devoted to his party and nation, would have played that card long ago.

"I think I understand everything you say, minister. The words, and the spaces in between the words."

"Good. I am making a bet that you are a trustworthy man. I hope that I am right." Carlos touched his heart in affirmation, as one of his Cuban heroes would have done.

"I have another secret I want to share with you. It's the reason I needed to talk with you."

"What is it, minister? If I can help, I will."

"I received a message yesterday from *Rukou*. Our agent in America. I had heard from her recently, but this was different. The woman says that she wants to leave America, immediately. They have discovered her identity. They are about to arrest her."

"I believe you said 'the woman,' minister. This is the first moment I have realized that *Rukou* was not a man. You live inside surprises."

"How soon can you get her out?"

"We have planned for such an 'exfiltration' operation. That is what the Americans call it. It will take me a week to arrange, maybe less."

"We don't have that long. She said it was very urgent. She asked to meet me overseas, so that we can take her 'in from the cold' outside America."

"That is possible. We can create documentation quickly."

"Carlos, listen to me now. She said one more thing. That was the most remarkable part of her message."

"I am listening, minister."

"*Rukou* said that the young CIA case officer you met in Mexico, Harris Chang who calls himself Peter Tong, was ready to defect. He has come under deep suspicion in America, as we had hoped, and now he wants to come over. To the motherland. And I must ask you: Do you believe that?"

Carlos Wang didn't answer for a long while. He walked slowly, hearing the grass crackle under his feet, watching his breath turn into a fog of tiny crystals. He did not want to get this answer wrong. His work was his art. His hero Leon Trotsky had written once that art wasn't a mirror to reflect life, it was a hammer to pound life into a different shape. Carlos Wang felt that way about espionage. It was an art, and a hammer. He exhaled one last cloud of crystallized breath, and then spoke.

"Yes, it is possible. This Chang was shaken by our meeting. I know how to read people, and I can tell you: He was changed. Whether he is sincere in his profession of loyalty and his desire to escape, I cannot say. But I know that he was altered by our encounter. And if he has taken the next step, and the next, well, he would not be the first."

"The CIA officer Chang offers something as a proof of his good faith. *Bona fides.* He says that the CIA has collected secrets about our ministry's enemies, which can help us survive. What do you think of that?"

Wang paused again before responding, weighing this information against what he knew about recruitment of foreign agents.

"Yes, that is logical, to make such an offer. That is what I would do, if I wanted to defect. The agent must have a prize that is too tantalizing to resist."

"But doesn't that worry you, *Xiao* Wang, when the package is so perfectly wrapped? Doesn't that make you suspicious?"

"Yes, minister, of course. We should always beware of provocation. If something seems too good to be true, then it is often false. But this information comes to you from *Rukou*, a source that you trust. Would she deceive you? That is the question you must resolve. If you trust your agent, then it follows that you trust what she brings with her."

Li lowered his angular body toward Carlos Wang. His face was creased with age and worry. He believed in his ministry the way he believed in China, but he was running out of time. He had needed a miracle, and now, perhaps, one was at hand. Should he accept it?

"*Rukou* wants to meet me in the next few days. She says that she can travel with Harris Chang to any city that I name, using false identities that they both have prepared, but I must go to meet them immediately. Otherwise, we will lose Chang. I am trying to decide how to answer this request. I have only a few hours."

"What is possible, minister? Do you have any foreign travel that would disguise this meeting?"

"A liaison trip was scheduled for this month. The plan was to go to Amsterdam and then to Brussels and London, then back home. Visit our stations. Talk with foreign services. My wife wanted me to buy presents for the holidays. The usual business. With all the commotion, I had thought I would cancel the trip. But maybe I could go. What do you think?"

"Yes, you could go. I can cover for you here. If there are any questions, I can deflect them. In that, I am adept."

"What city would be best for the meeting? Where would we have the best advantage, in terms of tradecraft?"

Carlos Wang pondered this request. He didn't know all the MSS stations in Europe, but he knew many of them.

"Amsterdam, I think. We are strong there, and our adversaries are not so strong."

"That's what I thought, too. Amsterdam. I could go there, and if the meeting goes well, I could abort the rest of the trip. I could fly directly to Moscow with our two assets and then safely back to China. I would not be very long in airspace that is not friendly."

"This operation could save you, minister. It would be a great prize and a triumph. Even your enemies would have to concede your success. It would be harder to destroy our ministry, if you achieved this victory. Your friends would sing late into the night in the Punjo Hotel."

"Stop the flattery, *Xiao* Wang. It makes me mistrust you. And are you sure this is your advice, and that you will protect it? I am putting my life in your hands, truly, and the future of this thing that we have tried to build."

"I cannot be certain that this is the correct course, minister. We never have such knowledge. But I can say: This is the course of action that I would take."

"And you will keep this secret?"

"I have no other loyalty but to you, and China."

They shook hands. Li Zian turned off the scratchy sound of the tape recorder and walked into the Ministry. His aides greeted him anxiously. His chief of staff giggled nervously. Li told him to confirm the travel plans for this month that had been made provisionally and to move up his departure for the next day.

Li went upstairs to his office and entered the shower stall of his private bathroom, where he composed and encrypted the personal message to his agent, *Rukou,* telling her when and where they would meet.

36.

LANGLEY, VIRGINIA

Denise Ford had a gold bracelet that her father had given her, the year she came back from Paris. He knew what she did for a living; it was a source of pride for him that his daughter was part of the secret world. When she put the bracelet on her wrist, it was as if her father were holding her hand. He had told her before he died that she was part of a "great chain of being," a Hoffman family tradition of independent, strong-minded public service. If he were still alive, would he understand that she was doing the right thing? Would he see that when her idealism had been blocked in one direction, she had found another? Would he forgive her for what she was about to do?

What would her Uncle Cyril say to her now? He had died of a heart attack two years before, after having been fired from a senior position in another intelligence agency. Cyril had at first been inconsolable, but Denise had cooked for him, read to him, shared gossip. She spent weekends at his big house in Great Falls, walking in his fields and gardens, listening to him sing arias from Philip Glass across his tomato plants. He had warned his niece, more than once, to quit the intelligence business. He said it was like a company in liquidation. She had nodded, but said no more.

Ford's bracelet clinked against her dressing table with that bright, hollow sound of pure gold. She arched her neck proudly as she looked at her face in the mirror. She clasped the bracelet to her chest and headed out the door.

Ford steered her Lexus up the George Washington Parkway toward her late Uncle Cyril's house in Great Falls, which was now occupied by a cousin. From a locked shed, she retrieved her transmission device. She signed on using a password generator that she had hidden in the fence behind the shed and prepared a message that could be sent to the person she described to herself as her "special friend" in Beijing. She pointed the communications north-northeast, to a precise compass heading, and sent a short-burst transmission to a well-hidden relay device a few miles away, which sent it on to a Chinese satellite in geosynchronous orbit.

It's done, she told herself. I'm gone.

John Vandel followed Ford's movements from the operations room in the basement at Langley. The surveillance was invisible but seamless. He knew the FBI would have wanted to arrest Ford the moment she sent her message, if they'd had the chance. But Vandel had talked to Miguel Votaw, the FBI deputy director. He agreed that Vandel's plan for a sting abroad trumped law enforcement.

The NSA was able to capture the encrypted signal, but a few hours later, a liaison officer reported to Vandel that the Chinese cipher was unbreakable, at least in practical terms. A brute force attack could take months or even years, given existing computing capabilities. A quantum computer could break such an encryption scheme someday, in theory, but not now.

Vandel was tired of hearing that "someday" refrain, but he could guess what Denise Ford had transmitted: She had told Beijing that she was coming out and that she was bringing a defector with her. What he badly needed wasn't the outgoing transmission but the return message from Beijing that would specify details about Ford's meeting point abroad. Knowing the city and day wasn't enough: He wouldn't have operational control if he couldn't arrive first at the rendezvous point chosen by his adversary. Vandel might be a gambler, but he was also a card counter.

Vandel was working out in his basement that night when an idea fell into his head. He recalled the man's round, earnest face. The name didn't come to him at first, but then he remembered it: Jason Schmidt, the man who claimed to have captured the quantum holy grail. Other computer scientists doubted him, but he had insisted to Kate Sturm and his other intelligence community handlers that his super-cold computing architecture could solve problems that were beyond any other existing machine.

Vandel dismounted his treadmill and walked to his secure phone. If not now, when? The chief executive of QED was busy in the lab and couldn't be located at first, but eventually he was summoned. He started off by apologizing, assuming that he had done something else wrong, but Vandel cut him off.

"I need help decrypting something, Mr. Schmidt," he said.

"Ask the NSA," responded the scientist. "That's not our department, yet. We're still in beta."

"NSA says it's impossible. They say the only way to factor an encryption string this long is with a quantum computer, which doesn't exist. But then I thought, wait a minute: I know somebody who says he has already built a quantum computer. So I was thinking, maybe you could try your baby on my decryption problem."

"Technically, it's not a quantum computer, Mr. Green. As I have told you and many, many of your colleagues, it's a quantum annealing machine. It solves optimization problems; it finds minimum values. It recognizes patterns. It's not Nirvana."

"Listen, I don't care about the technical shit. I just want to know if you could run an encrypted message into your machine and, I don't know, optimize it. So that I could read it. Or part of it. The message will be transmitted soon. I need this really fast. I'm in a jam. What about it? Can you do it?"

There was a long pause on the line, as the computer scientist turned the problem over in his head.

"How long will the message be?"

"Short, maybe five hundred characters. But it will be seriously encrypted. My guys said forget it. What do you think?"

"There's always a correct answer and a real answer. The correct answer is no, it's impossible. The real answer is maybe. If I can find a way to set it up as an optimization problem, so that it would collapse to a minimum value that was the answer, then it would work. Maybe."

"I'll take the real answer. Make it happen, Mr. Schmidt. Please. I'll have someone send you the encrypted message as soon as we get it. Give it a shot. That's all I ask."

That night, as Vandel was dozing off, he was awakened by the ODNI watch officer. He reported that at 10:30 a.m. Beijing time, one of the National Reconnaissance Office's low-orbit satellites over the Chinese capital had captured images of two men walking outside the Ministry of State Security compound.

The analysts believed that one of them was the principal target of their surveillance, Minister Li Zian; the other appeared to be Wang Ji, the chief of the American Operations Division of the Ministry. Beijing station had attempted to intercept their conversation in the garden, using close-in collection systems that were already in place. This effort had been unsuccessful, because of counter-surveillance efforts by one of the men, who appeared to be carrying a sound generator to cover his voice.

Vandel asked the watch officer if they had any other means of close surveillance. The Beijing station chief came back fifteen minutes later and apologized that they had no real-time access to Li's offices.

Vandel waited through the night for Minister Li to upload his message to a Chinese satellite for transmission to his agent on the ground in Washington. The transmission came just after 1:00 a.m. It was hidden in a stream of random signals, but the NSA analysts were able to detect the familiar addressing protocol, even though they couldn't decrypt the message itself.

Vandel ordered the watch officer to send these new signals to someone he described as a contractor with an experimental decryption technique. When the watch officer questioned sharing such sensitive information with green badgers, Vandel overruled him. "They're all I've got," he said, hanging up the phone.

Harris Chang awoke repeatedly through the night. He hadn't had an unbroken eight hours in several weeks. His father always teased him when he was a boy that he was addicted to sleep. The other youngsters in Flagstaff might smoke dope or drink too much beer, but Harris's secret vice was that he liked to sleep as long and as often as he could.

"You are *moyunga!* A lazy boy!" his father had said to him more than once, trying to get him up for church on a Sunday. When they got to church, he would often doze off again.

But now, when he waited for rest and release, it didn't come.

Why was Harris Chang anxious? It wasn't really that he was afraid of Vandel or the FBI investigators who had been following him, listening to his phone calls, reading a lifetime of his messages. The investigation was an insult, but he knew it would go away, and even if it persisted, he didn't care: A good lawyer would untangle this mess in court if necessary. No jury would convict him of espionage, whatever Vandel might threaten.

And it wasn't fear about the operation that lay ahead, either. The danger of kidnapping was real; so was the danger of a botched meeting that would end in gunfire. His friend Mark Flanagan had already been murdered, and a bad death, too, wracked by fever, his organs failing one by one.

But physical anxiety wasn't keeping Chang awake. As an Army officer in Iraq, he had thought more than once that he wouldn't survive a firefight or a suicide bomb attack. He had discovered that when it came to physical fear, his circuits went cold instead of hot as real danger approached. He believed in himself and his mission and, to the extent that anyone can be prepared to die, he was unafraid.

What had destroyed Harris Chang's tranquility was something else. He had lost faith. Serving his country had been his only dream growing up. West Point had been a kind of liberation, giving him an identity that wasn't racial or cultural. His service truly had been perfect freedom, as a chaplain had said to him one long night at a forward operating base. This identity had been shattered, and it couldn't be reassembled simply by Vandel's promise of rehabilitation.

The reason it had been so easy to voice the defector's script with Denise Ford was that it expressed what Chang had begun to believe. He *had* been betrayed. He didn't trust Vandel or the agency. He had fallen out of love.

———

Toward noon, as an early snow dusted Washington, Denise Ford posted a note on the CIA employees' classified "swap-mart," advertising to sell her 2014 Lexus Hybrid SUV. She said that she had purchased the vehicle in Amsterdam, and that it had just two thousand miles on the odometer.

Kate Sturm saw the message just after it was posted. She called Vandel, who was asleep on a couch in his office.

"They're meeting in Amsterdam," she said. "The day after tomorrow. What do you want me to do? Should I contact Support in Amsterdam Base?"

"God no," said Vandel. "Don't tell them anything. The Director would have a fit. Just get me on a black G-5 overnight tonight. You're coming, too."

"No way," said Sturm. "I have stuff to do here. Why bring me?"

"Because you know how to shoot a gun. Just get us on a plane, together, tonight."

Vandel called Harris Chang, who had just seen the swap-mart message himself and was already collecting his alias identity documentation.

"You're on," said Vandel. "She just posted."

"I saw it. I'm booking a KLM flight tonight from Dulles, in alias. Do we know where the meeting place is in Amsterdam?"

"I'm working on it," said Vandel.

"You mean we don't know yet?" asked Chang. The question hung in the air a moment.

"Working on it," repeated Vandel.

"Shit," muttered Chang. "Well, when she tells me where, I'll message you. If she tells me."

Chang knew that by the time Ford informed him where their clandestine defection would take place, it might be too late to make preparations. They would go to the meeting with Li blind, without operational control. What would happen then? That was unscripted. Maybe Chang would wake up in Beijing, or not wake up ever again.

"Keep cool," said Vandel. "We'll break that message."

"Un-huh."

"And listen, Harris, one thing to remember about Amsterdam. If you get stoned, don't fall into the canal."

Despite himself, Chang laughed. CIA officers never really had to grow up. Before he could respond, the line went dead. Chang removed his alias passport and credit card from the safe and booked the 5:50 flight for the Netherlands.

The analysts monitoring signals from Beijing confirmed that the Minister of State Security was readying his personal plane for overseas travel. A flight plan had been filed listing Schiphol Airport near Amsterdam as the initial destination, followed by Zaventem Airport in Brussels and Gatwick Airport south of London.

Minister Li's limousine had been tracked traveling to the headquarters of the Central Military Commission and back to the Ministry. Perhaps Li's enemies were surprised and happy to see him leave the country when his ministry was in such danger. Li was playing for table stakes, too.

Vandel called Jason Schmidt in Seattle to see if he had made any progress with the cipher. Vandel apologized for the pressure but said he needed the quickest possible decryption of the time-sensitive message Schmidt had been given. If it couldn't be broken in twelve to twenty-four hours, its value would disappear.

"Get off my back, please, Mr. Green," said the exasperated computer scientist. "Pressure from you is making this work more difficult. It's a technical problem, and it has a technical solution. But this isn't a classic computer. I can't just encode an algorithm. I have to tune the qubits so they'll yield the least-energy solution to my problem. It's like composing a piece of music. You can't make it better by trying harder. The way to set this up may come to me, but not if I keep having to answer the phone from Washington."

Vandel apologized. He couldn't help himself. He told Schmidt to take the time he needed.

"I'm asking the impossible," he said, knowing that this would be another incentive.

Schmidt tinkered at his whiteboard, writing formulas and then wiping them off as new programming steps occurred to him. Factoring a number could be an annealing problem, couldn't it? It was a set of unique, minimum values. His machine just had to tunnel through the landscape of numbers and let the solution reveal itself. Schmidt poured himself a Diet Coke, then a coffee, then a Red Bull. He played Rodgers and Hammerstein on his Sonos system, as he scribbled equations and notes and ran off to tune his machine.

Late into the night, he found himself thinking about the pictographs people used to illustrate the paradox of quantum computing. Things can be in two places at once. The coin is both heads and tails. The cat is alive and dead. A bit is zero and one. It's only the act of observing these phenomena that collapses their ambiguous state. Schmidt had spent his career behaving as if he understood this imponderable nature of matter, but did he? He wrote on his whiteboard in big, block letters the famous dictum of physicist Richard Feynman: "If you think you understand quantum mechanics, you don't understand quantum mechanics."

Schmidt fell asleep at his desk. As he dozed, his mind charted equations and code on the border of consciousness. "I am awake and asleep," he said to himself in the dream. Numbers formed in his head, the digits spinning like the rotor wheels on a code machine. They stopped at a particular value.

Schmidt bolted upright. He walked quickly to the whiteboard and began scribbling notations he had half-seen in his dream state. He looked for the puzzle pieces that had straight edges, which formed the borders of his problem. He looked for ways to tease out repetitions that might exist in the plaintext message before it was encrypted.

He simulated. His annealing machine might not be a quantum computer, but at very low temperatures, when electrons spin both ways at once, it was capable of quantum effects. He spooled up the logic threads and then unspooled them as instructions to his qubits and couplers. When the sun came up over Lake Washington, Schmidt thought that maybe he had begun to make a little progress.

———

A clean Gulfstream G-5 was ready at the Signature Air terminal at Dulles. It had been rented by a CIA proprietary from a time-share company. The tail numbers had never been used operationally. The crew wanted to file the flight plan. The pilot had just called the office of the proprietary in Rockville to ask for the names and passport numbers of the passengers.

Kate Sturm called the proprietary back and gave the supervising officer the alias that Vandel would be using on the passenger manifest and her own. She had decided that Vandel was right: He needed backup, and it was true that very few people at the CIA could shoot as well as she could.

Vandel had one last task before he left for the airport. He asked the ODNI watch officer at Liberty Crossing to request from the Defense Intelligence Agency's military attaché in the Netherlands the name and contact details of the most senior Chinese PLA officer in Amsterdam. Vandel asked that this information be prepared in a restricted-handling channel and waiting for him when he arrived at Schiphol the next morning.

Vandel composed in his mind the message he would send to General Wu Huning's operative, the representative in Holland of the PLA's Second Department. He was confident that it would be believed: The PLA and the CIA shared a common enemy.

Denise Ford carefully composed a note on her personal stationery. The thick sheets of paper were the color of clotted cream. She put the note in an envelope and addressed it to her former French teacher at Yale, and she mailed it at the corner box before she left for the airport. The Office of Security cleaned the box later that afternoon when they secured her town house. They put the letter in a plastic envelope and sealed it for later. The letter read:

"My dear Marie-Laure: This is a sort of farewell, I think. I am not a traitor, whatever the U.S. government may claim. I despise people like Aldrich Ames and Robert Hansen. They betrayed their country. Worse than that, they were vulgar. They sold secrets for money. They were an inversion of the Cold War; their secrets were putrescent. I am not an agent of a foreign power. I have never taken a penny from anyone. I serve the cause of one world and the free and open exchange of information. I hope you will be proud of me, always. Denise."

37.

AMSTERDAM

Harris Chang checked into the Amsterdam Hilton the next morning. It was a cool, clear December day that softened the old city's color in the low winter light. The purple waters of the canal behind the hotel were dappled by sparkling traces of the sun. Chang checked into his room and then descended to the lobby to wait for Denise Ford. She hadn't been on his flight, but there were other ways to reach Amsterdam overnight. He asked the front desk to call the room of Audrey Fingerhut. The clerk said there was a reservation in that name but that she hadn't checked in yet. Chang left a message to inform Miss Fingerhut when she arrived that Mr. Tong was in the hotel restaurant.

Chang found a table overlooking the canal and had a late breakfast. Small boats were berthed just beyond the grass of the hotel garden; they bobbed gently at their moorings, disturbed occasionally by the wake of a barge that moved along the Noorder Amstel. Chang looked at his watch every few minutes, and he ventured into the lobby several times. He thought about going upstairs to bed, but he knew he wouldn't sleep. The waiter brought a copy of the *International New York Times*. Chang ordered more coffee and scanned the newspaper. The lead story was about the widening political purge in China.

Chang was still seated at his table when, just after noon, Denise Ford entered the restaurant. She wore a blonde wig under a gray hat and a big pair of sunglasses. Heads turned. Even on the run, she maintained the tailoring and demeanor of a well-turned woman. The waiter tried to seat her at a table near the water, but she shook her head and walked toward Chang.

"Fancy meeting you here," she said. She removed her sunglasses. Despite the long trip, she looked remarkably fresh. Her skin had a faint blush.

"Hi Audrey," responded Chang. "How was your flight?"

"Long, but pleasant enough. I came via Copenhagen. The man in the next seat tried to talk to me, but I pretended I didn't speak English."

"How's your Chinese? Mine isn't very good, but I'm ready to learn. I just hope your friend will be here. We need to work out the details. They're going to realize soon that we're missing back home. We can't make any mistakes."

"Shhh!" She put her finger to her lips. A man at the next table was paying his bill. She wanted him gone before they talked anymore.

"Did you know that Amsterdam has more canals and bridges than Venice?" she asked blandly. "Yes. And do you know what the local people call this city? They call it 'Mokum.' The taxi driver explained it on the way in from the airport. Mokum. What an ugly name for such a pretty place."

The man at the nearby table had signed his check and left. Ford patted Chang's hand.

"I'm glad we both made it," she said. "I thought you'd be here, but I wasn't certain. Impressions are sometimes wrong. You look a bit tired. Are you okay?"

"I'm concerned, to be honest. I am about to walk over a line that I can't cross back. I want to be sure that your friend Mr. Li will be on the other side to greet me."

"Oh yes! He'll be here. He said he would be, and he's not a man who breaks his promises. Ever."

"Where are we going to meet? Do you know?"

She put her finger to her lips again.

"That's my secret. Personal protection. I trust you, of course. But a girl learns never to tell a man everything. I'll explain tomorrow morning on the way to the meeting. That's safer, I think."

Chang tried not to show anxiety. But this was the first piece of the plan that was going wrong.

"I don't know," he said warily. "I hate to go blind. Part of my Army training. Always do the recon."

"I understand, but it's just not possible. Relax. Curiosity killed the cat."

"I'm in your hands, Audrey, literally."

"No. Figuratively you're in my hands. Not literally, although I'm willing to consider a proposal."

She looked at her watch and then yawned.

"Gracious. I'm tired all of a sudden. I think it's time for a snooze. Soon we'll be on Beijing time. Can you believe it? Very exciting, really. A new world dawns."

She rose from her chair. "I'll call you if I wake up for dinner, but I think I'll stay in bed. Did you know that this hotel is where John and Yoko had their 'love-in' for peace, in bed? Historic."

She waved good-bye.

"What about tomorrow?" pressed Chang, still hungry for information he could pass to Vandel.

"Knock on my door at 8:00. Room 512. We'll go from there. Sleep tight."

Ford strolled off, dropping a five-euro note in the waiter's hand on her way out.

John Vandel traveled through the night in his Gulfstream jet. The flight attendant made up the bed in the aft cabin. Vandel offered it to Kate Sturm, but she said she had some paperwork to finish. He slept nearly the whole way.

When they landed at Schiphol, a car was waiting just outside the general-aviation terminal with a chase car behind. The military attaché's office had dispatched the vehicles, as Vandel had requested, along with a team of four U.S. Army warrant officers who worked out of the Amsterdam consulate on counter-terrorism support missions. The Director had ordered Vandel to stay away from CIA channels. He didn't want any paperwork that he would have to brief the intelligence committees about.

Vandel and Sturm stayed in a small hotel by the Amstel, just south of the old city and its concentric bands of canals. The lobby was dense with pimply tourists from Britain who had come for the legal dope and the sex shops. Many of them sported tattoos and piercings. They looked at Vandel and Sturm in their dark suits as if they were creatures from outer space.

Vandel waited until 6:00 p.m. that afternoon to call Seattle. It took an exercise of will, pacing in his small room above an Amsterdam alleyway. He didn't want to disturb yet again the contractor to whom he had assigned the decryption problem, but he was running out of time. By the next morning it would be too late. The Special Operations Forces officers were already asking where they should deploy. Vandel told them to be patient about the details, but that wasn't a military virtue.

When Vandel finally placed his call to Jason Schmidt, it was 9:00 a.m. Seattle time. Schmidt had been in his lab all night, working on the computations. His voice was shaky from exhaustion, disappointment, elation: Vandel couldn't tell. Maybe all three.

"So where are we?" asked Vandel. "Have you decrypted any of it? I need to know. If it didn't work, just tell me."

"Well, I can't say yes or no, exactly. I don't know." He sounded exhausted, otherworldly.

"That's a quantum answer, for Christ's sake! Give me a zero or a one."

Schmidt sniffled, then he choked back a sob. "I'm so close," he said. He was convulsed for a moment.

"Bear up, man. Did you get anything I can use? Anything at all?"

"Not yet. Please. I'm trying to make bits of niobium play a symphony. This is almost a quantum computer, but the encryption string is just too long. I can factor a five-digit number, maybe a ten-digit number. But this is too much." He sniffled again.

"Get some sleep, Mr. Schmidt. It's not your fault. You tried. We'll cope."

"I still believe, you see." Schmidt's voice was soft, apologetic, but still affirming the wonder of what he had built. "My machine can do so many quantum things. We can find optimal solutions. We can recognize patterns. There are so many ways we can help. We just can't do this."

Vandel summoned Sturm to his little room overlooking the alley. He looked exhausted, suddenly. Too much stress, too many bets, too little to show. His scarred face was sallow and his eyes were sunken.

"We're fucked," he muttered. "Our quantum guy can't break the Chinese code. Without that, we can't ID the meeting place. They hold the high cards. We're sending Harris in blind. He's screwed."

Vandel shook his head. He looked like a defeated man.

"Maybe we should abort," his voice cracked slightly as he said the words.

"What are you talking about?" Sturm took his limp arm and shook it.

"We could bail. Maybe that's the right call. We know where Chang and Ford are. We could go to the Hilton and grab them, put them on our plane, and fly them home. Sort it out when we get back. That's the safest thing to do."

"Stop it, John," said Sturm sharply. "This isn't like you. This is a puzzle. You have to solve it. You're too exposed now to retreat. Suck it up."

Vandel straightened. Nobody talked to him like that. He raised his hand, as if he might slap her, and then let it fall to his side. As he glared at Sturm, his pewter eyes began to glow again as his brain processed the problem. She was right. The buzzer was ticking down. He had to take the shot.

"Think, dammit." He put his hands to his head and closed his eyes. Sturm waited while he rubbed his temple and the synapses fired.

"Okay," he continued, his eyes still closed. "If someone chooses a city for a rush meeting, the chances are that he's been there before. Right? And so has the other person. It's a place that's special, where they both know the meeting point, and there's no chance of getting lost. That's what you would do, isn't it? You'd go back to someplace you know."

"That sounds right," said Sturm with a trace of a smile. "That's how I would set it up."

"Of course, you would! That's the only way. You'd go someplace in that city where you've both been before." He looked at her and then roared again: "That's it! That's what our targets would do."

"What?" asked Sturm. "I don't get it." But he was already in motion.

Vandel walked back to his desk and grabbed the communications device he had used before to call Jason Schmidt. He punched in the Seattle number again.

"I'm so sorry," began Schmidt, his voice shaky, when he answered. He was still floating in a pool of regret.

"Forget about that," said Vandel. "Pull yourself together. I have a new question for you, and this one could be a lifesaver."

"Okay, sir." Schmidt roused himself. "I'll try."

"So, listen, you told me a few minutes ago that your machine can do pattern recognition. I assume that means facial patterns. So how fast? It would take a couple of days for the NSA's best computers to match faces from a big database. That's way too long. Can you do it faster with your machine? I mean, like, are you *sure* that you could do it faster?"

Schmidt laughed. He was relieved. This was a problem he had already solved.

"My goodness, yes! Much, much faster. Pattern recognition is just optimization. It's in our sweet spot. The last test we ran with some of your people we solved a pattern-recognition optimization problem one hundred million times faster than a single-core classical computer did. Is that fast enough?"

"Sweet Jesus," said Vandel. "Brother Schmidt, I think you just found your Killer Application."

"Really?" The computer scientist, who had been in tears only a few minutes before, was still wary of flunking another test.

"Here's what you're going to do," said Vandel slowly. "Some people from the intelligence community are going to call you in a few minutes. They will help you connect to a very large database of facial pictures taken by surveillance cameras in a city in Europe over the last five years. When I say large, I mean billions of faces. Then they're going to send you two particular faces we're searching for. Understood? Then you get your quantum machine thing to identify, fast, where those two faces have been seen together in this city. Can you do that? Fast?"

"I think so. We've done it before. We have the basic tuning set for recognizing facial patterns. What's the city?"

"Amsterdam."

"Oh, I love that city. So pretty," said Schmidt, enthusing now. Vandel cut him off.

"We need to move. This is super urgent. People will be in touch with you to set up the data links right away."

"Yes, sir. I'm here. I'm ready. My techs can get started as soon as you get the data to us."

"That a boy," said Vandel. He rang off.

Vandel called the director of national intelligence himself to make the pitch. It didn't take long: They had served together in Iraq. The DNI instructed NSA to break its normal rules and gather a comprehensive Amsterdam facial-recognition database immediately, some data shared openly by the Dutch government and other data obtained by different, covert means. The NSA was told, further, to share this ocean of data immediately with the little Seattle company and its "beta" quantum computer.

Vandel turned back to Kate Sturm when he had finished the phone call to the DNI's office at Liberty Crossing. The wave of exhilaration and action had passed through his body, but now he was shaking his head.

"I don't know," he said. "We have, what, twelve hours? Maybe Schmidt will be a hero and maybe not. But we need some kind of backup. Do we have enough people to follow Ford and Chang when they head out to the meet?"

"Not on the ground. We don't have enough people, even if we borrow more SOF. We could try overhead monitoring. We wouldn't know where Ford and Chang were going until they got there. But that would be better than nothing."

"Okay, then that's our alternative tomorrow morning. We'll use the SOF team we've got, steal some more from DOD, and get some birds overhead. We'll track them to the location, wherever it is."

"And then what?" asked Sturm, looking into the bloodshot eyes of her boss.

"When the meeting goes down, we grab the Chinese minister and tell him it's over. We own him. He'll come with us. He's a dead man if he doesn't."

"If he's smart, he'll say yes," answered Sturm. "He's in a jam. With the right pitch, maybe he'll come over. What if he says no?"

"He'll say yes. Definitely. His world is falling apart back home. We can save him."

"One question: How are we going to move our Support team around town following these guys without it looking like a Blackwater reunion?"

Vandel pondered the problem for a moment. His answer, inevitably, was deception.

"Get some Dutch police uniforms for our SOF guys. As many as you can. And some vehicles that look like Amsterdam cop cars. Can you do that overnight?"

"Probably. But is this a good idea, John? The flap potential is huge. The Dutch won't be amused. They like us, but they take their sovereignty seriously."

"They'll never know, if we do it right. Chop-chop. We have a lot to do in the next twelve hours."

Vandel walked her to the door, gave her a pat on the back, and put an arm around her broad shoulder. The other arm he held aloft in a fist.

38.

AMSTERDAM

The sun rose the next morning a bright Dutch orange. The canals came to life with a rolling ripple of sunlight that illuminated the ribbons of water in the old city, one after another. John Vandel and Kate Sturm had been up all night in preparation. Vandel popped pills through the night to stay awake. Sturm caught him gobbling another tablet just before dawn and wagged her finger, but Vandel gave her a thumbs-up.

"Better living through chemistry."

The SOF detail in Amsterdam had months ago established a safe house near the old city, just below Willemspark. Vandel had turned that into a temporary command post overnight. His friends at the Defense Intelligence Agency had cobbled together a secure downlink for satellite reconnaissance, and thanks to more emergency tasking from Liberty Crossing, continuous low-orbit reconnaissance had been arranged starting at dawn. A dozen Dutch police uniforms had been found, along with three vehicles and, Vandel was assured, a Dutch speaker.

Harris Chang woke early. He had lain awake rehearsing his "defection" speech for the meeting with the Chinese intelligence minister. He retrieved from his room safe the manila envelope, with Vandel's special "gift" for Minister Li. That was his only weapon. He felt entirely alone, a sensation that on this morning was oddly reassuring. He might not be able to trust anyone else, but he trusted himself.

Denise Ford, true to her word, had slept through dinner and then taken a long walk along the canals at midnight. She strolled past the windows of the red-light district, observing the women in their garter belts and black-widow bustiers. Several of the women beckoned for her to come inside, but she kept walking. A drunk stopped her on the sidewalk, taking her for a hooker. She pushed him away so forcefully that he fell over.

Chang knocked on Ford's door at 8:00 a.m. She was wearing her blonde wig and a trench coat. She had packed her roller bag. She was smiling serenely, very like a person who was about to escape from one life to another.

"*Zaoshang hao*," she said brightly.

"And good morning to you, too," answered Chang. He wore a blazer and gray slacks, with a blue-striped shirt and red silk tie, perhaps dressed for a job interview.

"You're not packed!" she said.

"My suitcase is back in the room. I'll get it in a minute. I need to know where we're going. It makes me nervous not to know. We could get ambushed."

Ford shook her head, pushing some stray blonde hair from her wig off her forehead.

"I'll tell you en route," she said. "Safer that way. Now go get your bag. And I hope you brought some warmer clothes. They say Beijing is freezing in the winter. Meet me downstairs in the lobby in five minutes. I'll order a taxi."

"You do know where we're going, right?"

"Of course, I do. I've been there before. It's all good! Now get your things."

Chang met her downstairs, towing his bag and wearing his overcoat. "All in," he told himself, for the hundredth time. He should have been more worried, but the calm he'd felt the night before had returned. The current now was inexorable. It was better to relax and follow than to resist.

Vandel kept calling the DNI watch officer as dawn approached, hoping that QED's not-quite-quantum computer had done its work. But each time, all he got was a crisp "negative, sir." Finally, he called Seattle just after dawn.

Exhaustion had pushed Schmidt's voice up a register. He squeaked out a greeting and something between a promise and an apology.

"I need you now, brother," said Vandel.

"I'm almost there," answered Schmidt. "We've never worked with so much data before. It took longer than I thought to tune the machine. This is like climbing Everest, but honestly, I can see the top. A little more time."

"We're almost at H-hour, my friend. Call your NSA control officer the minute you have something. I mean, that minute. Got it?"

Schmidt answered in the affirmative, but Vandel was gone. He needed to make final arrangements for the ground and aerial surveillance on which they would rely, precariously, if Schmidt's machine failed.

Ford told the doorman to call a taxi from the queue outside the hotel. She directed the driver to travel south a half-dozen blocks to a tramway station in Minerva Square, and then ordered a halt.

The broad plaza was filling with people heading to work on a Wednesday morning from their apartments in the massive red-brick residential buildings that framed the square. A queue was forming for the tram. Ford handed Chang a fare card; she'd had the time, and wit, to purchase two cards the day before.

Chang scanned the tram car for watchers, hoping that Vandel had found some way to follow them. There were a few police outside, but the cabin seemed stuffed with commuters. The morning car traffic was thick alongside the tracks. Chang felt himself slipping toward the falls.

A long-ago memory came to Chang as the tramway car rattled north. He was in Tikrit, in a Humvee on a bluff high above the Tigris River, leading a convoy back to his local headquarters. "Rover" was the name of his little task force. The insurgency that nobody would talk about was in full sway. An intelligence message had come in over the combat radio. A "VBIED," meaning a suicide car bomb, had been spotted by the surveillance cameras in a blimp overhead. The vehicle was about a half mile away and heading toward Chang's convoy, which was about that same distance from the T-walled protection of the U.S. encampment.

"What do we do, major?" radioed the sergeant from the vehicle behind.

"Keep going," Chang ordered, his voice even. "Rover gunners up. Keep it tight."

Chang felt the nodes of command in every part of his body. Move, anticipate, attack. The soldiers manning the fifty-caliber machine guns swiveled toward the approaching vehicle, which was throwing up a storm of dust.

He didn't feel nervousness or fear in that moment, but a heightened sense of alertness; all the other systems in his body slowed down; the nerves, the sweat glands, even the heartbeat. He focused his eyes and ears on the approaching threat. The VBIED, a late-model Hyundai, was moving faster than the Humvees and was gaining slightly on them.

"Rover 3, fire fifty-cal," ordered Chang. The last of the Humvees opened up, an arpeggio of fire. They were now about three hundred yards from the entrance to the compound. If they continued, they would probably reach safety, but they would draw the car bomb toward the compound, where many dozens of soldiers and contractors were manning security.

"Halt and spread," ordered Chang, his voice loud and firm, leached of fear. "Rover 1, Rover 2, Rover 3, I need the fifty-cal, now. Take him out."

The VBIED approached faster, into a monsoon of bullets. A first spray caught the car, then another, and then a shattering, convulsive hail. The Hyundai exploded in a red ball of fire that reached fifty feet in the air. Chang felt the percussive force of the blast in his vehicle.

When they were safely inside the perimeter, Chang walked over to thank the members of his unit. There were tears in the eyes of several of the men. Each of them said pretty much the same thing: Thank you, sir. Chang hugged one of the men who seemed especially upset and told him that everything would be fine.

"Where are we going?" Chang asked Ford. "I don't like a drop zone that we haven't cleared. I thought you were going to tell me on the way."

"We're heading north," she said smiling. "Northeast. Look at my compass. You're like the donkey in *Shrek*, do you know that? 'Are we there *yet*?' Goodness. Don't you trust me?"

Chang rode in silence. The tramway eventually reached the Central Station in the northeast tier of the city. Ford directed them to a Starbucks coffee shop in the station. She claimed that nobody would ever look for them in such an obviously American place, and the location would allow them to watch for surveillance. Chang ordered a double espresso.

"You're too thin, Harris! Order something that's bad for you."

Chang stuck with his coffee. Ford ordered a "flat white," which she drank with a spoon.

At ten minutes after 9:00, Ford finished off the last of her drink and announced that it was time to go. They took a taxi from the red-brick pile of the train station. They were heading south now, through the old city. They changed cabs once more, ditching the first and traversing a walkway under Dam Square and then catching the second on the other side.

The surveillance team found Ford, then lost her, and then found her again.

"Thank God for that blonde wig," said Vandel. "We couldn't track shit, otherwise. She knows how to do a surveillance detection run."

"She's good," murmured Sturm. "She always was."

Sturm sat next to Vandel in the back seat of a Volvo van that had been "borrowed" from the Royal Marechaussee, a paramilitary unit that assisted the Dutch police. The blue vehicle, emblazoned at the front with white and orange stripes, was one of three that had been obtained through the SOF group's Dutch "friends." The American officers wore the deep blue uniforms of the gendarmerie, crested with the signature emblem of a flaming grenade.

Sturm tracked the overhead surveillance on a laptop, which mirrored the display facing the two Americans in the front seats, who were dressed in the blue gendarmerie uniforms. The other two vehicles had similar feeds of the overhead surveillance. With Sturm coordinating their movements, they tried to stay close to Ford and Chang, lagging at some corners, passing them at others, always staying just far away enough to avoid detection.

"This is never going to work," muttered Vandel. "They will have locked down the site by the time we catch up."

Ford stopped the taxi on a street called Marnixstraat, at a bridge that crossed a small canal called the Leidsegracht. To the east, the narrow waterway was bordered by leafless trees. A small white skiff was cruising under the bridge of the next street down; to the west, the canal opened to a broader waterway called the Singelgracht. Ford paid the fare and told Chang to get out of the car.

"Let's walk the rest of the way," she said, putting her arm through his.

"Where are we?" he asked.

Ford put her finger to her lips and smiled.

"Almost there," she said.

They walked down the Marnixstraat, past small hotels and restaurants and a movie theater. Chang walked slowly, but she tugged at him when he lagged.

"Stage fright?" There was a spark of anticipation in her eyes. "Come on, little brother. No time for cold feet."

They continued walking along the sidewalk until they reached the intersection of a big street threaded by tramway tracks. The street sign said Leidseplein. Ford carefully scanned the intersection, waiting in the shadows, and then pulled Chang with her as she took a right on the big boulevard.

The secure phone rang in Vandel's Volvo. Sturm answered it and then quickly handed it to Vandel.

"We've got the coordinates, sir," said the ODNI watch officer. "They just came in from your contractor, twenty seconds ago. We're plugging them into your mobile grid as I read them out."

"Thank God! Let's have them, quick." Vandel turned to Sturm. "Get our teams to move as soon as they register the location."

"Okay, sir. The destination point is 52.364039 degrees North, 4.881894 degrees East. It's an old theater called the Stadsschouwburg in Leidse Square. That's where the target faces were recorded four years ago."

"Roger that." Vandel took the radio and spoke to his team.

"Showtime, everybody. Move carefully. They've got people in place already. When we have operational control inside this theater, we'll take him down."

Versions of "roger" came crackling back from two other radios. The Volvo surged forward toward the target address, which was already plugged into its navigation system.

Sturm adjusted the strap of her shoulder harness and checked her gun.

"Give me the phone again," said Vandel. "I have to do one more thing. You're going to think it's weird, but it's not the first time, right?"

Vandel placed a call to a number that had been sent to him by a DIA contact the morning before. It was the private cell phone number of the senior representative in the Netherlands of the Second Department of the People's Liberation Army.

The phone rang twice. A Chinese voice answered warily.

"Colonel Bo, listen to me carefully. I am a friend of General Wu Huning. He knows me as 'Alex.' You understand so far?"

"What?" returned the wary voice.

"Just listen. I'm 'Alex.' I want to inform General Wu's representative of something important that is about to happen in Amsterdam. The Minister of State Security of China, Mr. Li Zian, is about to meet with his American case officers from the CIA. I'll say that again: Minister Li Zian is meeting his American case officers. He is going to defect to the United States. It's probably too late for General Wu to stop it, but I thought he would like to know."

"Repeat this, please," said a nervous voice on the other end of the line. The PLA officer didn't want to get the message wrong, and he hadn't recorded it the first time. So Vandel restated the essence: The Minister of State Security was about to meet with American intelligence handlers in Amsterdam.

"I can give you the location," said Vandel. "Do you have people in Amsterdam?"

"Yes, yes," said the military attaché. "Amsterdam address, please."

"The Stadsschouwburg Theater. S-t-a-d-s-s-c-h-o-u-w-b-u-r-g. Leidse Square. They're inside. Don't come with guns, or you'll get shot. But you might want to see. Just to confirm the evidence."

Vandel ended the call and gave Sturm a wink.

"Why did you do that?" asked Sturm. "It's our operation. Why tip off the other side?"

"Insurance," said Vandel. "They're my backup."

Sturm shook her heard. "You're right. I don't get it. We need to go."

Denise Ford and Harris Chang approached a neo-Gothic edifice, red brick trimmed in white stone. The building was as grand and well braced as a nineteenth-century matron: Turrets capped the corners, framing three broad stone arches. A portico out front was supported by columns of alternating red and white stone, gaudy as a barber pole. A red banner above advertised the current performance in the theater inside.

Ford turned to her companion. Her smile was radiant.

"This is the place," she said. "Lots of memories for me. This theater is where I first encountered the gentleman you're about to meet."

Chang looked around him, casting a fleeting desperate eye for someone he could signal. But he saw no one.

A minute before, at the back side of the building, two Volvos had discharged what appeared to be members of the Royal Marechaussee who moved quickly into the squat red structure.

"I'm inside the theater, sir," said the leader of the SOF team. "Moving upstairs now."

"Slowly," advised Vandel. "Don't panic anyone. You're a friendly cop on a visit. There's no emergency."

Vandel's car arrived a moment later. He and Sturm sprang from the vehicle. The two walked quickly to the building, accompanied by a SOF colleague in deep blue.

The theater had its usual crowd of tourists. Some were hanging out in a coffee shop to the left of the entrance. A group of school children was making its way upstairs on a tour. "I don't like it," muttered Sturm. Vandel ignored her.

"Dirk," the leader of the SOF team who had been traveling in another van, met Vandel and Sturm just inside the door. Another tall, muscular man stood next to him. They both wore gendarmerie officers' uniforms. Strapped to their belts were semiautomatic pistols and Tasers. The jackets displayed the name of the service, *Koninklijke Marechaussee*, under a coat of arms that showed two lions grasping a sky-blue medallion.

"Our people have gone upstairs to the theater," said the SOF team leader. "They're in all four corners. There's a Chinese man sitting in a box overlooking the stage. He's waiting for someone."

"Does the Chinese man have security with him?"

"Four guys. Two in the hall and two outside the box where the man is sitting."

"Can you take them down?"

"I think so. With these uniforms, and surprise. The Tasers have a range of forty feet. We're well positioned. I think we can disarm them before they start shooting."

"You have anyone who speaks Dutch?"

"I brought a friend," said the American, smiling. "This is Willem. He got us the uniforms and cars. He's actually one of the officers of this outfit. We've helped him out on some missions in the past. He was nice enough to return the favor."

"Good man," said Vandel, shaking the Dutchman's hand. He put his finger to his lips. "Deaf and dumb," he said. The Dutch officer nodded.

Vandel gave Dirk a fraternal knock on the shoulder. Life was about improvisation. The scripted operations were the ones that usually went wrong.

"Here's the drill," said Vandel. "We don't move unless our American targets are with the Chinese man. We take down their security, first, in coordination. Then I enter his box and bring them out. No gunshots, please. That would seriously mess this up. After we get inside, have people close the doors and make sure no one gets in."

"Yes, sir," said Dirk and Willem together.

Willem took Vandel and Sturm up a flight of stairs, followed by a member of the SOF team in one of the purloined uniforms. The steps were marble; the gilded walls were decorated with frescos.

The sounds of children's voices echoed from the far end of the mezzanine hall.

"Shit," said Vandel as he watched the Dutch boys and girls, bundled in their winter coats, walking two by two toward him. He grabbed his deputy.

"Kate, get them out of there, now. Have Willem talk to them. I don't care what you tell them. Say it's closed for a special performance. Say the Pope is coming. I don't care. But get the little ones out of the theater before this thing goes down."

Sturm moved nimbly, despite her bulk, alongside the Dutch officer. They approached the teacher who was leading the group. The big Dutchman whispered gently in her ear. The teacher nodded. The file of children turned and headed back the way they came.

Vandel walked with his SOF escort toward the entrance door to the royal loge, at the far right end of the corridor. He repeated to himself the lines of the pitch he had been waiting so many months to deliver.

39.

AMSTERDAM

Denise Ford had arrived at the loge door several minutes before, holding Harris Chang's hand as if she were afraid he would flee at the last minute. Chang took a last look for some sign that Vandel and his team had tracked them to the theater, but he saw only tourists. His raft was about to go over the lip. What would he do if Vandel couldn't close in time? He didn't know. He patted his coat pocket to make sure the envelope was there.

The two Chinese security men outside the door recognized Ford and her colleague from photographs. One moved to open the loge door, but Ford took the ornate brass knob herself and gave it a twist. She remembered the feel, from years before.

The door swung open, revealing the austere, angular form of Li Zian, sitting in a plush red velvet chair, flanked by two other seats that were empty. Behind him was the intricately decorated proscenium arm and the rich blue velvet of the stage curtain, which was partially opened to reveal an opera set, half completed.

"*Rukou!*" said Li, smiling. He stood and bowed. "We meet again, where our story started."

The Chinese intelligence officer's voice was animated. She had come, and she had brought her trophy. The two Americans stepped down into the box. The theater appeared empty, except for two Chinese security men, one in the orchestra just below the stage, one across the way on the far side of the mezzanine.

"*Wo de baobei*," said Denise Ford, speaking a Chinese term of endearment carefully from memory. She took his hand, but before she could shake it, he gave her a tender kiss on each cheek.

"I want to introduce my colleague," she said. "*Our* colleague. He has come with me, as I told you he would. He's one of the agency's best. But they made him their enemy. Isn't that right, Harris? You explain."

Chang was about to speak, but Li took his hand. He held it, silently, for perhaps twenty seconds, looking Chang up and down.

"You called yourself Peter Tong, I believe," said the Chinese intelligence chief. "But we know you are Harris Chang. We know a great deal about you. Yes, we know your whole life, as my assistant Mr. Wang explained to you in Mexico. But do we know everything? I wonder. Before I accept this gift called Harris Chang, I must know what it is."

"I'm here because they gave me no other choice, Mr. Li. They have accused me of being a spy. I'm not a traitor."

"Of course not," said Li. "We know of your bravery for your country. We feel sorry for you. Truly. Come, sit down. Let us talk."

Li gestured to the other two velvet chairs. The three took their seats in a tight triangle. Li took Ford's hand and squeezed it, then turned to Chang.

"So tell me," Li said simply.

"I am an American, Mr. Li. I have been an officer of the Central Intelligence Agency. Before that, I served in the U.S. Army. But I began to see that to my American colleagues, my former colleagues, I will always be Chinese. That is the first thing they see. The color of my skin. I've known that for a long time. But I couldn't admit it to myself until I came back from Mexico and found the FBI waiting."

"Yes, yes," said Li, nodding in sympathy. "A sad story. America is a country where race matters. The more people say they are, what, color-blind, the more it is a lie. But I must ask you, Mr. Chang, how can I trust you? It is very nice that my old and valued friend, Miss Ford, *Rukou*, has brought you here. But how can I be sure that this is not a trick?"

Chang stole a quick glance to the door. Where was Vandel? They were reaching the point of no return. He let himself think, only for an instant, that maybe it was true. They didn't care about him. He closed his eyes, no more than a long blink, and leaned toward the Chinese intelligence chief.

"I have brought something for you, Minister Li," said Chang. He reached into his pocket for the envelope. "I told Miss Ford to tell you I would bring something that would convince you I am sincere and would help you fight your enemies in China. I have it, here. I think it will surprise even you."

Chang removed from the envelope several photographs taken by a CIA surveillance camera in a hotel room in Dubai. They showed John Vandel, head of the clandestine service of the CIA, meeting with General Wu Huning, director of the Second Department of the People's Liberation Army. Between the two men, on a coffee table in the Dubai hotel room, was a leather-bound notebook.

Chang handed over the photographs to Li Zian. The Chinese man studied the pictures, held them close to his eyes to look for evidence the images had been doctored. For a long moment, he said nothing.

"*Baozang*," he said finally, quietly. "This is a treasure."

"You know who these people are," said Chang. "But you don't know why they met. Mr. Vandel traveled secretly to Dubai to give your PLA enemies the *mijian*, the secret notebook, of Dr. Ma Yubo. He wanted to destroy you, because of *Rukou*. So he gave your greatest secrets to the person who could hurt you most. Now, you can fight back."

Li held the photographs in his hand. His fingers trembled ever so slightly, a sign of the rage inside, barely controlled. His rivalry with Wu and the others in the PLA was deep, but he had never imagined they were capable of treason. As Li's eyes smoldered, Chang glanced once more toward the door.

"I didn't know you had that," said Ford.

"I didn't tell you. I wanted to save it for Minister Li. I hope you trust me now, Mr. Minister."

Li nodded. His face was grimmer. He was thinking, perhaps, of how he would use his two defectors, and the photographic evidence, when he returned to Beijing. He turned to Chang. He tried to smile, but it didn't come.

"Trust is something that an intelligence officer does not give on the first meeting. But I accept you. That is a start. And I am prepared to take you with me and *Rukou* when we return to China. I think it is time to leave, soon. My plane is ready. It is very comfortable, even on a long flight."

Chang swallowed hard as he nodded. Where was Vandel? He wasn't coming. In that moment, sensing that he had been abandoned, Chang felt an emotion that was, oddly, something like release. When we are truly alone, we lose our dependence on anyone or anything.

Li took Chang's hand. His eyes softened. He took Denise Ford's palm in his other hand.

"Perhaps, Brother Chang, when we all reach China, you will feel that you are at home." He rose, and they followed him up the red-carpeted stairs toward the door of the little box. Their backs were turned, so they didn't see what was happening behind them.

The first sign of the assault was a loud noise on stage, as a prop crashed to the floor. The four Chinese security officers all turned toward the sound. In that moment, ten men in Dutch gendarmes' uniforms sprang from hiding places near the Chinese guards. With the deadly agility that comes from years of SOF training, aided by surprise and distraction, they moved to disarm their targets.

The Chinese guard in the orchestra pit went down first, disabled before he realized what was happening. The officer standing in the far mezzanine was toppled second. He had his gun in his hand and was preparing to shoot, but the SOF officer hidden behind him was quicker, firing a disabling burst from a Taser gun. He was enveloped by two blue-clad giants before he could shout a warning.

Li was emerging from the loge as Vandel's team took the guards on either side of the entrance. The SOF team was swift and devastating. The Chinese, under orders like the Americans to avoid gunfire if possible, were a moment too late. They were smothered on the floor under blue-uniformed men who subdued them quickly.

Li Zian stumbled back toward the loge door when the attackers pounced on his guards. He wasn't a fighter; he didn't try. He shot a quick glance toward Harris Chang, one of bitter disappointment.

Denise Ford, always so composed, looked at Chang with the rage of betrayal in her eyes. She began to scream, but she was quickly muffled. The only sound Li made was a moan of anguish.

John Vandel emerged from behind the bulk of his special operators. On his face was a look of mastery. "Take Minister Li downstairs, backstage," ordered Vandel. "We'll talk to him there."

The Chinese intelligence officer glanced at Vandel and then turned his eyes back toward Harris Chang. He gave him a scornful look, bordering on contempt, and quietly said the words, "*Ni zenme neng?*" He repeated the phrase in English, in case Chang had not understood: "How could you?"

As Li spoke, two SOF officers took his arms and bundled him down the mezzanine stairs to the orchestra and then up a ramp and through a door that led backstage. The Chinese guards that had accompanied the minister had been tranquilized and were being carried, one by one, by the members of the Dutch-uniformed team toward the waiting vans.

In an alcove backstage, surrounded by a cordon of men in blue uniforms, stood three people: John Vandel, Harris Chang, and Li Zian.

Denise Ford was already outside. Kate Sturm had removed her from the theater, on Vandel's orders, in gag and handcuffs, and placed her in another of the vans. Sturm had summoned the legal attaché from the consulate to begin a formal extradition process on charges contained in a sealed indictment that had been handed up in the federal district court in Alexandria, Virginia, the previous day.

Li was silent, glowering at the two men facing him. He maintained his dignity rather than pleading or screaming for help. But he was angry, in part at himself for having walked into this trap. The armed men in blue backed away, leaving the three principals alone.

"We don't have much time," said Vandel. "I want to make you an offer."

"I demand to see an officer of the Chinese consulate," said Li. "I am being detained against my will. This is an illegal action."

"I think you should listen to my offer, Mr. Minister. I think you'll see it's your best option, under the circumstances."

Li shook his head. "I want to see the consulate," he repeated.

Vandel ignored his protest and continued with his pitch. He had fixed his intense, dark eyes on the Chinese intelligence officer and leaned his body slightly toward his rigid form. Harris Chang stood back slightly from the other two.

"Here's the situation, Mr. Li," continued Vandel. "We are in a position to make you a very attractive offer. Settlement in the United States. Full legal protection, security in a house we will purchase for you in a secure location. A handsome stipend of one million dollars, annually, with bonuses for information you may provide, which I hope you will do. You just have to walk out that door with me and sign a statement that you are traveling to the United States voluntarily."

The alcove was silent for ten seconds, but it seemed much longer. Through the walls, in the theater lobby, came the voices of Dutch regular police, who had arrived to inquire about the commotion in the theater. They were met with soothing reassurances from Willem, the officer from the Royal Marechaussee, that all was well.

"I refuse," said Li calmly. "I am a Chinese citizen. I demand that you release me so that I can go home."

Vandel looked him dead in the eye. They were on the edge of a blade.

"My offer expires in thirty seconds," said Vandel. "You will make a fatal mistake if you refuse. Your enemies know that you're here meeting with me. The PLA's Second Department has been informed. Their representatives are on their way. Either you come with me, or I'll leave you to General Wu."

Li smiled ruefully and shook his head. As an intelligence officer, he could only admire Vandel's coup. But still, that tall, angular form didn't bend.

"You understand everything, Mr. Vandel, except one thing. Which is that I am Chinese. I will never come with you freely."

"There's Plan B, Mr. Minister. If you won't come voluntarily, then we'll bring you out another way. That's a less attractive option, long term, I assure you. But it's your call."

Li looked at Vandel once more, the shrewdly calculating American who was determined to win this match. Li turned his gaze to Chang. He studied the tan, muscular face of the Chinese-American.

Chang returned his gaze. The calm he usually felt in stressful situations gave way in this moment to something different, a deep uneasiness, the agitation, perhaps, that a decent person feels when he is asked to do something wrong. Chang didn't speak, or move, but there was the slightest inflection in his eyes as he looked at the minister's unyielding posture.

The sound from the theater lobby outside was nearer and louder. The police were insistent. Vandel looked at Chang, with the first hint of apprehension, and then back to Li.

"Time's up. Last chance. What's your answer?"

"I refuse. This is illegal."

"Have it your way," said Vandel. He turned to the ring of SOF officers surrounding them and instructed the leader. "Dirk. Get him out of here. If he resists, subdue him, gently. Do it quick. Not much time."

The SOF team leader was halfway to Minister Li when Harris Chang stepped forward and pushed Vandel back with a forearm hardened by decades of training.

"Minister Li said no, sir. He refuses to leave. You can't kidnap him. That's illegal. The Dutch won't allow it. They'll stop you at the airport. Don't do it, sir."

Vandel knocked away his deputy's arm. People in the lobby were pounding on the backstage door, demanding entrance. The roulette ball was slowing on the wheel, about to fall into red or black.

"Stand aside, Harris, goddamn it. Now."

"No," said Chang. "I refuse to cooperate, sir. This is illegal."

"Which side are you on, you fucker?" screamed Vandel. The police were banging hard on the door now. They would be inside in a few more seconds.

"Neither," said Chang. "Both."

The backstage door came off its hinges with a rip of splintering wood. The Dutch police entered the room, guns drawn, followed by Willem of the Dutch gendarmerie and two Chinese military officers in uniform from the Chinese consulate.

"Sir?" barked the leader of Vandel's SOF team, seeking guidance from his boss.

Vandel's eyes narrowed, as he weighed the odds.

"Stand down," he said.

The CIA deputy director for operations turned to the commander of the Dutch police unit. He spoke to him in a low voice, confidentially.

"There has been a terrible mistake here," he said. "It's a matter of national security. I can explain everything to the AIVD."

The Dutch police commander said that an officer of the Dutch General Intelligence and Security Service was already on the way.

As the two men were speaking, the uniformed Chinese officers had approached Minister Li Zian and stood on either side of him. An observer might have thought that they were protecting him, but Li's posture told another story.

40.

LANGLEY, VIRGINIA

John Vandel tried to cover his mistakes. The public announcement of Denise Ford's indictment was played by reporters friendly to the agency as a triumph of counter-espionage that had exposed a Chinese mole in the heart of American intelligence. The leaders of the House and Senate Intelligence Committees were briefed in detail and informed about the CIA's secret campaign to undermine and topple the Ministry of State Security in Beijing. Rather than ask embarrassing questions, the members of Congress competed to appear on national television to offer inside details of a case on which the CIA and FBI were refusing to comment.

Li Zian reappeared in China. He was home less than a week before he was arrested. A commentary in *China Daily* said that investigators had discovered that Li's personal mistakes had led to the exposure of the Chinese penetration agent within American intelligence. A magazine that was known to have close ties to the Commission for Discipline Inspection published a story alleging that Li had maintained secret contacts with the CIA himself and may have acted as their agent. The magazine also alleged that Li had maintained foreign bank accounts and that he was the latest member of the dirty *Shanghai bang*, or "Shanghai clique," that had corrupted the Ministry of State Security.

Several days after Li's arrest, a new minister was named to head the Ministry of State Security. He was a PLA officer who had for many years represented the Second Department on the liaison committee of the Central Military Commission. As the new minister took office, he announced that the Ministry of State Security would henceforth operate more closely with the PLA, under the direction of the Central Military Commission.

A commentator at the *South China Morning Post*, who was known to have senior contacts in Beijing, wrote that the Ministry of State Security had, in effect, been abolished as an independent intelligence agency. The article quoted Warren Winkle, a former U.S. government official, who was now working as an adviser to the foreign ministry of Singapore.

Late one afternoon, John Vandel called a number in Seattle. He had news for Jason Schmidt, the chief executive of the computer company called Quantum Engineering Dynamics.

"Congratulations, my friend," said Vandel. "On authority of the Director, you have been awarded the Distinguished Intelligence Medal. The citation reads as follows: 'For performance of outstanding services or for achievement of a distinctly exceptional nature in a duty or responsibility, the results of which constitute a major contribution to the mission of the Agency.'"

"Wow," said Schmidt, momentarily at a loss for words. "When can I get my medal?"

"You can't, actually. It's classified. The medal will be held in a vault here for you. But I will be sending you a certificate that, although it doesn't mention the medal by name, notes your exceptional service. There's also a large financial reward, but you have to sign some paperwork to get that."

"What about my quantum computer? I hope you're not going to put that in a vault."

"Oh, no. We'd like to buy every machine you've got. Although, technically, I'm told we're not describing it as a quantum computer, even though it does quantum things."

"It is. And it is not," said Schmidt solemnly. "What do you want to use it for?"

"Pattern recognition, mostly," laughed Vandel. "You proved your point. And for encryption, too. The other side of the coin. Our people think your machine is better at jumbling than un-jumbling. But you'll figure out other applications. You just can't sell them to anyone else. Ever."

"What happens to all the other quantum researchers? All the different labs and contractors and project teams. Are you buying them out, too?"

"Let's just say that we have a lot of money to spend on national security. If people are confused about what works and what doesn't, that's fine, better, even. They can go down all the rabbit holes. Our Chinese friends may think they know all our secrets about quantum computing, but they don't understand the biggest one: Which is that we already did it. Sort of."

"You'll be lying," said the CEO. "But I guess that's your job. For you people, something really can be zero and one at the same time."

"That's where we live," said Vandel. "If people want simple answers, they should call the State Department."

A week later, a small fleet of trucks lined up outside the wire-fenced QED office on the southern shore of Lake Washington. Half a dozen FBI agents supervised a team of government employees whose uniforms didn't specify where they worked. This anonymous team packed and loaded every machine in Schmidt's laboratory, along with the peripheral equipment, monitors, backup systems, and research library. The trucks headed south in a convoy.

Most of Schmidt's senior researchers transferred to the company's new location at the campus of Lawrence Livermore Laboratory in northern California. They became government employees; they disappeared from social media; they had jobs and ideas and dreams, but they couldn't talk about them anymore.

Jason Schmidt refused to sign the documents that the government required as a condition for receiving a generous, multimillion-dollar bonus for the work he had done. He hired an attorney and, at that point, his negotiations with the government became adversarial. After a few more months of sparring, the legal talks collapsed.

Schmidt tried to send several messages to "Mr. Green" at Langley, Virginia, but the emails bounced and the letters were returned. All that Schmidt wanted to say was that he was grateful for the opportunity to have been helpful to his country and was happy now to be free once again to invent and create.

Denise Ford hired a very good lawyer from the same firm that had represented her Uncle Cyril. He managed to negotiate a plea agreement that would give her the opportunity for parole before she turned sixty-five. The Justice Department approved the bargain after the CIA warned that it might be impossible to argue the case at trial without disclosing national security secrets.

Ford's lawyers insisted that the evidence was ambiguous: Ford hadn't taken money from China, and much of the information she had shared was published in scientific and technical journals. She claimed that she had disclosed information that belonged to the world and had not acted as an agent of a foreign power.

Before her sentencing, Ford visited the best cosmetic surgeon in Washington; she looked youthful and almost glamorous at her sentencing. The newspapers found her story irresistible. "Sexy Mole!" was the headline in one tabloid. A long magazine profile examined the mysterious woman who was the first high-level female penetration agent in modern intelligence history. A Facebook page created by her supporters had over one hundred thousand "likes."

The FBI was disappointed that Ford was not more cooperative. But Ford did agree, as part of the plea agreement, to prepare for the CIA a manual on tradecraft, in which she would share what she had learned about Chinese operations. She wrote it in the form of a novel, which captured what she had come to understand about intelligence, not simply in her work with Li Zian but through her career at the CIA as well.

Ford's book was circulated widely within the intelligence community. It gave Ford what she had sought through her career but had only achieved after she became a foreign spy, which was a reputation as a brilliant and intuitive operations officer. She was a traitor, but not to herself.

John Vandel summoned Harris Chang a month after their return to Washington to offer him a promotion. Vandel was too smart to try to squeeze the one person who knew the entire story. The Seventh Floor seemed to have forgotten about the past accusations of disloyalty. The awkward moments at the theater in Amsterdam were history, too. Vandel wanted to keep Chang quiet and safely out of his way.

Chang arrived at Headquarters in a new suit, stylishly cut, the trim jacket and tapered waist showing off his physique. He had a new haircut, too, fuller than the military look he had favored for a decade after leaving the Army. He'd spent a few days back home in Flagstaff, visiting his family and skiing. His face was tanned and the lines and creases that had begun to form in recent months seemed to have disappeared.

"I owe you an apology," said Vandel. His manner was cheerful, but he looked worn at the edges, like a piece of paper that has been folded too many times.

"Thank you, sir," said Chang. "Apology accepted."

"I don't just mean about doubting your loyalty. I never did, really, but the Bureau was antsy and I had to play that out. No, what I mean is that I owe you an apology for not realizing how tough you are. I'm not used to people saying no to me. But you probably saved my ass in Amsterdam. If I'd tried to haul in Minister Li, I might have gotten fried. So you were right. I was wrong. Does that make you happy?"

Chang bowed his head a moment, then looked up.

"I did what I thought was right. That makes me happy. The rest, I don't care."

Vandel pursed his lips. He usually was good at sweet-talking people. He didn't like having his moment of generous self-criticism dismissed so abruptly. But he pressed on. Vandel had only a forward gear.

"I want to offer you a new job as head of National Resources. It's one of the best jobs in the agency. You'll run our collection from traveling professors and businesspeople. You're perfect for it."

"Why am I perfect?" asked Chang, with a wry smile. "Always good to have a Chinese face dealing with intellectuals and tech entrepreneurs, I guess."

"Stop it," said Vandel. "You don't know how to take yes for an answer."

"I have something to tell you, sir, if you don't mind," said Chang.

"Sure. Whatever. So long as you take my job offer. Otherwise, you'll hurt my feelings."

"I am resigning from the agency. I'd like it to be effective as soon as the paperwork can be processed. I wanted to tell you personally, but I've already gone over the procedures with Kate Sturm."

"Why? Are you nuts? This is a top job. If you do it well, you'll be in line to succeed me."

A look of sadness came over Chang's face.

"Working at the CIA was the only thing I ever wanted to do, sir, after I met you. But something got broken on this case, and it can't be put back together. It's like falling out of love. You can't talk yourself back into it. Sorry."

"That's bullshit," said Vandel. "You're either in or out."

"Then I'm out, sir. I'm sure that sounds stupid to you, but it's what I've decided."

Chang extended his hand to say good-bye. Vandel wouldn't shake it at first, but he did after a moment. Vandel was staying in the game, after all. He didn't need new enemies. If someone wanted to turn down a great job on a supposed stand of principle, well, that was their problem.

Chang walked out of Vandel's office with a more buoyant step than he had felt in many months. He was finished with trying to be the person John Vandel would admire. He shook hands with Melanie in the outer office and went down the hall to say good-bye to Kate Sturm. He took the elevator down to the main lobby, looked at the stars on the wall, the eagle's crest embedded in the marble floor, and the other totems of America's secret world, and kept on walking out the front door. His whole adult life, Harris had carried on his body, and in his mind, the words "Duty. Honor. Country." He had tried so hard to be faithful to those three values that he had almost forgotten to keep faith with himself. The Army had another slogan he hadn't paid attention to: "Be. Know. Do."

Harris Chang wasn't a zero or a one. He occupied a space where things are ambiguous, where people are simultaneously friend and foe, loyal and disloyal, impossible to define until the moment when events intervene and force each particle, each heart, to one side or the other. A binary separation between black and white might be the human condition, but it wasn't the natural order of things.

ACKNOWLEDGMENTS

In researching this novel, I was aided by many people who generously shared their knowledge.

Craig Mundie at Microsoft, one of the nation's wisest technologists, responded to my request for help by gathering some of his company's best experts on quantum computing, including Michael Freedman of the University of California at Santa Barbara, and Krysta Svore and Burton Smith of Microsoft. I can't do justice to the subtlety of their work, but I hope I shared their passion for the big issues that are ahead in computer science.

A quantum "annealing" machine actually exists today, in the D-Wave 2X. Vern Brownell, the CEO of D-Wave, arranged for me to visit the company's founder, Geordie Rose, and see some of the machines they've built in Vancouver, B.C. Colin Williams, D-Wave's director of strategy and development, kindly read and critiqued portions of the manuscript.

Despite this real-world background, I should stress that all the companies and people in this book are entirely fictional, as the researchers I consulted know better than anyone. I hope they will forgive my mistakes.

This novel explores how the U.S. government oversees technology. The Intelligence Advanced Research Projects Agency (IARPA) arranged visits to their offices in Maryland, and I am especially grateful to project manager Dave Moehring, who explained IARPA's unclassified investments in quantum computing and took me to the University of Maryland to see one of the technologies that may be a pathway to a real machine.

Maryland has become a world-class center for computer science; the university's brief fictional cameo in my book is a hint of their remarkable work. Norbert Mathias Linke, a senior researcher on the ion-trap project at Maryland, read portions of the manuscript and offered helpful suggestions.

The heart of this book is about the long-running spy war between the CIA and its Chinese counterpart, the Ministry of State Security. My mentors were several of the best-informed people on this subject outside China. At their request, they remain anonymous here, but they know my debt to them is immense, especially for reading and critiquing a draft of the book. I'm grateful to my old friend Lena Sun, former *Washington Post* bureau chief in Beijing, who read the manuscript and offered wise comments.

A sincere warning to the reader: This is a work of fiction. When I mention agencies, companies, technologies, or other bits of information, these references are to a fictional world of my imagination. Readers will make a serious error if they assume that anything in this book is "real." The people, places, and institutions exist only in the writer's mind.

Online resources are invaluable to a novelist these days, and my list of Internet citations could go on for pages, but I owe a special debt to Stanford University's "Chinese Railroad Workers in North America Project." I also drew on Iris Chang's narrative history, *The Chinese in America*, Philip Choy's guide to *San Francisco Chinatown*, Arthur Dong's *Forbidden City, USA*, and Eric Liu's memoir, *A Chinaman's Chance*.

During the course of research for the book, I visited Shanghai, Beijing, Tokyo, Kyoto, and Singapore in Asia; Amsterdam in the Netherlands; and Seattle, Newport Beach, Mexico City, and Vancouver, B.C., in North America. Thanks to my hosts in all those places. A shout-out to the superb online archive at the Leon Trotsky Museum in Mexico City.

Comments from family and friends shaped this book. I would like to thank my beloved computer scientist wife and first reader, Dr. Eve Ignatius; my father Paul Ignatius; my friend Garrett Epps, whose advice for this book was, as always, inspiring; and finally Lincoln Caplan, another close friend of more than forty-five years, who gave the book two subtle final readings and suggested some very helpful changes.

Special thanks to my editor at Norton, Starling Lawrence, and my literary agent for nearly forty years, Raphael Sagalyn. I am also deeply grateful to Bruce Vinokour and Matthew Snyder at Creative Artists Agency. W. W. Norton has been my publisher now for six books. A writer cannot have better luck than to be a Norton author.

The *Washington Post* has been my professional home for more than thirty years. I have been lucky enough to see the greatest handoff in journalism history, from Don Graham and his family, sublime newspaper owners, to Jeff Bezos, a visionary and iconoclast whose investment has given the *Post* new energy and readership. Thirty years ago, when Norton published *Agents of Innocence*, I thought I had to choose between being a journalist and a novelist. I'm glad that I didn't.